CW00857314

WHISPERS OF WAR

THE ILVANNIAN CHRONICLES BOOK THREE

KARA S. WEAVER

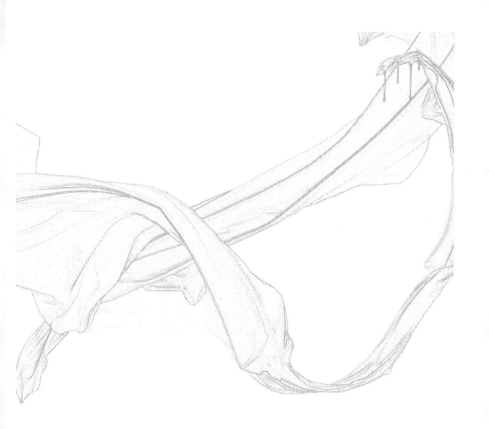

WHISPERS OF WAR

THE ILVANNIAN CHRONICLES BOOK THREE

KARA S. WEAVER

DEDICATION

To all of you who love to go on adventures without leaving your house.

ORIGIN STORY

If there ever has been a time where we Gods and Goddesses have strayed from our true purpose, it is now. My brothers and sisters do not wish me to speak of this, to confess that we may have made mistakes. If you ask me, the time for lies and deceit is long gone. The future of our children—our future—is in danger. If we do not get ourselves involved now, it will be too late.

Esahbyen, God of War

PROLOGUE

ESAHBYEN

*O*nce more I found myself staring into the globe, watching my daughter's life and those around her unfold in ways I had never imagined possible. She was stubborn, more so than her mother—*more so than myself*—and with a pride that would make my sister Nava envious. Yet there was a quiet power inside her I could not place, a will to see the world not as it was, but as it could be, even in the face of impossible odds.

She intrigued me.

"Watching her?" Xiomara's soft lilt sounded next to me. "Again?"

"It is all I can do, sister," I replied, "since you bound me to our home."

"It was for your own good. You are too invested in these mortals."

With a swipe of my hand, I shut the globe off and turned away from it, anger simmering underneath my skin. I ground my teeth, ignoring the familiar tic in my jaw as it began.

"How can you be so calm when their world is about to fall

apart?" I asked with a shake of my head. "Can you not see the shift in the stars, sister, feel the air thrumming with power like it never has before? How can we not interfere?"

"Esahbyen," she said, the tone of her voice suggesting she was talking to a child rather than to me, the God of War. "We've had this conversation thousands of times before. You know why."

"You've grown soft, brother," Eslandah observed as she glided into the room. "She has made you soft."

The scowl on my face deepened. A part of me wanted to yell at them, scream to the stars that they were *khirr* for not seeing what was right under their noses. One by one, I watched my brothers and sisters enter the room, taking up their positions until we formed a circle of twelve. The last time we gathered was when we decided six of us would produce heirs among the mortals.

Six children.

One prophecy.

In time, when evil would awake, they would fight in our stead. Now, I almost laughed at the idea. We had expected them to be strong—stronger than most, but we had not accounted for the fact that not all of them would inherit our powers.

Only two of them had.

Aeson's son possessed the ability to heal, but it had come with a catch none of us had foreseen. Xiomara's daughter could catch glimpses of the future but would never know if they were accurate. None of the other children had shown direct powers. One of them had died at a young age. My daughter had shown prowess in fighting skills, and she picked them up faster than most, but she was not extraordinary.

It had been disappointing, I admit.

The same went for Nava's son. As handsome as his mother was beautiful, he was a master hustler and drove the hardest of bargains, but he had shown no particularly interesting powers either. Vehda's daughter, a fierce, skilled huntress who had gone far beyond the borders of her country because of a dream had perhaps the barest trace of magic in her veins, but she possessed none of her mother's remarkable skills.

Our only solace lay in the fact they would all be connected. Soon.

"Xalara is stirring." I watched each of my siblings in turn. "Our children do not have the strength we had expected they would. They cannot defeat her."

"Speak for yourself," Aeson replied in a soft, musical voice.

"And what good is it doing him?" I snorted. "His power is flawed."

"Better flawed than non-existent."

"It doesn't matter whether they have powers," Nava interjected, "flawed or not. If Xalara is stirring, if her power is awakening, it means destruction to the world as we know it."

"Is that really such a bad thing?" Seydeh observed. "Our children have become greedy, power-lusting monstrosities who kill each other out of jealousy, hatred or a hunger for power. Perhaps the world needs a new start."

"If that is so," Xiomara said, "we have failed."

"What do you propose we do?" It was Xanthier, the most level-headed of us all.

"I agree with Esah," Vehda folded her arms, drawing attention to the bow on her back and quiver at her hip. A show of intimidation, no more. "If we do not help them, we have forsaken our children—we will have failed ourselves."

"We agreed not to interfere," Arran observed. "I still stand by that decision."

Murmurs arose until one outshouted another to be heard and getting nowhere in the process. At this point, I knew no decisions would be made today, or anytime soon for that matter, so I quietly bowed out of the conversation and slipped out of the grand hall. While we did not exactly have bedrooms in the conventional sense of the word—they were more like halls, fashioned after our particular predilections—it was the only place we could call our own. None of us could enter without the other's approval.

I entered my hall, but not before I took notice of light footsteps behind me.

My lips curved into a smile. "Come in, Nava."

As I turned to look at her, she sashayed into my domain, the corridors and grand hall behind her disappearing from sight. With one hand propped on her hip, she regarded me, head tilted to the side.

"So," she began. "What are you going to do?"

"What makes you say that?"

She chuckled. "Because I know you, Esah. You have never cared about our opinions, have always done what you felt like doing consequences be cursed, and you have not changed a single bit. If anything, I'd say having met your daughter has only strengthened that resolve."

I harrumphed in response.

"Again, I ask, what will you do?"

"Why do you want to know?" I asked somewhat suspiciously.

None of us usually did anything if they did not stand to gain. Seydeh had not yet collected the debt I owed him for saving my daughter's life, but he would. Maybe not today, maybe not tomorrow, maybe not even a century from now, but he would.

"Because I may be inclined to help you," she replied, staring intently at me. "Like you, I do not wish my son to die in this war."

"What will be my debt?"

She shrugged. "If my son survives, consider your debt paid."

"And if he doesn't?"

Nava winced, her voice wavering when next she spoke, "It will no longer matter."

"In that case," I replied, pulling a sword from the wall, "I am about to do something I may regret for the rest of my existence."

CHAPTER 1

SHALITHA

I killed an innocent woman.

The blood pounding in my ears drowned out the catcalls and jeers from the audience. My chest rose and fell with ragged breaths. I spat blood on the dirt as I wiped my nose with the back of my hand, my eyes never leaving my opponents. With deadliness apparent in their moves, the tigresses circled me, stalking me like the predators they were. A low growl rumbled from their throats almost in unison, making the hair on the back of my neck stand on end.

The odds weren't in my favour.

My only chance of survival lay in outsmarting them, but how do you outsmart a beast that's ten times as fast, as strong, and as agile? My chances were slim indeed. Out of the corner of my eye, I caught movement. One of the ginormous cats came pelting my way, paws pounding the ground in a deathly beat. I was running before I made the conscious decision to do so, casting about to look for an elevated position.

How stupid do you think they are?

One of the metal gates that had kept the *tigresses* confined loomed in the distance like a gaping maw of death, but it was my only chance. I pushed down to gain momentum, just an inch more with every step, pumping my arms to be that little bit faster. The stitches in my side were nothing compared to the pain in my chest, but unless I wanted to be dinner, I had to keep moving. I didn't dare look back.

I knew what I'd be seeing.

Nevertheless, the sudden impact from my left came as a surprise. My sword clattered from my hand as the encounter sent me sprawling into the dirt. Ignoring the pain in my side, I scrambled to my feet and resumed running, straining my ears to listen. One of the beasts was behind me, the other somewhere to my right, their growls testimony to the imminent danger I was in. I'd soon realised Kehran was crazy—I'd been mistaken in downplaying his insanity. This was nothing but a game to him.

The fury coursing through me fuelled my determination, adding a strength to my legs I didn't know I still had. Only a few more steps until I reached the gate. The growls behind me turned deeper, more vicious, and I knew like by some deeper instinct I had perhaps the count of five heartbeats before they were on me. Just as the tigresses made to pounce, I jumped at the gate, slamming my chest hard against the iron bars. It knocked all the air from my lungs, and I hung there, clinging on for dear life while regaining my senses. I scrambled up without looking down, going as high as the structure of the *herrât* allowed me.

At least I can fall to my death now, too.

The gate rattled underneath the felines' assault, jarring me with every collision until they tired of it and made themselves comfortable. I stuck my legs through the bars and hooked my feet behind the rungs. It wasn't the most ideal position to be in, but it was better than the alternative. As I clamped a hand around the most recent injury, it came back bloodied.

What's a few more scars for the collection?

Keeping one hand on the injury, putting as much pressure on it as I had the strength for, I surveyed my surroundings. There was no chance of going up—the arc around the gate was too deep for that, the walls too high to scale and too smooth to climb. My only way out of here was down. I held onto one of the rungs and twisted in my makeshift seat, hissing at the fierce sting above my hip. One of the tigresses had lain down, paws folded as if she were waiting. The other was pacing up and down beneath me.

Going down isn't the problem. Going down and staying alive is.

I needed to distract them, but I had no idea how, and I was running out of strength fast. A sudden rattling noise alerted me, and I realised with horror that they were pulling up the gates. The only mercy was that the gates were heavy, and they were pulled up manually. As quickly as I could, I unhooked my feet and scrambled from my sitting position. My hands were slippery, which made clambering down problematic. I risked a glance at the felines, both of whom were now pacing rapidly, giant heads turned up.

My chest tightened as irate anger began to pulse deep inside of me, fighting its way up. In a moment of clarity, I remembered the dagger in my boot. I climbed down to the last iron bar, estimating the distance between myself and the feline below me. Without taking my eyes from it, I slipped the dagger into my hand, holding it tight.

I can do this.

As I dove, my other hand wrapped around the hilt of the dagger, too. One of the tigresses jumped to meet me. My ears roared. My heart pounded. All I had eyes for was the predator below me. When we collided, everything was silent for a heartbeat—the crowd, the feline, the world. I sensed rather than saw the dagger hit its mark and plunge deep into her neck. I felt the roar starting in her stomach and going through marrow and bone as it left her muzzle.

9

She roared in pain.

In the momentary confusion, I let go of the dagger, rolled out of harm's way, and to my feet. Ignoring the throbbing sensation underneath my ribs, I started running to the sword I'd dropped after one of them had jumped me. With every step I took, the pain increased as my strength decreased. I pushed forward, cursing myself in Ilvannian and Zihrin alike. The sound of thunder was fast approaching, and I realised then it was a furious feline bound and determined to make dinner out of me.

My sword lay only a few feet away.

The hairs on my neck prickled as if I was being watched. Obviously, everyone was watching me, but this felt different. It felt like a warm blanket on a dark, wintry night. A shudder went through me, and as it did, the pain dissipated, and a renewed burst of energy shot through me.

It was the last push I needed.

I skidded to my knees, grabbed the sword from the ground, and by instinct, turned on my back, holding up the weapon in defence. The second tigress speared herself on the blade. With a hard pull, I yanked my sword up, cutting the feline open. Blood and guts oozed on top of me, coating me in whatever the tigress had digested. I shuddered at the thought. The feline fell on top of me as it died growling and huffing. I tried to push it off me, but the strength I'd had before melted away, as did the comforting presence I was now sure I'd felt.

Esahbyen!

There was no response, of course, but it couldn't have been anyone else. Sheer effort of will had me push the carcass off me. With a grunt, I pulled my sword from its chest and looked around for the other feline. It lay on its side near the gate, still breathing from the looks of it, but judging by its whimpers, it was in pain. Instead of putting it out of its misery, I turned to

Kehran on his balcony, my eyes briefly resting on the man sitting next to him.

Elay was watching me intently.

The *Akyn* had risen to his feet, gold attire flashing in the sunlight. My vision was blurry, but I wasn't sure if it was because the sun made my eyes water, or because of the amount of blood I'd lost. Either way, he'd better decide what he wanted with me before my body would do it for him. If he turned his back, I was dead. If he bowed, it meant I'd earned his respect and would live another day.

He took a long time deciding.

Bow already, grissin.

I pushed the tip of my sword into the dirt and leaned on it, clenching my jaw at the sheer agony that was my waist now that the adrenaline had dissipated. Tremors started in my legs and built up until I was shaking all over. It wouldn't be long before shock would set in, if I remembered Soren's lessons correctly.

Where are you when I need you?

Above, on the balcony, Kehran bowed.

I dropped to my knees, gulping in lungs full of air while trying to hold on to my awareness. The crowd burst into a cacophony of cheers and yells I didn't care to make out. Instead, my focus turned to the severed foot lying a few feet away from me, an arm even farther. I couldn't bring myself to look at the mangled corpse I knew was there.

A woman—I'd guessed her not much older than myself—had been brought into the *herrât* with me, and before we'd even made it to the centre, she'd soiled herself. The difference between us had been astounding. She'd been a warm summer's day—I a cold winter's night. I only had to watch her hold the sword to know she'd never held one before, let alone had any idea how to wield it.

I had refused to fight her.

Kehran had sent in the tigresses.

11

Although I had tried to get her to run to safety, the sight of the predators had paralysed her, and between one heartbeat and the next, the felines had pounced on her, tearing her to shreds. Her screams still echoed in my head.

Despite refusing to fight her, I had killed her.

Sick to my stomach from the memory and faint from the loss of blood, I barely managed to get to my feet. I looked up at the balcony one more time. Kehran was reclining on his throne, accompanied by a handful of courtiers and servants. Elay had made himself scarce. With a light nod, I acknowledged Kehran. Under the deafening shouts of the crowd, I left the *herrât*, one hand covering the wound, the other barely holding on to the sword. The only way I would leave this place without a weapon was if I were dead.

Once in the cool sanctity of the tunnels, I slumped against the wall, sliding down until I was sitting. I would have collapsed had two hands on my shoulders not arrested my fall. A hiss escaped my lips as the world tilted into a more upright position. Looking up, a pair of emerald eyes twinkled in what little light there was in the tunnel.

"Elay," I murmured.

"*Mithri*," he said softly. "You did it."

"No," I whispered. "We did it."

CHAPTER 2

TALNOVAR

a bell tolled.

It sounded urgent, but it was so distant I paid it no heed. At first. The distinct sound of heavy footfalls of people running on a wooden deck accompanied the urgency of the bell.

Something's wrong.

I struggled out of my hammock, which was quite the challenge with my arm in a sling and cursed when the *nohro* piece of fabric suddenly gave way, dropping me to the deck. My stomach lurched in the same rhythm as the ship did, and after I staggered to my feet, I held on to one of the support beams until the nausea dwindled to a more bearable level. After the first two nights on board, I'd considered taking up residence in Zihrin just so I'd never have to be on these floating death-traps again. I slipped into my boots and leather overcoat and began making my way up top to see what the mayhem was about, stopping every few steps to allow my stomach to settle

I'd rather die before setting foot on a ship again.

Navigating the ladder on wobbly legs was a challenge all by itself. When the ship suddenly lurched to the left, I barely managed to grab on to something to keep from being thrown down the rungs. I slammed into the wall, hitting my injured shoulder against a protruding piece of wood. My vision blurred, and I sank to my knees, holding on to a rope for dear life.

The ship lurched again.

This time I couldn't hold on anymore. I curled in on myself, tucking my arms close to my body as I fell. A loud grunt escaped my lips when my head slammed hard on the wooden deck, and as the darkness took me, everything fell silent. When I came to, the patter of footsteps on deck had increased. Blinking away the stars in my vision, I rose to my feet, unsteady like a newborn colt.

I took a tentative step forward, and another, waiting to the count of ten before taking another step, in case the ship would heave sideways again. Just as I grabbed hold of the rope for the ladder, the ship took another sharp turn to the right, leaving me skipping on one leg to keep my balance.

Nohro! What in Esah's name is going on up there?

Expecting to be tossed around like a ragged doll made it somewhat easier to navigate the rung this time. Although I was thrown left and right at every sharp turn, banging my hips and shoulders into the walls, I managed to make my way topside. The crew scurried across the deck in frantic mayhem to the belted commands from the captain. How they understood what he yelled was beyond me. I stared around in confusion, wondering what was going on until someone ran into me.

Hard.

I caught myself barely in time.

"Oi! Watch it, *metâh,*" the crewmember muttered.

He was gone before I could ask what was going on. If anyone could give me news, it was the captain, but before I could take a step in his direction, he shouted something, followed by another lurch of the ship. In my peripherals, I saw the crew hold on to anything that was within reach and anchored to the ship. Being a second too late to comprehend the order, I began sliding starboard, but before I would be thrown overboard, I grabbed hold of the ropes. My stomach dropped and clenched, the muscles in my jaw tingled, and saliva flooded my mouth. I breathed in through my nose, counted to ten, and focused on something else. None of it helped.

The nausea increased as the ship dipped deep into the waves.

By some miracle, I managed to keep it inside, but my stomach heaved and burned. I didn't think I'd manage a second time. As the ship straightened, the crew let go of whatever they'd latched onto and resumed their duties on deck. It took me every ounce of will to uncurl my fingers from the rope and regain proper footing. As soon as I did, I staggered back against the railing, turned around, and vomited over the side of the ship.

Howls of laughter sounded up from the crew, but I'd stopped caring after the first day.

Someone slapped me on the back. "Here *mahnèh*, have a drink."

I looked up into the face of an Ilvannian man. A scar ran from his right eye down to his jaw, pulling up the left side of his face into a sneer. He was holding out a flask to me.

"Thanks," I murmured, wiping my mouth.

I threw my head back and took a swig, grimacing as the liquid burned down my throat, but at least it took the taste of vomit out of my mouth.

"Go see the healer," the man offered. "He'll have something against the sickness."

I nodded mutely, handing the flask back. "What's going on?"

He gave a curt nod to the other side of the ship. "She's been on our tail for the past few days. Started gaining speed a little while ago. Cap'n's not pleased."

I cursed silently. "Where's she from?"

The man smirked. "Ilvanna, *mahnèh*, and I doubt she's here for me."

He left me with those words. A cold shiver travelled down my spine as I settled my gaze on the ship in the distance. If what the crewmember said was correct, and it was indeed an Ilvannian ship, it could only mean Azra hadn't ceased her pursuit.

Or she's just trying to prevent you from finding Shalitha, by any means necessary.

My gaze travelled to the captain who was staring in the distance through a spyglass. Wanting answers, I made my way to him, keeping my hands close to whatever I passed in order not to fall over. I still felt ungainly walking across a deck that dipped and rose beneath me, my stomach dipping and rising with it, but at least the nausea had settled a bit. One thing was sure. Once I returned to Ilvanna, or any country on Ilvanna's side of the map, I'd never set foot on a ship again.

Ever.

"*Mishan*, to what do I owe the pleasure of your company?" Captain Fehran asked, spotting me coming up.

The tone of his voice held a note of mistrust which hadn't been there before. I inclined my head and went for a smile, hoping to ease whatever tension was between us.

"I came up for some fresh air, *Irìn*," I replied, glancing at the ship in the distance, "and to see what all the ruckus was about. I heard the bells."

"Of course, you did," he said, sarcasm in his voice,

I arched a brow. "Is something the matter, Captain?"

"You tell me." He turned to me, folding his arms in front of him.

Captain Fehran was a short, stout man, at least half a head smaller than I was, but there was no mistaking his authority on this ship. Every man obeyed him without question—every man was loyal to him. One only had to look at how they worked for him to notice that. It was whispered he was one of the best Captains in the world, although I had no idea how they measured that. I supposed he had to be as a smuggler, but I couldn't tell whether he was one because he was such a good captain, or whether he was a good captain because he was good at running contraband.

Either way, he wasn't a man to trifle with, and I had no intention of doing so.

"Eamryel told me you could be in trouble." He tilted his head. "He never mentioned trouble would follow you."

"I doubt he thought she'd go as far as this," I replied, shifting my weight to find my balance.

"So, she is after you."

"Depends on who you mean by 'she', Captain."

He huffed. "You and I both know who I'm talking about, *mishan*. I may spend a lot of time on my ship, but news reaches me."

I didn't reply at first.

"Now what?" I asked after a while, returning my gaze to the Ilvannian ship that seemed to have slowed down.

"Now we try to keep outrunning them until we arrive in Portasâhn. They cannot follow into the harbour if their objective isn't trade. It'll be considered an act of war."

I shuddered at the thought. "I wouldn't put it past her."

Captain Fehran smiled, a genuine one this time. "Not to worry, *mishan*. I have yet to be caught by any ship in these waters. Now, do me a favour, and see the ship's healer. It'll be a rough fare from here on out, and I cannot have you throw up all over my decks."

It wasn't a favour.

It was a command.

Arav, the healer, was a man who from the looks of him had seen quite a few centuries. Ilvannians—and judging by the looks of him Kyrinthan's, too—didn't start showing signs of old age until the last hundred or so years of our lives, but once it happened, it happened fast. Arav's skin was wrinkled and dry, and he stooped when he stood and shuffled about as if his legs were about to give way from under him any moment, but his lively hazel eyes and physical strength belied the frail look.

I'd learned he was anything but frail the first night on the ship.

"Talnovar, good to see you," he croaked, flashing me a gap-toothed grin as I stepped into his cabin. "How's the shoulder?"

"As if I got hit by an arrow," I replied with a wry smile.

Arav narrowed his eyes and puffed out his cheeks. "Ha... ha."

"My apologies," I replied, rubbing my jaw. "It's sore, but it could have been worse."

"Sit down."

I perched on the stool Arav pushed my way, trying to make myself comfortable with my knees almost up to my neck. It was made for children, not grown men. Arav took off the sling, holding my arm to keep it steady. I gritted my teeth at the sudden weight on my shoulder, biting back a curse.

"Still just sore, *eshen?*"

"No," I hissed. "This hurts like a *hehzèh.*"

"A what?"

"Never mind. Please, get on with it."

Arav chuckled, obviously quite pleased with himself. I closed my eyes, balling my good hand into a fist while he set about checking my shoulder. Although I'd been mostly out of it when they brought me aboard, I'd woken up screaming the moment Arav had pushed the arrow through and snapped it. I'd been lucky the arrowhead hadn't been barbed.

It had hurt beyond any imaginable pain.

"Take off your shirt."

"And dislocate my other shoulder?"

Arav harrumphed, assisting me where necessary. "Humour an old man. How did you get shot in the first place?"

"With a bow," I remarked without thinking.

He slapped me upside the head. "You might want to refrain from those smart-ass comments, *eshen,* or you can deal with this on your own."

"Apologies."

He's not Soren, khirr.

If he had been Soren, I wouldn't have felt as banged up as I did, of that I was sure, but he wasn't here, and Arav was the only one between me and a functional arm. As he took off the bandages, humming a merry tune to himself, I couldn't help but smile. He made an effort to put me at ease despite my remarks.

The ship heaved to the left.

Arav remained steady on his feet. I all but flew to the other side of the cabin, skidding to a halt once I reached the wall.

"*Nohro ahrae,*" I grunted, rubbing my other shoulder. "What in Esah's name is the Captain doing?"

"Saving our lives, I presume," Arav commented drily. "Come, sit. I wasn't finished yet."

I snapped my mouth shut to keep the retort from passing my lips and stumbled over to the stool Arav had placed back on its legs. Once I sunk on it, he continued as if nothing had disturbed his administrations.

At least he wasn't as sadistic about them as Soren.

In fact, he was gentle, lulling me into a sense of safety I hadn't felt since before this mess started.

"Wound looks good," Arav said while dressing it. "It'll hurt for a while, and you will definitely need the sling even longer if you have any hopes of using that arm again."

I grunted. "How long?"

Arav shrugged. "Weeks? Perhaps less if you heal as fast as I've been told."

"Not as fast as I would like," I replied with a heavy sigh. "But thank you anyway."

"No matter. No matter."

He shuffled away from me and started cleaning up his cabin. With difficulty, I managed to slip my shirt on. Arav helped me with the sling.

"On a different note," I ventured. "The Captain sent me here... for seasickness?"

Arav tilted his head. "Seasickness? Hm, yes, of course."

He turned to a cabinet and began rummaging through a multitude of small drawers. I leaned against the desk, my feet planted wide and my good hand curled around the edge on the off chance the ship would yank to one side again.

"Arav?"

"Yes?" he croaked.

"How long have you been on this ship?"

He chuckled. "Not as long as you might think, *eshen*, but I've been on ships for a very long time. Sailed the world beyond Zihrin, beyond Geâhr, seen things you couldn't possibly even dream of."

I smiled. "Have you always been a healer?"

"Nay, *eshen*. I was a warrior like yourself."

"What happened?"

A sad smile touched his lips as he turned to me, a bundle of something forlorn in his hand as memories flitted across his face.

"I lost my fight," he said at length, his voice soft.

"I'm not sure..."

"She was everything to me, *eshen*. The love of my life. I'd have died for her... I should have died for her—instead of her. When she did, I vowed never to take up arms again."

I felt the muscles in my jaw and neck jump under my skin, my hands clench into fists, and stuffed the toe of my boot into the carpet.

"You know of what I speak."

Arav didn't ask. I didn't reply. Swallowing the lump in my throat, I returned to look at him. There were tears in the corners of his eyes, but he was smiling.

"I'm sorry for your loss," I said, pushing myself to my feet.

"Don't make the same mistake I did, *eshen*," Arav said, placing the leather bundle in my hand. "Take this twice a day, before eating or drinking anything. It tastes vile, but it'll help against the nausea."

I nodded. "Thank you, *Irìn*."

"I'm no lord." He clucked his tongue. "Now out with you, you need to re—"

A loud bang cut off his sentence seconds before the portholes shattered into a thousand pieces.

CHAPTER 3

SHALITHA

*P*ain.

I knew pain in most of its glorious forms, but what I was experiencing now pushed all rational thoughts to the background while my mind amplified the fiery sensation in the area underneath my ribs, focusing on how it spread to my leg, chest, shoulder, and arm as if it were hungry for more. What my mind didn't register were the shrieks of pain and cries for mercy as my own.

The healer, if he was that, was doing his best to clean and stitch the injuries I'd sustained after the giant cat had sunk its claws into me. Although Kehran had given him permission to do that, he'd not allowed for him to sedate me. More than once, I wished for Soren to magically appear at my side and make it all go away.

But thinking of Soren made me think of home and thinking of home guided me down a dark path I had a hard time coming back from. With nothing else to do but daily training and sitting in a cell, waiting to be called for another round of fights, it was easy to get lost in my own head.

A sharp sting yanked me back to my current reality.

"*Nohro!*"

Tears ran down my cheeks in steady rivulets, soaking the hair and shirt in my neck. Even if I tried, I knew I couldn't stop them. I bit down on the leather strip as another wave of agony surged through me, and I had to grab the table with both hands to keep myself from hitting the healer.

It wasn't his fault I got mauled by that tigress.

If only I'd killed that woman.

You wouldn't have been able to live with yourself, qira.

I hissed at a needle-sharp jab just above my ribs and glared at the healer. He smiled at me cheerfully.

"Almost done, *shena*," he said, patting my hand gingerly. "You are very lucky."

I grimaced. "I don't feel lucky."

"The *Akyn* didn't have you killed after you gutted his pet." He clucked his tongue. "I call that luck."

His version of luck and mine were clearly at odds, but I wasn't going to argue with the man stitching me up. Past experiences had taught me that was never a good idea.

My throat seized up and my stomach clenched as a sudden sense of loneliness overwhelmed me. I gulped away the lump in my throat, pushing back another onslaught of tears. In combination with the pain, I was having a hard time altogether, so when this darkness threatened to pull me under, I allowed it.

I came to when something pressed against my lips, and a cold liquid trickled down my chin until I opened my mouth. The first drop of water on my tongue felt almost foreign, but after the second drop, I began to drink greedily.

Someone took the cup away.

"*Taleh, taleh*," a woman murmured. "Let's not get you sick."

Although I didn't recognise the voice, it sounded friendly enough for me to ease up. I opened my eyes, but the difference between them being closed or open was negligible. What little light illuminated the cell came from bowls of candles in the corridors. The small window, if it even deserved that name, barely allowed any air through, let alone light.

This isn't my cell.

"Where am I?"

I pushed myself to a sitting position, but a sharp pain in my side stopped me halfway up. Lowering myself took a great deal more effort than I'd thought, so by the time I'd lain back down, sweat beaded my brow.

"They brought you in a while ago," the woman spoke in heavily accented Kyrinth. "He told me to watch over you."

I snorted. "I doubt Kehran cares whether I live or die."

"Not the *Akyn*," she said. "His brother."

I turned my head in the direction of her voice, but she was barely visible in the dim light.

"His brother?"

She might have sounded friendly and given me water, but for all I knew, she was on Kehran's side, and she just wanted to establish how much I knew.

It's what I would do.

The thought startled me.

"Tall, dark, and handsome," the woman said, her voice holding a note of amusement. "He looked as if he would murder the world if anyone would harm you."

Elay.

Turning my head away, I stared up at the ceiling, my thoughts chasing each other in circles. When we planned all of this, I made him promise not to do anything to compromise our plan. If we wanted to make this work, Kehran had to believe Elay had sold me out. He couldn't go and threaten people on my behalf. His meeting me in the tunnel had been tricky, but his visiting me down here was outright stupid, and I resolved to give him a piece of my mind when I saw him again, provided I would.

"What's your name?" I asked, desperate to change the subject.

"I am Z'tala of Nihbehra."

"Nihbehra?"

She hummed under her breath before she spoke as if contemplating whether she would answer or not. "It's a country far beyond the endless desert. Farther even than the Chellay Mountains to the west."

She sounded as if I were supposed to know where that was.

"How did you come to be here?"

"That," she began, rising to her feet, "is a story best told to friends, *k'lele*, and you need to rest."

I pressed my lips together, ready to argue with her, when a sudden yawn overtook me, and my eyes began to feel heavy.

"Why didn't he just let me die?"

The question was to no one in particular. It was rather a passing thought as sleep dragged me under, but I could have sworn Z'tala answered.

I just never caught it.

"I am not sure whether you are brave, stupid, or both," a deep voice purred from behind me.

I groaned, dropping my arm over my eyes so I didn't have to look at him. "What are *you* doing here?"

"Do you always greet old friends like that?"

"You're old but hardly a friend."

He huffed. "Harsh. I see you still have to work on those manners."

"I will once they are necessary."

Esahbyen laughed a deep, smoky laugh that reverberated inside my head. "I see you have gotten your priorities straight."

With a heavy sigh, I turned to him, my eyes widening and my breath hitching when I realised 'here' wasn't where I thought it was.

"Where are we?" I asked.

"That is not important," Esahbyen replied, suddenly serious. "We need to talk."

"Like we talked last time?" I folded my arms in front of my chest. "Because last time I checked, you still owe me about a dozen answers, at least."

He had the decency to look at least guilty.

"I am not going to apologise for that." He straightened his shoulders. "Come, walk with me, *dochtaer*."

Although his way of familiarity still raised my hackles, his words about my temper still rang in my ears, and I refused to prove him right.

I can control it.

"I don't think it's wise if I do," I replied. "All things considered."

"Your injuries will not trouble you here."

His off-hand manner fed into my irritability, but rather than giving in to it, I pushed myself to a sitting position tentatively, relieved to find he wasn't lying. The smug smile on his lips did nothing to help the situation.

Grissin.

I rose to my feet expecting to be unsteady. In truth, I hadn't felt this strong in a long time. Both the old pain and the new were gone, as if it had never existed at all, and for the first time in forever, I felt ready to take on the world. I caught Esahbyen smiling out of the corner of my eyes, but there was a sadness to him that hadn't been there before.

"Do not get used to it," he said. "Once you are back, it will return tenfold."

"I'll take what I can."

Even if it's only for a short while.

"So," I began, rolling my shoulders in a feeling nothing short of awe, "what is so important that you dragged me down here?"

"Your life, *dochtaer.*"

I harrumphed. "It's been on the line for more than two years now. Why is it suddenly so important?"

He glared at me. "It has always been important."

Folding my arms, I watched him. "Really? Why then has nobody come to find me? For all I know, they believe I'm dead and just didn't bother."

"If you believe that," he said, sounding thoroughly annoyed, "you are a *qira.*"

Biting my lip, I regarded him quietly as he started pacing up and down, something I'd never seen him do. His face had turned ashen, and a vein was pulsing visibly just below his jaw.

He's afraid.

The thought was disconcerting at best. I wrapped my arms around myself to stave off the sudden cold snaking down my spine. If Esahbyen, the God of War, was afraid, something terrible had to be going on.

"All right," I said at length. "I'll humour you."

He all but rolled his eyes, then motioned for me to follow him. As soon as we started walking, our surroundings changed until a myriad of colours and scents assaulted my senses. I stopped and stared in awe, twirling around step by careful step to take in the natural garden. Flowers in all shapes and sizes grew along a well-tended grassy path. Pink flowers were interspersed with purple, white, and yellow. I recognised peonies and foxglove, and lavender by the scent alone, but there were many more, most of which I couldn't put a name to. Not that it mattered—this garden was stunning.

It reminds me of Mother's garden at home.

Thinking of her felt as if someone stabbed me in the heart and I gasped, staggering backwards a step. Esahbyen laid a hand on my shoulder.

"Shalitha? Is everything all right?"

I nodded, not trusting my voice.

Esahbyen clasped his hands behind his back and started walking without looking to see if I was following. Wiping my nose on the back of my hand, I composed my features, straightened my shoulders, and fell in step with the God of War. For the longest time, we did not speak. He seemed to be content with my mere presence alone if the smile on his face was anything to go by.

He guided me along a path, past a bush of blooming red and pink wild roses which fragrances reminded me even more painfully of home. Up ahead, sparkling in the sun—it could have been a trick—a white gazebo perched on a small hill overlooking the garden. Vines crept up its side and around its posts in a manner that suggested someone took painstaking measures to make them grow that way.

I didn't have to guess as to whom.

"You have asked me questions before," he said as we reached the gazebo, "and I denied you the answers you needed because I was bound by my word."

"And now you're not?" I arched a brow.

One side of his lips tugged up as he took a seat. "No, I still am, but my siblings and I no longer appear to have the same goal in mind."

"Which is?"

"To save the world." He looked at me solemnly. "At all costs."

"How dramatic."

His deadpan expression almost made me chuckle, but I

managed to keep a straight face. My eyes must have betrayed me because he snorted and shook his head.

"Take this seriously, or not, *dochtaer*," he said, "but I am giving you the opportunity to be prepared."

"Apologies." I bit my lip. "Bad habit."

He smiled at that, but the smile never touched his eyes.

"How well do you know *our* history?"

I smiled ruefully. "Depends on which part."

He gave a short bark of a laugh and shook his head, watching me out of the corner of his eyes. I could have sworn amusement made them shine. I looked away and into the distance, leaning against a beam for support, my mind returning to what religious classes I had attended.

They weren't legion.

It wasn't that I was entirely ignorant of our pantheon, or the stories around them—I'd just chosen to write them off as myths and legends devised to keep children out of trouble. Mother had always said there was some truth to them, but I'd discarded it as her trying to persuade me, so I'd go to my lessons. Considering where I was and, in whose company, I'd give anything to turn back time and accept her words for truth.

"Do you know how our world came to be, *shareye*?" Esahbyen asked after a while.

"If we are to believe the stories," I began, pursing my lips, "you created it. You and your... siblings."

He inclined his head. "And do you know what happened to *us*?"

"You left."

Esahbyen winced as if I'd slapped him. Whether they had or not, I didn't much care. I was more concerned with why he had chosen to show himself now, and why he kept interfering with my life.

"If we had not," he said, sounding defensive, "we would have destroyed the world."

His fists balled at his side, his jaw clenched, and the look on his face was as if he'd bitten into something sour.

I placed a hand on his biceps. "I'm not judging."

His expression softened when he looked at me, but the hard lines around his mouth hadn't gone. A sudden sound behind us made him turn a shade or two paler.

"Hide," he hissed. "Quickly."

I all but dove into the bushes next to the gazebo and turned to him just in time to see him wave his hand and mutter something. Everything around me dimmed, as if a veil had been placed over my eyes. My hearing, on the other hand, had amplified.

"Sister," Esahbyen purred. "What a pleasure to have you here."

I stilled completely.

"I thought I could find you here, brother." The woman's voice was smooth, almost silky, but there was an undertone of haughty command. "You have grown soft over the years."

Esahbyen was silent for a while.

"What brings you here, Mara?" His tone of voice was short and clipped.

Mara. That must be Xiomara then.

A sudden sense of vertigo threatened to engulf me. Not only was Esahbyen real—I'd still been entertaining the idea this was some kind of delirious dream—but so was Xiomara, and if she was...

So is the rest.

A cold shiver slithered down my spine and settled in my stomach. I hardly dared breathe in fear she would hear me.

"I am worried about you," she remarked.

There was something in the way she said it that made me wonder if she was worried about Esahbyen or about something else. He burst out laughing—a deep kind of rumble that didn't sound entirely too unpleasant and reminded me of my father.

I swallowed hard.

"There is nothing to be worried about," he assured her. "I just come here to think."

She snorted. "You are only fooling yourself, Esah. We all know you come here when you miss *her*."

Although I couldn't see him from where I was crouching, the silence stretching between them was long enough for me to know she hit a nerve.

I wondered who he was missing.

Do Gods fall in love?

"I should not have to remind you of what will happen should you endeavour to pursue this... issue," she observed, the tone in her voice not unlike Mother's when she expected to be obeyed without question. "In any regard," she continued. "I came to tell you a decision has been made. You are expected back."

Esahbyen let out a heavy sigh. "Can you give me a few moments alone to say goodbye? Something tells me I will not see this place again."

Xiomara didn't respond straight away. "Very well. I will give you until dawn, brother, because despite what you think, I *do* care."

I strained to hear more, but either none of them spoke or Xiomara had already disappeared.

"You can come out now," Esahbyen said at the same time as my sight returned to normal and the world suddenly sounded as if I'd submerged. "We do not have much time."

"Really?" I couldn't help the sarcasm lacing my voice as I began picking leaves and twigs from my hair.

"Someday," he muttered, rubbing his jaw, "that tongue will get you in trouble."

"It already has."

The amused look in his eyes had returned, but there was more, and I could not quite place it. It was almost like a parent watching their errant child backpedal out of a situation so fast they tripped over their own feet.

"What you need to know," Esahbyen said, glancing over my shoulder, "is that history is repeating itself, *dochtaer*. There is a war coming, and you must win it, not just for Ilvanna, but for the world."

Had he pierced me with a sword and told me I was immortal, the effect would have been the same. I stared at him, vaguely aware of my mouth hanging open.

"I knew you were mad," I said, my voice like a stranger's, "but I see now I was wrong. You are at an entirely irremediable stage of insane."

"Shalitha," he began. "Please—"

"No." I cut him off, running a hand through my hair. "No. You don't get to do this. You don't get to tell me I need to win a war for the sake of the world and still leave me with nothing. I want some *nohro* answers!" Anger rose with every word until I spat the last ones at him.

"Do you not think I want to give them to you?" he yelled in return, composure forgotten. "Do you not think I want to give you every little detail so you are prepared as best as you can? What do you think I brought you here for? Xiomara must have known, and she must have come here to stop me."

"From doing what?" I shouted, placing my hands on my hips.

"From telling you the truth." He clamped down on his anger. "She was giving me a warning, *Tarien*. Tell you, and I would forfeit my immortality."

"But you were risking it before," I replied, my anger deflating, "when you brought me here you said you wanted to give me the answers I was seeking. Your life was on the line then. What has changed now?"

He inhaled sharply, pressing his lips together. "Because she threatened yours, too."

"What's the worst that could happen? I'll die?" My body felt suddenly heavy, my throat thickened, and my vision blurred. "Wake up, Esah, I could have died today. I could have died a week ago, a month ago. If you hadn't brought me back, I'd have been dead twice already. Why does it matter all of a sudden?"

"I told you," he said, his voice strained. "It has always mattered."

"Then tell me the truth."

The pained expression in his eyes nearly took away my resolve, but he'd promised to give me answers, and I wasn't going anywhere until he did.

"I cannot risk it," he whispered, stress audible in his voice. "I cannot lose you, too."

"But—"

Before I could finish my sentence, the scenery changed, and he had disappeared. Coming back was like slamming into the ground after falling off a ten-foot ridge. Pain assaulted me from every direction. Screams of agony tore through my haze of torture.

All I wanted at that moment was to die.

CHAPTER 4

HAERLYON

*W*ith dawn not far off, the air held a crispiness to its touch, biting what little skin I hadn't been able to cover as I made my way to the training fields. A pang of loss went through me as my mind conjured images of my sister training with her *Arathrien* this time of day, every day, for years. I'd always enjoyed watching them from a distance. Tal had made sure their training was fast and rigorous, not allowing for even the slightest mistake, challenging them to be the best they could be. Challenging Shal to be the best she could be.

None of them were here.

I made my way down the steps with a heavy heart, my eyes on the hills behind which the sky began to turn a light purple. With Cerindil gone, the position for *Ohzheràn* had opened up, and although I had expected Azra to give it to Yllinar, or any of her other loyal men, she had instead bestowed it onto me. My first act as *Ohzheràn* had been to assemble our army. What little remained was now trickling on to the fields, and my chest tightened.

I was to wage a war, and they were far from prepared.

Now is not the time to get soft, Haer.

I pulled my lips up at one corner. My inner voice had taken up sounding like Tiroy, which made chiding myself bittersweet. That night at *Hanyarah* was etched in my memory like a finely detailed painting. Whenever I closed my eyes, even if it was for just a moment, I could still see him sitting propped up against a cottage, face slick with sweat and blood, his hand clutching his abdomen. The scent of blood had never quite washed away, although, under current circumstances, there was so much of it on my hands that I almost felt certain it was oozing from my pores. Everything from that day was burnt into my memory—everything except one thing.

Our last kiss.

It was slowly fading from memory, as was his scent, and the way he used to curl up against my back. I could barely recall his voice, and the sound of his laughter dimmed with each passing day. What I wouldn't give to remember them, let alone hear them. But Tiroy was dead. He wasn't coming back, and although he'd made me promise not to mourn him, he'd also told me to be strong.

I had to be more than just strong.

The moment my feet touched the grass, I composed my features, pulling my lips down in a sneer while I surveyed the small assembly. Most of them were young—younger than I liked —pulled from families who had nothing left to lose and every-thing to gain. After Azra's killing spree, a lot of *àn* had died. When I pointed this out to her, she'd sent her men to round up every and all who would be able to hold a weapon.

A sour taste coated the inside of my mouth.

Between holding a weapon and knowing how to use it was a chasm of years of knowledge and training, and I didn't have that time. So, I did what I had to do in order to prepare them to the best of my abilities—bully them until they were obedient enough to actually want to learn, and then run them down until they at least knew how to defend themselves.

I'd be impressed if they survived the war.

"What are you waiting for?" I yelled. "Get running. Ten laps, and if you can't make it, I'll add another five."

Startled from their barely awake stupor, they began to trudge across the field. Ten laps were a lot, and more than half wouldn't make it, but I didn't do it to make them miserable.

I needed to know which of them could be trained.

"You're taking well to your new position," Azra said from behind me. "Almost as if you were born to it."

"That's because I was," I said with a confidence I rarely felt these days. "And I finally received what I was owed thanks to you, *Tari*."

She smiled, but it never reached her eyes. Instead, a distant, haunted look swirled in their depths, testimony to the fact that her thoughts were not here. I didn't have to guess where they were.

"They'll find him," I offered, clasping my hands behind my back.

I couldn't afford for her to see they were trembling.

"Oh, I know," she said in a lazy purr lacking conviction. "But I don't want them to just find him. I want them to capture him and bring him to me, so I can torture him until he begs me to kill him."

The hatred in her voice should have come as no surprise, and yet, an ominous feeling settled in the pit of my stomach upon hearing it. Talnovar had defied her more than once, but none of what he had done warranted such a deep-rooted animosity. But then, Azra didn't need a reason to respond the way she did.

She's a monster.

A sudden gasp startled me from my momentary revelry. Looking up, I caught the colour draining from Azra's face seconds before she sank to all fours and retched. I was at her side and on my knees in an instant, resting my hand on her shoulder.

"*Tari.*" I feigned shock. "Are you all right?"

She grimaced, wiping her mouth on the back of her hand. "Fine. Turns out growing babies is a nauseating, tedious affair."

I narrowed my eyes but didn't comment as I helped her to her feet, surprised by the constant tremor going through her. Out of the corner of my eyes, I saw the rookies had slowed down on their laps and were watching.

"What are you looking at!" I yelled, turning to them. "Get those feet moving or you'll get lavatory duty for the rest of this moon."

Only a few hesitated at first, but it wasn't long before all of them were moving, even though some occasionally cast glances our way to see what was going on. I took off my cloak and placed it around Azra's shoulders.

"Perhaps you should lie down, *Tari,*" I suggested. "You're not looking well."

Her eyes flashed. "No. I will not show any weakness. Come see me after you're done training them. I need you to do something."

I stepped back and inclined my head, pressing my lips together. "As you wish, *Tari.*"

The kitchens were busy this short to noon, and I knew it was a terrible time to be pestering the kitchen staff. Even as a royal son I had no business there, and Sihra would make sure I remembered that fact by chasing me out with a large, wooden ladle if he caught me in his kitchen. He may have had a soft spot for my sister, but he had none for me, and judging by the looks on everybody's faces when I walked inside, none of them did. Some stared at me in fear, forgetting about their job altogether. Others stared at me quite possibly wondering which kitchen utensil would be most lethal.

None of them acted on it.

Kalyani, Xaresh' mother, was busy chopping onions and didn't notice me until I was by her side. Her eyes widened when she looked up, only to narrow. Instead of fear, defiance shone in them.

"What can I do for you, *Irìn?*" she asked, turning back to cutting the onions with more fervour than before.

I did my best to ignore the stinging in my eyes.

"I'd like to have a word with you, *Irà,*" I said, my voice low enough so only she could hear. "I need a favour."

She hesitated in her movements for a minute before continuing, practically slamming the knife into the onions. I was afraid she would hurt herself.

"And why would I help you?" Her voice wavered slightly, but the set of her shoulders told me she wouldn't be easily persuaded.

"Because otherwise your son and daughter will have died for nothing," I replied, fidgeting with the hem of my sleeve absentmindedly.

Her hands stilled. Carefully, she placed the knife down and turned to me, several expressions crossing her face until she settled on something relatively neutral. I straightened, looking down at her. Before she could open her mouth to speak, I did.

"I mean no disrespect," I whispered quickly. "And I will explain everything if you agree to meet me tonight."

She closed the distance between us, peering up at me. If she'd still had the knife, it would have been buried between my ribs.

"Don't you *ever* pull in my children like that again," she

hissed, fighting to keep her voice under control. "I am not beholden to you in any way, *verathràh.*"

I winced and stiffened and was about to respond when Sihra finally took notice of me and stomped in my direction.

"Midnight," I said hastily. "The pergola in the south-west rose garden. Do it. For the *Tarien.*"

I was barely in time to duck out of the chef's reach and made a hasty retreat from the kitchen without looking back. If Kalyani decided not to show up, I had to come up with a better idea. The thought twisted my stomach in a knot so profoundly I had to use the wall for support. As I breathed in, I told myself I did what I had to do—I was doing it for the greater good.

Whatever that was.

It didn't take away the fact I had allowed her youngest daughter to die. I'd stood by with a smirk on my face as people trampled each other to death to get to safety. The memory made my blood run cold. I leaned back against the wall, closing my eyes, thinking of days long gone.

I don't know how long I can keep doing this.

CHAPTER 5

TALNOVAR

y ears were ringing, my vision was blurry, and my body felt as if someone in full armour had slammed into me. Twice. Smoke coated the upper part of the cabin, but even at ground level breathing in felt as if my lungs were on fire. A second ear-splitting explosion that was not too far off shook the ship, and it took me a moment to realise we were under attack.

"*Nohro ahrae.*"

I turned on my side with a grunt, pushing myself to my hands and knees while keeping my head low.

"Arav?" I croaked and coughed.

There was no response.

"Arav." I shuffled left and right on my knees, keeping my head low as not to inhale more smoke, using my good arm to feel around.

It didn't take me long to find him, but when I did, he was unresponsive. One of the things I'd learned in the army was to check for vital signs first. If your own life was on the line, you didn't want to waste time trying to revive a dead man. To my relief, Arav was still breathing, but judging by the wheeze and gurgle on every breath he took, I wasn't sure for how long.

"Tal?"

"Here," I said, resting my hand on his shoulder. "I'm here."

"Don't... don't make the"—coughs wracked his body, leaving him breathless—"same mistake I made. Go. Find her."

"I can't leave you," I replied, already looking for a way out.

"You can," Arav wheezed, "and you must. Another blast, and... and the hull might tear apart. You don't want to be below deck when... when that happens."

"What about you?"

He managed a weak smile. "My time has come, *eshen*. Go... now. Don't look back."

Rubbing the back of my neck, hesitation kept me where I was. This man had saved my life. I was doing him a disservice by leaving him here to die.

There's nothing you can do for him. His chances of survival are slim to none.

"Go." Arav pushed me feebly. "Unless you want Seydeh to take you after all."

A grunt escaped my lips. Deep down inside, I knew he was right, but it still felt like the wrong thing to do. It wasn't my decision to make, I knew this, too, yet somehow, I couldn't tear myself away from the old man.

"Xiomara, forgive me," I murmured, more to myself than to him. "May Seydeh be merciful, *mahnèh*."

Before he could respond and I could change my mind, I moved away from him, burying my nose and mouth in the crook of my arm while trying to find the exit. It took me longer than I liked, and when I did, it was blocked.

I cursed.

Visibility was limited due to the smoke, and with only one arm available to find my way around, I was at a serious disadvantage. For a moment, I considered taking off the sling until I remembered Shalitha's struggles with an improperly healed shoulder.

Use it for as long as you can.

My lungs ached fiercely with each indrawn breath, and the dizziness hadn't quite subsided yet. In fact, it was getting worse. I had to get out of here fast, or I would be joining Arav in a seaman's grave. A deep shudder went through me at the thought and combined with my serious dislike for ships, it fuelled my determination.

More by luck than anything else, I found an opening large enough to squeeze through. Although the smoke was not as bad as it had been in Arav's cabin, I still had to stay low. When the ship suddenly lurched to the right, I smacked into the wall on my left. There was resistance first, and then there was none. I stumbled into a small cabin barely lit by an oil lamp swinging from the rafters.

Something moved in the shadows.

"Who's there?" a voice croaked.

"A friend," I replied, having no idea whether this was true. "I'm not here to harm you."

"You're here to free me?"

"Free you?"

A rattling of chains followed. "I'm not here for fun."

"What did you do?"

"Not exactly of importance right now, is it?" the stranger scoffed.

I harrumphed and opened my mouth to reply when a third explosion shook the ship, slamming me into a wall for the second time.

"Nohro ahrae," I muttered. "What in Esah's name is going on up there?"

"Sounds like we're under attack," my companion offered. "All the more reason to help me out of these chains, don't you think?"

Hesitation settled in the pit of my stomach, but only for a moment. If I hadn't wanted to leave Arav behind, how could I contemplate leaving a chained man on a ship bound to sink?

"Anytime now," he drawled.

A low growl escaped my lips in response, but I did move closer to the prisoner, wondering how in the world I was going to get the cuffs off. I'd never developed any lock picking skills, and even if I had, I had neither the tools nor the time to even try. The only way to get him out of the chains would be to break his thumbs.

"The ring on the wall is somewhat loose," the stranger offered as if he'd heard my thoughts. "I've been working at it for the past three weeks, with little result, I might add."

"Why haven't you pulled it out then?"

He snorted. "I mentioned the little result, didn't I?"

I grunted in response, grabbed the chain close to the wall and began to pull. At first, the ring didn't budge. My left hand was hardly my strongest hand. Two hands wrapped around the chain behind mine, and between the prisoner and myself, we pried it loose. And not a moment too soon.

A loud crack resounded through the ship.

"We need to go," I yelled over the noise.

Without waiting for the man I'd just freed, I moved into the passageway and started making my way to the ladder leading to the next deck. Footsteps behind me indicated he was following.

"I never caught your name," he said.

"Tal."

"Halueth," he replied. "Thanks for getting me out of there."

I waved my hand in dismissal, focusing on where I stepped instead. The explosions had left the ship in bad shape, and I didn't fancy falling into a dark hole I'd missed.

"Not very talkative, are you?" Halueth commented.

"Trying to stay alive, if that's all right with you."

Whether it was or wasn't didn't matter.

Shouted commands and frantic cries reached us by the time we'd made it to what was left of the ladders. My heart was thumping erratically, stealing the air from my lungs in an almost painful way. I tried to gulp it down, but it didn't matter. It had lodged itself in my throat now.

"This way." Halueth tapped me on the arm as he moved past me. "There's another way to get above decks."

I nodded and followed him.

Skulking through the passages of the ship with Halueth up front, I felt like a thief in the night, and the knowledge that this ship was under attack because of me made this feeling infinitely worse. I'd expected Azra to go to great lengths, but I hadn't expected her to come fetch me from a ship. Sweat trickled between my shoulder blades, and I clenched my hands to keep them from trembling.

This is all my fault.

And as much as I wanted to make it right with the captain—I would do anything to keep his crew safe—the only thing that would ensure their safety was the one thing I couldn't do.

I couldn't surrender.

I couldn't go back.

If I'd thought the normal creak and sway of the ship was horrible, it had nothing on the desperate attempts that were made to keep it afloat. A sudden lurch of the ship sent me crashing into a wall, and as my head connected with a wooden beam, stars danced in my vision. Blinking them away, I observed Halueth hadn't faired any better. Blood trickled from his temple, but the injury didn't look too serious.

"You all right back there?" he muttered, wiping the blood away.

"Well enough."

I checked my head for injuries and was glad to find that aside from the headache building behind my eyes, there was nothing more than a lump the size of an egg. I did feel as if my stomach was about to flip over. Saliva flooded my mouth, and although I kept swallowing, it didn't cease.

I needed to get on top.

Fast.

"Just a moment," I gasped, leaning against a pole, trying to calm my stomach by taking deep breaths.

"Are you sure you're all right, *mahnèh?*" Halueth asked.

"Positive."

"If you say so, but we've got to move unless you want to have dinner with the fish."

The image Halueth painted was too much. I averted my head and added the contents of my stomach, what little I had inside of me, on the deck until all that was left was the bitter taste in my mouth and a severe ache in my abdomen.

Halueth clapped me on the shoulder, a tone of under-standing in his voice when he spoke. "Come on."

The ladder was close—I could see it from where we were standing. Only a few more steps and we could make it topside, but the ship suddenly groaned as if it were under a lot of strain and tilted dangerously far to the side. A loud creak like the sound of a tree falling tore through the frantic screams coming from above. The ship bounced back as if it had been loosed by a sling, throwing us to the other side. I managed to grab a hold of something, but Halueth lost his footing and slammed into a support beam. This time, he was less lucky, and he crumpled to the floor, his eyes rolling to the side.

The ship swayed from side to side like a drunken sailor, and I was glad there was nothing left in my stomach when another wave of nausea hit me. If I'd thought I couldn't feel worse than I already did, I was sorely mistaken. After the ship had more or less settled, I skidded over to Halueth, careful that I wouldn't be tossed another way should the ship make another unexpected move. I slapped his cheek, but he gave no response. Shaking his shoulder didn't work either.

I cursed.

At that moment, another loud crack resounded throughout the ship, followed by it tilting sideways. I grabbed onto a rope and held on for dear life, watching crates and sacks that had come undone from their bindings slide past, watching Halueth glide back the way we'd come from.

I had to get topside.

Now.

As soon as it appeared the ship was going to hold, I dashed to the ladder, taking the rungs two at the time. The sound of fighting reached my ears along with the scent of fresh, salty air. I snuck closer to where the fighting had come from, staying as low as I possibly could. Smoke from fires on the deck provided me with some cover, but it wasn't enough to stay out of sight completely.

"Hand me your passenger," a voice boomed across the deck, "and I shall leave you and your crew alone."

I knew that voice.

Yllinar.

A part of me was surprised at it not being Haerlyon—Azra had loved sending him after me—and with it came the sickening feeling that perhaps it was because he hadn't survived the injury I'd delivered. Crouching low, I crept closer to hear what the captain had to say.

"If I had a passenger," he said. "I'd hand him over, but as you can see, there's only me and my crew."

Yllinar scoffed. "This would all go so much easier if you would just cooperate."

"You destroyed my ship," the captain said, unimpressed.

I couldn't see either of them from where I was hiding but imagining them facing off against each other wasn't hard. Yllinar was a tall, wiry man, but he was fast and stronger than he looked. Captain Fehran, on the other hand, was a small man, and he had looked as if he hadn't wielded a weapon in a long time. Yet something told me he knew perfectly well how to defend himself when it came to it.

"These were warning shots," Yllinar said, his voice slick as always. "My demands are clear."

"Well, I don't have what you're looking for, so get your ass off my ship before I'll make you."

My conscious warred with my heart. I could save these people, but it would mean everything Eamryel, my father, Soren and Mehrean had done would be in vain—everything the rebellion was fighting for would be a lost cause, and Azra would win.

I couldn't let her.

Two pairs of hands grabbed me from behind and yanked me to my feet. They twisted my arms behind my back, eliciting a howl of pain, drawing the attention of everyone on board. My vision swam, and I would have fallen forwards had it not been for the death grip on my arms. With my line of sight clear, I could make out both Yllinar and the captain. The first looked as if he'd been given the best gift at *Wannenyah*, the second as if someone had just gutted him.

I struggled against the men holding me, but to no avail. They were stronger than I was and most likely uninjured. Before I knew it, I was on my knees in front of Yllinar in a similar fashion as at *Hanyarah*.

My blood ran cold at the hatred in his eyes.

"Did you really think you could escape?" Yllinar asked.

"Of course," I replied, my lips quirking up at one side of their own accord. "She's not as smart as she thinks."

He backhanded me. "Show some respect for your *Tari*."

"She's not *my Tari*."

"Ah yes," he drawled. "You still believe in the *Tarien*. She's hardly a threat. Between you and me, I don't think she was ever fit for the throne. She's better off wherever she is."

I smirked. "If you really thought she were no threat, you wouldn't be here."

"I'm here because Azra has a plan for you," he replied. "If it were up to me, I'd finish what I started two years ago."

"She has no plans for me. She just doesn't want me to find her niece."

Yllinar shrugged. "I really don't care what it is she wants or not, to be honest, but you're coming with me."

"I don't think so," the captain said. "You have no authority on these waters, *mishan*, and this man is my prisoner, not my passenger."

Yllinar narrowed his eyes as he looked at Fehran. "Prisoner, you say?"

"I intend on selling him as a slave in Zihrin."

But Yllinar wasn't easily fooled. He straightened his shoulders, cocked his head imperceptibly while tugging at the cuffs of his coat.

He was getting ready for something.

"I'm not sure what your sentiment is over this man," he said pointedly, "but he's coming with me, so you can either hand him over, or I'll kill every last man on this ship and take him."

Without waiting for any kind of response from Fehran, he ordered his men to do as he threatened with a flick of his wrist. Judging by the sound, several of the captain's men lost their lives before they had found their weapons, and then the fight started in earnest. The pressure on my arms lifted, but before I could get out of the way, Yllinar's sword was at my throat, and I knew he'd be faster.

"Don't even think about it."

For a moment I considered his words as well as the pain flaring through my shoulder. My eyes darted left and right, surveying my surroundings to see what was happening, but there were precious few people in my periphery. The captain was fighting off two of Yllinar's men, blood trickling down his cheek from a cut. If I couldn't save them by handing myself over, I could at least help give them a fighting chance. Keeping

48

an eye on Yllinar, I waited until his gaze flicked away from me. When it did, I rolled out of his sword's reach and made an attempt to sweep his feet from under him. He staggered back, surprised by my action, but before I'd gotten steady on my feet, he was upon me.

"You really need to learn your place," he hissed, raising his sword.

"I know mine," I replied, assuming a fighting stance. "Do you?"

He snarled and brought down his sword. I dodged his first strike, and on my instep, planted my shoulder in his ribs. Yllinar grunted and gasped for air, clutching his chest while staggering back. I grimaced at the fierce pain emanating from my shoulder but pushed it to the back of my mind. I couldn't get distracted by it. His second attack was less confident, his swing wide and uncontrolled.

It left him exposed.

Without thinking twice, I charged at him and grabbed him around the waist, using my momentum to topple us both over-board. Everything happened both slow and fast. Yllinar yelped and dropped his weapon as we went. The wind assailed me from every direction as I fell, battering my ears in the process. Yllinar grappled onto me. I kicked him off.

He hit the water hard.

I was barely in time to straighten myself and go underwater feet first. Something latched onto my leg, dragging me down while I tried swimming up with one arm. I kicked, but it— Yllinar—held on. A sharp pain in my leg registered somewhere in the back of my mind, but the heaviness in my chest and the burning sensation in my lungs were far more pressing. He was pulling me down. I kicked, pushed, shoved, but he wouldn't let go.

There was only one way to get rid of him.

CHAPTER 6

SHALITHA

I awoke screaming.

Every fibre of my being was on fire—every muscle in my body felt as if I'd been fighting for a week. A pounding headache had taken up residence in my skull, and even though I tried, I couldn't move. Reality twittered about me like a nervous bug, jerking from left to right, undecided where to settle, and colourful spots were dancing in my vision.

Son of a hehzèh.

If Esahbyen ever showed up again, I'd kill him.

"*Taleh,*" a familiar voice said. "Calm down."

As reality finally settled and the spots slowly disappeared, I could make out a woman's face hovering above mine. Her brow was furrowed, her lips pressed in a tight line.

"Z'tala?" I remembered her from the night before.

"Praise Temarìn," she murmured. "You scared me, *k'lele.*"

"I'm sorry?"

She raised an eyebrow and retreated to her side of the room. A thin bar of light filtered through the small window, barely illuminating the cell we were in. I hadn't noticed how small it was the night before. There were two bunks—one for me, one for Z'tala, with a path half as wide as a bunk between them.

One could hardly move.

I pushed myself to a sitting position, ignoring the sharp stabs in my side and the off kilter feeling in my stomach. Z'tala was watching me through narrowed eyes but didn't say anything.

Rubbing my temples to ease the headache, I let my thoughts wander to the encounter with Esahbyen, and how he had left me with more questions than answers, but as anger rose within me, I remembered the desperate look in his eyes just before he sent me back.

Why would the God of War look so terrified?

"What happened?" Z'tala's voice drew me out of my reverie.

I frowned. "What do you mean?"

"In your sleep," she said. "What happened?"

"Just a bad dream."

"Do you have them often?"

I regarded her quietly, curious why someone I'd only met the day before was so inquisitive. Just because Elay had me placed with her didn't mean I could trust her.

"Often enough."

It wasn't a lie, but it wasn't exactly the truth either. I'd had enough dreams over the past few months to last me a lifetime, but they'd never been as vivid as this one. Then again, I wasn't sure whether this had been a dream or something else.

How could it have been something else? You were asleep.

"I'm sorry if I've woken you."

Z'tala shook her head. "*N'era.* I do not sleep much anyway."

Her words reminded me of the question I'd asked her the night before, of how she came to be here, and I was about to ask it again when a loud clamour alerted me.

"Guards," Z'tala muttered. "Get up. Look down."

"Why are they here?" I whispered.

"Food. Whatever you do, don't look up and don't make any sudden moves."

The cell I'd been in before had had a latch through which they'd shoved food, making this development progress. Getting to my feet wasn't as hard as staying on them while waiting. I strained my ears to listen to the shuffle of feet, the rattle of keys, and the creak of metal bars being opened. Cries of pain and whimpers followed curses. As the doors were slammed shut, the sound of metal hitting metal reverberated through the tunnel. It felt like forever before they reached our cell, and by that time sweat beaded my brow, and I was swaying on my feet.

"Stay still," Z'tala murmured.

"Trying."

Gruff voices appeared at our cell. I closed my eyes, counting to twenty and back to focus on something other than how faint I was feeling. Hot flashes surged through me, and if I didn't know any better, I'd say I was spiking a fever. Keys jingled, and a moment later, the door was opened.

Don't move.

I swayed and moved one foot to remain standing. The guard yelled incomprehensibly, his voice coming from far away. I think they were orders, but I wasn't sure. Another voice chimed in, a female voice, and then there were hands on my shoulders to support me. Looking up, I found Z'tala's face inches from mine. Her lips were moving, but her words were nonsensical.

Everything happened at a snail's pace.

She turned to the guard, said something, and turned back to me. I had the sensation of floating, then realised she must have helped me lie down because I'd stopped swaying. Instead, I started shaking uncontrollably. As warmth seeped into my body, lessening the trembling just a little, I thought it was a blanket, but blankets were a rare commodity in here. When I opened my eyes, I found Z'tala lying next to me, covering me with most of her body.

KARA S. WEAVER

"What are you doing?" I whispered.

"Keeping you warm, *k'lele*," she replied, sounding as if I'd just asked a stupid question.

"Why?"

She snorted. "You are welcome."

"Where are the guards?"

"They left," she said. "Be glad, too."

I was about to ask another question but decided against it. This place worked in ways I had yet to uncover, and although I would get a long way by inquiring, I didn't want to appear like a dimwit. The moment Z'tala moved away from me, another blast of cold hit me, but at least the uncontrollable shaking didn't return.

"You need to rest." Z'tala sounded stern. "And eat."

She offered me a bowl with something that looked even less appetising than *ch'iti* and smelled a whole lot fouler. Z'tala set to her breakfast unperturbed, ladling the porridge into her mouth with her hand. They hadn't provided us with spoons. I turned on my side and followed her example, a shudder going through me at the taste.

It's food. Be glad they're giving you something.

Z'tala halted mid-scoop.

"What?"

"Just surprised you'll eat without a spoon," she commented. "Most who come here for the first time would rather starve than use their hands."

I shrugged. "I'm not going to starve myself over something as trivial as eating utensils. My hand is fine, although a bit messy."

She smiled at that. "Good. You may yet survive this place."

"Why is that?"

"Because you'll do whatever it takes."

"How can you be so sure?"

54

Z'tala's lips quirked up at one side. "We are not so different, you and I."

The rattle of keys alerted me from my slumber, and I sat up as fast as my injury allowed me. Z'tala's hand shot out to steady me as I rose to my feet and swayed but was gone just as fast. I glanced at the door, unsurprised to find two guards standing there.

"You," one of them said, pointing at me. "Come."

I risked a look at Z'tala, but her gaze was firmly fixed on the ground. Straightening my back, I side-stepped over to the guards, but instead of looking down, I looked right at them. It earned me a backhand across the cheek.

"Raise your arms," the guard growled. "The *Akyn* wants to see you."

I bit the inside of my cheek to keep myself from replying I was in no mood to see him, but I wasn't that stupid. Besides, with a bit of luck, I'd be able to see Elay. My heart ached for him, which was made worse by the fact it reminded me of Tal and how my feelings for him were changing. Whenever my thoughts turned to him, the pain was indescribable, and yet, that pain was overshadowed by what I felt for Elay.

The heaviness of the cuffs snapping shut around my wrists startled me back to the present.

Worries for later.

My eyes locked with Z'tala's moments before the guard closed the door, and I barely caught her imperceptible nod. I had no idea what it was for, but I felt reassured all the same.

As the guards marched me through the corridors, I did my best to memorise the turns we took, but there were so many, I lost count after the fifteenth. A rush of fresh air indicated we were moving up to ground level. The *herrât*, or arena in my tongue, was a grand affair built to impress visitors, looming high atop the rocks overlooking Akhyr. The holding cells for the prisoners were underneath it, hewn out of the same stone as the tunnels connecting them. While it kept the cells cool enough during the day and cold during the night, it also retained the heavy, stale air reeking of dirt, blood and sweat.

I inhaled deeply the moment we emerged from the tunnels.

Curiosity made me wonder why Kehran wanted to see me, but I wasn't fool enough to disregard a punishment for killing his cat. A deep shudder ran through me at the memory of the beast, drawing out a low hiss from me. As I stumbled over my own feet, the guards' hold on my arms prevented me from smacking into the cobbled street face first. Their grip tightened, and by the time we arrived at the palace, my arms were numb, and I was sure that come morning, my biceps would sport finger-shaped bruises.

A patch of white caught my attention as we passed the training site, its out-of-place appearance dancing on the edge of my vision, tugging at my senses. I strained to see who it was. Although my guards didn't relinquish their death grip, I got a good look at the fighter.

An Ilvannian.

His hair was pulled back in a ponytail, revealing tapered ears of which the one I could see was missing its tip. From this distance, I couldn't make out his features, but he was watching me, too, and judging by his stance, the sight of me surprised him as much as the sight of him did me. I kept looking at him until I could no more and resolved to ask Elay to look into it.

If I could.

They didn't take me into the palace proper like last time, but through several corridors until I'd lost any sense of direction, and out into a garden. It reminded me of Elay's garden back in Zihrin, except this one was much bigger and much more luxurious. Four recliners stood in a half-circle facing a stage on which three scarcely clad women were dancing. They weren't naked, but their attire was mostly gauze except across the more delicate places.

My attention snapped to the two men on the middle recliners. Kehran was watching me with open curiosity. Elay made it his mission not to look at me at all. My stomach did a backflip upon seeing him.

"Release her," Kehran ordered in a bored tone of voice. "No reason for restraints here, or is there?"

He was looking at me pointedly.

"Of course not, *Akyn*." I inclined my head slightly and placed my hands behind my back once the guards relieved me of my shackles.

If I'd had a weapon, he'd have been dead the moment my hands came free, but it would have destroyed our carefully laid plans. Its success was contingent on Kehran still being the dictatorial narcissist Elay had painted him to be. Straightening, I risked a glance at Elay studying his nails meticulously, a positively bored expression on his face.

"That was quite the performance," Kehran purred, looking at me. "The crowd absolutely loved you."

I stared dead ahead, lips pressed tightly together.

"Unfortunately," he continued, and I stiffened. "I wasn't much impressed with you killing my pets."

"Then you shouldn't have sent them in."

The words were out of my mouth faster than I had a chance to think them over. Elay's head shot up sharply, emerald eyes boring into me as to inquire to my degree in stupidity. At that point, I'd say it was at death wish. To my surprise and Elay's, judging by his brows shooting up, Kehran chuckled. It wasn't a pleasant sound by any account, but there was a twinkle in his eyes.

"I like her spirit," he said, looking at Elay. "Shame she landed on your doorstep first, brother."

Elay's lips twitched up in a smile, but his eyes remained cold as he regarded the man next to him. "She sure has a way with... words." He was grinning, watching me as if I were a prized possession.

The look didn't go unnoticed by Kehran.

"You seem... interested, brother?" he asked.

Elay observed me with a wicked look in his eyes. "How can I not? Have you not seen her?"

Kehran pulled up his nose as if he'd smelled something disgusting, looking me over. "You'd share your bed with a beast?"

"Without a doubt," he replied without batting an eyelash, looking at me now. "After all, if she's as wicked in bed as she's out in your *herrât*, I'll be in for a night of fun."

My stomach plummeted as if I were dropping out of the skies. My legs felt a little unsteady, but a familiar and not quite unwelcome tingle made its way down between my legs. It took me every bit of self-restraint I had not to move a muscle.

Kehran's eyes narrowed, his mind obviously working on something—Elay's confession, I assumed. I didn't blink, trying to push down the elation soaring in my chest while at the same time battling the fear of what-ifs.

What if Kehran decided Elay's words were worth something, and he'd take me to his own bed instead?

"As much as I'd like to indulge you, brother," Kehran said at length. "Your sexual escapades must wait until she's recovered. Until then, see to it that she does."

"As you wish, *Akyn*." Elay bobbed his head.

"As for you." Kehran turned his gaze back on me. "You've done well. You did what any other fighter in the *herrât* would have done. Keep fighting like that and you might earn privileges. Until then, you'll go back to the dungeons. Kick up trouble, and you'll end up dead. Understood?"

"Yes, *Akyn*," I replied, my voice sounding strangely detached.

"See to it that she returns, brother. Take two guards."

Elay inclined his head as Kehran turned his attention away from me. Graceful as a cat, Elay rose from the recliner, a secretive smile on his lips as he stalked towards me. My heart was thudding in my chest, remembering another time where he had been the graceful predator and I'd been his more than willing prey.

I swallowed hard.

His hand came around my bicep, and he steered me away from the garden, keeping a firm enough grip to make it look like he was hurting me. Two guards fell in step behind us.

None of us spoke on the way back.

The Ilvannian male I'd seen practising earlier was still at the training grounds, fighting off four others with a deadly grace I'd seen only in Talnovar. My chest tightened. Two of his opponents were down before they knew what hit them. A third got in a good blow to his side, but the Ilvannian twirled and knocked him out with a punch to the nose. I winced as the man crumpled to the ground. The fourth attacker, a mountain of a man ready to tear the Ilvannian in two, attacked with brute force. He danced out of the way, light on his feet, clearly playing with the mountain.

"Who's that?" I asked.

I realised Elay had stopped to allow me to watch.

"Not here," he murmured.

CHAPTER 7

TALNOVAR

Did she feel like this?

A strange feeling of tranquillity enveloped me, reminding me of my mother's embrace that time I'd almost died after Azra tried to kill me. The thought summoned a feeling of discomfort—gave the impression that something wasn't as it should be. I kicked my feet in sheer desperation, swept my arms through the water in pure terror.

I swam as if my life depended on it.

The moment I broke the surface, I felt as if I drew air into my lungs for the first time since forever. I took a deep gulp at the same time as a wave broke over my face, and I coughed and spluttered at the mouthful of water going down my throat. My legs felt heavy, each kick to stay above the surface becoming increasingly more difficult. It was as if a dead weight hung from them even though I'd made sure he was gone. As it turned out, despite my injuries and the lack of air, I'd been more determined to live. All it had taken was keeping him under water long enough until he'd lost consciousness.

The sea had done the rest.

Yllinar was dead.

Exhaustion pulled at me, calling to me like a lover, begging me to surrender and ease into its embrace. Considering my recent experiences with lovers, that option held no appeal. The ship lay ahead—a dark outline against the darkening sky—its mast leaning forward in an unnatural angle. It wasn't going anywhere soon but judging by the distance—if my judgement was anything to go by these days—it was quite the swim, and I wasn't sure I would make it.

The Ilvannian ship was much closer and from the looks of it, my only chance at survival. If I could somehow get on board and in one of their skiffs, I might have a chance to escape. Again. All I had to do was keep swimming until I could no longer, which was quite the undertaking with my injured shoulder and deadweight leg. Every stroke was pure agony, every kick unprecedented torture.

But I had to keep going.

For Shal. For Ilvanna.

The words became a mantra with every stroke forward—a steady drum in my mind to keep me going. The ship increased in size the closer I swam. By the time the outlines of the cannons on the starboard side of it came into focus, I was dragging myself through the water with one arm, my shoulder having given out miles ago. Despite kicking my feet, I barely made any progress. Or so it felt.

Desperation clawed its way up my chest, tightening the muscles in my throat as I laboured to get air into my lungs. My head dipped under more frequently now, but I came back up each time.

For Shal. For Ilvanna.

By a miracle, I reached the ship without drowning first. The challenge was now to haul myself up somewhere. Making out anything in this darkness was hard, let alone finding something to hold on to, but it was either that or the depth of the sea.

I had no wish to become better acquainted with Seydeh.

Nohro. I should've paid more attention during Naval History.

Biting back the pain, I explored along the ship until my hand brushed against a protruding piece of wood. Mustering all the strength I had left, which wasn't much to begin with, I hoisted myself up with one hand and threw out the other, hoping to catch another bar.

I did.

The effort it took to haul myself out of the water and onto the rungs was enormous. My arms were shaking. My legs felt too heavy. One misstep and I'd plunge back into the water.

If that happened...

Don't go there, mahnèh.

I grabbed hold of the next bar, and the next, and the next, pressing myself close to the ship to keep most of the weight from my arms. More than once, I had to stop and catch my breath. More than once, I almost slipped, sending my heart into a wild frenzy.

For Shal...

For Ilvanna...

On my right, the dark shape of a cannon appeared. If I could climb through that small opening, I wouldn't have to drag my ass up these small wooden bars all the way to the deck. Just these few had drained me beyond any feeling I knew existed. Closing my eyes, pressing myself against the side of the ship, I deliberated my options.

Neither climbing up all the way nor squeezing through a cannon hole had any certainty of success. If anything, both were doomed to fail.

I had to make a choice. Fast.

The cannon hole it was.

I listened carefully for any sounds coming from the small opening, and only when I felt certain there was no one there did I inch closer. Saying a prayer to any God to keep me safe this time, I first stretched out one hand, biting back the roar of pain as my shoulder locked up.

Not now.

I pushed beyond the torment, beyond the blockage, and wrapped my hand around the opening. I stretched out my leg, hooking my foot behind it, and bit by bit I edged closer, keeping myself from falling by sheer effort of will and the last bit of strength I possessed. The moment I slipped inside, I slumped to the floor.

I barely had the strength to crawl to a less conspicuous spot before I passed out.

THE HARSH CRY of seagulls close by and the gentle dip and sway of a ship on the move startled me awake. My stomach responded almost immediately, and I was just in time leaning over in my hideout. Aside from water I must have swallowed the night before, nothing came out. As in response to this notion, my stomach growled.

Mind your own business.

Overhead, the sound of people moving around the ship highlighted my predicament. At this time of day, there was nowhere to go without being discovered, which was the last thing I wanted to deal with it. Getting off fast was my objective. I had no desire to be captured and taken even farther away from my end goal, and closer to the last place I should be.

Ilvanna.

The thought of returning to Azra made me break out in cold sweat, sending shivers rolling down my spine in uncomfortable waves. Yllinar said she had plans for me, whatever that meant. I intended not to find out.

I needed to get to the skiffs.

I need a plan.

Peering out of my hideout—not much of one I realised, looking around—I was relieved to find the gundeck abandoned.

For now.

It was when I tried to get to my feet and found I couldn't stand on my left leg properly that I realised this plan hinged on a whole lot more than finding a skiff. Lowering myself to the floor, I inspected my leg with trembling hands, wondering what caused this paralysis.

Remembering last night, I had a pretty good idea.

Yllinar must have gotten me somehow.

My fingers found the cut along my leg, and I traced it from the upper half of my calf almost down to my ankle, shivering. I'd thought swimming had been so hard because of how tired I'd been, not because of yet another injury. If Yllinar had cut into muscle, or even tendons, no wonder I couldn't feel it.

It's a miracle I haven't drowned.

At least it had stopped bleeding—a small mercy in the grand scheme of things. It could have been a lot worse, but I needed my leg to work. It was as simple as that. As long as I wasn't dying, I'd find a way. I had to.

Sitting back, I listed the things I needed to do before I escaped the ship. First, I needed to find the ship's healer's cabin and get something for my leg, perhaps my shoulder, too. I would have to find food and water as well if I wanted to survive out on the sea—I already didn't like my chances—and if possible, something to cover myself with during the night. I had no doubt it could get cold, plus the weather could turn ugly just as easily. There were only two problems with my plan.

One, I had to find all these items without being caught. Two, I didn't know the layout of this ship.

Or any ship, for that matter.

THE PASSAGEWAYS WERE empty save for a few drunken stragglers on their way to their hammock. What had surprised me upon my first encounter with some of them from the safety of my hideout was that they weren't mostly Ilvannian as I'd expected. In fact, they looked a lot like Captain Fehran's crew. If my assumptions were right and they'd indeed taken over the ship, I would probably be all right if I made myself known. But after what happened the day before, I couldn't be sure.

I couldn't risk it.

I went from cabin to cabin in a desperate attempt to find the healer's quarters. Although my knowledge of ships was passable at best, I knew they should have one aboard. Arav had been killed in the first attack, so Fehran would have asked this ship's healer to join him, provided he had survived. With a bit of luck, the healer would still be busy treating the injured and wouldn't be in their cabin.

It was a long shot.

Up ahead, a door to a cabin stood ajar and voices drifted from it, urgency in their tone. Checking the passageway and finding it mercifully empty, I snuck closer, using the wall for support. The numbness in my leg was a constant distraction, and I had to focus on not sinking through it every step, but it was also a reminder of why I was doing this. I wasn't doing this for me.

"The *Tari* won't be pleased," one man said.

"She never is," another replied. "But I, for one, am glad it's over."

"Be careful what you speak of, *mahnèh*," the first hissed. "Your words could be considered treason."

The second man huffed. "She's not here, and both Arolvyen and Imradien are dead."

"Presumably."

"You saw them go overboard," the second man objected, and

I thought I detected awe in his voice. "Neither of them has come up. I've been watching for a long time."

How long have I been under?

The two men were silent for a stretch until the first man broke it. "Do you think there is merit to the rumours?"

"Which ones?"

"That *Tarien* Shalitha is still alive?"

"Now you're talking treason," the second man muttered. "But yes, I do. Not that it matters now that Imradien is dead."

The first man let out a heavy sigh, which was followed by a creak as he lay down on something. "I suppose you're right. What do we do now?"

"With some of his men dead, I assume this new captain could use additions to his crew. I'm not going back to Ilvanna."

"Nor me, *mahnèh*. Nor me."

The door closed, trapping the light within, and shrouding the passageway in semi-darkness once more. Their words had triggered something inside of me, giving me new hope where previously I'd felt none, and I realised I hadn't been fully convinced of the possible success of this mission at all.

The thought was unsettling.

I slipped past their door quietly, feeling a smile tugging at my lips.

So, not everyone in her army is loyal to her after all.

Logic dictated this made sense, but it did something for me. In the time I'd been with her, she'd made me the villain in everyone else's story, an accomplice to her atrocities, and I'd gone down a dark path I should have had the sense not to. It had discouraged me, stolen from me the belief there were still good people in this world. I had thought my faith in them had been mended after Father, Soren and Eamryel rescued me, but the feeling hadn't lingered.

I hadn't realised until now.

Arayda had chosen me for a reason—she had believed I

could bring her daughter back and restore her to the throne. If she were still alive, she would have sent me again and again for the simple reason she'd believed in me.

It was time I returned the favour.

For Ilvanna, mey Tari.

With newfound strength, I continued my prowling of the corridors in search of the healer's cabin and the galley. Surely, they couldn't be far now? As I turned a corner, another set of voices drifted my way, growing louder with each passing moment. When I turned back in the direction I'd come from, I realised it was the only way—they'd have to pass me to get to the other side.

Nohro.

I tried one door. Locked. A second. It opened, but the moment it did, snoring erupted from inside. I quickly closed it. A third door was locked as well. The voices grew steadily louder, as did the footsteps. Aware I was running out of time, I slipped inside as soon as the fourth door opened and closed it behind me, listening to the voices and footsteps moving away.

I let out a sigh of relief and closed my eyes.

"Move and you're dead," a voice hissed suddenly near me.

The tip of a dagger nestled uncomfortably against the hollow of my throat. I stilled and opened my eyes one by one. As I did, a grin spread across my lips, mirrored by the person standing opposite me.

"Vaen! I thought you were dead!" I clasped his hand.

Ruvaen smiled wryly. "By all accounts, I should have been. Here, have a seat. You look like you fought *Esahbyen's* hounds."

"Close enough," I replied, lowering myself to sit on the small bed, massaging my leg even though there was no pain.

His eyes narrowed, but he didn't say anything. Instead, he poured two cups of *ithri* and handed one to me. I took it gratefully and gulped most of it down, barely tasting it.

Ruvaen snorted. "Never seen you this eager on *ithri*. Not since you joined the army, anyway."

"Desperate times," I said with a lopsided smile. "So, how did you survive?"

He scratched the back of his neck, his brows knitted together in consideration. "It was the strangest thing," he began. "We were preparing for the attack when I received an anonymous letter. It stated our endeavour was compromised. If I continued our plan, I'd surely die."

"So, you stayed back?" I scowled.

Ruvaen's lips pulled up at the corner in disgust. "No. I gave my men a choice. Cease our activities and fall back or attack, pray some of us would get through to start the fires, and risk getting killed."

"I take it they chose the latter?"

He nodded, a harried look flitting across his features. "They did. Few of them survived, including myself. Your father ordered us to retreat."

"He told me you had died."

At that, Vaen smiled bitterly. "They thought it best to make you believe that."

"You don't agree?"

"Who am I to question the *Ohzheràn*, Tal?" He shrugged. "Things were hectic at the time. I figured he had his reasons."

"Where did you go?"

He pressed his lips together. "Of that I cannot speak, *mahnèh*, but you must believe me when I tell you I'm on your side. Always have been."

I nodded and took another sip of *ithri*, mulling over his words. Knowing my father, he'd had a thousand reasons to tell me Vaen had died, the most obvious the fact he'd never liked him. In hindsight, I suppose I couldn't blame my father, although I did wish he would see Ruvaen had turned his life around as well.

Unlike Cehyan.

"Listen." I bit my lip, twirling the cup in my hands before looking up at him. "I need your help."

Ruvaen arched a brow. "All right."

"I need to get some healer's supplies, food, and a skiff," I said, "and leave the ship before they either find out it's missing or discover me here. I can't go back to Ilvanna."

"Figured as much," Ruvaen replied drily. "You'll be dead if you do. Where are you going?"

After his comments about not being able to tell me where he'd gone after the failed attempt of setting the palace on fire, I briefly considered not telling him either, but that was a childish response if anything.

"Zihrin," I replied. "Thought I'd go enjoy some culture."

Ruvaen snorted and pushed himself off the door he'd been leaning against. "Let me see what I can do. Stay here, I'll be back soon."

Before I had a chance to respond, he was gone.

BY THE TIME RUVAEN RETURNED, the sun was already dipping into the ocean, and I'd been pacing up and down the cabin for the better part of that time, agitation fighting a winning battle with my self-control. My leg kept giving out, sending me stumbling to hands and knees. Each time, I pushed back to my feet, praying that it wouldn't happen again, and each time when it did, I cursed, praying even harder it would hold me up long enough to leave this ship. Several times, I stopped myself from going out of the room and getting things myself, and it had taken a massive amount of restraint not to do so. With Vaen's arrival, most of the unease settled, until I saw the troubled look on his face.

"Here," he said, tossing a cloak at me. "Put that on, and"—he rummaged through a trunk beneath the bed and pulled out a dry pair of leather trousers, a clean shirt, and a fur-trimmed jacket that would be infinitely warmer than what I was wearing now—"this. It's not much, but it beats whatever you're wearing."

"*Teralé,*" I murmured, and began to strip my clothes off.

I managed to get out of my jacket and shirt without too much hissing and cursing, but it was another matter entirely when it came to my trousers. It soon occurred to me the frayed edges of the cut had dried up along with the blood, effectively melding wound and cloth together. There was no way to get it off without ripping the injury open.

"By Esah," Ruvaen breathed. "You need a healer, *mahnèh.*"

"No time," I said through gritted teeth, perspiration beading my brow as I began the ungodly process of teasing the scraps of fabric free. My head swam, my stomach lurched, and more than once I had to catch my breath before I could continue.

At some point, Ruvaen stopped me. "Leave on the trousers, Tal. This isn't going to work, and it'll upset the injury only further. The best we can do is pour the rest of the *ithri* on it, bandage it, and pray to the Gods you'll survive long enough to find a healer in that *nohro* desert."

I grunted in response, unable to form a coherent sentence. There was merit to his words. Rising to my feet unsteadily, I hoisted up my trousers and fastened them. With help from Ruvaen, I pulled on the blouse and fur-lined jacket before sitting down on his bed.

"This'll hurt," he warned, uncorking the *ithri* with his teeth.

"Get on with it," I rasped.

The howl of pain erupting from my lips was cut short by a hand clasping over my mouth. I gasped and hissed, cursing Ruvaen to the end of the world and beyond. Only when the feeling of liquid fire rampaging through my leg dwindled did I regain most of my senses. Ruvaen had bandaged my leg, looking a few shades paler than he normally did.

"We'd best get going," he said, glancing out the porthole. "It's properly dark. Best time to sneak a fugitive off the ship."

Without wasting any more time, I rose to my feet, grunting as I put weight on my injured leg. I threw the cloak around my shoulders and fixed it with a clasp. Before leaving the room, I pulled the hood over my face to hide it.

"What will you answer when they ask you questions?"

"That it's none of their *nohro* business." He flashed me a grin.

As we made our way through the ship and up to the main deck, a good deal easier now that we weren't shot at, Ruvaen handed me a small pouch with coins, a leather bag with food, and a wineskin. Rummaging around, I found the bag didn't contain enough to last me a few days.

It's better than nothing.

"Wait here," Ruvaen murmured as we arrived at the ladder leading above decks.

He made his way up the steps with an easy swagger, producing a second wineskin from his coat. I couldn't help but chuckle when I realised what he was about to do. Some things never changed. I waited while raucous voices drifted down to my hiding place, beginning to believe Ruvaen had forgotten all about me, until there was a sharp whistle, and I knew it was time to go. He was waiting for me above deck, looking out over the ship stretching out before us.

Even in the moonlight, she looked magnificent.

"Stay low," Ruvaen murmured, pushing the hilt of a sword in my hand. "Go left and find the last skiff. Get into it. I'll be there shortly."

Being on a ship had the benefit of not having many places to go topside—below decks was another matter entirely—so I found the last skiff Ruvaen mentioned quite easily.

Almost too easily.

Looking over my shoulder to make sure I wasn't being watched, I slid underneath the canvas and into the skiff. The deep darkness was suffocating, but it was a good deal better than inside the belly of the beast. After what had happened on the other one, never would be too soon to set foot on a ship again. I made myself comfortable on the bottom of the skiff as I waited, wondering what in *Esah's* name Ruvaen was up to.

A sudden lurch and jolt startled me back to awareness—I must have dozed off—and to my side, I heard Ruvaen order someone to help hoist the skiff down. My heart was beating rapidly as they lowered me to the water, my stomach heaving at every shocking movement downwards. It wasn't until the skiff hit the water that I released my breath.

I began pushing the canvas overboard. While it would certainly be good to have should there be a storm, it was also heavy and would weigh down the skiff. It was almost off when I felt something sharp pressed against that sweet spot just below my ear.

"Give me one good reason why I shouldn't kill you, *verathràh.*"

CHAPTER 8

HAERLYON

*D*espite the time of year, the night air held a winter's chill to it. I wrapped my cloak tighter about me, pacing the length of the pergola, praying to Xiomara that Kalyani would heed my plea. As much as I hated dragging her into this, I needed an ally, but I would understand if she wanted nothing to do with me. My sister had offered her and her daughters a job after Xaresh was killed, a safe place. Not only was he dead now, but so was one of her daughters, the other was gone, and there was no safety to speak of.

I need to tell her about Samehya.

I ran a hand over the shaven side of my head, the sensation of the light stubble underneath my fingers reminding me of Tiroy. Sadness clutched at my heart but steeled my resolve. The orders I'd received from the *Tari* that afternoon bordered on insanity, but unless I wanted to blow my cover, I had no choice but to obey them.

My skin crawled as if invested by a thousand bugs at the thought.

As the sound of approaching footsteps reached me, my hand went for my sword instinctively. Even though I was expecting someone, one could never be too careful, so when the hooded figure came closer, my hand remained firmly on the pommel.

"Is that a way to greet someone you invited?" Kalyani's soft voice reached me before she did.

"In these times," I replied, "one must always be on his guard."

"In your case especially, *Ohzheràn*." She pulled back the hood of her cloak.

The slumped shoulders and dark circles under her eyes were testimony to how tired she was, but there was a fierceness in her eyes as she looked at me. Tired she may be, but she would fight.

"Talk," she said. "Fast, or I'm gone, and there won't be a second chance."

I blinked at her. "Gone? Where?"

"As if I'd be telling you."

"Fair enough." I regarded her quietly, sitting down on the pergola's fence, stretching my legs in front of me. "Samehya is safe, and I need your help keeping an eye on the *Tari*."

Kalyani watched me coolly, folding her arms in front of her. "And why would I do that?"

Pinching the bridge of my nose, I thought hard about how to phrase my next response. It was obvious she didn't trust me and so far, I had given her no valid reason to accept my request. In truth, I wasn't completely certain what it was I was asking of her exactly. All I knew was the importance of having someone in Azra's inner circle.

Call it gut-feeling.

"Listen," I began, rubbing my hands on my thighs. "I may be privy to a lot of information, but not to all, and if we want to win this coming war, we need all we can get. With the *Tari* pregnant, she will need more help than before, so I wanted to ask you if you would agree to become one of her ladies-in-waiting and spy on her."

She observed me from under a frown, lips pursed in

thought. "You want me to risk my life, too? As if my children weren't enough?"

Without thinking, I pulled my dagger from its sheath in one swift movement. Kalyani took a startled step back. I took the blade between thumb and forefinger and held it out to her, watching her.

"Take my life if you want repayment for your daughter's death." I pushed myself away from the fence and knelt at her feet, turning my head up. "If you could get revenge for Xaresh, for Tynserah, would you?"

She narrowed her eyes at me. "Maybe, but it wouldn't bring them back."

"No," I whispered, my voice tight, "it would not. But their murderer would no longer be alive either."

Kalyani pressed her lips in a tight line. "You're as much of one as she is, standing idly by, murdering on her command."

"Yes."

There was no denying it.

I lifted my chin, craning my neck so she had full access to my jugular. I was even so kind as to point out where to thrust the dagger. "Just... make it fast."

Knowing Xaresh had faced his assailant with his eyes open, knowing her daughter had died fully aware of what was going on, I didn't blink, focusing instead on the light passing through the pergola, illuminating the woman standing in front of me with a dagger. I swallowed hard and inhaled deeply the sweet scent of the roses surrounding us.

If I were to die today, at least I'd do so on my terms.

I stilled as Kalyani pressed the cold blade against my throat and winced at the stinging sensation underneath my jaw.

I'll see you soon.

"No." A loud clatter disrupted the silence as she threw the dagger to the ground. "I will not be like you—like *her*. I will help you, not because you deserve it, but because she doesn't."

I bowed my head low. "*Teralé, irà.* Thank you."

"Let me know where and when," she said, her voice strained. "This is the one and only thing I'll do."

"Of course."

Without another word, she turned around, pulling the hood back over her head. I let out a sigh of relief and sat down promptly, unable to bear my weight any longer. Leaning back on my hands, I stared up at the sky, aware of blood trickling down my neck, deciding on my next course of action.

A small price to pay, indeed.

As I rose to my feet, I grabbed the dagger from where Kalyani had dropped it, but rather than putting it back into its sheath, I lay it flat against my lower arm, grabbing the hilt tight.

I knew what I had to do.

THE SOUND of my heartbeat drumming in my ears kept me going, helped me put one foot in front of the other, held my focus on the task ahead. Nobody still prowling the corridors dared halt my progress, not even the guards posted throughout the corridors. Instead, they inclined their head in acknowledgement. I didn't return the favour.

Gone was Haerlyon an Ilvan.

The *Tari's* right-hand man had returned, the scowl on my face a permanent deterrent for anyone who stepped in my way. All that withheld me from losing my determination was a memory—a distant whisper in the back of my mind, an order I could not refuse. My lips pulled up at one corner as I strode through the hallways of the corridor, the call for revenge humming just below my skin. As I rounded a corner to the royal wing, one of the guards stepped forward, chest puffed out to look more important. It deflated rapidly when he saw who I was.

"*Ohzheràn*, apologies," he mumbled, stepping out of the way. I inclined my head, glowering at him.

A quick once-over told me he was one of the original Ilvannian guards and not one of Azra's hired men.

Good.

"What's your name?" I turned to him, lifting my chin half an inch to add to my authority.

"Erlahn," he answered.

"How long have you been around?"

"Fifty years," Erlahn replied, somewhat steadier than before. "I served under your mother and *Ohzheràn* Imradien."

"Why are you still here?"

Erlahn's eyes widened, a stricken look on his face. He masked it quickly and pulled himself up to his full height. "Because it's my job, *Ohzheràn*. It's not my decision whom I serve."

Admirable, but wrong.

I didn't quite believe him. "I'm glad you managed to switch your allegiance."

He regarded me as if trying to solve a puzzle, but again, he rearranged his features fast, as if afraid of what would happen if I caught on to them. That alone gave me a reason to doubt him.

"For the *Tari*," I said.

Ehrlan squinted before replying. "For Ilvanna."

I continued my way into the royal corridors, my mind whirling around the conversation with Ehrlan, a smile tugging at my lips. Information was good to have. When I rounded the corner to the servants' side of the royal wing, I glanced back. Ehrlan had taken up his position again, stifling a yawn.

No guards paroled these parts of the palace—not anymore.

Azra simply didn't care what happened to the people in the palace as long as nothing happened to her. With her current agenda, I wouldn't be surprised if there was another attempt on her life soon. A part of me wished there would be, but for the sake of Ilvanna, it could not be me. People were growing desperate under her strict rule, and more and more Ilvannians fled the city every day, seeking their fortune either in Therondia or Naehr.

It made her go berserk on a good day.

She was convinced they were rallying forces against her, which was why she sent out patrols to round them up and bring them back to the city, and if they rebelled, have them killed.

Anything to keep her throne.

I halted in front of a nondescript door and opened it without thinking twice. The room was small compared to the royal chambers, barely large enough to house a bed, a wardrobe, and a table and chair. The occupant of the room sat up in her bed when the door clicked shut behind me.

"Hello?"

I remained silent.

"Who's there?"

Rather than responding, I took a step forward, allowing her to see me in the moonlight entering her room through the small window.

"*Irín,*" she murmured, rubbing her eyes. "What are you doing here?"

"I know of your treason, *Irà,*" I replied gravely. "The *Tari* has ordered me to see to your punishment."

The woman stilled like a hare which had caught the scent of a hunter. With her face shrouded in shadows, I couldn't quite make out her expression.

"Make it fast, please," she whispered as she lay back down.

I slit her throat without a moment's hesitation.

It had to be done. For the greater good.

CHAPTER 9

SHALITHA

*A*fter meeting Kehran that afternoon, I felt out of sorts. The man was as mercurial as Ilvanna's and Kyrintha's weather combined, which made reading him, predicting his actions, more difficult. I'd just gone to bed when a hand clamped over my mouth at the same time as a deep voice told me to be quiet. My heart was hammering in my chest. Opening my eyes, I found Elay's face inches from mine. Behind him, Z'tala sat quietly.

"Elay?"

"Shush. Come with me."

I frowned. "Why?"

"You'll see."

"Z'tala?"

"Go with him," she whispered, sounding as if this was the most normal thing in the world.

We both knew that if we got caught, we'd be lucky if Kehran had us killed on the spot. Nodding softly, I slipped to my feet and allowed Elay to guide me out of the room, wincing as the sound of him locking the door echoed through the corridors. His warm hand slipped in mine, sending a jolt of longing

KARA S. WEAVER

through my body. I shut off the feeling as quickly as it had come up. Now was not the time to give in to any kind of desire.

The corridors were surprisingly devoid of guards as we moved deeper into the dungeon, if the sounds and smells of were any proof. I was still wondering where Elay was taking me when he suddenly halted in front of a door. Our breathing and the soft jingle of keys were the only sound.

"You have an hour," Elay murmured, his lips brushing my cheek. "I'll come for you when it's time."

"But—"

Before I could finish my sentence, he nudged me into a cell at least twice as wide as the one I shared with Z'tala. Moonlight lit up most of the space, giving me a chance to look around. There was a table and a chair on the right and judging by the softness underneath my feet, a carpet. A book lay open on the table, an unlit candle not far away from it. In the darkness to my left, somebody stirred.

Instinct had me at attention and ready for a fight in a heartbeat.

"Who's there?" a deep voice croaked.

The tall Ilvannian man I'd seen training earlier that day stepped into the moonlight. Up close, he looked familiar, but I could not remember where from.

His eyes widened when he saw me and a moment later, he was on a knee in front of me, head bowed, fist against his chest over his heart.

"*Tarien*," he murmured.

"Please," I whispered, discomfort edging its way up my spine. "There are no titles here."

His lips quirked up in a lopsided smile as he rose to his feet. "No, there are not."

He cocked his head to the left, curiosity twinkling in his eyes. His scrutiny would have felt uncomfortable had he not smiled.

80

"Please," he said, inviting me to sit down at the table with a wave of his hand. He made himself comfortable on a stool I hadn't noticed when I came in. I avoided looking at him, wringing my hands as if I were washing them, all kinds of questions racing through my mind.

He beat me to it.

"How did you end up here, *Tarien?*" he asked.

I glanced up at him. "That's a long story we don't have time for."

"Tell me the short version."

"Azra."

He narrowed his eyes. "What about her?"

Bile rose in my throat at the memory of her, of everything she had done. Inhaling deeply, I steadied my nerves. Exhaling slowly, I spoke, "She's the *Tari* now."

The stool he was sitting on crashed into the wall behind him as he jumped to his feet. I watched him pace up and down his cell, glancing at the door, praying to all the Gods that nobody had heard.

"What about your mother?" His voice was barely a whisper.

"Dead." The lack of emotion in my voice came as a surprise, not just to myself, but from the looks of it, to him as well.

"I'm sorry."

I shook my head. "I can't do anything about it." Bitterness crept into my tone, and I pinched the bridge of my nose. "Have I seen you at court before?"

He shook his head, a wry smile on his lips. "I do not think so, *Tarien*. I left before you were born, but the name is Jaehyr Imradien. It may sound familiar, perhaps."

I stilled, forcing away the tears that came unbidden at the name. "Family of Cerindil?"

"Yes."

Judging by the look on his face, I thought it best not to inquire any further into their relationship.

"Why did you leave?"

"*Tari's* orders," he replied with a heavy sigh, retrieving the stool from where he'd kicked it to.

I frowned. "Surely she didn't order you to be a slave here?"

He smirked. "How astute of you, *Tarien*. No, she did not. She sent me to kill her sister."

There was no mirth in his voice, no indication he was joking or otherwise trying to be hilarious. He was dead serious.

"Why?"

He let out a snort, looking at me as if I'd grown two heads. "Have you met your aunt?"

I grimaced. "I get why she'd want Azra dead. Why did she send you?"

"To get my vengeance on her."

My brows shot up in surprise. "Vengeance?"

Jaehyr let out a heavy sigh, turning his lambent gaze on me. "Azra killed the woman I loved. Murdered her own sister and got away with it."

"You were in love with my mother?"

He stared at me, confusion knitting his brows together. "Your mo—" His eyes widened, and he shook his head. "No, no, *Tarien*. Your mother and Azra had another sister. Azra is part of a twin."

My mouth dropped open, and I blinked at him stupidly. "I —what?"

Jaehyr watched me with something close to compassion in his eyes and shook his head, muttering something to himself. "Her name was Shaleira," he began softly, looking at me with a faint smile on his lips. "If I'm not mistaken, your mother named you after her, partially anyway. She was the oldest of the three and heir to the throne of Ilvanna. She was killed during the last war between Ilvanna and Therondia."

"*Ohzheràn* Shaleira was a *Tarien*?"

"She was, indeed."

82

"They don't mention that in the books," I muttered, then frowned. "Why?"

He shook his head. "Rumour has it *Tari* Xeramaer went mad after losing two daughters so shortly after one another that she had everything in relation to them scrapped from the records. I suppose whoever wrote that book of yours thought Shaleira was worth mentioning."

"You said she was killed in battle," I said. "But you also said she was killed by Azra. That doesn't add up."

"During the last battle, Shaleira was brought to the infirmary with a knife injury. She died of blood loss."

"From a knife?"

Jaehyr scowled. "According to Gaervin's reports, the kni—"

"Gaervin? As in, my father, Gaervin?"

I fell silent. Gaervin wasn't my real father according to Esahbyen. But Gaervin had practically raised me, and for that alone, he'd forever be exactly that—my *real* father.

"Yes," Jaehyr replied with a heavy sigh. "According to his reports, she'd sustained the injury hours before and had just gone on. Knowing Shaleira, it was because she didn't want her people to perceive her as weak. She was their *Ohzheràn*, she had to lead them into battle—and she did. Rurin found her half-dead on the battlefield."

My stomach twisted and turned at his words. Everything I had believed in the last couple of years had been a lie. My father had been a lie. My mother had lied to me. Azra had betrayed us and mother had suspected—she must have. I swallowed over and over, but try though I might, I couldn't keep the queasiness at bay. I all but flew off the chair and emptied my stomach in the bucket near the door.

Jaehyr pulled my hair away from my face without comment until I was done, and when I sat back on my heels, he offered me a scrap of cloth to wipe my face.

"Not the response I expected," he said in a half-chuckle. "Are you all right?"

I nodded. "I'm fine."

I got to my feet and straightened my back. This was hardly the worst thing I'd ever heard in my life, but it was a surprise all the same. "You and Shaleira?"

"We loved each other." Jaehyr shrugged, leaning against the wall. "Even though we knew we might never be together."

"I thought *Tari* could marry whomever they wanted as long as their men were nobility?"

Jaehyr pursed his lips. "Yes and no."

I arched a brow.

"Probably every other *Tari* in the history of Ilvanna could, but your grandmother, and her mother before her, had been very picky whom their daughters would marry. One had to be of impeccable breed to pass her requirements."

I'd never known my grandmother. She had died before I was born, and judging by the sound of it, I didn't have anything to be upset about.

"That explains why Mother married Father rather than Rurin," I replied, sitting back in my chair, chewing the inside of my cheek.

Jaehyr smiled faintly.

"You said Azra killed Shaleira," I continued after a while. "How did they know it was her?"

Jaehyr opened his mouth to reply when a light double-knock on the door and the click of a lock being opened halted him. A moment later, Elay stepped in.

"Time to go," he said, glancing at Jaehyr with his lips pressed in a thin line.

Jaehyr had his fists balled at his side.

"No," I said, looking at Elay. "I can't. There's more. I need to hear it."

"No time. The guards will be renewed in a matter of

moments, and they'll be doing their rounds. They cannot find you here. Or me, for that matter."

"But—"

"Please, *Mithri*," Elay said, sounding tired. "Listen, for once."

Out of the corner of my eyes, I noticed Jaehyr's look of surprise at the endearment Elay offered me. He rather looked as if he were ready to tear Elay's head off. Raising my hand in warning, I rose to my feet and inclined my head to Jaehyr.

"*Teralé*," I whispered. "I hope we meet again."

"Take care, *Tarien*."

I smiled at hearing the title. He'd offered it before, but it was strange to hear my title in a place like this. Elay clicked the lock back in place and rested his hand on the small of my back almost possessively as he guided me through the corridors back to my cell.

"You know this place well," I murmured.

"I grew up here, *Mithri*. Of course, I do."

I let out a heavy sigh. "I need to see him again. Soon."

I felt Elay tense beside me.

"Why?"

"I just have to."

Jaehyr knew more about my family than I did. If I were to get rid of Azra, I had to know everything I possibly could about her, and something told me he could provide me with a lot of answers. Considering the place we were at and Kehran's unpredictability, we could be dead in a few days.

Elay stopped in front of my cell.

"I'll see what I can do," he murmured, "but know that I'm already at risk for arranging this meeting. I was able to call in some favours, but I might not be able to the next time."

"Let us train together."

"I don't think Kehran will allow that."

"Why?"

"Because you're both Ilvannian, *Mithri*," Elay murmured,

cupping my face in his hands. "And he might not be the brightest, but he isn't stupid enough to let two of his enemies—his mother's enemies—together."

"Well," I began. "We have to come up with something, or he'll be forever on your throne and she on mine."

Elay placed a light kiss on my lips after unlocking the door. "We'll figure it out."

The click of the lock echoed in the darkness.

CHAPTER 10

TALNOVAR

"*Y*ou're alive," I breathed, relief flooding through me. "Thank the Gods."

Halueth pressed the dagger hard enough against my skin, but not hard enough to draw blood. "Why wouldn't I be?"

Holding up my hands in surrender, I considered my next words carefully. "Because I thought you died on that ship. You hit your head hard, and when I checked..."

He interjected me with a scoff. "It wasn't that bad. I came around just as you fled up the ladder."

He couldn't have.

And yet, here he was, alive and ready to slit my throat.

Verathràh.

Halueth wasn't the first to call me that and would most likely not be the last, but I was at a loss as to what I could possibly have done to him. The easiest way out would be to surprise him and throw him overboard, but I was tired of running. My shoulder was on fire and my body felt broken and bruised from being tossed around like a sack of grain. If I couldn't talk myself out of this, perhaps I deserved to end up at the bottom of the sea.

"The *Tarien*," I said in response to his question, halting on the rowing even though I was hard-pressed to get away from that ship as fast as possible. "I'm looking for the *Tarien*."

Halueth hesitated for a second, and I could feel the dagger withdraw from underneath my ear.

It was back a moment later.

"She's dead," Halueth replied. "You're running."

I closed my eyes. "She's not dead, *mahnèh*. She's alive somewhere in Zihrin."

And even if she were, running doesn't sound like a bad idea.

"You're lying," he seethed, adding pressure to the blade. Where I'd expected he'd break the skin in doing so, I didn't feel it. The pain in my leg undoubtedly drowned it out.

"*Nohro*," I grumbled. "Why in Esahbyen's name would I lie? What do I stand to gain?"

"You work for that *hehzèh*," he spat. "For Azra."

Despite the anger spiking inside of me, I managed to stay calm, breathing in through my nose and out through my mouth.

"Then answer me this," I said, glancing at him. "Why does she want me dead?"

Out of the corner of my eye, I noticed Halueth hesitate, a frown on his face he worked through my words. I remained silent, allowing him the time to decide for himself.

"Why would she?" he asked at length.

"Because I'm going to find the *Tarien*," I said firmly, "and bring her home. Whatever it takes."

Halueth considered my words, his mouth working as if he were about to reply, but then his jaw set, and the tip of his blade was back beneath my ear.

I held my hands up in surrender.

"You killed them," he growled. "That day on the streets. You killed them. All of them. For *her*."

It took me a moment to realise what he was referring to. Cold dread slithered in my gut, but I bit it away. It didn't do to dwell on the past.

"Please," I said in a hoarse voice. "Before you kill me, hear me out. If you're not satisfied by the end, do what you must do."

The slight tilt of his head and the fact he didn't kill me straight away were the only indication he was willing, but something told me I had to be fast.

"That day," I began, "I fought on your side. The moment I saw what she'd done, I knew I had to try something—anything —to keep her from succeeding. That woman"—I swallowed hard—"she's evil. The things I've seen her do, just because she... could."

A cold shiver ran down my spine, and I grabbed the oars in a death grip. The pressure of the blade against my neck eased somewhat, suggesting that Halueth had noticed.

"I tried to save people," I said softly, swallowing a lump in my throat. "Tried to give them a chance to flee, but it was for nothing. And when they caught me..." I shook my head to dispel the memories. "She made it look like I'd done what she ordered me, but I would never do that. My allegiance lies with *Tari* Arayda, with the *Tarien.* I'd sooner die than pledge allegiance to that *hehzèh.*"

I looked at him, and whatever he saw in my eyes was enough to withdraw the blade and tuck it back in his boot. With a heavy sigh, I released the hold on the oars and slumped forward.

"I don't know what happened," Halueth said in a soft voice. "I'd been out on a mission with my squad before *Tari* Arayda died. Nareth said you were involved. Said you instigated the rebellion on Azra's orders. I... I never thought you were capable of it, but then I saw you with her, how you obeyed her, and I..."

"I don't blame you," I replied. "I will never forgive myself for everything she's made me do. I'll spend my life making up for it."

"You really believe she's alive?" he asked after a while. "The *Tarien*, I mean?"

"I do."

"Let me come with you, *Anahràn*."

I stilled at the title and turned to him, sadness washing over me. "I'm nobody's *Anahràn*, Halueth. I don't deserve it."

"Perhaps, but you are my *Anahràn* now."

I pulled the oars in silence for a while, both of us caught up in our own thoughts. Although Halueth had decided not to feed me to the creatures of the deep, a part of me wished he had. His story hurt worse than anything Azra had put me through. It was exactly what I'd tried to avoid, and I had failed.

Dinner was a sober affair—some curated meat Ruvaen had provided me with and half an apple each. It wasn't much, but I had no idea how long we'd still be at sea, and the last thing I wanted was to run out of either food or drink. If we weren't careful, the sea would toss the skiff in any direction and Seydeh knew we'd end up where.

At least there was the small reprieve of me not feeling too nauseous now, even though I didn't feel too well. Hot and cold interchanged, but I put it down to the fact it was freezing on a skiff out on sea. It had to be the reason for the tremors rolling through me as well.

"What will you do when you find her?" Halueth asked, startling me from my contemplation.

"I don't know." I shrugged, the familiar ache in my chest blooming. "Take her home, I suppose."

"You'll need an army to get into Ilvanna, *Anahràn*."

I flinched at the title. "Please, call me Tal. And I know. I didn't say it would be easy."

Halueth snorted. "It sounds impossible."

"Maybe." I sighed, rolling my shoulders. "But I've come this far."

"Well." Halueth made himself as comfortable as he could on the bottom of our skiff. "Let's try to get to land first. None of that will matter until then."

I snorted. "I suppose."

"Goodnight... Tal."

"*Mehra saen*," I murmured. "Sleep well."

Halfway through the night, I caught myself nodding off more and more frequently. Halueth appeared deeply asleep, and after what had happened, I didn't have the guts to wake him. I knew I should sleep, but I didn't dare. With a new burst of energy, I pulled the oars, ignoring the warning flares in my shoulder and the fiery sensation in my leg. Perhaps if I'd focus on that, I could stay awake—I could get us to shore. By the time dawn arrived in a pale hue of grey and purple, I'd surpassed feeling tired.

Halueth woke up shortly after, looking as refreshed as if he'd slept in the best bed in the palace, not a dark thought to mark his dreams. When he looked at me, he frowned.

"Didn't you sleep?"

I shook my head. "No, couldn't allow us to drift off course."

The sound of seagulls in the air and the splash of the oars on water was the only sound around us. The shore was visible on the horizon, just a dark line against the rising sun, but if I'd learned anything while on a ship, it was that the distance at sea could deceive you.

"Do you know where she's supposed to be?" Halueth asked after a while.

"Y'zdrah. Wherever that may be."

He nodded. "What if she's not?"

I stared at him, opening and closing my mouth like a fish out of water. While his question made perfect sense, and it was a possibility I'd considered somewhere in the back of my mind, hearing it spoken aloud made cold sweat trickle down my back. I rubbed my neck and clenched my jaw.

"We'll find her," I said resolutely. "One way or another. If it's not in Y'zdrah, then somewhere else."

Halueth was grinning.

"What?"

"It just reminded me of how you sounded on the training fields whenever anyone wasn't doing what you instructed."

I snorted. "I didn't train you, did I?"

"No. I was under *Zheràn* Haerlyon's command," he said, his lips pulling up in a snarl. "Before he decided to work for... *her.*"

My own sentiments regarding Haerlyon were as colourful as Halueth's from the looks of it, but whenever the royal brother appeared in my thoughts, there was a feeling I couldn't quite place. Perhaps it was the fact I had no idea whether he was still alive or not, or perhaps it was the words he'd spoken at the very end. Something about them had sounded grim, but I couldn't for the life of me explain the feeling.

"It's a shame he did. We lost a good man."

"It makes no sense," Halueth muttered. "Of all the people in the palace, he's the last one I'd expected to become a turncoat."

"Grief does strange things to a person."

He winced at my words.

"Sorry, I didn't mean to—"

"It's fine."

A soft chuckle escaped my lips, and I shook my head, trying to ignore the stab of pain in my heart.

"What's so funny?"

"She used to say that," I replied, looking up, "a lot. Even if she wasn't fine."

"By she, I assume you mean the *Tarien*?"

I nodded. "Yeah."

"She was quite the character around Ilvanna," he said after a while. "I don't think people were sure what to make of their future *Tari*."

A snort escaped my lips. "Trust me, nobody could. I'm pretty sure she didn't even know herself."

Halueth's brows shot up in surprise.

"She was respected though," he remarked. "Among the army at least."

I tilted my head.

"The common men and women respected her because she trained like us every day, no matter the weather. She wasn't like most noblewomen or men for that matter. Nor were her brothers. Which is why Haerlyon's betrayal—"

"Stings?" I offered, a faint smile on my lips.

He nodded. "Don't get me wrong, we all respected and revered the *Tari*, and we followed our orders because of it, but ever since seeing the *Tarien* on the training fields, I knew I'd follow her to the end of the world if I had to."

A smile tugged at my lips. "Yeah, I know what you mean."

Silence settled over us again, broken only by waves lapping at the skiff and seagulls crying overhead. Halueth's words were a kindness I felt I didn't deserve. Not many people had cared to see Shalitha like I did—had not bothered to get past that tough exterior and look at what was on the inside. Not that many had gotten that chance, considering who she was, but even those who did never tried. Insecurity and fear had been most prominent when she was alone, but she'd never allowed either of them to rule her, had never allowed either feeling to consume her, but we, her *Arathrien*, had known.

We'd seen the toll it took on her.

I'd stood by and watched as her relationship with her mother grew tenser by the day, watched as she rebelled against a destiny she wanted no part of. If only I'd made it clear much sooner how desperately I wanted to be in her life as more than just her *Anahràn* perhaps all of this would have run a different course, but I'd been too blind to her pain and anguish, too focused on her safety that I'd missed all the signs.

If I'd just paid more attention.

Halueth let out a whoop of delight, jerking me back from my pitiful thoughts. I looked at where he was pointing.

"Land! We've made it!"

Relief the likes of which I hadn't felt in a long time spread through me.

Land. I'm coming, Tarien.

CHAPTER 11

HAERLYON

*I*t had been almost a moon since Azra sent us off. In her perpetual paranoia, she had ordered me to deal with Ilvannian refugees to the south. According to the reports from scouts, they were headed to the mountains to join up with the rebel forces at *Denahryn*. Whatever the cost, nobody—not even children—could reach them on the off-chance my sister would return. The fact Azra believed this to be a possibility was both exciting and terrifying.

Her return would mean war.

Azra would stop at nothing to kill my sister despite the multiple failed attempts. She'd do anything to keep the throne, including killing everyone in Ilvanna if that was what it took. Shalitha was a threat, and Azra was afraid of her. She wouldn't go through all of this if that weren't the case. A smile tugged at my lips. Shalitha had always been the toughest of us three, and definitely the most determined if nothing else. Whether it came from growing up with a prophecy to her name or being heir to the throne, I wasn't sure, but if anyone could defy the odds, it was her. If Azra was indeed so frightened of her, I would keep praying to the Gods for my sister to remain fighting.

If she can do that, I can do this.

The steady click of hooves on the cobblestones eased my discomfort somewhat, but not by much. Cries still rang in my ears as if I'd just heard them. The coppery scent of blood still clung inside my nose, transferring me to another time—another place. A shudder ran down my spine, leaving goosebumps in its wake. This massacre—I couldn't call it anything else—had been like *Hanyarah,* yet so much worse.

There had been no children at *Hanyarah.*

My thoughts returned to the night at the beach with Talnovar. The hatred in his eyes had been more painful than the knife between my ribs. We could have easily overcome him, but I'd held back after we captured Eamryel. I had my men make sure he wasn't bleeding to death to give Tal time to escape. When we caught up, I'd had to make it believable.

He hadn't disappointed.

As if in memory, the scar began to itch. Underneath the layers of armour I was wearing, I had a snowball's chance in summer to reach it. I could wiggle in the hopes of it working, but with there being no guarantees, I decided to ignore it as best I could.

It was hard.

To make matters worse, it began to rain with big, heavy drops, slow at first but gradually increasing in strength and speed until we could barely see a hand in front of our faces. It felt as if the Gods were punishing us for what we'd done, and I couldn't help but wish their punishment was more severe. Had Mother still been alive, we would have been hung like common criminals instead of being welcomed back like heroes.

My shoulders hunched at the prospect, and I found myself fidgeting with my necklace.

Our arrival at the stables was a quiet affair. None of my men spoke. None of them joked or boasted. They hadn't done any of that the entire journey back—unlike the men I'd had with me when we chased Tal and Eamryel—and for that alone they had my respect. Stable hands scrambled to their feet, taking the reins and helping us dismount. I grabbed my saddlebags, ordered my men to find food and take their rest, and made my way inside the palace to report to Azra.

I wasn't looking forward to it.

Seeing Azra on the throne, her pregnancy too obvious to hide, made my stomach do an uncomfortable backflip. It wasn't as much the pregnancy that made me feel that way, but rather the idea of whose child she was carrying. She hadn't told me, I doubted she'd told anyone, but I'd seen her going to Tal that night. I'd heard his pleas. His screams. It was a good thing Cerindil arrived when he did, or I would have blown my cover. I'd never understood why she'd done it, but she did everything without any rhyme or reason to it. This time, I just wasn't convinced this had been one of her whimsical ideas.

She'd planned this for a reason beyond my imagination.

"Haer!" she chirped when she saw me. "You've returned."

I inclined my head, unsure of how my voice would sound if I opened my mouth. I needed a moment to collect myself and don the façade of the merciless *grissin* Azra believed I'd become.

"How did it go?"

I felt my lips pull up in a sneer. "As easy as could be expected from a group of refugees."

"Survivors?"

"None."

She all but clapped in glee. "I knew I could count on you."

"Of course, *Tari*," I replied. "If you would excuse me, it's been a long journey."

Surprise washed over her until she took a good look at me and saw me dripping water on the tiled floor.

"But of course," she purred. "You have the night off. Come see me in the morning."

"As you wish, *Tari*."

I turned on my heel and left the throne room in large strides, desperate to reach the silence and sanctity of my own bedroom. I only hoped she didn't see the despondency. If she noticed anything off…

Don't think like that.

Thoughts like that would leave me unfocused and allow for mistakes. I couldn't make mistakes, or this war would be lost.

We couldn't lose the war.

When I stepped inside my bedroom, candles had already been lit, but only just enough to chase the shadows away and provide me with sufficient sight to reach the adjacent bathroom without walking into furniture. With a heavy sigh, I dropped my saddlebags where I was standing, my limbs suddenly heavy, like my head and my heart. Getting out of my armour proved a struggle, and I was too tired to even curse when the chainmail snagged on my hair halfway over my head. Under normal circumstances, someone would have been here to help me— now, nobody dared come close to me out of fear I might kill them.

I couldn't blame them.

"Let me help you," a soft voice sounded from close by moments before a pair of hands lifted the chainmail from my head and deftly loosened my hair.

"You're not supposed to be here," I whispered half in shock.

"I know," Mehrean replied, "but I needed to see you."

"You're the only one in Ilvanna who does." I deadpanned.

"Not entirely true."

"You and Azra then."

She pressed her lips in a thin line at the mention of the current *Tari*. "That's why I'm here."

"Can it wait? I desperately need a bath."

"You can listen perfectly fine from there," she observed. "It's already been prepared."

I stared at her. "How—"

"Surely I do not need to tell you how a bath's drawn up?"

"But—"

"Nor how to get in it?"

"How did you—"

"If you want to keep a shred of dignity, I suggest you get out of those clothes and into that tub before I help you."

I stared at her. She glared back, hands on her hips.

Deciding I was in no mood to argue with her, and distinctly wondering if my sister had put up with this attitude every day, I made my way into the adjacent room, grateful to see steam billowing from the tub. I stripped out of my wet garments rapidly and was just lowering myself into the water when Mehrean stepped inside, towels in hand.

"You really do not care for privacy, do you?"

"Such ideologies are trivial when the fate of the world is at stake, don't you think?"

I grunted in response.

"Anyway," she continued as if I'd made no sound at all. "Azra."

"You have to be more specific," I muttered.

Mehrean stared at me, unimpressed, but there was a twinkle in her eyes that belied her seriousness. "She'll be giving birth soon."

My jaw dropped. "How did y—"

"Stop asking foolish questions, Haer," she interjected. "Shut up and listen."

I snapped my mouth shut and lowered myself to my chin into the water, almost folding myself double.

"As I was saying, Azra will be giving birth soon, and we cannot allow her to have that baby."

That made me sit up straight, staring at her. "What are you saying?"

"I'm saying that we have to make her believe the child died at birth."

I contemplated her words in silence, making a steeple of my fingers. For a moment I thought she'd say we needed to kill it, so I was relieved when she said we only had to make Azra believe it had died at birth, but therein lay the crux.

Azra wasn't stupid.

"She won't fall for that."

Mehrean smiled in that mysterious way of hers, almost as if she knew things I did not. "We just have to show her a dead baby."

Her words sent cold shivers down my spine.

"I'm not killing babies," I whispered in shock. "That's insane."

"Nobody's killing babies." Mehrean sighed in exasperation. "They die in childbirth more often than you think."

"What are the odds another woman gives birth to a dead baby on the same day as Azra does to a living? Who says it'll live?"

She shrugged. "Nobody does. If it dies, it makes our job easier."

"When did you become so cruel?"

Mehrean pressed her lips together, narrowing her eyes. "I don't have to remind you of *Hanyarah*? Shal? Tiroy?"

I stilled, anger bubbling up inside of me. "Don't pull him into this. He's innocent. As are babies!"

"Keep your voice down," she hissed, anger flaring in her eyes, "before you say something you regret. I do not wish the child to die. On the contrary, it needs to live, which is why I'm staying at the palace."

"You're insane."

"Just pragmatic," she replied. "It's at least a two week's travel back to *Denahryn*. We maybe have two moons, less if we're unlucky. I need to be here when it happens."

"She'll kill you when she finds out you're here."

She smiled ruefully. "That would mean she believes I am still alive, and if that were the case, she'd have strung you up next to your mother."

I winced.

"I obviously cannot move around," she continued. "So, I was hoping I could stay here with you and have you bring me something to eat and drink."

At that, I smiled. "I may not have to do it myself."

"Oh?"

"You remember Xaresh' mother?"

Mehrean nodded.

"I've been able to convince her to help me. She's Azra's maid-in-waiting, one of the many. I'm sure I can convince her to bring food and drinks here."

Relief washed over her and until now, I hadn't realised how much had been riding on my agreement. I sighed, rubbing my face.

"So," I began after a while, "what's your master plan?"

She smiled like the cat who'd just caught the mouse. "Leave that to me. The less you know, the better. I heard Azra's quite fond of torture."

I scowled at her words but said nothing. Mehrean wasn't wrong in that observation, and I didn't like to find out how far Azra would go with a *verathràh* like myself.

"Just make sure I'm kept fed and hydrated," she said, looking amused, "and I'll take care of the rest."

As she rose to her feet, a thoughtful expression crossed her face, but it was gone as fast as it had appeared. I opened my mouth, a different question on the tip of my tongue, but rather than asking it, I closed my mouth again.

"I'll leave you to your bath," she said in a soft voice. "I'll be in the other room. Would you like some tea?"

"Sounds like something stronger is in order."

She chuckled at that. "Perhaps, but tea will help you sleep and drive away the soreness of your journey."

I stared at her, again. *How does she know?*

After she'd left, I inhaled deeply, closed my eyes, and submerged. The silence around me was as deafening as it was welcome. Whatever Mehrean's plans, they were dangerous. Not just because Mehr could be caught, but if that happened, so would I, and that would bring down everything.

Best not get caught, an Ilvan.

CHAPTER 12

TALNOVAR

I all but kissed the sand once I'd pulled the skiff
ashore. Never in my life had I been so happy to have
solid ground underneath my feet as I was at that moment, even
if it did make me slip and slide as I walked. When I rose, I staggered back a few steps back, unused to steady ground.

Halueth chuckled softly. "You really weren't made for the
sea, *mahnèh*."

"Really? I hadn't noticed."

He snorted as I pulled the sack of rations out of the boat,
what little there was left of it, and hoisted it over my shoulder. I
adjusted the sword at my belt and looked at my companion.
"We'd better find shelter before nightfall. Something tells me
staying out here at night is as deadly as the Ilvan mountains in
winter."

"I wouldn't know," Halueth replied falsely cheerfully. "Never
been here."

"Neither have I, and I'll be happy if I never have to again."

He smirked but said nothing. We started away from the sea
to what I hoped was more inland in silence. The loose sand and
my leg made my walk hard and painful, and more than once

while trekking up the dunes, I lost my footing and slid back a few steps. By the time I managed to get on top, I was winded, my shoulder was burning, and I was in the foulest mood.

Halueth was grinning like an idiot.

"What are you so happy about?"

He pointed behind me. "I think finding a place to stay might be easier than we thought."

Sure enough, in the distance, I could make out smoke billowing into the sky lazily from tiny structures. The air shimmered in the heat, reminding me of the hot summer days in Ilvanna.

"Best get going," I said, starting forwards. "It'll be a good few hours before we reach them."

"You really know how to motivate people."

"Not my intention."

Halueth chuckled. "Yeah, I've noticed."

I awarded him a wry smile. His words held no malice, no judgement—something I was grateful for. For the past two years, my every step had been watched, my every choice and decision criticised. *Nohro*, even my personality had been found wanting. People believed I was someone I knew I was not, and to most of them, I was a *verathràh*.

My redemption was to bring the *Tarien* home.

Not just my redemption.

My saving, too.

Azra had broken me. Not entirely. Not completely. But parts of me. I would never admit it to anyone out loud. By Esah, it was hard to admit it to myself in silence, but it was there, deep inside of me. It was different from when Varayna had died. I'd blamed myself for a very long time, and even though my parents had long since forgiven me for it, I doubted I ever would. It had changed me, but this, what Azra had done, was much more severe. She'd taken something from me I knew I could never get back. Not my innocence, exactly, the Gods knew I was way past that, but my confidence. Confidence that I could take care of myself no matter what the situation.

"Tal." Halueth's voice pulled me from my thoughts.

When I looked up at him, my eyes settled on a dust cloud not too far from us. In it, I could just make out the outlines of riders.

"*Nohro,*" I hissed.

It was futile to try to hide. There was nothing for miles around to even do so. Dropping the sack of rations, I drew my sword, grunting at the pain lancing through my shoulder.

"You really should give that injury some rest, *mahnèh,*" Halueth offered, glancing at me. "It will never heal this way."

"I'll live."

"Sure you will, but that arm might be of no use to you if you keep this up."

I scowled at him. "When did you turn into a healer?"

"Common sense, *mahnèh.*"

Rolling my eyes, I switched the sword to my left hand instead, tucking my injured arm against my chest. Halueth wasn't wrong. Between fighting on the ship, swimming for miles, and pulling oars for days, I'd already done more wrong than good. Using it now could mean permanent impairment, if I hadn't already done that. It was a good thing I'd trained for ambidexterity for years, a skill Shalitha had been more than envious of, or I'd not have stood a chance here.

The thought made me smile as determination rose within me.

Whatever came next, I wouldn't go down without a fight. I was here for a reason, and nobody was going to take that away from me.

"Look alive." I grinned.

Before long, a dozen people on humpbacked animals surrounded us. Every man wore a garment that protected their head from the sun and covered all but their eyes. It was unsettling. One of them rode forward, the rest slid from their mounts, curved blades in their hands, eyes hard.

A man who I assumed to be their leader spoke, his voice all lilt and musical. "Drop your weapons, unless you wish to die."

"Are we going to comply?" Halueth asked under his breath.

I smirked. "What do you think?"

By silent agreement, we attacked, even though we were sorely outnumbered. Now that I was finally on the other side of the map, I wasn't going to let anything keep me from my goal. If I had to kill everyone I came across on my journey to find Shal, I would without a moment's hesitation.

I parried a strike and dodged another attack by jumping out of the way before a sharp pain erupted in my arm. Gritting my teeth, grabbing my sword tight in my left hand, I attacked. Left. Right. Parry. Dodge. Parry. Right. The motions were as much practise as it was muscle memory, and once my mind caught on with what was happening, my movements turned into a dance.

One I'd sorely missed.

My attention never wavered. The pain in my body turned into a distant thrum I could ignore and for the first time in a long while, I felt alive until a fierce pain shot through my head, and my knees buckled. I snorted and coughed at the cloud of sand rushing past my face.

"Stay down," Halueth lisped from my left.

I coughed again. "You all right?"

"I've had better days."

Several voices were arguing over our heads, but the building headache prevented me from catching what they were saying. It took me great effort to make sense of the words.

"They're arguing what to do with us," I muttered. "Most want us dead."

One of the men frowned as he looked down at me.

"Why haven't they killed us then?" Halueth remarked.

"Because their leader wants us alive."

"Why?"

I remained silent for a while. He shifted beside me, a soft grunt escaping his lips as he did so.

"He wants to sell us," I whispered, straining to listen.

Had they said they'd wanted to toss us into the ocean to see how long we'd stay afloat, my response would have been the same. Anger built inside of me so fast I was on my feet in an instant. I spun towards my captor, kneed him where it hurt, and swung my fist into his face almost in the same instance. He fell backwards, limp like a rag doll.

A sword was at my throat another heartbeat later.

"Turn around," the owner of the sword grunted. "No funny business or I'll cut your throat."

I complied, clenching my fists together. Up close, the man looked less menacing than he had from atop his mount. He was a good half a head shorter than I was, which made this situation rather absurd, in my opinion, but I wouldn't make the mistake of doing anything funny. Short he may be, but I didn't doubt for a moment he'd do as promised.

"What's your name, *irtehn?*" he asked.

I looked at him, cocking my head slightly. "I'm Tal. This is Halueth."

Confusion marred the man's features as he shared a look with his men. They shrugged and shook their heads.

"State your business," he ordered, looking less than amused.

I shrugged. "We're looking for a job."

The man's brow furrowed. When he spoke to one of his men, intentionally hard so I could hear it, I caught him saying I wasn't right in the head.

"I'm not mad," I commented, forcing myself to stay right where I was rather than give in to the urge to make him see otherwise.

Halueth snorted but didn't comment. Neither did our captors, but they did keep up their conversation in rapid Zihrin, sparing me the occasional glance or two that suggested they weren't sure what to make of me. After a while, the leader turned to me. "You're our prisoner now. Fight, and you're dead."

Prisoner. Singular?

I shook my head to clear it. Somehow, I must have misunderstood him, his words lost in translation. Aware I stood no chance, I raised my arms in surrender.

"I'll come quietly."

The smoke we'd seen in the distance came from a camp that didn't quite deserve that name. It was nothing more than three shoddy tents that looked as if they'd seen better days. In the Ilvannian army, we'd have considered them useless for the sheer size of the holes at the top. One downpour and everyone inside would be soaked.

Here, I wondered if they even knew what rain was.

Two men pushed me inside one of the tents with a growled command. *Don't try to escape.* Between the ropes binding our hands and feet, and the endless amount of sand I'd seen walking to this camp, escaping equalled death. I didn't need to know much of Zihrin to know that to be the truth.

"Joyful bunch," Halueth commented, sitting down with a grunt. "Great fighters, too."

I snorted, trying to make myself comfortable. "I suppose."

"So," he began at length, shifting his weight. "Now what?"

Stretching my legs, wincing at the strain it put on my injured one, I contemplated his words in silence. Now what, indeed? If these men wanted to sell us, it meant they were slave traders. Although uncommon in Ilvanna, stories of men, women and children gone missing from the shore settlements did occasionally reach the palace. I'd been sent on more than one mission in the past to find them.

We'd never recovered any of them.

"Let them sell us," I replied eventually, my words slow and deliberate.

"Have you lost your mind?"

"Hardly, but let me ask you this," I said. "How well do you know Zihrin?"

Halueth looked up at me, lips lifted at the corners. "All right, fair point. But what if they take us even farther away from the *Tarien?*"

"It's a risk we have to take."

He whistled low under his breath, shaking his head. "That's quite a risk, *mahnèh.*"

"Not more so than trying to escape in the middle of nowhere." I glanced sideways at him. "Besides, mayhap the Gods will favour us for once, and we might actually get closer. It's a fifty-fifty chance."

"I'd say more like a ninety-ten chance and not in our favour," Halueth commented drily. "But if you're willing to risk it, who am I to argue otherwise?"

"Not a gambling man?"

"Just not a very lucky man," Halueth said. "Never had much faith in the Gods to begin with."

Neither had I, but ever since *Denahryn*, I'd come to believe there may be more to the world than I initially believed. After Soren, after what I think he did… No, it wasn't possible. Healing magic was something out of fairy tales.

At first, I'd put it down to delirium until I remembered the morning after the lashing Azra had given me and the lack of pain. Of how Soren had looked the way I should have looked, or how Shalitha should not have been able to walk at all after that attack from the wolf. And then there was the fact she had not died after Haerlyon found her at the gates after she'd gone missing for a month. I remembered seeing my mother and Varayna, remembered how I was dying.

And I hadn't.

That night at *Denahryn,* Soren had clutched his side in the exact same place where my injury had been. What he had done or how he had done it was beyond me, but he had done—something. Of that much I was sure, but I could hardly tell Halueth.

I still wasn't entirely sure myself.

"What if we get sold separately?"

Considering his words, I began shaking my head slowly and looked up at him, a grin spreading across my lips.

"We just have to make sure they understand we're much better together."

"How?"

"I don't know yet, but I'll figure it out."

Halueth tilted his head. "You'd better be fast. Something tells me we don't have a lot of time."

Not a lot of time and everything's riding on the sheer size of our luck.

I didn't feel as confident as I made it look.

CHAPTER 13

SHALITHA

*M*y shoulders were aching fiercely, my arms felt heavy, and my lungs felt fit to burst, but Z'tala wasn't letting up. She continued battering into me with her quarterstaff. Left. Right. Right. Left. Left. I was barely in time to parry half of her blows. The other half landed on my shoulders, my arms, and even on my face once. She never stopped to check if I was okay.

"Defend!"

She attacked again, but not with her staff this time. Instead, she was a flurry of arms and legs as she came at me full force. I dropped my staff, blocking her attacks with my arms and legs, grunting at the effort. A wicked gleam appeared in her eyes. Z'tala was nothing if not fanatic, and she treated every training as if she were in the *herrât*, fighting for life or death.

It was great to practise. Painful, but great.

Z'tala suddenly stepped back, ceasing her attacks mid-strike. Around us, the sound of fighting desisted as the other *herriatâre* all but dropped their weapons.

"Stand by me," she murmured. "Keep your eyes down."

I did as she instructed. If I'd learned anything in the few

weeks since my arrival, it was to do as she said without questioning it. So far, it had kept me alive and out of trouble. She reminded me of Mehrean in a way, except that Z'tala was infinitely more lethal. Then again, I was sure Mehrean wasn't quite as nice as she'd have us believe.

With my eyes and head slightly lowered, all I could see were a pair of legs in the finest silks and slippers. I didn't need to look up to know it was Kehran. Other footsteps alerted me. Before long, a small group of people, murmuring and gasping, was standing not too far away. I risked a glance up. Sure enough, a gaggle of men and women dressed as if they had too much money to spend had accompanied Kehran.

"*Eshen, Shena*, these are my finest fighters." Kehran's voice boomed across the training area. "Have a look now, so tonight you may choose one for your company."

"*Herriatâre*, attention," *Dekiatâre* snapped.

I clasped my hands behind my back, set my feet apart at shoulder width and raised my chin, staring dead ahead. It had been one of Z'tala's first lessons after we began our training together. Apparently, these kinds of exhibitions were a common thing.

My eyes locked with Jaehyr's across from me, and more than ever I wished Elay hadn't interrupted our conversation. I understood why he had done it, but there was so much more I needed to know. I hadn't been able to get close to him—there was always someone blocking me or keeping me from Jaehyr, as if they knew what we had done, but I doubted anyone other than Elay and Z'tala did.

My train of thoughts was interrupted by a man stepping into my vision. He was handsome, like every Kyrinthan—like every child of the Gods. His skin was as dark as Z'tala's and there was a calculated look to his eyes that sent shivers down my spine.

"Who is this?" he asked in a musical lilt.

Kehran stepped closer, a big smile on his face. "This, *eshen*, is none other than the *Tarien* of Ilvanna. One only needs to look at her face to know this to be truth"

The man's brows rose in surprise, his amber eyes suddenly alight. "Is that so?"

Kehran nodded, even though the question had been rhetorical. The man stepped closer, his eyes roving over me as if he were sizing up a piece of meat he'd like to purchase from the local butcher's on market day. I grabbed my wrist tight, fighting to keep my composure. Something gave me away though.

The man chuckled. "She's got spirit."

Kehran glared at me, quickly schooling his expression while returning his attention to the stranger.

"She's one of my best fighters, *eshen*," he said. "Almost as good as Z'tala."

The man inclined his head and glanced in her direction. Z'tala perked up almost imperceptibly.

Interesting.

I returned to stare off into the distance, but this time it was Jaehyr who locked his gaze with mine. Judging by his posture and the look in his eyes, he was ready to pounce. The notion amused me for half a heartbeat until I noticed one of the women making her way towards him.

If they'd catch him like that, he'd be in trouble.

I couldn't speak, couldn't move lest I wanted to get a beating, so I opted for lifting my chin and staring him down. He tensed at first, then eased as if he'd understood my message.

Ai sela. Stand down.

This was neither the time nor the place to start a fight and definitely not worth the punishment Kehran would have *Deki-atâre* dole out.

"You have seen what I have to offer," Kehran almost purred. "Let us retire."

While the rest followed Kehran like a compliant gaggle of geese, the dark-skinned stranger lingered, his eyes on Z'tala.

She cocked her head slightly, almost as if she were listening to him, which considering the distance should be impossible. And yet...

Gods aren't supposed to actually exist either.

The man's amber eyes turned on me, highlighting the mysterious smile on his face. He inclined his head before he left. As soon as they were all gone, we let out a collective sigh of relief. Poses eased, arms and legs stretched, and a low murmur rose among the small group of *herriatâre*. From across the yard, Jaehyr was watching me, and when he noticed me looking, he inclined his head.

A gong startled us all.

"Head back to your cells," *Dekiatâre* called. "You'll be picked up shortly to prepare for tonight's festivities."

"What's happening tonight?" I asked Z'tala quietly.

The pity on her face did nothing good for my nerves.

"No," I said, pacing up and down the small path in our cell. "I'm not doing it."

"You have no choice," Z'tala replied. "If you don't, the *Akyn* will have you killed."

I clenched my jaw and balled my hands. "I'd rather be dead."

Z'tala tilted her head, looking at me curiously. "You would rather give up on your country by dying than do what you must to survive?"

"Yes. No. I..." I jerked my hands through my hair, hissing as I hit a few knots, then breathed out heavily as I sunk down on my bed. "How could I live with myself?"

"How could you not? Women and men have done this for thousands of years to survive. What would you lose?"

"It sounds as if you condone what he does."

She looked at me without judgment. "I am not, *k'lele*. It's a vile practice, but not one I will allow to break me. I have done what I must to survive, and now that the end is near, I know my fight has not been for nothing."

"What end? What are you talking about?"

Z'tala smiled at her own secret. "Do you believe in destiny, *K'lele?*"

"I didn't think I did."

Just as she opened her mouth to reply, the locks to our cell clicked and the door was opened. Four guards awaited us.

"Come," one of them said gruffly.

We complied in silence, keeping our hands where they could see them. Before they took us away, they cuffed our wrists to ensure we wouldn't attack them. Between Z'tala and myself, we could take them out even with our hands bound, but we both had reasons not to attempt it... yet.

My thoughts returned to her words as we made our way through the corridors. By now, I knew the way they would take. For the most part, it was the same direction as the training area and the *herrât*, but before we left the dungeons, the guards escorted us left instead of right and out into the blaring sun.

I squinted at the sudden bright light.

The bulk of the palace, and by extent the *herrât*, now lay to my right rather than my left, and I'd lost all notion of where we were going. I'd realised we wouldn't go straight to the palace and going back to the training area made no sense, but I knew too little of the rest of the layout to know what our destination was.

"Where are we going?" The words were out of my mouth before I could think it through, earning me a shove in the back that made me stumble, but not fall.

"You only speak when you're spoken to," a guard hissed, giving me a shove for good measure.

Unfortunately for him, I'd expected it to happen and had braced myself before his hand connected with my shoulder. I stepped back into him and slammed the back of my head into his nose.

He howled in pain.

Within the space of two heartbeats, the other guards had wrestled me to the ground, pushing my forehead firmly in the sand, twisting my arms painfully. I refused to cry out.

"Let her go," a stern feminine voice spoke.

The pressure on my arms and head lifted, and I was hauled back to my feet. Strong hands wrapped in a vice-like grip around my biceps to keep me in place. I supposed I deserved that—all of it—but I was getting sick and tired of being bossed around by men who wouldn't even last five minutes in the *herrât* with me. One just had to look at them to know they weren't in their best shape.

"She broke my nose," the guard said in a muffled voice. "The *tekka* deserves punishment!"

"Perhaps," the woman replied, "but that is not for you to decide. Get back to your posts, I will take it from here."

The guards released their grip, bowed from the hips and turned on their heels. I could hear the one with the broken nose curse all the way back to where we'd come from, and I smirked.

Served him right.

"Wipe that smirk off your face," the woman ordered.

Looking up at her, my heart skipped a beat. She looked so similar to Elay, I thought for a moment it was him dressed up as a woman and pulling off a marvellous act. But there were subtle differences. Her eyes were a lighter green, her nose more delicate, her lips fuller. Her attire was clearly that of a noblewoman, but unlike the women I'd seen that afternoon, she wore a shawl that draped over her hair and down her back but kept her face uncovered.

"He never said you were twins," I whispered, staring at her.

She pressed her lips together, glaring at me. "Follow me, both of you."

Z'tala and I fell in step behind her. My cellmate was looking at me with brows knitted together as if she were trying to solve a puzzle. I just shrugged, focusing on the back of the woman walking in front of us. She was Elay's sister, of that I had no doubt, but I felt out of my depth how to go about this. I needed to talk to him, sooner rather than later, but our meetings were based on his schedule, not mine. Biting my lip in frustration, I tried to push away the annoyance coiling inside of me like a restless snake.

I knew our relationship—our marriage—was based on secrets and the belief we both had ulterior motives to see it through, and yet I couldn't shake the feeling of there being more between us. Trust was too big a word, but we shared something.

Just not that one of his sisters happened to be his twin.

I pushed the thought aside and focused on the present instead. Before I could consider them, I needed to think of tonight, of the festivities, and how I was going to keep myself from murdering any person who wanted me for company. A part of me wished—hoped—Elay would be there, but I hadn't seen him in the training area today.

Or anywhere, come to think of it.

Then again, he knew Kehran's *herriatâre*. He'd seen them on more than one occasion, so he might simply have foregone the obligations.

We'd arrived at a large, rectangular building set completely apart from all the other structures. Both the *herrât* and the palace were now well behind us, and I wondered momentarily if we were still in the palace grounds. Logic dictated we had to be —there was no way Kehran would allow us off his property, especially without guards.

When Elay's sister pushed the double doors open, however, all questions ceased to exist, and I was certain we were still on palace property. Just by looking at the extravagant design inside, I could tell no noble in Kyrintha, Zihrin or Ilvanna was wealthy enough to pull off a decor like this.

Gold pillars ran along the length of the black marble floor. The walls, painted such a deep red it reminded me of blood, were decorated with intricate drawings in gold and silver. We stepped inside on a heavy, crimson velvet carpet stretching the length of the floor all the way to the end. Following it, I observed the arches hidden just behind the gold pillars. A soft light came from rooms hidden behind them, and I could swear I heard music drifting from one of them.

There was no time to marvel at it all as Elay's sister guided us through another set of double doors and into a spacious, circular room. My jaw dropped. Four massive palm trees towered over the room like giants, creating a square in the middle where four loungers, reminding me of Kehran's personal garden, occupied each side.

They were currently empty.

"This way," Elay's sister said and guided us to another set of double doors, behind which was a dressing room.

"Undress," she said, "grab a towel, and follow me."

Too curious to disobey, I undressed—not that it was much— and wrapped a towel around myself. Z'tala did the same, only she looked a lot more comfortable wearing it.

"Stop worrying," she whispered. "Nothing bad is going to happen."

"You never know. Someone might try to drown me."

Z'tala looked amused. "You really don't trust people, do you?"

I shrugged. "After what happened, not particularly."

"If you want to survive here, you may have to trust a few."

We returned to the circular room where Elay's sister was waiting for us. She guided us past several baths, each of which seemed different. One had steam billowing above it, another smelled heavily of lavender, and a third gave off an icy chill as we passed it. We stopped at none of them. Instead, she brought us to a door on the other side of the accommodation. It was dark and unwelcome inside, but Elay's sister seemed confident in stopping here.

"Z'tala, you know how it works. Take her through it, explain if you must. Make sure you're both prim and proper by the time I come to pick you up."

"Yes, *Shena*." Z'tala bowed.

I followed suit.

After she left, Z'tala unwrapped the towel and placed it on a wooden table next to the door, motioning for me to do the same. Less certain than her, I let the piece of fabric slide from my waist, trying not to be too conscious about my appearance.

It wasn't as if she hadn't seen me naked before.

That was different.

"Come." Z'tala smiled. "You'll enjoy this."

When she opened the door, the scent of eucalyptus reached us along with a cloud of fog. It enveloped us in a warm, welcome mist, and without hesitation, I followed Z'tala inside. The mist was heavier here, as was the smell of eucalyptus, and it was pressing on my chest uncomfortably. Beside me, Z'tala inhaled deeply.

"Sit down. It'll make breathing easier."

In the low light, I could barely make out the bench she was sitting on, but sure enough, when I took a seat, the air became less humid and I, too, took a deep breath. The eucalyptus seared the inside of my nose, my lungs, leaving a tingling sensation in its wake, but it wasn't unpleasant. In fact, for the first time in months, I felt I could actually breathe again.

"What is this place?"

"They call it a *Tazur*," Z'tala replied. "A fancy word for steam house."

"*Tazur* does sound better."

Z'tala didn't respond to that. Neither of us was proficient in small talk of any sorts. I'd always been a straightforward person. She was cut of the same cloth. Often in our cell, we would be silent for a long time even though we were both awake. Sometimes, we'd talk, which meant she spoke of how things were done around here, and I listened. Instructions from Kehran, I assumed.

Or Elay.

During our time together, either in the cell or in training, I'd learned she and I were much alike, just like she'd said.

We were fighters.

We didn't give up.

"Why did you do it?" Z'tala asked.

"I felt like it," I replied, not needing to ask her what she meant. "They pretend to be better than us just because we're in a cell, but we could take them out in the blink of an eye if we wanted to."

"Do you?"

"Not yet."

Z'tala moved, but I wasn't sure if she was looking at me or not. "Come, time for the next step."

As soon as the cooler air outside the *Tazur* hit me, goosebumps rippled across my arm, legs, and spine. I wasn't cold, not by far, but the sensation was odd, to say the least. Z'tala didn't bother with a towel when she crossed the distance to the cold bath. I wanted to warn her but stood transfixed, watching her walk into the water like it was nothing. She motioned for me to join her, and I instinctively took a step back.

"It's just cold water," she called.

It wasn't so much the cold I was afraid of as it was the memories it would bring. Never would I forget the cold depths of the sea in which I should have drowned.

Get over yourself, qira.

It wasn't as if I would be tossed into the water—I could go

at my own pace, step by step. Rationally, it made no sense to be this afraid of a cold-water pool. It wasn't the sea, and I wasn't alone, yet every step I took sent my heart in a frenzy and turned my limbs heavier. By the time I'd reached the steps into the water, I was gasping for air while fighting the urge to run.

Z'tala was watching me, brows knitted together in confusion.

"Nothing will happen, *k'lele*."

You don't know that. Instead of speaking the words that had come to mind, I nodded.

The first step caught me by surprise. It was jarring, painful even, yet strangely comfortable on my skin. I took another step and another, until I was in the water to my waist. By then, the temperature had turned almost comfortable, but the fear held my throat in a vice-like grip. Z'tala hoisted herself up the side, keeping her legs in as she watched me.

"You need to submerge."

I glanced at her. If I'd learned anything it was to do something painful as fast as possible, but fear held me back. What if I went under and my heart stopped beating from the sudden shock? What if I went under and I accidentally breathed? What if I'd drown?

I breathed in—once, twice, three times—and forced myself underwater. As soon as the water closed over my head, panic took over and I breathed. Water rushed into my mouth, and I began to cough. I mowed my arms, kicked my legs, but nothing I did helped until I kicked off against the floor by lucky accident. The water over my head broke, and between coughs and splutters, I drew air into my lungs.

Z'tala was right next to me, eyes wide.

"In Temarin's name, what happened?"

"I panicked."

She arched a brow. "Panicked?"

"Long story," I muttered between coughs and began wading out of the pool.

I felt as if I'd spent time standing outside during an Ilvannian winter storm without any clothing to call my own. My fingers were stiff, my limbs were heavy, and I moved as if I'd frozen over. Z'tala was at my side quick enough and guided me to another bath. It was hot at first, but as my body thawed and got used to the temperature, I began to relax.

Somewhat. I was still surrounded by water.

"What did you mean by 'not yet'?" Z'tala asked, cocking her head.

"Just that I'm not planning on staying here forever," I replied, sitting as still as a mouse.

"What have you got planned?"

"Nothing specific yet. Why?" I looked at her curiously.

She smiled, showing off a row of perfect white teeth. "Again I ask you, k'lele, do you believe in destiny?"

"Maybe."

"When your answer is yes, you will understand."

AFTER WE FINISHED BATHING, we returned to the dressing room, only to find our clothing had been replaced by robes. Z'tala put hers on without hesitation, so I followed her example, guessing that it was still part of whatever was going.

"What's happening next?" I asked in a low whisper.

"We'll get dressed."

I frowned. "Then why did they take our clothing?"

Z'tala's lips curled up in a wry smile. "Because they will be dressing us, k'lele, for tonight's festivities."

My heart sank at the idea. The last time I was dressed up was at *Hanyarah*, and that hadn't ended well. I bit the inside of my cheek and nodded as if to tell myself it was all right, that everything was going to be fine. Inhaling deeply, gathering my courage, I looked at her.

"Very well."

After all, it could never turn out as bad as *Hanyarah*.

Z'tala guided me out of the circular room and back into the rectangular hallway with its gold decorations and hidden archways where Elay's sister was waiting for us. At her side stood another woman dressed in simple attire, marking her as a servant.

"Inhra goes with Z'tala," she said. "Shalitha comes with me."

I followed her into one of the antechambers. Too surprised she knew my name, I missed the signs, and she had pushed me up against the wall with a dagger at my throat before I could respond.

Nohro.

"What have you done to my brother?"

CHAPTER 14

TALNOVAR

The stench of unwashed bodies and excrement hit me before we even arrived at the slave camp, although I doubted we smelled any better after our time at sea and trudging through this godforsaken desert. My skin felt as if I'd washed myself with sandpaper, my lips had cracked until they bled, and my eyes were so dry that blinking hurt more than not blinking at all. At that point, I hadn't yet decided what I disliked more—the desert or the sea.

"Give me snow any day," Halueth muttered at my side. "This sand gets *everywhere.*"

I grunted in response.

He wasn't wrong there.

The rope around our arms jerked taut when our captors urged their beasts of burden to move faster, leaving us stumbling after them. I bit back my curse. Halueth did not. Thankfully, our captors didn't seem to notice, a mercy all on its own as they didn't hold back from doling out punishments. My back was testimony to that. They'd made sure not to break the skin— my value would be less if that happened—but enough to make it uncomfortable. With all that sand everywhere, uncomfortable didn't even begin to describe it.

On top of that, my shoulder was burning as if a fire had been ignited inside it, melting the ligaments of my bones. Arav's words resonated in my mind. *Don't put too much strain on it, or you won't be able to use it again.*

I didn't have a choice now.

I didn't think about the consequences—didn't want to think of what it could mean for the future if my shoulder never healed properly. I had to keep faith that it would work out somehow.

"Look at this place," Halueth murmured.

Row upon row of lean-tos spread out before us, offering its occupants minimum shelter from the merciless sun. Dirty, emaciated men sat side by side, cuffed together at the ankle. Thin women huddled together with scared, bony children whose eyes had widened in permanent terror. Anger roared inside of me, but as much as I wanted to level this place to the ground, there was very little I could do. They watched us as we passed, the men with eyes narrowed, mistrust radiating from most of them, the women in fear.

I wasn't entirely sure whether it was directed at Halueth and myself, our captors, or all of us.

They took us to a lesser occupied part of the camp with only a handful of men. In contrast with the others, they looked strong and healthy, which explained not only the chains around their ankles but around their wrists and necks as well. Their skin colour varied from a rich dark brown to the pale pink of Therondians. There had been no Ilvannians amongst them until now.

Like them, we were chained and cuffed at the wrists, ankles, and neck with enough room to move our arms and legs almost comfortably. After our journey, I didn't mind sitting at all. Our captors placed us with two others, neither of which appeared happy having to share what little solace the lean-to gave.

"Ihr ena den kelar," one of them said, drawing a chuckle from the second.

"Den kelar sen k'irai," I snorted.

The man who had spoken surged forward, hands up to throttle me, but the other man grabbed hold of him. I stood my ground, albeit unsteadily.

"What in Esah's name was that about?" Halueth frowned.

I shrugged and winced. "He insulted us."

"Why?"

"Your guess is as good as mine, *mahnèh,*" I replied, making myself as comfortable as I could get on the hard-packed dirt. Halueth grimaced and opted to sit on my left side rather than close to the other captives. I sat down next to the guy who'd restrained his friend and nodded gratefully. He awarded me with a faint smile.

"I'm Tariq," he said in Zihrin.

"Tal," I replied in kind, then pointed at Halueth. "Halueth."

Tariq looked puzzled for a brief moment, opened his mouth, but decided against it with a shake of his head, mumbling something under his breath.

"Nazeem," Tariq pointed at his companion.

Nazeem scowled in response and turned the other way. Out of the corner of my eyes, I saw Halueth responded much in the same fashion, and I rolled my eyes at him. If he was going to be a *khirr,* he could do it on his own terms.

"Where are we?" I managed, digging deep to find the words, no doubt mispronouncing all three of them.

Tariq's eyes sparkled in amusement. "Zihrin, of course."

I'd have rolled my eyes if I weren't afraid of it being an insult, so opted for a deep sigh instead, forcing a smile on my face.

"Where in Zihrin?"

My pronunciation the second time was horrible enough that

it drew a wry smile from Nazeem and made Halueth snort behind me.

"You're murdering their language," he commented.

I smirked. "Now you care?"

Halueth lifted his shoulders in feigned disinterest.

"We don't know where we are exactly," Tariq replied eventually, looking almost apologetic. Halueth translated. "We live here until they take us. Most never come back, so we assume they're sold or killed."

Despair knotted my insides. "Why killed?"

"They are too weak." It was Nazeem who spoke. "Most of them are."

"I noticed the division when we arrived," I replied, glancing in the direction we'd come from. "Why the separation?"

"We're worth more," Tariq said. "We're strong. Capable. Good for a number of things."

"Such as?" Halueth asked.

Neither of them responded to him, so I repeated the question. Nazeem ran a hand through his shaggy hair. Tariq rubbed his jaw. Watching them more closely, I noted both the differences and the similarities between them. They shared the same hazel coloured eyes and the somewhat hooked nose, but where Tariq's looked straight, Nazeem's looked as if it had been broken more than once. Tariq's left ear was stumped as if its tip had been cut off, whereas Nazeem's were still perfectly elongated. Their smiles were alike, but Nazeem had a darker look about it than Tariq did. Of the two, Nazeem had a bulkier build. Tariq looked more athletic, much like Halueth and me. The number of scars running across Nazeem's chest rivalled my own, and I would have bet anything he'd been a fighter, too.

Of Tariq, I wasn't so sure.

"We've heard rumours," Tariq began, "of men being sold to fight or work the mines, the strong ones anyway. The weaker ones? It's anyone's guess."

"The women and children?" I wasn't sure I wanted to know that answer.

"Often bought by *Gemsha*," Nazeem growled, making the universal sign for sex with his hands.

A sudden feeling of vertigo washed over me upon the realisation this could have happened to Shal. My stomach twisted itself in a knot at the thought of her having been sold for *that*.

She's nothing here, mahnèh.

That harsh truth sobered me up faster than any of Soren's concoctions ever had, and it took me a moment to find my bearings. Somehow, subconsciously, I'd laboured under the delusion she could be somewhere safe, but as I considered that thought, I knew deep down it might be far worse than anything I had imagined. It wasn't that I didn't trust her to survive—I'd trained her hard, harped on her relentlessly, pushed her more than I'd pushed anyone else. It was the simple fact that I had no idea where she was or what she was going through—what she had already gone through—that made thinking of her momentarily unbearable.

I must find her.

Eamryel had told me to go to Y'zdrah, find a man called Elay, and get answers there. Instead, I was in the middle of nowhere, in a camp where death lurked in its shadows, shackled to three other men, two of which were as likely to kill me in my sleep as they were to help me out. The only one I trusted enough was Halueth, but despite his promise to help me find the *Tarien*, what happened to his family by my hand still lingered between us.

I was on my own.

"Tal?" Halueth's voice cut through my moroseness, and I looked up.

He looked taken aback, but quickly recovered his composure and jerked his head in the direction of Tariq and Nazeem. "They're asking how you got here."

I told them our story, using my hands when I couldn't find the proper word. Sometimes, I added an Ilvannian term, much to their amusement. I felt more at a loss than when I was hanging over the ship's side to add the contents of my stomach to the sea. Even so, I got the message across, and by the end, they looked satisfied with my explanation.

"What happened to your leg?" Tariq asked, the kind of intrigue I'd seen on both Soren's and Arav's faces while tending the injured lighting up his eyes.

A healer, perhaps.

"A knife," I replied with a grimace. It was as if his question had triggered the worst of the pain. "Someone didn't want to die."

Tariq blinked rapidly. Nazeem huffed.

"I'd say that goes for most people," Tariq offered, a gentle smile curving his lips upwards. "Including you."

I scowled for a moment, then lay down with a heavy sigh, grunting at the fresh jolt of pain flashing through my shoulder and leg.

"How bad is it?" Tariq moved closer, brows knitted together.

"I-wish-they'd-take-off-the-*nohro*-leg bad," I muttered through gritted teeth. "The journey here did me no favours."

"Can you move it?"

"Rather not." I awarded him a wry smile. "It just needs some rest."

Tariq didn't look convinced by my words, but whatever he saw on my face stopped him from asking more. Draping my good arm across my eyes to ward off the sun, I heard the voices of Nazeem and Tariq, but didn't bother listening to their words. A sudden drowsiness settled over me, and I had to fight to keep my eyes open. No doubt the heat in combination with the pain and lack of sleep was taking its toll, but no matter how hard I fought, my eyes fell shut, and my mind wandered off to other places.

NEXT MORNING ARRIVED with the pungent scent of too many people in one place and breakfast. Several women carrying bowls were shuffling by, handing them to the other captors. Their hunched appearance and skittish moves were indicative of their fear, although I wasn't sure that sentiment was towards the men following them at a leisurely pace or to us. They handed us the bowls fast and efficiently, avoiding eye contact at all costs. As they approached, I noticed the guards brandishing bullwhips at their side and felt a sudden heat creep across my skin as if in memory of the lashes I'd received. At the same time, fury boiled to the surface at the mere thought of those whips being used to discipline these women.

Or are they for us?

The thought was disconcerting.

When one of the women handed me my bowl, she glanced up, and her eyes widened as if in recognition. I tilted my head slightly, offering her a smile, but it only served to scare her off. She nearly tripped over her own feet as she made a hasty retreat.

"*Diyenka,*" I murmured, thanking her even though the chance of her hearing me was slim.

Somehow, she had. When she looked back, the scared look on her face momentarily made way for surprise, and she managed a faint smile before returning to her duties.

My lips lifted at the corners.

"What was that all about?" Halueth asked, looking from the woman at the men.

I shrugged, sitting down cross-legged, placing the bowl in my lap. "No clue."

"Looks like you scared the poor woman," he commented, mimicking my position.

I arched a brow. Halueth just grinned and turned his attention to his bowl, his lips curling up. Had he been a cat, his hair would have stood on end and his tail would have tripled in size. A snort escaped me.

"What in Savea's name is this?"

"Looks like *diresh*." I frowned, sniffing it. "A much watered-down version of it, if anything."

Halueth grunted in disapproval. "It looks like something someone dragged up af—"

"Don't finish that sentence," I interrupted, glaring at him. "It may not look like much, but it's all we have, and I'd rather it goes down."

"I'm not su—," Halueth began.

"Eat," Tariq interjected in heavily accented Ilvannian, a slight frown creasing his brow.

Halueth's scowl deepened even further if that were at all possible.

"*Ch'iti's* very nourishing," Nazeem remarked. "Tasteless, but nourishing."

I inclined my head and set the bowl to my lips. As forewarned, the taste was bland indeed, but it was the texture that almost made me regurgitate the contents of the bowl. The graininess sliding down my throat reminded me of the amount of sand I inhaled on our journey here, but it was preferable over the slimy lumps that followed. Its only redeeming quality—and that was stretching the notion—was the amount of liquid that helped wash it down. Nourishing it may be, but if I had any say in the matter, this was both the first and the last time I'd have it.

"Not a fan either, I take it." Halueth snickered, regarding me with an amused expression on his face.

I scowled at him. "It doesn't matter, does it? It's either this or die."

"I haven't quite decided what I prefer though," he replied, giving his bowl a look of disgust. "Something tells me dying might be the better choice."

A snort escaped my lips. "You've certainly got a flair for the dramatic."

"That's what my mother used to say."

"Did you just compare me to your mother?" I asked, incredulity creeping into my voice.

A wide grin spread across his lips as he shrugged, neither confirming nor denying my question. With a heavy eye roll, I turned away from him, settling instead to watch the camp. Although there wasn't much to be done in chains, there appeared to be a quiet routine among the denizens that added a certain buzz to the place. Under the lean-to across from us, two men were playing a game of dice while their companions were having a heated conversation if their volume and wild gesticulations were any indication.

In other lean-tos, men lay with their arms folded behind their heads, eyes closed while others were speaking in muted voices. Some had gotten to their feet to stretch their legs, and yet others sat cross-legged with their eyes closed. Nazeem and Tariq squatted beside me, drawing something in the sand with their fingers that looked remarkably like a map. Halueth had made himself comfortable on my other side, basking in the sun like a well-content cat.

A prickle in the back of my neck made me look up, my vision spinning as I did. One of the men who was stretching his legs was watching us with an intense look in his eyes. When he caught me watching, he rolled his neck from left to right, followed by his shoulders as if he were preparing for a fight. A wicked grin spread over his otherwise dark features, revealing pearly white teeth of which some were missing.

"Get ready," Halueth murmured, sitting up at my side, looking in the other direction. "Incoming."

Half a dozen men carrying whips and weapons strode into our little camp, barking orders in Zihrin. Beside me, Nazeem, Tariq, and Halueth rose to their feet, as did the men around us. I followed their example, surprised at the sudden change of events.

"Where are we going?" I asked softly.

"We're allowed a bit of time out of chains," Tariq murmured. "Stretch your legs, run laps, stand there underneath the scorching sun praying for water. Whatever you prefer. I wouldn't suggest trying to escape though."

An uneasy feeling settled in my stomach, and I couldn't help but glance at the captive who'd been sizing me up as if I were dinner only moments before. He was watching me, a look of glee in his eyes. I squared my shoulders and felt my lips lift in a smirk, refusing to be the one to break eye-contact first.

"Don't," Halueth hissed.

"Not doing anything," I muttered in response. "He started it."

Although I couldn't see it, I was sure Halueth rolled his eyes at me. The dark-skinned stranger looked away as one of the armed men walked his way just as another arrived at our lean-to.

"*Havv*," he grunted, motioning for us to follow.

In six groups of four, they escorted us through the camp at such an incredibly slow pace, I wondered if we'd arrive before we would be taken back again. Each step sent agonising flares of pain through my leg, making me wish it would go back to being numb again. Sweat trickled down my back in steady rivulets, and not just from the sun either. The only upside of this trip presented itself as an opportunity to get a good look at the layout of the camp. Not that it did me any favours. All I could see in any direction were tents, lean-tos, and even some wooden huts, suggesting this camp had a more permanent nature.

I couldn't help but wonder about the size of it.

At a junction, our captor guided us to the left, following a group in front of us, whereas the group behind us turned right. A tug on my chains warned me to move on, and I quickly followed Halueth in a shuffle.

"You all right, *mahnéh?*" he cast over his shoulder.

"Why wouldn't I be?"

"Because I've been talking to you since we took this path, and you haven't bothered responding."

"I'm sorry," I replied, not entirely sure that I was. "Just, caught up in my thoughts."

His shoulders shook with silent laughter, and his head swivelled from left to right as if he were asking the Gods to bear witness to my stupidity. I knew for a fact I wasn't being stupid. Goosebumps rose all over my arms, and there was this prickling underneath my skin I'd long since come to associate with danger.

I had a good guess where it was coming from.

We arrived at a clearing surrounded by rope for a fence on the outskirts of the camp. There were no guards aside from the ones who'd brought us—nothing to keep us here aside from the chains binding us together. Beyond the clearing lay the endless desert, glittering in the sun as it climbed through the sky. It appeared as if the air were moving, distorting the image of the mountains far beyond the horizon. I understood why they hadn't bothered fencing this part off.

Fleeing equalled suicide.

The guard released the chains, yanking them from the cuffs around our arms and legs without consideration for injuries. Not that I cared—we were momentarily free from each other with enough room to move and stretch our arms and legs.

As soon as the guards released him, the dark-skinned man strode in my direction, clenching and unclenching his fists as if he were holding himself back from doing something stupid. I held up my hands in the universal sign of surrender—I hadn't come here to fight.

When he spoke, the words came at me in rapid succession, stringing syllables together I assumed made up words, but they were in a language I'd never heard before. I stared at him, feeling like the biggest *khirr*, and blinked.

He poked me in the chest.

"Would you say that's cause to hit him?" Halueth mused, standing idly by.

I stared at him, blinking. "Are you out of your *nohro* mind?"

Something knocked the wind right out of me, and the next thing I knew, I was measuring my length across the sand, my forehead connecting painfully with the hard-packed dirt. Stars burst in my vision. Before I could find my bearings, I was hauled to my feet and spun around so I was face to face with the stranger.

I'd expected this.

"Fool me once," I muttered in Ilvannian.

I dodged his next swing, hopping on one leg to regain my balance, and punched him in the ribs with all I had. I staggered back while a fierce pain shot through my arm and shoulder. Biting back a cry of anguish, I fought the dizziness, trying to stay on my feet. Going down meant I'd lose. The fact he barely flinched registered in my mind quite unwelcoming. It meant one of two things. Either I didn't pack the punch I once did, or the man's pain threshold was much higher than I'd anticipated. In any case, it made for trouble.

He swung again.

I threw my arms up so his hand connected with the metal of the cuffs. There was a loud cracking noise, which I was sure came from him, but he didn't look perturbed. His gaze shifted to my face, indicating where the next attack would come. I ducked and planted my good shoulder in that sweet spot just underneath the ribs. He stumbled backwards with a grunt, clutching his chest, and it was then I realised he wore no cuffs.

"What the—" I began, not taking my eyes off him.

Enraged by my attack, he charged me like a bull on a rampage. Rather than stepping out of the way, I sunk to one knee as he reached me and pushed up just as his momentum would have made him trip over me. As I did, I grabbed one of his arms with mine. He flipped over my shoulder and landed flat on his back next to me, my foot on his throat.

"Yield," I growled in Zihrin.

He tried to get back up, so I twisted his arm. His face contorted, but he made no sound.

"Yield."

He tried to twist himself out of my hold, but to no avail. As a result, I twisted his arm farther. He turned a few shades paler. Tariq spoke up beside me, his voice distorted and coming from far-away. When I looked at him, my vision swam, and I had to blink a few times to straighten it. Below me, the man went limp, resignation on his face. I let go of his arm and staggered out of his reach, fighting another spell of vertigo.

Relief washed over me when he stepped back after getting to his feet.

The reason why became clear when a man appeared in my vision. Dressed in an abundance of silks, his familiarity with wealth was strikingly apparent. He was young from the looks of him, not much older than me, and he carried himself with an air of importance I'd long since linked to people who are used to being obeyed.

His easy swagger reminded me of Haerlyon.

I straightened my shoulders, clasping my wrist in front of me with my other hand. Pain lanced through my shoulder, but I didn't want him to think I would attack him like I had the captive. I wasn't stupid. Murmurs rose around me, but I wasn't sure if it was directed at me or the stranger.

Golden hoops and earrings glinted in the sun, giving him the appearance of a bad guy from one of Shal's books. Reading had been one of her favourite pastimes aside from training and letting us chase her, but she hadn't spoken of it often. On more than one occasion, she'd discussed the books with me, or rather kept up a one-sided conversation while I pretended to listen and know what she was talking about. She hadn't liked to share that softer side of her, afraid it would make her look weak.

It was one of the many things I loved about her.

I felt certain that if she could see this guy now, she'd be delighted.

The thought was amusing at best—the reality much less so. Shal wasn't here, and this man looked as if he had a bone to pick with me, despite the smile on his face, which I was sure could charm fish out of the water. No, it was the shrewd look in his eyes that convinced me otherwise.

"That was quite some skill," he said in flawless Ilvannian. "Especially with an injury like yours."

I perked up, locking gazes with him. "I'm not sure what you're talking about."

His lips quirked into a lopsided smile, eyes twinkling in amusement. We both knew I was talking out of my neck.

"Ilvannian army?"

There was no point in denying the obvious, so I inclined my head, forcing a small smile to my lips.

"Position?" he asked.

"*Anahràn*," I replied.

Something told me this man knew perfectly well when he was being lied to. What I hadn't expected was the widening of his eyes before they narrowed, almost as if in recognition of something. I tilted my head, but he didn't grace me with an explanation. Behind me, Halueth hissed something under his breath, but the man didn't bother to respond.

"Why are you here?" he asked.

"Your men captured us," I replied simply.

His eyes narrowed as he cocked his head to the side, regarding me with a wary expression. For a moment it looked as if he was about to backhand me. It wasn't a lie. He sighed and awarded me with an expression one would give a young child after they said something entirely inappropriate.

"Oh, you mean why are we in Zihrin?" My lips lifted in a lazy smile. "Fled the country. Decided to seek fortune elsewhere."

"Did you now?"

I merely inclined my head, not caring whether he believed this part or not. I'd be honest about a lot of things, but my reason for being in Zihrin wasn't one of them.

"Well, *Anahràn*," he began. "Although I admire your skill, I cannot have you beat up other slaves while in this encampment just for the fun of it."

"I di—"

"As punishment," he continued, staring me down. "I think two days without food should do."

I opened my mouth to protest, but he cut me off short again.

"Try not to get into trouble, *Anahràn*," the man remarked. "You will not like the consequences."

He pivoted and stalked off like a man on a mission. I'd half-expected to be chained to Halueth and the others again, but to our mutual surprise, our captors stepped back and allowed us time to stretch out legs.

Nobody dared come close to us.

CHAPTER 15

SHALITHA

"*W*hat are you talking about?" I hissed through gritted teeth, glaring at her.

"You heard me," she growled, pushing the blade harder against my skin.

Blood trickled down my neck. "Last time I checked, he was still very much alive if that's what you mean."

She slammed me against the wall again. Her strength surprised me—she didn't look like much. A grunt escaped my lips, and I began to feel annoyed. First the guard shoving me so I stumbled and now her slamming me into a wall. What was I, a rag doll?

"What in Esah's name do you want?" I growled.

"What have you done to my brother?" she seethed.

"Maybe if you're a bit more specific," I retorted, fighting to push the knife away from my throat, "I'd be able to answer you."

She stepped away with a growl of her own, keeping a firm hold on the knife in her hand. I brought a hand to my neck where she'd nicked me, assessing the damage while keeping a wary eye on her. She paced up and down the small chamber, reminding me of a caged animal.

"He's lost interest in the cause," she said eventually, sounding defeated rather than angry.

I arched a brow. "What cause?"

She glared at me. "Don't play stupid, *Tarien*. You know the story. Elay said he told you."

"Fine," I replied. "Then what am I supposed to have done."

"You tell me," she hissed, taking a step forward. "He's lost interest because of *you*."

I snorted. "Hardly. He's more determined than ever if you ask me."

"All he talks about is you." She sounded offended. "How he needs to look after *you*. Take care of *you*. Make sure *you* don't die."

Laughter bubbled up inside of me, and it took me a lot of effort not to allow it to burst out. She was still holding the knife, but I didn't feel like explaining to Elay why his sister was dead.

"And he's doing it all for *you*," I replied, keeping my voice calm and steady. "When he learned what Kehran had done to your parents, to his brothers and sister, well... furious doesn't come close to describing it. He'd have torn down this place with his bare hands had he been given the chance."

Naïda lifted her chin, giving the impression she was looking down her nose at me. "Then why didn't he?"

I arched a brow. "You're joking, right? Rumours say he has an entire army at his disposal."

Her lips formed a thin line as she regarded me, her expression of someone who was deadly serious. I let out a heavy sigh and shook my head.

"If he'd done that, he'd be dead," I said. "And he doesn't have that army."

"Why do you care?"

The sudden change of subject caught me off guard, and for a brief moment, I considered hitting her full in the face, if only to satisfy the need to strike something. I doubted that would go over well with both Elay and Kehran. Instead, I pushed myself against the wall, hands flat. My heart beat frantically in my chest, but I wasn't sure if it was because of the anger surging inside of me, or something else. When I spoke, my voice was softer and kinder, yet restrained.

"Because," I began. "I do..."

I couldn't say I loved him, not to her.

Not to myself.

By saying I cared, I wasn't lying. I cared deeply for Elay, more than I should for the mysterious stranger whom I'd married out of necessity, for the man who'd offered me kindness in a world where everyone wanted me dead, for the man who'd shown me more of himself, and who had taught me more about the intimacies between a couple.

Was it love, though?

"You love him," she whispered, staring at me.

I didn't respond, staring down at my feet.

Guilt gnawed at my insides like a rat trying to escape. I'd tried to deny it for a long time, even more so when I learned Tal was still alive, but he wasn't here and Elay was. He had extended his hospitality to me when I needed it most, seen to me when I was injured, cared for me when nobody else had.

"He was desperate," I said after a while. "Frustrated even. With himself, with the situation. No matter what he came up with, he couldn't devise anything that could save you and your brother. He was convinced Kehran would kill him on the spot."

Naïda clenched her jaw, tightening the grip on the knife. "It doesn't explain why he brought *you* along."

I laughed this time, but there was no humour in it. She'd used my title but apparently had failed to comprehend the meaning of it, surprising considering the fact she was a princess in her own right. With a shake of my head, taking in big gulps of air, I forced myself to calm down. This time when I spoke, there was no kindness, sadness, or restraint. It was hollow and detached. If Elay had not confided in his sister, I wouldn't either.

"I'm leverage," I said. "A mere slave in your half-brother's *herriatâre*. Ask Elay why he brought me. I do not know."

She didn't seem to believe me.

I didn't care.

"Elay's not here," she said in resignation, "or I would have."

Air rushed out of my lungs as if she'd punched me in the gut. In a heartbeat, I decided I couldn't show her what it did to me, so I straightened, keeping my face blank.

"Let's not keep the *Akyn* waiting."

Her head snapped up in surprise, but judging by the look on her face, she realised she wasn't going to get anything more out of me. I knew this move could make an enemy out of her, but right now, that wasn't my main concern. She wouldn't kill me for the same reason I wouldn't kill her.

Elay.

"Let's not," she replied in a strained voice.

Four guards escorted me through the corridors of the palace, and I couldn't help but feel as if they were leading me to my execution. A part of me wished they did. The news Elay wasn't at the palace had seized up my throat and constricted my chest, but it had soon cleared with the knowledge I wasn't going to be alone. Z'tala would be there, as would Jaehyr.

It was a small comfort considering Kehran's ambitions.

I hadn't forgotten the surprise visit at the training field that morning, nor the dark-skinned stranger who had shown too much interest in me. Z'tala's words still rang clear in my mind —her explanation, her warning. Even so, discomfort crept down my throat and settled itself in my stomach like a heavy stone.

It was perhaps a good thing I hadn't eaten.

When we arrived in the garden, music and voices drifted on the wind towards us, lulling me into a false sense of security. A shove between the shoulder blades shattered the spell, and I stepped forward, reluctance turning my limbs heavy and my thoughts rebellious. Z'tala had spoken of survival, of doing what had to be done no matter what it took, and although a part of me agreed, the other part wanted to fight. I inhaled deeply, wrestled down the warrior inside me, and exhaled.

Now was not the time.

Given my upbringing, I was prepared to be put on display, but not in the actual sense of the word. One of the guards guided me to a low marble pedestal—the other guided Z'tala to another—and muttered at me to step up. While it gave me a good view of the party revellers, it gave them a good view of me, too. As it was intended, of course. Discomfort itched across my skin and it was only my rigorous training that kept me from wriggling.

I stood with my arms alongside my body, my chin lifted, back straight like Tal had taught me.

Opposite me, Z'tala stood rigid, her pose like mine—at attention—eyes on something far beyond this place. I kept a close watch on the people around us without it looking suspicious. The *Dekiatâre's* instructions had been crystal clear—if we even so much as twitched, our punishment would be severe. Movement out of the corner of my eyes caught my attention, and risking a glance aside, I saw Jaehyr step on his pedestal, the expression on his face indecipherable.

This probably wasn't the first time for him either.

Three others joined us—all of them men, all of them looking as stoic as Jaehyr, if not more. One of them had the look of a Therondian to him, a pinkish hue to his skin. Like Jaehyr, he wore nothing more than a piece of fabric around the waist, covering the most essential parts while highlighting the rest of his well-toned body. The second man had the same dark skin as Z'tala, and his braided hair was pulled back, giving his look a dangerous edge.

He, too, wore next to nothing.

It was the third man who caught my attention. Something about him looked familiar, but I could hardly stare at him to find out. It was in the way his jaw was set, in the way his body tensed before stepping on to the pedestal, in the way he surveyed the people below him, almost as if they were beneath him. When he glanced in my direction, I quickly looked away, pretending I hadn't just been ogling him.

I caught him smirking out of the corner of my eyes.

Cocky grissin.

Despite myself, I kept throwing glances in his direction, trying to figure out what it was about him that made me feel as if I'd seen him before. A sudden touch on my foot made me tense, and I clenched my jaw, trying for all I was worth not to move. A man reminding me too much of the *Gemsha* was pulling up my trouser leg, presumably to uncover the *Araith* underneath. In my peripherals, I saw Jaehyr pull up his lips in a silent snarl. I'd have liked nothing more than to kick the man in the teeth.

It wasn't worth the punishment.

"Checking out the merchandise?" A man's voice sounded from a slightly different angle.

Glancing down, I saw it was the dark-skinned stranger I'd seen earlier that day, regarding the man groping me with jovial indifference.

"Of course," the man replied without looking at him, his eyes on me instead. "I'd pay good money for a night with this one."

"You've always liked the dangerous ones, Ma'lek."

"Just like you, R'tayan," Ma'lek replied, one hand clasping around my calf.

I stilled and closed my eyes briefly.

"The *Akyn* has surely outdone himself this time." R'tayan sounded gracious, but there was an undertone in his voice that belied this.

I caught his eye, and he smiled.

"Come." R'tayan placed a hand on Ma'lek's shoulder. "I think the *Akyn* is about to announce something."

Both men turned away, and I let out a shuddering breath. Although Z'tala had told me what would happen tonight, I wasn't by any means prepared for the next part.

Kehran, standing out among the crowd in his golden attire, drew the attention of his guests merely by lifting his glass into the air. A hushed silence fell over them as they turned to watch him, which made us stand out even more.

"*Eshen, Shena,*" Kehran said in the silkiest voice he could manage. "I bid you welcome to this humble party. I shall not bother you too long for you are familiar with this custom. The bidding shall commence when the sun lowers beyond the walls."

His words sent a thrill through the crowd, eliciting soft murmurs and sneaked peeks in our direction. It sent chills down my spine. Even though I knew he wasn't there, I couldn't help but look for Elay.

You don't need him. You never needed any of them. Don't start now.

Whatever came next, I could face it. I couldn't leave Ilvanna in the hands of my psychopath aunt, so if that meant putting my pride aside for a few hours, so be it. But as I gave myself this inspirational talk, I couldn't help but feel sick at the notion of someone bidding for my company, however he or she decided.

With a heavy heart, I watched the sun sink in the distance until it was barely visible over the wall and felt my courage sink along with it. My gaze flitted from Z'tala across from me to Jaehyr on my right. Both looked as unperturbed as ever.

You can do this. Don't let it get inside your head. Survive. For your brothers. For your friends.

For Ilvanna.

The bidding was a strange event with the ritual intensity of a *harshâh* but without the accompanying insanity. Servants placed bottle-shaped vases—wide at the bottom, narrow at the neck— at our feet while Kehran addressed his guests in a voice unstable from too much wine. As he explained the proceedings, my gaze shifted from the man called Ma'lek, whose eyes bore into me as if he were trying to see through me, to R'tayan, whose composure was of a man confident in his conquest.

I had the distinct feeling I was that conquest.

The moment the crowd dispersed on Kehran's orders, my eyes snapped up to gaze into nothing, but my ears were pricked to pick up the voices closest to me. A vase to my right jingled as someone dropped something in it.

Not once.

Not twice.

Several times.

The sound reminded me of a ritual back home at the temple. Although it had been a long time since I set foot inside one, I still remembered the polished white stones the *Haniyah* offered upon our arrival. Its smooth surface had felt like silk under my thumb as I stroked it, and the longer I continued, the more at ease I had felt. I'd been about to pocket the stone when Evan murmured in my ear it would be sacrilege to do so, and I couldn't possibly want the Gods to punish our family. At forty-three, a child still in the eyes of our elders, his words impressed me enough to offer the stone to the Gods instead, murmuring an apology under my breath. After that encounter, and for many years after, I'd considered my brother's words and had concluded that if the Gods would punish a child over taking a pebble, they must be evil indeed. As soon as it was no longer mandatory to visit the temple, I stopped going.

Voices at my feet cut through my silent reverie, but I didn't dare glance in their direction.

I knew what I would see.

Stone after stone was dropped into my vase, the sound musical and echoing at first, but turning duller with every stone they placed inside until no more stone would fit. I'd somehow expected a squabble between the two men to happen, but nothing of the sort came. I glanced at Z'tala, watching in curiosity as a bid for her company between two men and one woman was well underway. One by one, they dropped a stone inside the vase. I thought it made no sense to do it this way because surely, they could count, until I noticed the different sizes another guest was going through in his hand.

The bigger the size, the higher the price.

They had no way of knowing who had won until the stones had been counted, which left me to wonder how they knew which stones belonged to whom. In the dim light of the torches, their colour was hard to distinguish. Logically, they'd be different, but I'd long since learned Kehran and logic did not go hand in hand.

If anything, he was as unreasonable as they came.

But he does stick to his rituals.

Somehow, that notion stuck in my mind as important. Kehran liked his rituals. I'd noticed that whenever something didn't go the way he wanted it to, the chances of a tantrum increased per every passing heartbeat. No, Kehran didn't go about things logically—he went about them emotionally. I felt my lips curl up in a smile at the thought.

That's how we'll defeat him.

Turning my gaze to the man in question, I watched him conduct business with another guest, a man dressed in the finest silks. He laughed at something Kehran said, which sent the golden hoops in his ear swinging. They caught the candle-light and glittered, or so it appeared, and for a moment I was reminded again of Elay.

It was like a punch to the gut.

As much as I had convinced myself I didn't need any of them —needed *him*—I became aware of the notion that I *wanted* him here, walking around, stealing covert glances my way, reassuring me with his presence. He'd been there when I was utterly alone.

What about Tal?

The thought was like a knife to the chest—painful, unbearable, mind-numbing. Whatever had been between us had been stolen that night at *Hanyarah*. It had been new, fresh, enticing and oh so intoxicating, but it hadn't lasted.

And I'd believed him dead.

When Esahbyen had told me he was still alive, I'd felt relieved—happy even—but now that I thought of it, I wondered whether it had been relief because my *Anahràn* was still alive or because the man I loved was.

Was it possible to love more than one?

Kehran clearing his throat jolted me back to the present, and it was then I realised the six vases had been collected and were now displayed in a row behind him. In front of them, servants had placed smaller bowls. Some vases had only one, some two, and one even four. I assumed they were filled with the rocks the bidders had dropped into the vases.

My heart picked up speed.

The Therondian and the Zihrin had both been bought for the night by the same woman. They didn't seem too perturbed by the notion as she shamelessly led them away inside the palace. The other Zihrin—the one who looked so familiar, but I could not place—went with a more dignified woman. He followed her obediently as she left the garden area, her posture straight, head lifted.

When Jaehyr stepped off his pedestal and walked over to the well-dressed man I'd seen converse with Kehran earlier, my heart went out to him. He caught my eye before he turned to follow, and I could see the anguish in them.

"Ai Sela'àn," I whispered under my breath.

At ease, soldier.

Whether he had heard me or not, a little tension appeared to leave his body as he passed the rest of the crowd, holding his head high. I watched them leave until long after they'd gone, and I almost missed who had bought Z'tala's company for the night.

My stomach lurched when I saw her leave with R'tayan.

Ma'lek had bought me.

CHAPTER 16

HAERLYON

A scream that went through bone and marrow tore me
from my sleep and had me on my feet with a dagger in
hand and running in the space of a few heartbeats. My bare feet
padded the cold floor in the otherwise silent hallway. Outside,
night still lay over Ilvanna, casting its darkness on the corridors
of the palace save for where the lit lanterns chased the shadows
away. At this time of night, those were few, but I needed no light
to navigate my way through the hallways. I knew them like the
back of my hand. Just as I reached the *Tari's* door, a second
scream full of agony rang out.

I kicked down the door, unprepared for what I came face to
face with.

Blood spattered the room from left to right, leaving nothing
untouched, least of all the *Tari* herself. She wore nothing but a
robe which she hadn't bothered to tie—or maybe it had come
undone—her pregnancy showing, her hair haloing her face in a
wild, frantic mess. Below her, barely alive, a man attempted to
lift his hands, but he was too weak.

She hardly noticed.

I stared for what felt like hours. Azra tore into him as if she were a hungry, savage animal, heedless of the conventions of our kind. Her hands were dark against her otherwise pale skin, but it wasn't the reason why I fled. It was when she looked up—her eyes feral, her mouth covered in blood—that I took a step back.

When she lunged at me, I sprinted into the corridor.

A part of me wanted to yell for help, but it was the other part—the flight part—that took over and kept me running, trying to get away from what was chasing me. Glancing over my shoulder, I found Azra was still on my tail. Despite the huge belly, she was fast—faster than I would have liked. I skidded around a corner too sharply and almost lost my balance.

I lost precious time.

Something heavy slammed into me, sending me to the marble floor. A sharp pain lanced through my side a moment later. Without hesitation, I turned on my back and used my hands and feet to push her off me. She slammed into the wall, hitting her head hard enough for any person to lose consciousness.

She didn't.

Instead, she shook her head and rounded on me as fast as any predatory animal I'd ever encountered. Not that they were many, but the few I had seen had reacted in an eerily similar fashion. When she lunged at me just as fast, instinct took over. She barrelled into me, and we went down together. A wail of anguish tore from her lips, and she scrambled away from me, staring at the blood gushing from her side. I stared at her, shaking my head as the realisation of my action dawned on me. I'd stabbed her. To my surprise, she made no attempt to stop the flow, merely looked at it with her head tilted, curiosity warping her features into an almost animalistic mask.

"*Tari.*" I scrambled over to her, half-expecting she would knock me out of the way.

The wicked smile contorting her lips into something

straight out of nightmares had me stagger back, and I fell on my ass, staring at her as she straightened. The injury should have brought her to her knees. My mouth slackened, and I felt all colour drain from my face when I realised she was no longer bleeding.

"What in Esah's name," I whispered.

She looked at me, her usually dark eyes now swirling with an intense darkness reminiscent of the night sky. A deep shudder ran through me as I pushed back from her, kicking off against the tiles to find purchase. Her laughter echoed through the hall as she looked down on me, and for a brief moment, I felt certain I was drawing my last breaths.

"You're no match for me, *q'lerahn.*" She sneered. "And you never will be."

She stepped forward, hand raised to strike me when suddenly her eyes widened, and she dropped to her knees with an audible gasp. The thump as she fell made me wince. I scampered over to her as quickly as my trembling limbs could carry me and checked for a pulse. To my relief, I found a slow, steady beat underneath my fingers. With a grunt of pain, I rearranged her robe and lifted her in my arms, conscious of the jitters going through me at her proximity.

If she woke up in my arms…

I hoisted Azra a little higher, but as I carried her to her room, a sudden thought struck me, and rather than going to hers, I went to mine. It was undoubtedly a fool's decision, but if anyone knew what had gone on, it would be Mehrean, and as long as Azra was unconscious, she need not fear.

Perhaps...

"SHE *WHAT?*" Mehrean hissed through her teeth.

"Cannot be killed," I replied, rubbing my forehead in an

attempt to ease the building headache. "It... it was self-defence. I used my dagger like I would have on anyone attacking me. She was bleeding, Mehr, until"—I swallowed hard, staring at the stranger in my bed—"she was not. It just stopped..."

"That's impossible," she murmured, more to herself than to me. "Unless..."

"Unless what?"

Her head snapped up, bewilderment in her eyes as she looked at me. "Nothing, unless nothing." She waved her hand in dismissal and shook her head while moving about the room to gather what little belongings she had brought.

"Going somewhere?" I arched a brow.

"Yes, I—" She stopped, her mouth half-open as she stared at me. "What happened?"

I frowned at the sudden change of direction. "What are you talking about?"

Her brows knitted together, and her lips pressed in a thin line. "You're injured."

It was as if her words triggered my body to respond. I dropped to one knee, clutching my side as pain flared out, enveloping me, and the adrenaline left me in a powerful whoosh. I felt bereft, as if I'd just lost someone dear to me. Mehrean placed my arm over her shoulders, wrapped her arm around my waist and helped me to my feet.

"Come," she whispered, guiding me to the antechamber.

"What about her?" I asked, glancing at Azra over my shoulder.

"Between her ordeals and my sleeping draught," Mehr said, "I doubt she will wake up soon."

Reassured by her words, I allowed Mehrean to escort me to the other room and onto a stool. For a change, I was glad not to be wearing a shirt. I watched Mehrean bustle about quietly, and I felt a smile tugging at my lips. Something about this was so comfortable, so familiar, it felt as if everything had turned back to normal, and I half expected Shal to burst through my door at any moment.

The thought of my sister stopped the memories short.

She wasn't here. She was somewhere in a country beyond the sea doing Gods know what. Surviving, I hoped. The last news we received, which had been a while, I realised, was that she'd been seen in Portasâhn, Zihrin's largest harbour. From there on, all leads had gone quiet.

As far as I knew, at least.

I didn't doubt Azra kept information behind. No matter how much I played at being her man, I would always be Shalitha's brother. Although I fully believed Azra had no idea what such a connection meant emotionally, what kind of allegiance and loyalty it brought out in people, she wasn't stupid.

She trusted me. She didn't trust me completely.

"Can you raise your arm, please?" Mehrean murmured.

I did as instructed, biting back the anguished cry as the movement stretched the injured area beyond comfort. Glancing down, I found Mehrean kneeling at my side and felt her deft fingers gliding around the wound to assess the damage. She stifled a gasp as she leaned closer.

"What is it?" I asked, feeling much less certain.

"What did she attack you with?"

I furrowed my brow, trying to remember what it had been, only to come up blank.

"She didn't have a weapon..."

A chill rolled down my back as an eerie image sprang to mind—the image of her blood-covered mouth. My stomach twisted in a knot as I looked down at my side and saw my skin hanging loose where she'd torn it with her teeth.

"By Esah," I whispered, my voice feeble and weak.

"Don't look then." There was an edge to Mehrean's voice I hadn't heard before.

"Can you... fix it?"

She glanced up at me briefly and shrugged. "I don't know, Haer. I will do my best."

"Where is Soren when you need him?"

Mehrean poked me gently in the ribs. "A bit more faith, please."

I grunted in response.

She set to cleaning the injury with the quiet determination I was used to seeing in her but was surprised to find her hands trembling as she proceeded with her administrations. It wasn't like her to be nervous about something. Rather than ask her, I opted to keep quiet, not trusting myself to stifle a cry of pain at any point. The last thing I wanted was for Azra to wake up and find Mehrean here.

There would be no forgiveness.

"How..." I hesitated, biting my lip while I tried to find the words. "How is everyone?"

Mehrean glanced up, pity at my expense reflected in her eyes. "As well as can be expected."

I swallowed hard. "Soren?"

"His usual pragmatic self."

"Cerindil?"

"Quite ready to level the palace," she replied, a tone of annoyance lacing her words. "Who knew the man had such a temper?"

A faint smile tugged at my lips. Talnovar used to be quick of temper, too, but over time he had managed to turn around completely. He'd somehow gained everlasting patience, although, I supposed, it had come with the job of protecting my sister.

She hadn't made it easy for any of them.

My chest felt suddenly tight, stealing the air from my lungs. Tears pricked my eyes, but I refused to let them fall. If I fell apart now, I would never be able to do what I must.

"Evan? Nath?" I asked quietly.

Mehrean stilled so completely, I thought for a moment she had just disappeared. I belatedly realised my mistake—she and Evan had been together before he decided to play the hero and marry Nathaïr. Mehr let out a shuddering breath, her voice barely a whisper when next she spoke. "Nathaïr died in childbirth. Evan's... doing what he can, considering the circumstances. You know him. Doesn't show any signs of weakness."

I stared at her, my jaw hanging open. "What about the child?"

"She lives." Mehr smiled, but it never reached her eyes.

She was about to say more when a sound from the next room stopped her. I strained to listen, trying to discern whether Azra was waking up or not.

"Hide," I hissed as I rose to my feet.

I was at the doors to the garden in three strides and opened one without a sound—over the years I'd perfected this—allowing Mehrean to slip outside.

"Stay low," I muttered.

Without waiting to see if she listened, I closed the door, grabbed a roll of bandages and while wrapping it around my waist, strolled back into the bedroom, my lips pulled up in a little sneer. As suspected, Azra had woken up, looking for all the world like a lost little girl. I'd never thought I'd attribute any of those words to her, but there I was. Her eyes were wide, unfocused, looking around the room in what I could only describe as fear. Her hands were clutching the blankets tightly.

"Haer?" she whispered in bewilderment. "Where am I?"

"My room."

She blinked. "Why?"

The moment of truth. Was I going to tell her what she had done, or should I err on the side of caution?

"What do you remember?" I asked instead.

A frown creased her brow, adding years to her age. "I'm... not sure. I remember a messenger at my door with news and then..."

If at all possible, she looked even more confused, her mouth working as if she was talking herself through something even though she made no sound. I almost pitied her.

Almost.

Something in her gaze shifted. The woman staring at me now was not the same as the one I'd been looking at before—it was the same one who'd called me *q'lerahn*. Gone was the fear in her eyes, the slouched posture—returned was the predatory smile, the wicked sparkle in her eyes.

I took an involuntary step backwards as she slipped out of bed.

"What's wrong, Haer? You look like you've seen a ghost."

I pulled myself together in a heartbeat, lifting my chin slightly. "Nothing wrong, *Tari*," I replied. "Glad to see you up and about."

"Why am I in your room?"

"It was closest after you collapsed. No offense, *Tari*, but you aren't exactly light right now."

I'd expected her to sneer at me. Instead, she laughed, but the lack of mirth surprised me every time. It was as if she knew no emotions, and yet, I'd seen fear on her face just now. Together with the not dying part, something didn't add up. Didn't she remember what had happened, or did she pretend not to?

"Escort me to my chambers," she ordered, looking around my room, her nose pulled up as if she smelled something funny.

I pulled a shirt over my head and guided her out of the bedroom and into the hallway. Dawn was fast approaching in light purple hues, and it would only be a matter of time before the palace denizens began to stir. Azra, indecently dressed with blood still on her hands and face, would be quite the sight if people saw her now. I was thankful my room wasn't far from hers.

The stench of death reached us moments before we arrived at the door. My insides twisted, and I gripped the handle of the door so tight I was afraid I'd break something. The smell of blood and excrements hung heavy in the air. Azra didn't seem perturbed as she stepped inside, barely sparing the corpse on the floor a second glance. As I passed him to open a window, I couldn't help but look down. I wished I hadn't. If I'd had any hope of identifying him, it went out the window straight away. She'd left nothing of his face to recognise him by.

"What happened anyway?" I asked, trying to sound indifferent.

"Yllinar is dead."

Despite her sounding casual, there was an underlying tension in her voice, and I wouldn't have been surprised to see it mirrored on her face. After all, if the rumours were true, Azra and Yllinar had been lovers a long time ago, and he had been the only one she ever fully trusted.

Or had he been the only one who had as wicked a soul as she did?

"Dané il ruesta," I murmured, then continued loud enough so she could hear. "How did he die?"

Her shoulders tensed considerably at my question. She turned to me slowly, deliberately, several expressions crossing her face before she settled on utter hatred.

"Talnovar killed him," she said, her voice oddly hollow. "He will pay for it."

My heart skipped a beat at hearing his name. He'd been alive then.

"How?" I asked. Azra narrowed her eyes before looking away.

"There has been a naval battle, or so I've been told. They encountered the merchant ship harbouring the *verathràh*, but they weren't as outnumbered as my men had been led to believe —I will have to punish Eamryel for that—and were overpowered. Talnovar pulled him overboard, and neither has been seen since."

The same faith as you had us believe happened to my sister. Serves you right, hehzèh.

I grimaced. "Well, at least there's a chance Talnovar is dead, too. Did they recover Yllinar's body?"

"No," she said. "The merchant and his crew hijacked my ship, offering my men either a place on board or sending them off in a skiff."

A growl escaped my lips. Azra offered me a wry smile in return. I hadn't meant to make the sound, nor had I meant it to be in defence of what she'd said, but she seemed to take it as me being on her side.

"How did he get to be here?" I asked.

Azra shrugged. "He said something about having been let go."

I arched a brow.

"I didn't exactly wait for his excuses," she snapped, scowling at me. "Wouldn't you have done the same if they'd killed someone you loved?"

I clenched my jaw, staring hard at her. Considering the fact she was still drawing breath, the obvious answer was 'no', but I could hardly tell her that. I'd love nothing more than to kill the person who murdered Tiroy, even if it hadn't been by her own hand.

"I suppose," I replied, looking at the body on the floor. "Although I may not have gone to such extremes."

The body, or rather what was left of it, looked as if it had been mauled by a wild animal. Had I not seen it with my own eyes, I would have believed a bear had entered Azra's chambers and had this man for breakfast. The truth was a lot more disconcerting. Yet, even as the thought crept up on me, I couldn't shake the memory of her looking lost, fragile, and frightened shortly after she'd woken up, almost as if she couldn't remember where she was or what had happened. The switch to this woman had been so fast, however, I wasn't entirely sure I hadn't just imagined it.

"Let me call your ladies-in-waiting to help you dress and a few men to get rid of this body," I said, starting for the door.

"No."

Her voice stopped me short, and I turned to her slowly, brow furrowed. "*Tari?*"

"You get rid of it," she ordered. "Don't call anyone in until this is taken care of."

"How do you propose I get rid of a body by myself?" I asked, trying to keep the incredulity out of my voice. "People are starting to wake up."

She folded her arms in front of her, ignoring the fact her robes had come undone again, and pressed her lips tightly together. "Get rid of it however you see fit but do it on your own. Let my ladies-in-waiting come when you are finished. I'm going back to bed."

Without waiting for a reply, she turned her back on me, dropped the robe to the floor and slid underneath the blood-stained covers of the massive bed. I shuddered and watched as she made herself comfortable on her side, listened as she muttered about the pregnancy, waited until I heard her breathing slow down and deepen before I slipped out of the room and stormed back to my own. Mehrean was sitting on my bed, looking up the moment I closed the door behind me. The look in her eyes stopped me short for a second time this morning.

"What's wrong?" I asked.

"I need to leave."

I frowned. "I figured after you started gathering everything. What about your reason for staying here?"

"You must do it," she replied, rising to her feet. "There's something I must investigate. Something that may alter the outcome of... well... everything."

"That is not vague at all."

"Listen. If Azra goes into labour before I return, you must ensure she never sees the baby. Give it to someone you trust and tell them to leave for *Denahryn*. Tell them to find Cerindil, Soren, Evanyan, any of them. Whatever happens, Azra must believe the child was born dead. Can I trust you to do that?"

I nodded.

"Good," Mehrean said distractedly, pulling the hood of her cloak over her head while walking to the garden door. "In case I do not return... do not worry about me. I'll be fine."

She was gone before I could even ask what that was supposed to mean.

What is Esah's name is going on?

CHAPTER 17

TALNOVAR

*I*t wasn't as much the drought that made the situation intolerable as it was the everlasting heat weighing down upon me. My lips had cracked days ago and were bleeding almost constantly. My fingers felt stiff, as if the skin had dried up and shrunk, constraining mobility. My body, once a pristine white where the *Araîth* didn't mark it, had turned a dull red everywhere it was exposed to the sun.

The itch was insufferable.

To make matters worse, after my showdown with one of the other captives, those closest to me kept a careful watch, almost as if they expected to be next. Even Nazeem and Tariq were keeping their distance.

At least Halueth doesn't quite fear me.

Not that I knew of, anyway.

In all truth, this situation suited me. Whether they feared me, hated me, or otherwise had feelings for me, as long as it repelled them, I was content. It gave Halueth and me time and privacy on our walks during our free time. There were only two people who spoke to me under the pretence of normalcy—

Halueth and the well-dressed stranger who had spoken to me after my fight.

He was there now during our free time, sitting in the shade provided by a luxuriously decorated pavilion. Although I couldn't be entirely sure with him sitting too far off, it appeared he was keeping an eye on me. Once or twice, I caught him staring at me, his lips pursed, eyes narrowed. When he caught me watching, he smiled.

There was something about him I didn't like. I just couldn't put my finger on what it was.

This morning was no different from the other mornings. I'd woken up early from the sun, had gone behind the lean-to to relieve myself—the chains allowed for that at least—and came back to find the rest waking up, too. My stomach had protested at the sight of the others having breakfast. I'd scowled at mine as if it had done me a great disservice and managed two or three spoonfuls before setting the rest aside. After breakfast, it was time for our daily walk around the smaller sandbox where I kept well out of everyone's way. It wasn't that I was scared to fight, but my shoulder was finally getting the rest it needed, and day by day, the pain diminished.

I prayed to the Gods it would heal properly.

"I heard them discuss an uprising," Halueth remarked, stretching his arms behind his back.

"When?"

He held up his hand, palm uplifted, and shrugged. "They didn't say."

"Of course, they didn't," I muttered, pinching the bridge of my nose.

Three men nearby were watching me curiously and began whispering among themselves. One twirled a finger next to his temple, suggesting I didn't seem to have my faculties in order, but I shrugged it off. I was fine aside from the constant dizziness and feeling as if I were frying out here in the sun. Halueth

163

continued his narrative, and I responded when I thought I should, but my gaze was drawn to the figure sitting underneath the pavilion, his gaudy attire twinkling in what little sun dared make its way inside, and the man talking to him.

Tariq.

At that moment, the stranger turned to watch me. From this distance, I couldn't read his expression, but the way he'd folded his hands and was tapping his fingers against his lips told me he was considering something.

Something Tariq is telling him.

"Tal?"

"Hm?"

"You're not listening," Halueth said reproachfully, but there was a twinkle in his eyes that belied his sentiment. "I could have been pouring my heart out to you, or given you my mother's cookie recipe, and you would have responded the same way."

"I'm sorry, *mahnèh*," I said. "What were you saying?"

"They intend to kill you, too."

I blinked at him, slowly, stupidly, as if he had spoken in a different language, and I was trying to figure out the meaning. But it wasn't that. There was something in the words he'd spoken that caught my attention. My gaze travelled to the stranger and Tariq standing at his side, leaning forward to whisper in his ear. Something at Tariq's side flashed in the sunlight, and I noticed his hand hovering dangerously near.

Kill you, too.

"*Nohro!*"

Before I had consciously decided to do so, I was running in the direction of the pavilion, my feet kicking up a cloud of sand as I went. My eyes scanned the area, looking for the Gods know what. The stranger sat up in his chair as I charged towards him, confusion marring his features. He rose to his feet as I approached him. Tariq turned in my direction as the guard behind them took a step closer, his hand on the hilt of the curved sword at his side. He looked vaguely familiar.

Regardless, I kept going, pushing my feet down to gain momentum. I saw the stranger step aside just as Tariq stepped forward, drawing his weapon.

"Watch out!" I yelled.

To my surprise, he didn't move, even as Tariq stepped forward and the guard moved up on his other side. I knew him, but I couldn't recall his name. The notion disturbed me only briefly—I'd never forgotten names before, not while sober anyway. Before Tariq had his weapon fully unsheathed, I barrelled into him, and we went down together, kicking, growling, cursing. I tried to wrestle his blade from him, but he was stronger. At that moment, I was desperate. The stranger knew where I'd served, and something told me that I would need him in the future.

I couldn't let Tariq kill him.

He hadn't expected the man to get out of his way.

With a strength I didn't even know I possessed, I forced the knife out of his hand and pinned him to the ground, applying my weight to his chest. A moment later, a sharp pain lanced through my head as the world tilted, and the carpet rose to meet me.

When I came to, a headache the likes of which I hadn't experienced since coming off *sehvelle* pounded in my skull. I squinted against the sunlight, my vision blurry. When I tried to sit up, and my arms and legs refused to cooperate, I realised they were tied together.

I was trussed up like a hog.

"Ah, awake, are you?" the man's voice sounded above me.

The man just smiled as he sat down in his high-backed chair, his eyes surveying me unabashedly. The scrutiny was uncomfortable and made me painfully aware of both my position and attire, or lack thereof. Like every other man in our camp, we'd been made to wear wide trousers and nothing more. Although more comfortable than the Ilvannian leather outfit I'd worn, the exposure to the elements—and this man's gaze—was a good deal less enjoyable.

"I'd release you of your bonds if I trusted you wouldn't attack me again."

I blinked.

I hadn't attacked him, had I?

Surveying the pavilion, I noticed Tariq had gone. At the motion of the stranger's hand, a young woman arrived carrying a tray with a pot of tea and two cups. The man barely glanced at her as she placed it on the single table and began to pour the tea. I watched her from my position on the ground. Her skin colour was the opposite of mine—black where I was white. Dark hair lay in a single braid across her shoulder.

"Like what you see, *Anahràn?*" The man smiled at me.

A frown creased my brow as I looked up at him, grimacing at the uncomfortable strain movement created between my shoulder blades. I wasn't sure what to reply, so I went for an ineffective, "She's a beautiful woman."

"But not the woman you are looking for, is she?"

My head snapped up as if he'd hit me. "Excuse me?"

"I know who you are, Talnovar Imradien," the man said, the smile gone. "*Anahràn* to the late *Tarien* Shalitha an Ilvan."

I fought against my bonds despite feeling weak and gritted my teeth. "Tales of her death have reached even these shores?"

"You wouldn't be here if you believed those rumours," he observed, looking highly amused at my efforts to get free from my restraints.

"Wouldn't I?"

He regarded me, stroking his chin while pursing his lips as if

166

considering whether I was being serious or pulling his leg. Leaning forward, with his elbows resting on his knees, he brought his face inches from mine.

"How far will you go to find her, *Anahràn?*"

My title on his lips sent a chill down my spine, although I wasn't sure why. Perhaps it was because it reminded me of Azra and how she had used it to get under my skin.

"To the end of the world," I replied, meeting his gaze. "I'll tear it apart on my way if I have to."

His lips quirked up in a quick smile. "Of that, I have no doubt. Shame you might not live to do it."

I stilled, staring at him. "What?"

"You attacked me, Talnovar," he said, picking up the cup of tea before leaning back in his chair. "The question now is not what you will do to find her, but what you will do to stay alive."

With a flick of his wrist, the bonds around my wrists and ankles were cut away. Looking up, I found myself staring at Nazeem. He awarded me a wry smile and a shake of his head before stepping out of sight. If he were any good at what he did, I knew he'd be close.

"Have some tea," he said, gesturing for me to take the second cup from the table.

As I began to settle in a cross-legged position, a sudden pain in my leg stopped me, and I remembered there was something wrong, but when I looked at it, my vision swam, and I had a hard time staying up. A pair of hands steadied me.

"Drink your tea, Talnovar." The stranger's voice came from far away. "You'll feel better afterwards."

Something to drink in this scorching heat wouldn't go amiss, even if it was tea. Its scent was surely inviting. I took a sip, and another, until I'd emptied the cup. I'd been thirsty indeed. When after a couple of minutes a sudden drowsiness hit me, I snapped towards the stranger, opening my mouth to say something, but it was as if I were no longer able to form words.

When the sensation of falling washed over me, I became aware of hands underneath my shoulders. I wasn't falling—somebody was helping me lie down. Over my head, voices spoke in hushed tones in a language I couldn't comprehend, but I understood the urgency. Whatever was going on, whatever made them so worried, however, was beyond me. It was the strangest sensation—it was as if my mind had disconnected from my body and both were operating on their own.

"Hey, *Anahràn.*" Halueth's voice turned my attention away from myself. "See you on the other side."

CHAPTER 18

SHALITHA

There was a hollowness in my chest where my heart used to be. In the distance, I heard a woman's voice like an echo throughout time, familiar yet outlandish, pleading, begging for it to stop. It was like a memory of days long past in a world beyond the sea—a place where I knew there were others who had my best interest at heart, who had loved me.

Here, I was alone.

Small.

Nobody.

My mind drifted away from hands greedily exploring my body, pulling away whatever fabric hampered their endeavour. The hot, foul breath on my neck and cheek was repulsive, but much less so than his fingers fumbling around where they did not belong. I wanted to snake my hands around his neck and squeeze until he no longer drew breath, but remembering Z'ta-la's words, I kept them firmly clutching the bedsheets.

Do what you must to survive.

I'd done everything to survive. I'd married a stranger, followed him farther away from Ilvanna, allowed myself to be captured by his mad brother to fight in his *herrât*. But now? He'd left me in the hands of this vile creature whose life depended on my willpower. I could do it—it would be all too easy—but where would it leave me? Kehran would serve me to his tigresses for dinner before the night was done.

Would it be worth it?

Would it be worth to die just so this beast would be stopped from having his way with me? Was my virtue worth the price of a country? Two countries? I resigned myself to the fact that it was not and turned my attention elsewhere, hoping Elay could forgive me—that Tal could forgive me.

Wish you were here.

A sudden yet familiar warmth spread through my body, a warmth I'd felt only once before, a warmth that had saved my life that day, and not just from the tigresses. At first, I allowed it to envelope me, welcoming it as if it were an extra blanket on a particularly cold night. I relaxed into it, closing my eyes, shutting down my senses.

None of this mattered, did it?

Too soon, I became aware of a presence. It had been there that day, but it had remained in the background. Now, however, it was gently nudging me aside, lulling me into a sense of safety my subconscious craved more than anything. I began to struggle, to fight, but realised the other presence was too strong.

"Do not fight me, dochtaer," Esahbyen spoke in my mind. *"You are too weak."*

"I'm not weak!" I spat, his words rousing me.

In my mind—it couldn't be anywhere else—Esahbyen appeared dressed in his full warrior regalia. He stood silhouetted against a light background, highlighting the sword protruding over his right shoulder. Although I couldn't see his face, I knew he was angry.

"I can do this myself," I said, but I didn't sound as strong as I would have liked.

"You cannot."

"I won't let you fight my battles," I retorted. *"You promised me not to save my life again."*

"So, you expect me to stand idly by as this man disgraces you?"

I gritted my teeth or thought I did, anyway. *"Yes."*

"I cannot allow that to happen, dochtaer," he said mournfully. *"Please, forgive me."*

The sensation was that of falling from a great height in a dream moments before I'd wake up with an awkward leg-jerk, except it didn't happen. I kept falling, only vaguely aware of what was happening on the *outside.*

The sudden stop made my stomach plummet, and I felt momentarily disoriented.

My surroundings were dimmer than they'd been before, the outlines of the world blurry as if I were watching through tears. Somehow, I knew it wasn't that. I knew I was still in the room with Ma'lek, but rather than feeling what he was doing, I was a spectator to what was happening.

As Ma'lek fumbled around with his breeches, I loosened my hand from its death grip on the sheets—or rather, Esahbyen did —and I hit him on the nose with the palm of my hand. There should have been a crunching sound as I broke it, but there was nothing. Blood gushed from his nose, but I couldn't smell it. The sensation was eerily uncomfortable. In this world between worlds—or was I already in the afterlife—no sound passed through, which made this whole experience oddly disconnecting.

I spoke—no, Esahbyen did—but I couldn't hear more than a muffled sound. Ma'lek paled further, leaving him a sickly grey colour. It was then that I noticed Esahbyen holding the *grissin's* wrist at a painful angle, and judging by the look on his face—my face—he wasn't yet done. Cold snaked itself down my spine and into my gut.

This wasn't going to end well.

The events unfolding in front of me were mesmerizing.

Esahbyen grabbed the man's hand, snapped his wrist as if it were a twig, and punched Ma'lek square in the chest a heartbeat later, sending him flying back against the wall, breeches halfway to his knees. Ma'lek clutched his chest, gasping for air as blood welled up at the corner of his mouth. Two images blended. One of myself—haggard, haunted, unsteady on my feet—the other of Esahbyen in his war regalia, reaching behind him for a sword that wasn't there.

Until it was.

"No!" I yelled as loudly as I could, scrambling to my feet.

Esahbyen—I—turned to look at me, sadness crossing our features. *"His heart is dark,* dochtaer. *A man like this will not be missed."*

"I know," I replied, *"but death will be much too easy for him, don't you think?"*

The God of War regarded me with his head tilted. *"What do you propose?"*

"We make him suffer."

Esahbyen's lips curled into the wickedest grin I'd ever seen on anyone. My eyes lit up with a malicious glow, torture written in their depths. While I may never have been capable of such a thing, he was, and Ma'lek deserved every single punishment the God could come up with. For that, I would happily take a backseat and watch.

"If he is doing this to me," I said. *"He'll have done it to others. Perhaps he should feel what he has done."*

"I like your way of thinking, dochtaer."

I didn't. When Esahbyen exacted his first punishment upon Ma'lek—a stick up a place nobody should ever feel one—I winced, but I forced myself to watch. The look on the man's face was one of pain, his open mouth suggesting he was screaming.

For once, I felt relieved to have no hearing.

By the time Esahbyen finished, Ma'lek was sobbing like a

little girl, his mouth working fast as if he were either praying or begging.

"Now what?" Esahbyen asked, looking too smug.

If I could have, I knew I would have felt sick at the suggestion. *"Make him feel the terror they make us feel."*

Esahbyen arched a brow. *"What a curious suggestion,* dochtaer. *Are you sure?"*

"Yes," I said through gritted teeth.

He pressed my lips in a thin line, turning my silver eyes stormy. *"Turn away,* shareye," he murmured, waving his hand. As he did, I went blind on top of being deaf. The sensation was terrifyingly surreal, and I had a hard time not to lose my mind.

When it returned, a short time seemed to have passed, but as I laid eyes upon M'alek, I knew it had been longer than I'd thought. He lay curled on his side, pain twisting his lips down, his hands covering his essential parts, his eyes darting to me whenever he thought I wasn't looking—Esahbyen wasn't looking.

"What will you have me do next?"

I shook my head. *"That's enough. He's been punished, humiliated, hurt."*

He tilted his head, curiosity stealing over him. *"After what he has done to you, you want me to let him live?"*

"I won't let you make a murderer out of me," I replied.

He fell silent, considering my words, a look of confusion in his eyes. *"But you have killed before?"*

"Killed, yes. Murdered, no."

"What's the difference?"

"Everything."

If he could not understand that difference, he was no better than the man he intended to kill. He was frowning at me, as if the words I'd spoken were foreign to him. Then he shook his head, a bitter look contorting his otherwise handsome face. *"Enough? I've barely even begun. No,* dochtaer, *this is not enough."*

"If justice still prevails, he will not get away with what he has done," I said. *"But I cannot allow you to kill him. In doing so, you will sign my death warrant in my own blood."*

His posture turned rigid, like the look on his face. It was as if this concept was hard for him to understand. *"How is that justice, dochtaer? Had I not intervened, he would have molested you, maybe even killed you."*

"He wouldn't have," I replied. *"Molest, absolutely, but he wouldn't have killed me. Kehran will have his life for that."*

"But you don't understand." He sounded frustrated now. *"This man has no remorse. I can see it in his heart! He will do it again and again and again if given the chance, not just to women..."*

"But it's not up to us to decide his fate, Esahbyen," I said, releasing a heavy sigh. *"If you kill him, Kehran will punish me for my insubordination and with luck, he'll have me killed. If I'm unlucky, he will let me die of my injuries."*

"Then we should kill this Kehran."

"Yes," I replied. *"But now is not the time. Stop interfering in this world or you will start events that will ultimately, I'm sure, lead to the destruction of our kind. If you want me to succeed, let me do it."*

He looked at me as if considering this request, but something in his gaze shifted, turned stony, and before I could stop him, he thrust his sword inside Ma'lek and twisted it. Ma'lek's eyes widened. He coughed once, twice, blood staining his lips in what I knew to be a dark red. His breathing came in pained wheezes, and he looked at me—at *me*.

Esahbyen had relinquished control to me.

I stared at him, my mouth open in horror, my hand wrapped around the hilt of the sword. The feel of it in my hand returned my confidence as well as the pain and the anger roiling inside of me. With one great heave, I pulled the sword from Ma'lek's chest and stepped back, watching as he bled to death at my feet.

"Finish him."

At first, I thought the voice belonged to Esahbyen, but I

realised it was too deep—too sinuous for it to be him. I dispelled the notion with a shake of my head and made to take another step back, but instead, I raised the sword in my hand, gripped the hilt with both hands and prepared to drive it through Ma'lek's heart.

"*That's it,* shareye," the voice purred at the same time as somebody shouted, '*Tarien, no!*'.

The spell broke, and I staggered back, my legs no longer capable of supporting me. Strong arms caught me before I fell to the ground. I blinked up, looking at a face I thought I'd never see again, and my heart soared.

"Tal?" I whispered.

"*Do not lose the sword,* dochtaer."

"The sword," I murmured. "I need that sword."

I reached for it, but my fingers grabbed nothing but empty space. Frustration rose in me, and I twisted to look for it, only to find my body wasn't entirely willing to cooperate.

"I've got it, *Tarien,*" a voice murmured in my ear. "Let's get you out of here."

Despite the face being so similar, the voice didn't belong to Talnovar, and it took me a moment to remember this had to be Jaehyr—Tal's uncle.

"Where are we going?" I asked, feeling as though I had to fight to get the words out.

"Back to where we belong," Jaehyr said.

"Home?" I asked in a faint voice. "To Ilvanna?"

I never caught his reply. I felt a stranger in my own body, aware of where Ma'lek had touched me and of what he had tried to do, but my body was growing heavy, languid. My mind was disconnecting, returning to memories long past, but every time a vision cleared, something jerked me away from it.

"I'm here, *Tarien,*" Jaehyr crooned as if he were talking to a child. "You're safe."

There were other sounds, voices rising in pitch, commands

being shouted through the hallways, footsteps echoing against the walls.

Something was wrong.

A STRANGE HUMMING inside my head disrupted the image of the palace back in Ilvanna, of Evan and Haerlyon, of Mehrean, of my mother and Azra, of Tal. The sound was almost like a bee zooming around my head, but the pitch was off—it was too high, too sentient for it to be an insect. I realised it wasn't just humming a random melody—it was humming the tune of Ilvanna's anthem, if it could be called that. It was only ever played in wartime, something which hadn't happened during my lifetime.

"*Until now, Tari,*" the sinuous voice spoke in my mind. "*There are whispers of a war, and I've been ordered to guide you through it, no matter what.*"

I remained silent, certain I was making this voice up. It was received by an amused chuckle. "*I'm very much real, shareye.*"

"Who are you?" I asked, surprised to hear I'd spoken out loud.

Waking up felt as if I'd been asleep for so long, I couldn't remember what it was like to be awake. For all the comfort of the bed I was in—I assumed I was, at least—it might as well have been the floor. It was hard, unforgiving, and my body felt bruised in the spots where bone connected with the harsh surface.

"*K'lele.*" Z'tala sounded relieved. "You're awake."

"Why is that so surprising?" I asked, opening one eye to look at her.

We were back in our cell.

Z'tala was frowning at me, looking everything but amused.

It somehow reminded me of the last time I woke up injured after my fight with the tigresses.

"I'm fine," I said, sitting up with ease.

Much to my surprise, I felt fine indeed. After Ma'lek, I had expected to feel a good deal worse, but despite feeling bruised from the plank I slept on, nothing felt out of the ordinary.

How odd...

"Are you sure you are fine?" she asked, looking unconvinced.

"Yes. Why wouldn't I be?"

She pursed her lips, then let it go with a shake of her head. I was glad of it because I had no idea what had happened. It hadn't felt like scratches, but I wasn't going to tell her that. I hardly understood what Esahbyen had done, and there was no way of explaining what had happened without telling her I'd been possessed by a God.

She'd think I was insane.

"Where's the sword?"

I began to look around frantically, but there was no sign of the weapon anywhere. Z'tala looked even more confused than before.

"What sword, *k'lele?*"

"Jaehyr said he brought it along," I replied, confused.

"He was only carrying you when he came in."

"I'm only visible to those I deem necessary."

I blinked stupidly. "Excuse me?"

"I didn't say anything," Z'tala said, her confusion making way for annoyance. "What is going on with you?"

I'd like to know that, too.

"How did Jaehyr know where I was?"

Z'tala's gaze darkened as she sat down on her bed cross-legged, folding her hands in her lap. "Your screams echoed through the palace. Jaehyr must have left the man who'd purchased his company to get to you, said he found you poised to kill *your* man."

"I wanted to help him out of his misery," I lied.

"The misery you put him in in the first place?" She sounded curious rather than accusatory.

It had been her who'd told me to do anything to survive, but I doubt she'd meant this. Technically, I hadn't killed him, but mentioning being possessed by a God sounded like a bad thing to admit to even to me.

"He shouldn't have done what he did," I muttered. "Kehran can punish me all he wants."

"He won't be punishing you," Z'tala said quietly.

"What? But wh—"

The question died on my lips as I realised there was one another person he could, and most likely would punish.

Jaehyr.

"Where is he?"

"In his cell," Z'tala replied. "They'll hang him when the sun is at its highest peak."

"That's not punishment. That is murder!"

"It is, *k'lele*, but there is nothing we can do for him. You and I are slaves. Your... husband is not here to change his brother's mind. Jaehyr knew full well what he was doing when he came to your aid. He knew the consequences."

I cannot let him die.

"Then we won't."

CHAPTER 19

TALNOVAR

"*Do you think a person's destiny can change?*"
    "*I think destinies don't exist.*"

It had been a glorious summer afternoon a long time ago—
an unusually hot day for Ilvanna. My father, newly appointed
Ohzheràn at the time, had cancelled all training, and many
people had sought solace in the cool water of the palace lake.
The *Tarien* still needed protection, but times had been peaceful,
so I'd permitted Elara, Caerleyan, and Queran to join in on the
fun. I'd have let Xaresh go, too, if he hadn't confided in me he
had never learned how to swim and would be much more
comfortable on the shore.

Shal had been of a similar mind.

The three of us had made ourselves comfortable on the
banks of the lake, Shal lying on her back, Xaresh and I seated on
either side of her, weapons close at hand. She'd asked the question out of the blue, but my response had come fast.

I think destinies don't exist.

I still didn't think so, but I couldn't deny the horrible truth
about her destiny being real somehow—prophecy included—
which by extent meant *I* had a destiny, and I wasn't sure I was

prepared for that. After Varayna's and my mother's death, I'd turned my life upside down, I had fought to get better, be better, do better, but now I wasn't so sure any of that still mattered.

I'd relapsed into old habits.

They made me do it. Azra. Cehyan.

I WOKE up to a jolt before becoming aware of the creak and groan of wooden wheels. When I tried to raise my hand, I realised I was much too weak. Not just my arm felt heavy—my entire body did, as if all the strength had left me. I felt as sick as I had on the ship, and if it hadn't been for the endless amount of sand surrounding us, I'd have believed I was back on one. I managed to turn my head and found Halueth huddled in a corner, watching me intently.

"Where are we?" I croaked, licking my lips to moisturise them.

"Not sure," he replied. "On our way."

"Where?"

Halueth's frown deepened. "I just said I don't know."

As the sun began to set in the distance, a cold wind picked up, kissing my naked skin every chance it got. I curled in on myself, somewhat surprised at how much colder it felt here than back at the camp. Halueth had wrapped his arms around himself, jaw clenched so tight it was as if he was scowling at the wind.

A blanket wouldn't go amiss.

The wagon lurched to a sudden halt. I pushed myself up on my elbows, or tried to anyway, but barely managed to turn myself on my side.

"Why are we stopping?"

Halueth shrugged, sounding annoyed. "Making camp for the night, I assume."

It sounded more than logical, and I was annoyed I hadn't come up with it myself. What was wrong with me? It was as if I was so far removed from myself that my brain couldn't even jump to these kinds of conclusions anymore. I was a stranger in my own skin.

To myself. To Shal.

My body was aching all over, my lips were cracked and bleeding, and my tongue felt like leather in my mouth. I shivered, wishing for a blanket or someone to keep me warm. If that wasn't enough, my thoughts alternated between wishing for this to end and begging to stay alive to finish my mission. My ruminations almost made me miss the fact someone came in and began to check my vitals.

Halueth had gone from the looks of it.

"How is he?" The familiar voice drifted over to me, worry in its tone.

"Better than expected," another replied. I knew that voice, too.

Who do they belong to?

When I opened my eyes, Tariq's face came into vision, and I frowned. "What are you doing here?"

He merely smiled at me. "Just rest. You're safe."

Am I?

"What did you mean, better than expected?" I managed, clenching my jaw to keep the shivers from making my teeth chatter. I felt exhausted—the kind where your brain feels heavy and thinking becomes the most strenuous exercise, so I wrapped my arms around myself against the cold seeping into my bones. I'd thought at some point that I couldn't get any colder aside from when I died, maybe.

By Esah, was I wrong?

The tremors came on gradually, starting with a tremble in my leg I couldn't shake. At first, I thought it was perhaps from hunger, until the tremors increased, spreading out from my leg to the rest of my body. The sensation was oddly familiar. At some point, the trembling subsided as a deep calm stole over me.

I must have fallen asleep.

"I've been waiting for you," a sensuous, feminine voice said.

Upon opening my eyes, I found myself staring at the most beautiful woman I'd ever laid eyes on. If I'd been a poet—or anywhere near as good with words as Haerlyon used to be—I could have accurately described her. White hair that shimmered in the sunlight cascaded down her back in light waves. Her eyes appeared to change from one colour to the next depending on how she moved them, never quite settling on any one colour, and her legs seemed to go on endlessly.

Then again, from the flat of my back, I assumed everyone's legs went on.

"Please, rise," she said, not unkindly. "It will make our conversation much more enjoyable."

I got to my feet with ease, only mildly surprised at the lack of cold. The pain and tremors were gone, too.

"Where are we?" I asked, looking around.

The sight was nothing short of disappointing. White was the dominant colour all around—even the floor was a white marble tile and reminded me painfully of the palace. I wondered if I'd ever see it again.

"We're in my... house," the woman said, a pleasant smile on her lips. "You're quite safe here."

"And who are you?" I asked, feeling as if this was the stupidest question I could ask.

Her eyes flashed in amusement. "There was a time our children were grateful for meeting us, but I suppose those times have changed, indeed. My name is Xiomara, Goddess of—"

"Life, women, childbirth, and marriage," I interjected. "We're taught our pantheon."

"And yet you had to ask who I was?"

I shrugged. "The lectures don't come with pictures. Besides, what would you do if you woke up somewhere unfamiliar with someone strange standing over you when you were pretty certain you fell asleep in the desert somewhere?"

"Quite likely the same, Talnovar."

I wasn't even surprised she knew my name. "Why am I here?"

"You do not sweet talk, do you?"

"Only if I'm courting," I replied. "And I doubt that's what's happening here."

She laughed, the sound soft and kind on my ears. It was nice to hear something as sophisticated as this for a change.

By Esah, when did I become so shallow?

"You're not being shallow," she said in answer to my thoughts. "Merely longing back for easier times."

"How did y—," I began but thought better of it. "No, never-mind, I don't want to know that, but I still want to know why I'm here."

"It's not looking good," a voice sounded from far away. *"He needs a proper healer. I can't do much more."*

Xiomara remained silent, regarding me with those unnerving, ephemeral eyes that I was sure could see straight into my soul.

"What's all this?" I asked, somewhat unsettled by the fact I was being discussed as if I weren't there.

"You're dying," Xiomara stated matter-of-factly. What was the life of one mortal to her, after all? "I'm giving you a choice."

"How long... ride... Portasâhn."

"What choice?"

There was a hint of sadness in her eyes as they swept over me. She released a heavy sigh and pulled herself up to her full height, exuding such a regal air I bowed out of instinct. A distinct snort escaped her lips.

"Either you die," she began, "or you live."

I frowned, folding my arms in front of me. "How is that a choice?"

"Must go now..."

"Because one will leave you indebted to me."

"Indebted how?"

Xiomara tilted her head as if I'd just asked her the silliest thing in the world. In my defence, it sounded like the proper question to ask. I had the impression that being indebted to a Goddess might be even worse than dying.

"One day I may call upon you for a favour," she said. "Until then, you will not know what this shall be."

"Do you?" I asked.

She flashed me a lopsided smile that looked remarkably attractive on her. "As a matter of fact, I do not."

A groan escaped my lips. "I can't seem to win, can I?"

"There's only one thing that must be won, *Anahràn,*" she said solemnly, "and that's the war against Azra. Choose wisely."

"He's dying..."

CHAPTER 20

HAERLYON

*B*etween my nightly ordeals with Azra and her order to get rid of the body, a pounding headache had begun in the back of my head, expanding stealthily until even the smallest movement caused me to groan in agony. It was noon by the time I finished cleaning up her bedroom and sent for her ladies to help the *Tari* dress. She hadn't woken once in the time I'd been busy.

A day of rest for Ilvanna.

A curious thought, if nothing else, but one I couldn't help feeling rang with truth. If Talnovar was successful, and if Shalitha somehow found her way home, rest would be the last thing on the list for a long time to come. Already, Azra was preparing for a war that would be Gods know how long from now. The tricky part wasn't in not knowing the when, but in learning the where and the how. The world's greatest strategists could come up with a thousand plans, and none of them could be successful if the conditions were unknown. In that regard, my sister had the upper-hand, and Azra knew it. I looked back at the sleeping *Tari* once more before I slipped out of her bedroom, closing the door quietly behind me.

There was something I had to do before she awoke.

With time not on my side, I moved fast. I gathered clothing and boots from my bedroom and wrapped it in a cloak, nicked some apples and bread from the kitchen, and made my way to the garden. My heart was thundering in my chest, afraid someone would catch me doing something I shouldn't be. Even so, I strode to the part of the garden where Shal had once sucker punched Eamryel and hid the package of clothing in one of the high decorative vases along the way. I tucked one apple in my pouch and kept another in my hand.

Without stopping, I returned to the palace. Holding my back straight and lifting my chin, I plastered a sneer on my lips that was enough to make everyone scatter as I approached. I liked it that way. Only a brave few dared step in my path to ask me a question, but even they dispersed as soon as they got what they needed.

I hated it as much as I loved it.

A short while later, I arrived at the dungeons. Two of Azra's men were leaning back in their chairs, feet kicked up on the table, a permanent scowl on their faces.

"What's your business here?"

I arched a brow, staring down my nose at him. "None of yours."

They knew why I was here. I knew they didn't care as long as Azra paid them for their troubles. It was a simple formality none of us felt was needed but complied with anyway.

"What you got that apple for?" the second man asked. "Not thinking of feeding the prisoner?"

I grinned and took a bite. "Of course not."

I grabbed a lantern from the wall and descended the spiral stairs, my footsteps echoing above and below me. The farther down I went, the colder the air became. These dungeons had once been built to house the traitors, the murderers, and those too dangerous to the realm. In Mother's time as *Tari*, they'd rarely been used. Not because there hadn't been any traitors, murderers, or otherwise shady people, but because Mother had believed in a fairer justice system than letting them rot in a dank, dark cell.

Azra on the other hand...

A muffled thud signalled I'd reached the floor. The darkness was so intense that my little lamp barely chased away the shadows. An odour of sweat, excrement, and vomit infused the air. The combination was altogether unpleasant. A small wonder people went insane down here.

I halted in front of the last door on the right, produced a key from an inner pocket, and slid it into the lock. The click as it unlocked seemed to reverberate throughout the hallway—in truth, it barely even registered with the inhabitant of this cell. As I stepped inside, Eamryel looked up from where he sat huddled in the corner. In the little light I had brought, I could see the bruises on his face, the near translucency of his skin, his emaciated body.

A deep shudder went through me.

"Haer?" he croaked.

I closed the door behind me and placed the lamp out of harm's way before kneeling in front of him, my brow creased in worry.

"I'm sorry, *mahnèh*," I whispered. "I couldn't come sooner."

Eamryel gave a little snort. "It's fine. I'm not going anywhere."

I inhaled sharply and pressed the apple I'd taken a bite out of in his hand. "It's why I'm here."

He took the apple, cradling it in his hand, bringing it to his face to inhale its scent. The look of hunger in his eyes twisted my stomach. How he endured this was beyond me. He took a careful bite and closed his eyes.

"I'm getting you out of here," I said softly. "Tonight."

Eamryel stopped halfway through the bite. "Tonight? Is it safe?"

"I'm afraid not," I replied. "But it's either that or sure death."

"What happened?"

I settled back on my heels, wringing my hands in front of me as I considered how to tell him his father was dead. Not that I thought he'd care much, but he should know. His last living relative—as far as I knew anyway—was dead. He was the sole heir to the Arolvyen estates and assets and to his father's questionable business. I'd think he would want to know that, at least.

"Your father passed away."

Eamryel looked unperturbed. "How?"

"Talnovar killed him."

I swore I saw a smile tugging his lips up, but it was gone as fast as it had appeared.

"Good riddance," Eamryel murmured. "I take it the *Tari* isn't pleased?"

"She blames you."

He snorted, then sighed. "Maybe I deserve to die."

"We all deserve to die at some point," I replied. "The Gods know I do, but if we want to stand a chance of winning this war, we need every man we can get. Even you."

"Even me?" he scoffed. "At least you're being honest about it."

"You know what I mean." I scowled.

He shrugged. "How do you propose getting me out of here?"

"By giving you the key," I replied, making it sound simple.

It would be anything but. Eamryel was weak—weaker than I would have liked—and he would have to do the actual escaping. All I could do was create diversions to ensure he had a chance, even if it was a small one.

"Remember the garden where Shal and you faced off?"

He nodded. I'd expected him to scowl, but instead, he just smiled. "What I wouldn't give to have her punch me again."

I arched a brow, wondering quietly if he still had all his faculties in order.

"It would mean she's here, *mahnèh*," he murmured. "Where she belongs."

After *Hanyarah*, he hadn't surprised me very often, barring perhaps the few months where he'd gone missing and then showing up out of nowhere as if nothing was wrong. Wherever he'd been had changed him, more so than *Hanyarah* had either of us, but he'd never spoken of it. I never pushed. We all had our secrets, which was why hearing him say such a thing surprised me much less than it would have done before.

"Life sure would be a lot easier," I murmured. "Although, after what we have done, I wouldn't be surprised if she'd hang us."

Eamryel chuckled darkly. "We'd deserve it, too."

I merely nodded, my thoughts returning to the matter at hand. "We've got a long way to go before that becomes a reality. Remember the decorative vases at the entrance to that garden?"

"I'm sure they're hard to miss."

"There's a package in the right one. Clothing, boots, a cloak, food. Everything you'll need not to blend in."

"And then what? The gates are closed. There's no way out of the palace."

"Actually," I said, looking at him. "There is, but you won't like it."

AFTER ALL THE killing I'd done, I thought the copper scent and the wetness of blood would no longer perturb me, and yet, as I slit the second guard's throat, a shiver ran down my spin. I wasn't sorry to see these *grissins* go, but I was sorry it had come this far. I hooted like an owl—a skill I'd had to develop because I couldn't whistle to save my life, Eamryel's signal it was time. I placed the dagger in the guard's hand, did the same with the other, and stepped over his dead body, smirking at the sight.

Two can play this game.

Xaresh' and Elara's killer had never been found either, so I had the hope they wouldn't discover me either. Although they had never been brought to justice, I was certain he'd operated on Azra's orders. Not that she'd ever mentioned it, but she had a history. Curious, come to think of it—she'd boasted about everything else. With a shake of my head, I dispelled the thoughts and made my way to the stables, confident in the notion most people would be asleep by now.

And if not, who are they to question me?

The stables were empty save for a stable lad who sat slumped against the wall, an oil lamp at his side, obviously fast asleep. All the better for me. I scooped a handful of oats from one of the sacks and tiptoed over to Meadow's stable. An excited whinny reached me before I'd even come in sight of her. As soon as I slid into her stall, she nuzzled my hand, eager for the oats I was holding.

"Not even happy to see me then?" I murmured, stroking her flank with my empty hand.

Meadow let out a snort.

"I'll take that as a no."

I poured the oats into her feeder and left her stall to gather her equipment. When I returned, my eyes fell on the two empty stalls next to hers. Orion's and Hadiyah's. Orion hadn't been seen since the day Shal was kidnapped, and I assumed Evan had taken Hadiyah when he fled the palace.

And now Meadow would leave as well.

With a heavy heart, I saddled her as quickly as possible without making too much noise. Every now and again, I peered around the corner to see if the stable boy was still asleep. He didn't disappoint—not until I guided Meadow out of her stable, wincing at the clopping of her hooves on the cobblestones. The stable boy was up in seconds.

"H—halt! Who goes there?"

I stepped into the light of his lantern, the look on my face solemn.

"*Ohzheràn*," he murmured and bowed. "Apologies."

"Tell no one you saw me," I said. "Understood?"

"Y—yes, *Ohzheràn*."

With a bit of luck, the boy was impressed enough not to sound the alarm unless he'd be ordered to, and he was more afraid of them than of me. Although I didn't think that was the case, I couldn't be sure—not with Azra. She'd been upset enough when I told her I'd seen to Eamryel's punishment that afternoon, so she didn't have to. For a moment, I had thought she would take my head instead of his, but she had deflated and complimented me on my fast thinking. My luck had to run out at some point. Once out of the stables, I pulled up the hood of my cloak to cover my face, mounted, and urged Meadow into a trot.

I had no time to lose.

Getting out of the palace was easier than expected—I'd have to do something about that if only to give Azra the idea our men actually bothered with their job. I didn't like to imagine what she would do if she found out security was not up to standards.

Worries for another time.

Once on the Main Street, I nudged Meadow to a gallop and thundered underneath the Circle gates to the one leading out of the city. The streets were eerily empty, courtesy of Azra's curfew, giving Ilvanna the atmosphere of a ghost city. A part of me wondered if it ever would return to the way it was when Mother was still *Tari*. There would be changes, of that I had no doubt. I just hoped they would be for the better.

When I arrived at the Main Gate shouting for a guard, a

groggy looking Ilvannian stepped out of the guardhouse, looking as if I'd woken him.

"Open the gate."

He blinked at me, the look on his face suggesting I'd ordered him in a different language.

"Tonight," I said through gritted teeth.

The guard scurried forward and opened the single door. I had to duck my head to pass through and even then I almost hit the post, but I got through without being contested, something that bothered me even more than the slow response of the guard to open the gate. I really had to do something about it.

Not now.

I rode a little away from the gate, waited until I heard it being locked again, and continued in the opposite direction, taking me off the beaten path. I had to be waiting when Eamryel arrived—if he did—and although his journey would be longer than mine, I couldn't risk not being there.

It was a matter of life and death.

PACING BACK AND FORTH, my gaze on the brightening sky, my thoughts went over everything that had gone wrong. Eamryel must have gotten caught, or worse, drowned. I flexed my fingers to release the stiffness from balling them up too long, but it did nothing to relieve the tension in the rest of my body.

I should have gone with him.

I would have risked it all if I had, and the logical side of me knew this. By Esah, I was already risking everything by staying here. According to my own plan, I should have returned to the palace hours ago. I had waited instead—was still waiting.

Perhaps for nothing.

Risking another glance at the distance, I decided to stay a little longer. Maybe he'd just had to find his strength before attempting his escape. There were a lot of maybes and what-ifs, but it was all I had to go on.

"If you're mourning me, you can stop now," Eamryel said from behind me.

I spun on my heel, my heart skipping a beat at hearing him. He stood dripping wet before me, wearing only a pair of trousers, holding a bundle of something in his hand. Long white hair stuck to his face and chest, and rivulets of water ran down his torso. In the pale morning sun, despite his incarceration, he looked quite magnificent.

Seriously, Haer? That's where your thoughts go now?

With a shake of my head, I took in his appearance once more, noting the blue lips and tremors ravaging his body, and took off my cloak. He stilled when I stepped close to wrap it around him. It wouldn't do much, but at least it would keep off the worst of the cold.

"You're late," I said, stepping back.

His lips pulled up in a sneer, but there was no malice in his eyes. "You'd be too if you'd felt that water. Took me five tries to stay in the water and dive under. It's *nohro* freezing."

"I'm sorry, *Mahnèh*. It was the only way I could think of where they wouldn't come after you."

"What about you?" he asked, narrowing his eyes. "What if they find you gone?"

I grimaced. "I've got that covered."

"You do?"

I chuckled softly and ran a hand through my hair, regarding him with my head cocked to the side. "I need you to hit me. Kick me. Stab me. Just... don't kill me."

Both Eamryel's brows shot up, his eyes twinkling in amusement. "Just that?"

"Just that," I replied. "And then steal my horse and flee. Don't look back. Don't come back. Stay out of harm's way."

"It almost sounds as if you care, *an Ilvan*."

My heart stuttered at the sound of his husky voice—or had I imagined that—and I pressed my lips together, folding my arms in front of my chest. "It would have been a waste of time getting you out of that prison otherwise. I'm a busy man."

Eamryel smirked. "I'm sure you are."

Before I could register his movement, he punched me in the face. I heard a crack moments before my sight went white and blurry. Tears streamed down my cheeks as blood flowed down my mouth and front. I spat it out, trying to catch my bearings. Eamryel was fast for someone who had been starving and had just swum underwater for the Gods know how long.

He shouldn't have been this strong.

A punch to the gut sent me staggering backwards. I tripped over something and fell back, the air whooshing out of my lungs as I landed on the stones beneath me. Eamryel kicked me in the side. I curled up. He kicked me in the stomach for good measure. I gasped, wrapping my arms around my abdomen. A part of me wondered at the fierceness behind it all. His foot connected with my lower back, and I howled in pain. He continued his assault until I lay curled up in a ball, gasping for him to stop. He knelt in front of me, although I couldn't see more than a blurry outline, courtesy of my broken nose and—although I wasn't quite sure—broken eye socket.

"Don't trust anyone," Eamryel hissed and spat on me.

I passed out to the sound of hoofbeats disappearing in the distance.

CHAPTER 21

SHALITHA

*A*n oppressive silence hung in the dungeon corridors, as if its denizens knew what was about to transpire when the sun was at its zenith. Perhaps they did—chances were they did, but I liked to think they didn't and were most likely just fast asleep. Only a few of us had been invited to Kehran's twisted party, but news travelled fast and rumours even faster.

I'd not be surprised if they *knew* what had happened.

Down here, we pretended to be friends, or at the very least tried not to stab each other in the back. Up in the *herrât*, it was every man and woman for themselves. Rumours and lies were the currency needed to topple your opponent before the fight even started—nothing happened for free. But Jaehyr had risked his own life to save me, a *Tarien* he didn't know, a woman who partially shared a name with the love of his life.

It made no sense.

After all this time and everything that has happened, he's still loyal.

"Loyalty is severely overrated."

"I wasn't asking you," I muttered under my breath.

The sword—now a locket around my neck and hidden

beneath the ragged shirt I wore—chuckled in my mind. Somehow, it didn't even bother me that it did. It had been a surprise to find out it had been the one talking to me. It had been an outright shock when it transformed into a key to open the door to our cell, so the fact it could chuckle was a minor disturbance.

"What do you gain by saving him?" it asked, curiosity in its voice.

Is it really a voice, or just my thoughts?

The sword all but made a snorting sound in my head. *"I'm as real as the air you breathe."*

"Even that might be an illusion."

I had the faint impression that if it'd had eyes, it would have rolled them. Again, just a minor disturbing thought—another bizarre aspect of my everyday life. If living and breathing Gods no longer bothered me, why would a talking sword? All my life was missing was a mythical creature from one of my books, and the picture was complete.

"Do you always think so much?"

"Not as much as you talk," I retorted in a hiss. "Now, shut up."

Hushed voices up ahead caught my attention, taking me back to a moment long gone into memory when I snuck upon my brother cutting off his relationship with Mehrean. The urgency in these voices reminded me of that day.

"You've got a depressing mind, you know that?"

I rolled my eyes, deciding not responding was the best course of action. A beam of light fell from Jaehyr's cell as I rounded the corner, and it was from there the voices had come. Jaehyr's was obvious, but it was the second voice that caught my attention.

Naïda?

That was an interesting development, but not of importance right now. Discarding the niceties, I slipped inside the bedroom, catching the lovers mid-kiss. Jaehyr dropped to his knees the

moment he laid eyes on me, murmuring a reverent *Tarien* as he
lowered his gaze.

Naïda looked far from impressed.

"We need to go," I said as she opened her mouth. "Now."

She stared at me.

Jaehyr's head snapped up as if whipped. "*Tarien*...what ar—"

"If you think I'm going to let that *grissin* kill you, you're
mistaken."

"And how do you propose we do that?" Naïda asked
scornfully.

A grin spread across my lips. "You'll be taking him."

The look on her face couldn't have been much different than
if I had accused her of murdering someone. Jaehyr rose to his
feet, his brows furrowed in thought.

"Forgive me, *Tarien*," he said. "But there is no leaving this
place. Besides, I knew what would happen if I disobeyed
orders."

"How is this man a fighter?"

I scowled, earning a surprised look from both Jaehyr and
Naïda. I waved my hand in dismissal, cursing the sword in my
mind. It reciprocated with a reverberating laugh in my skull.

Nohro ahrae.

"As I was saying," I continued, looking at Naïda, "you must
take him away from here. I'm certain we can get him out of the
dungeons, but that's as far as I can get. You have freedom of
movement. If we go now, you may be able to leave without
getting caught. By the time they find you missing, you'll be long
gone."

"And where do you propose we go?" Naïda folded her arms
in front of her.

"Go to the mountains just across the border. Find Dûshan of
the mountain people and tell him Elay and Shalitha sent you."

"The mountain people?" Jaehyr asked with a frown.

"The *T'erza Mahrzal*..." Naïda's voice trailed off, a thoughtful expression on her face. "Our stories tell of their savagery—how they kill travellers when they trespass. We are taught to steer well away from them."

"Which is why they're a perfect hiding place," I said. "Kehran won't think of finding you there."

"You must come, *Tarien*," Jaehyr said, stepping forward.

Naïda narrowed her eyes at me, a warning flashing in them. A snort bubbled to the surface. As if.

"I cannot," I said, turning to him with a wry smile. "There's something I must do before I can return home."

Jaehyr looked confused. "But... what about Ilvanna? The throne? You said Azra is *Tari* now. Our people are suffering!"

I clenched my jaw. "I'm well aware of that fact, but what good will it do if I show up at the gates alone?"

"You wouldn't be alone."

I couldn't help but laugh. "And what good would the two of us do, Jaehyr? No, I made a promise, and I'm keeping it."

"Then I'm staying." Jaehyr folded his arms in front of him. *"Who says chivalry is dead?"*

A low growl escaped my lips in response. Jaehyr was looking at me, jaw clenched, lips pressed in a thin line. Naïda glanced from him to me and back, confusion etched in the lines around her mouth.

"What did Elay promise you?" she asked.

"The same I promised him," I replied. "My throne back."

She let out a heavy sigh, dropping her arms alongside her body, glancing at Jaehyr. "If you wish to help your *Tarien*," she said not unkindly, "you should leave."

"You don't understand," he murmured, turning to her. "I already failed one *Tari*, I cannot fail another."

"Which is *exactly* why we must go," Naïda said. "You won't be any good to her dead."

A part of me felt sorry for Jaehyr. Had I been in his position,

I would have wanted to do the same, but Naïda was right. He was no use to me dead.

"I order you to leave, Imradien," I said, lifting my chin. "Find the *T'erza Mahrzal*, find Dûshan. Prepare for war. When I am done here, I will come to get you, and we'll go home together."

He didn't look convinced, but he eased his pose and let out a heavy sigh, rubbing his jaw. The look in his eyes was one of exhaustion.

"As you wish, *Tari*."

"Grateful, isn't he?"

"Will you shut it?" I hissed through gritted teeth.

"Tarien?" Jaehyr looked puzzled.

I shook my head. "It's nothing. Come, we'd best get moving now. We've lost precious time as is."

As I EXPECTED, getting out of the dungeons wasn't a problem. At this time of night, the guards didn't venture inside unless there was trouble or after a change of shifts, and there was only one exit, so whoever decided to try to escape would have to go through them. I was certain it wasn't what they expected when I stepped inside the guard's room and knocked two of them out before the third could even get to me. While I was wrestling with the remaining two, Jaehyr slipped behind the man I was facing.

He broke his neck without much effort.

Before my opponent could raise the alarm, I pulled the locket from my neck and swiped it across his chest, expecting there to be a sword. To my surprise, there wasn't. I stared dumbfounded at the locket, then my eyes darted to the man looking just as stunned and back to the locket. Before he regained his senses, I clipped him under the jaw and watched him crumple to the floor in a heap of limbs.

"I said no killing," I hissed as I spun to face Jaehyr.

His eyes sparkled in amusement. "What in *Vehda's* name were *you* doing, *Tarien?*"

"Nothing." I stepped over the men's bodies and into the corridor where Naïda was on the lookout, keeping the locket in my hand. Although it shouldn't be visible to either of them, putting something around my neck that wasn't there would look highly suspicious, and I didn't feel like explaining anything.

"We have to go," she hissed, glancing over shoulder. "Now."

She guided us through the darkness, past walls and other obstacles, sticking to the shadows as much as possible. With the dungeons and the *herrât* as far from the palace as possible, it took us a while to get there. Sentinels were patrolling the palace walls, their outlines barely visible in the moonlight. At the gates stood a dozen guards, six on either side, their postures rigid and alert. Something told me slacking on the job meant either beheading or hanging, depending on whichever Kehran felt like. I wouldn't be surprised if guards ended up in the *herrât* just for fun.

A large, circular plaza stretched out before us, its vastness interrupted only by a grand fountain in the middle. I remembered from my arrival the majestic statue of a man in the middle. He held a curved blade in his right hand, offering it to the heavens in salute. His other hand was open, reaching for something, and from that hand, the water flowed into the fountain.

It was a peculiar statue.

"If we can make it to the other side unseen," Naïda murmured, "we should be able to get out of one of the side gates rather easily. At this time of night, there's only one guard stationed on the inside and none on the outside. There are patrols on the outside."

"Leave it to me," I whispered, a grin spreading across my face. "Wait for my signal."

Before they could ask where I was going, I sprinted back the way we'd come, keeping to the shadows for as long as I could. Jaehyr's strangled protest followed in my wake. I swallowed hard and pushed on. If I didn't create a diversion, getting him out of his cell would only lead him to his death sooner.

I just hoped he listened better than his nephew.

A part of me longed to go with Jaehyr and Naïda, find the *T'erza Mahrzal,* find Dûshan and come up with a plan to go home—see my brothers, Mehrean.

Talnovar.

To my surprise, my heart skipped a beat at his name, and with it came guilt for not thinking of Elay first.

"Esahbyen told me you were worth it." The sword sounded disgusted. *"I'm beginning to question his sanity."*

"I didn't know he had any," I muttered.

The sword pretended to snort in my mind. *"She has a sense of humour."*

"Could you stop mouthing off," I said through gritted teeth. "Trying to focus here."

"On what?"

Again, the only viable response was to roll my eyes. I had the distinct impression we could keep going at each other until eternity.

"Not a chance, resha," the sword crooned. *"I'll beat you easily."*

"In your dreams," I thought. *"Do swords dream?"*

It remained quiet—the question was for how long. Inhaling deeply, I pushed myself off the wall and stalked in the direction of the palace as if I owned the place.

"Technically, you do?"

A snort escaped my lips at the comment. I suppose, in a way, the sword was right, but I didn't doubt for a moment Kehran failed to see it that way. It was the single reason why I was here, making my way to a probable punishment instead of running away with my kinsman and his girlfriend.

"In case you think you're being heroic, I'd like to think you're delusional. Why keep a promise to someone who has obviously abandoned you?"

"You wouldn't understand if you tried."

"How insulting."

As if I cared. Each step carried me closer to the guards, closer to Kehran, closer to Jaehyr's escape. The sword scoffed at my thoughts but remained mercifully silent.

"Halt!"

Four guards turned to me, weapons at the ready. I raised my arms to show I was unarmed.

"You're funny."

"You're useless," I thought, then continued out loud. "I demand to see the *Akyn*."

They glanced at each other before responding. "The *Akyn* is not receiving at this hour."

I smiled in amusement, folding my arms in front of me. "Are you sure? Not even me?"

Murmurs arose among them. It was like watching a child seconds away from pushing over the first *Denm* stone to topple all others. Once it went, there was no stopping it.

As it was in this case.

As soon as they realised who I was, they had me surrounded, swords and staffs raised and ready. My heart rate spiked, my breath quickened—my body was preparing for fight or flight. I willed it to calm down through the breathing exercises Cerindil had once taught me.

Would he be happy to see his brother?

"Walk, *zrayeth*," one of them growled, pushing his staff in my back.

Another time, I would have pivoted, grabbed it and either shoved it back in his gut or disarmed him—whichever was easiest—for calling me that. My temper might win skirmishes, but it would never win battles, let alone a war.

"Look who's catching on."

I was hard-pressed not to hit the guard who pushed me forward and made me stumble—only my quick reflexes saved me from measuring my length against the cobblestones. Willing myself to calm down, I allowed them to guide me through the gate, keeping my chin lifted in a display of arrogance I'd seen my Mother use on more than one occasion.

It's all about presentation, nothing more.

Presentation or not, the moment they marched me through the doors to Kehran's chambers, it made way for passionate fury and a sheer desire to kill. The feeling disappeared as fast as it had appeared, leaving me breathless and confused.

"What is this?" Kehran asked.

"She demanded to speak with you, *Akyn*." One of the guards thumped his fist against his chest in salute and bowed.

Everyone followed but me.

Kehran arched a brow, confusion marring his spotted visage. "She demanded?"

"Yes, *Akyn*. She walked up to u—"

It was clear he realised his error. My lips tugged up in a smirk as I watched him sink to his knees and bow as deep as he could, forehead touching the floor, arms outstretched. My joy wouldn't last long, so I took what I got for as long as I could get it. Anger flitted across Kehran's face, but rather than giving in, he turned to me. He clenched his jaw so tight I was afraid he'd break his teeth.

"How did you get out of your cell?"

"With a key."

He balled his fists, presumably to keep himself from hitting me. "And where did you get that key?"

"This will be interesting."

"I stole it," I replied, looking at him. "From one of your guards. Wasn't too hard."

It could have been the truth—I'd stolen enough in the past

year and a half to make it plausible, but Kehran didn't know that. Elay did. A lump wedged itself in my throat just thinking of him. I missed him more than I cared to admit, but at the same time, I was angry—furious even. He'd left me without telling me. He'd gone and left me to my own devices—left me to Kehran's mercy, just like Tal had left me at *Hanyarah*, how Mother had left me forever. Although I had no idea where my brothers were, I had no doubt they were gone from me also.

Time to sort it out myself.

"Finally!"

I'm not sure what gave me away. Between the moment I moved and pulled a sword from the guard next to me, and the moment they were wrestling me to the ground, I was sure only the space of a few heartbeats had passed. But two men lay dead, and Kehran was clutching his chest as a dark stain spread across his garment. I could tell it was severe enough to be painful, but not enough to kill.

He would live.

Will I?

"Get a healer!" someone shouted.

"Tie her up! Take her away."

Everything passed by in a daze. I shook my head, but the haziness didn't go away, and in the back of my mind, there was a faint chuckle.

"What have you done?" I thought, wondering how even the voice in my mind sounded drugged.

"I have done nothing, resha."

CHAPTER 22

TALNOVAR

$\mathcal{T}$he sound of seagulls in the distance pulled me from the strangest dream. My mind felt as if I were back on *sehvelle*, and I wondered briefly if my voyage across the sea and my fight with Yllinar had been in my imagination, but the soft bedding underneath suggested I was no longer on a ship, in a slave camp, or a prison cart. I was sure that when I opened my eyes, I'd be back at *Denahryn*.

Or worse, the palace.

"Glad to see you're awake," a male voice spoke from somewhere to the right.

I cracked one eye open, looking for the speaker. Seated in the corner of the room—a spacious one at that from the looks of it—was a man dressed in the finest riches I'd ever seen, and I realised I'd seen him before.

In my dream.

But if he were here, it meant it couldn't have been one, and everything that had happened was real. Why then did everything feel so warped? In that moment, I became aware of the pounding in my head made worse by trying to sit up. The room spun with nauseating ferocity, and I fell back, pushing the heels of my palms against my eyes to ease the pressure.

Of course, it didn't.

"You might want to take it easy," the stranger said. "You've been out for a while."

"Out?"

My voice came out not unlike the croak of a frog, and to my surprise, the sound hurt.

"How long?"

"Twelve days, give or take," said the stranger. "We weren't sure if you were going to make it."

His words made little sense as I tried to wrap my head around the few things he'd said. Who were 'we'? In fact, who was he? Neither in that dream nor the reality—whatever it had been—had he given me his name. He was the caravan master, but that was as far as my recollection of events went.

"Can we start from the beginning?" I muttered. "My memory of things is a bit obscure."

"I suggest," he began, "you eat, get freshened up, and dressed before we talk. I assume you have a lot of questions, and I will answer them to the best of my ability."

"So." I rubbed my neck. "What will you do with me?"

"We'll talk business later, *eshen*. I'll ask for someone to bring you food and escort you to the baths."

I wanted to ask more, but he stepped out of the room before I had a chance. Stiff from lying down, I pulled the sheet off me, finding I was stark naked under the covers.

Perfect.

It wasn't until I rose to my feet that I realised how weak I felt and promptly sat back on the bed, staring dumbfounded at the floor. A fortnight? I'd probably barely eaten in that time, barely drunk, so getting up was too much. Even so, I tried again, slower this time. After the initial dizziness subsided, I took a few tentative steps forward, surprised at the lack of pain shooting through my leg.

When you wake, your injuries will be healed, but do not overdo it. The process has merely been hastened, and it can be undone.

I'd made a vow.

Taking a few more steps forward, I placed a hand on my shoulder and raised my arm. I moved it up and down, left and right, but all I felt was a faint tug where the arrow had pierced my skin, no more.

Interesting.

A cough from the doorway made me spin around to face a woman standing there, eyes raking me from head to toe, lips curving into a smile as her eyes settled south of my hips. I hastened to grab anything within reach to cover myself and ended up holding a vase. She burst out laughing and made her way into the room, careless of my sensibilities on the matter.

"Here," she said in a sultry voice, tossing a package on the bed, "clothing. Thought you might want t'get dressed." Without stopping in her stride, she placed the plate she was carrying in her other hand on a side table before moving over to the window to pull open the curtains.

I stepped forward to protest, stretched out an arm, and nearly dropped the vase. She didn't seem perturbed at all by the idea.

"Thank you," I replied with a frown. "I think?"

She clucked her tongue. "Get dressed. Have some food. I'll be waiting to escort you to the baths."

"Can't you bring them here?"

A loud snort escaped her as incredulity marked her features. She put her hands on her hips, appearing bigger than she was— she was actually quite small, not something I was used to in women—but I didn't doubt for a moment her personality more than made up for it.

"You're obviously not from 'round here, so I'll forgive you."

Amusement twinkled in her eyes. "Get ready. Boss doesn't like to wait."

"He'll be there, too?"

She laughed again, a kind, gentle, honest laugh—a sound I hadn't heard in a long time. Both Elara and Shal had that same kind of way of laughing.

Does she still laugh?

"Get dressed."

The words jolted me back to the present just before the door closed with a click. I put the vase back where it belonged, unwrapped the package and pulled on the enormously wide trousers and simple shirt the woman had provided.

I should have asked her name.

The plate held an assortment of fruits, half a loaf of bread, nuts, a pitcher and a cup, and something I couldn't put a name to, but looked and smelled delicious. I poured myself a drink, grabbed the bread and a few slices of apple, and walked over to the window.

The view outside was breath-taking.

To my left, in the distance, the desert shimmering in the afternoon sun spread out beyond the horizon. Much closer on my right, the sea sparkled. Small ships bobbed lazily in the harbour down below. Farther away, the dark outlines of bigger ships were visible, and I wondered for a moment if Yllinar's— Fehran's, I reminded myself—ship was there with Ruvaen on board. I took a bite of bread as I settled on the windowsill, enjoying the simplicity of life such as it was. For once, there was no pain, and there were no demands on my time and person— unless you counted my appointment with the woman to take me to the baths.

There was a gentle knock.

"Are you ready?" She asked, poking her head around the half-open door.

I wish she'd had that decency before. With that thought

came the unsettling feeling it might not have been the first time she'd seen me naked. A heavy sigh escaped my lips as I slipped back to my feet, popping the last slice of apple in my mouth. I gulped down the contents of the cup, grabbed a handful of nuts, and sauntered over to the door, a smile on my face.

"Let's go then."

She gave me an appraising look. "You could be a right Zihrin nobleman if you weren't so white."

"I am a nobleman."

"Could've fooled me, *eshen*."

Her lips curved up in a tantalising smile that sent all kinds of feelings racing through my body, most of which were purely physical. I watched her as she skipped down the steps, her dark, curly hair bouncing on her back. An elongated ear peaked out on either side of her mane—just the tips, but enough to give her a whimsical air.

It reminded me of Shal enough that it hurt.

I peeled my eyes away, trying to focus on anything but her hips as they swayed from left to right on her walk out the door. Failing at even that, I made myself look around. As I'd seen from the window, the place we were staying at was situated in the harbour. Once outside, I could better establish my surroundings. The building looked quite derelict on the outside, and the sign reading Scarlet Queen was barely visible.

What an odd name.

Some would have said ominous, perhaps. It made the hairs on my arms and neck stand on end. With a shake of my head, I turned my attention to the present moment, to the woman by my side speaking in rapid Zihrin to another woman as we passed.

"It's not far," she said, turning back to me. "Just across the street."

"Thank you..."

"Sadereh," she said, "but you can call me Sadè."

"Thank you for your kindness, Sadè."

She chuckled. "Kindness? No, *eshen*, not kindness. Money. Although I have to say, you're easy on the eyes. Made my job a lot easier."

I stared at her and snorted. "I like honesty as much as the next guy, but you sure don't beat around the bush, do you?"

"No point is there?" she chuckled, taking another good look at me. "Takes a terribly long time to get what you want then."

I arched a brow, getting a good idea of what she wanted, but not being arrogant enough to think she'd act upon it. The suggestive wriggle of her eyebrows as she regarded me, however, was more than enough answer. My lips pulled up in a lopsided smile.

"I'm no good for you, *Irà*," I said, inclining my head.

"*Irà*?" She looked amused.

"I believe it is akin to your *Shena*," I replied.

"I'm no *Shena*," she said, her voice taking on a note of annoyance despite the blush on her cheeks.

"I meant no offense."

The rest of our way to the baths was silent. Sadè escorted me through an intricate archway, across a small garden, and into the building behind it. A distinct aroma of herbs wafted in our direction through the humid air.

"As much as I'd love to join you," Sadè said. "Your... employer made it clear I was merely to bring you here. Enjoy your stay."

"Will you be here when I return?"

She chuckled, a mischievous smile ghosting on her lips. "Nay, *eshen*. I have an actual job to do, and it is not here. When you step outside, you will see the inn where you were staying. Your employer will be waiting in your room."

I arched a brow at the mention of my employer but decided now was not the time to argue trivialities. As Sadè made to leave, my hand shot out of its own accord, and I turned to face her.

"I do not believe your words of money and no kindness, *Shena*," I said softly. "You've been at my side since I was brought in, haven't you?"

Quiet delight flickered in her eyes, and she cocked her head to the side. I'd have expected her to pull her arm back, but she didn't.

"What makes you say that?"

A smirk tugged at my lips, and as I leaned forward, I whispered, "Because you would have stared longer if you hadn't."

"Cocky," she murmured, her eyes staying on mine for a change. "I like that." She stepped back, slipping her wrist from my hand, a smile on her face. "He asked me to look after you while he was away which, between you and me, was a lot. He's paid me to stay with you all day every day until you woke up. Wouldn't tell me why. He only returned last night."

"Who is he?"

"He'll tell you," she replied. "If you go have that bath soon. He'll not pay me if you don't, and I'll come back for that payment." A grin spread across her lips as she gave me one last look-over before walking away.

I hoped they had a cold bath.

THE BATHS WERE QUITE UNEXPECTED. It was like one of the hot water springs in the Ilvan mountains but better. Warmth suffused my muscles until all remaining aches and pains were gone and my body felt weightless. Nevertheless, there was unease inside of me. Partially because of what Sadè had told me, partially because of how my body had responded to her. I groaned as it did the same just thinking of her, and I turned to hang from the pool's side, considering drowning myself then and there.

After Azra and Cehyan, one would think I'd never want a woman again.

You could try a man.

I could just imagine Haerlyon saying that and snorted, but the thought of him immediately sobered me up enough that I could get out of the pool without things looking awkward.

I wasn't the only one there.

Granted, I was surrounded by only men, but I was painfully aware already of how much I stood out with my pale skin, white hair, and an *Araîth* coiling from my foot to my shoulder, covering my arm. More than once, I'd caught some staring at me, but it wasn't that which bothered me either—it was the curled up lips and clear disdain on their faces that made the experience less than enjoyable.

I was a stranger here, an outcast.

At least that feels familiar.

Murmurs arose as I hoisted myself out of the pool. As I snatched the towel I'd been given from where I left it, I couldn't help but overhear their whispered words.

"Looks dangerous...," one said.

"Like that *tekka* Queen," another added.

"There are whispers of war coming from there," a third muttered. "No good, the lot of them."

After drying my face, I wrapped the towel around my waist and made my way from the communal area to where I could change into my clothing. The words I'd overheard kept playing in my mind as I dressed. Whispers of war? They might as well have shouted it from the rooftops. There were no whispers, no rumours. That war was coming, whether we liked it or not.

I just hoped we'd be on the winning side.

By the time I stepped outside, the sun had sunk behind the city, bathing it in an orange glow. More people were about now than there had been in the afternoon. Some were just standing about talking, others were carrying sacks or rolling barrels from the docks to the warehouses. I dodged small children chasing each other and women carrying laundry baskets.

It was as if the city had only come alive now.

I marvelled at it as I returned to the inn, looking from left to right with a smile on my face. Ilvanna had been like this in *Tari* Arayda's time. With Azra, the streets had been deserted after dark, lending an eeriness to the city I'd never seen before, so seeing one so awake now was welcoming.

It reminded me of better times.

Those feelings faded as soon as I stepped into the room I had been staying in and was faced with my so-called *employer* lounging in a chair as if he owned the place.

Perhaps he does.

The thought sobered me up. "Thank you for everything."

"Don't thank me yet," he said. "Care for a walk, Talnovar? Portasâhn is magnificent this time of night."

I narrowed my eyes at him. "I'm not sure that's a good idea."

"What have you got left to lose?" he asked, lips curled up in a dashing smile. He could convince anyone with that. "Besides, you wanted to talk."

"Fine. Let's talk."

CHAPTER 23

SHALITHA

*D*odge. Parry. Step back. Parry. Step aside. Dodge.

It was all I could do to keep my opponent at bay. With each hit jarring my arm, a flair of pain rushed through my body, antagonising injuries I'd sustained during the past fortnight. After five fights, I'd given up counting the cuts, scrapes and bruises—after ten fights, I'd given up trying to ignore the pain. Kehran in his fury after my attacking him allowed only the most basic of treatment so I wouldn't die of my injuries. They were supposed to slow me down, to dissuade me from taking up arms. Instead, it served to fuel my fury.

Kehran wanted me to die in the *herrât*.

Not if it's up to me.

"Don't stop. Not until your enemy is dead. They won't either." Tal's voice echoed in my memory. It sounded different—I knew he sounded different—but it was all I had. With newfound energy, I angled inward, releasing my blade from underneath my opponent's, going for a downward swing to his shoulder. He parried the first strike but wasn't in time to block the second to his hip.

My sword hit his kidney belt with force.

He staggered back, clutching his side.

"Let me join in on the fun!"

"Not yet," I replied in thought.

The sword muttered in a language I didn't understand. Without waiting for my opponent to recover, I attacked again, giving him no time to use his sword for anything but deflecting my strikes. Around us, the crowd jeered, calling for more, calling for blood. Before, it did nothing to me. Now, their combined voices echoed through me as if they were calling to something deep inside of me.

And that something responded.

A loud roar foreign to my own ears answered them, and it was almost as if Esahbyen was taking me over again, except this time, there was no warning, no feeling of a warm blanket covering me. It was cold, unfriendly, sinister, but it gave me strength.

I charged my adversary, heedless of keeping up my defence. In the back of my mind, I knew the stupidity of this stunt—I could almost hear Tal chide me for this—but it felt like the right thing to do. It startled him enough that he staggered back, but not enough that he went down. I went for his chest, but he regained his footing faster than I'd expected and stepped out of my headlong flight. Without him to temper my speed, I shot past and stumbled over my own feet, going down with a grunt. A blinding pain shot through my shoulder. My sword skittered from my hand, resting just out of reach.

Nohro!

Pushing myself to hands and knees proved to be harder than I'd thought. My body was ready to give up. I wasn't. Pain blossomed in my abdomen, and the world spun. My stomach churned with it, and I coughed. A coppery taste lingered in my mouth, and as I turned over to spit on the ground, I noticed the blood.

The next thing I noticed was the sword hovering above my chest.

Kohpé!

"Can I join the fun now?" The sword sounded impatient.

I grunted and began slipping the ring from my finger. It had a habit of changing into everyday items as it suited me. Despite others being unable to see it didn't mean I didn't have to carry it. Since I had no sheath for a weapon, everyday items that I could wear were the next best thing. With the hand holding the ring, I stretched towards my other sword, knowing it was out of reach, but I had to make it look less suspicious.

"Better not fail me again," I muttered under my breath.

"Say your last goodbyes, princess," the man above me hissed, anger flickering in his eyes.

My lips quirked up at the corners as I looked at him. "Goodbye."

The moment I jabbed my hand into the air while pushing myself up to a sitting position, the ring turned into a sword and pierced his throat. Disbelief washed over his face as blood gushed from the wound. His sword thudded to the dirt-packed ground, and he staggered back before dropping to his knees. I scrambled out of the way, rose to my feet, and stabbed him again. My chest heaved with every gulp of breath I took. I barely had the strength to pull out the sword and staggered back when it released.

My opponent fell forward.

Dead.

I sunk to my knees, gasping. My head felt as if it were ready to explode—my body as if it were giving out, but if I didn't face Kehran on my feet, if I didn't salute him and make my way to the tunnels, my life would be forfeit.

Those were the rules.

With my last bit of strength, I regained my footing and turned to Kehran. He was standing on his balcony, his gold attire glittering in the sun. Although I couldn't see his face from this distance, I knew he was angry.

I had survived.

Again.

Lifting my chin, I balled my fist and brought it to my chest before bowing from the waist down. The crowd exploded into applause and roars of approval. Fourteen fights in fourteen days.

Fourteen wins.

Kehran inclined his head, knowing full well he was in no position now to do anything. The crowd had spoken, calling for my life—calling for another fight. The only thing he could do was schedule that fight tomorrow with a fresh opponent.

One of these days, my luck would run out.

My sole focus went to putting one foot in front of the other. Nothing else mattered. I just had to get to the tunnels. By some miracle, I got there, but once I was inside, I dropped to my knees. Unlike the first time, and just like the past thirteen times, Elay wasn't there to catch me, to tell me I had done it.

Like every other time, I was alone.

"You have me," the sword said entirely too cheerfully.

"Not the same," I mumbled, my voice heavy with exhaustion. I could sleep for a week.

"Come," a soft voice said as a pair of hands helped me up.

"Z'tala?" I murmured.

"Right here, *k'lele.*"

"What about Kehran?" I asked, a little confused as to how she could be here.

"He sent me."

"That promises nothing good."

"Shut up," I hissed and felt Z'tala tense beside me.

I could hardly apologise without explaining why I'd said it, so I kept my mouth shut and staggered alongside her, grateful for her support.

THE HEALER—I still didn't quite believe he was one, but maybe I'd been spoilt with Soren—tended to the worst of my injuries like a butcher dealt with its meat. I wasn't sure whether he was trying to lessen the damage or add to it, and by the time he stuck the needle into my leg a third time, I grabbed it from his hand and shoved him aside, ignoring his protests. Soren had taught me enough about stitches to manage rudimentary basics.

I was nearly finished when Kehran entered the small chamber, stopping dead in his tracks a few feet away from me.

"What in Laros' name are you doing?"

Glancing up, I smirked at him, holding up the needle. "Doing what your healer is incapable of doing, *Akyn.*" I couldn't help the sarcasm dripping from the last word.

His lips pulled up in a sneer, his brows knitted together, and he clenched his jaw tight enough the light splotches on his skin turned red.

"Danger! Abort!"

"You're a pain in my neck," I thought grimly. *"Can't Esahbyen take you back?"*

The sword harrumphed. I returned my focus to the stitches on my thigh, conscious of how much this would enrage Kehran.

I cared no longer.

"Look at me," Kehran commanded.

It was too easy. It didn't matter what I did. If I looked, he'd be mad at me and punish me. If I didn't look, it would have the same effect, but at least I could get these last stitches in before things really took a turn for the worse. I'd just tied it up once when he pressed his fingers into my jaw and forced me to look up at him.

"I said," he hissed through gritted teeth. "Look at me."

So, I did.

Defiantly.

I drew upon my hatred for him and made sure he could read it in my eyes. Something deep inside me roared to life, just as it had in the *herrât*. It would be so easy to hurt him—so easy to kill him even. All I had to do was take off the circlet and tell it what I wanted it to be. I could slice his throat, pierce his heart—by Esah, I could jab him behind the ear with the needle, and it would all be over.

The thought both amused and startled me, but I was no murderer.

"Aren't you?" the sword purred in my mind.

Am I?

Kehran gripped my jaw tighter. "I asked where they are."

"Where who are?" I must have missed his first question.

"Naïda and that *veràthrah* Jaehyr." Spittle flew from his mouth in my face.

"Verathràh," I amended. "You stress the last part, not the middle part."

I was pushing it. His grip on my jaw was like a vice, and I had no doubt he was adding more bruises to the colourful collection on my body. To my own surprise, I still didn't care, and I wondered if I would care if he killed me.

Not really.

If killing me was the worst he could do.

The thing about not caring is that it makes life a whole lot less complicated. It took worrying about anything out of the equation, and it wasn't exactly as if I had anyone left to care about. Yet deep down inside, I knew that to be untrue, and something inside of me shifted again. Hopelessness returned to hope—blatant recklessness to carefulness.

I needed to survive.

Not for me. For Ilvanna.

"I don't know where they are," I said quickly, only then noticing the fierce pain in my jaw.

His grip tightened before he released it. I'd been sure he'd break my jaw first. I sagged in relief. Next thing I knew, the world toppled sideways, and I hit the ground hard. Blood pooled in my mouth and trickled down my cheek. As I brought my hand to my face to check for damages, I noticed how badly I was trembling.

"We are stronger than him."

I wanted to agree, but before I could react, Kehran kicked me. Instinct made me roll out of his reach, but the room was small, and I ended with my back against the wall. Kehran towered over me.

"Where are they?" he hissed.

"I don't know!"

I wasn't exactly lying. I knew where I had sent them, but I had no way of knowing if that was where they had gone. If Jaehyr was as loyal as he'd shown me to be, he would have pushed to find the *T'erza Mahrzal*. If Naïda had had her way, it was anyone's guess.

Kehran made to strike again, but something stopped him.

Z'tala.

"*Akyn*," she said, her voice kind, gentle, like how one would speak to a wayward child. "Do not exert yourself. Surely you do not wish to harm yourself by harming this *tekka*."

I scowled at her.

She glared back, warning in her eyes. Kehran coughed and tugged his coat straight, stepping away from me. I propped myself up against the wall—I couldn't call it sitting—and wiped the blood from my face with the back of my hand.

He'd hit me hard.

Out of nowhere, I began to laugh. The situation was far from funny—there was not a place on my body that didn't hurt, my head felt as if it were about to explode, and I was so *nohro* tired I was afraid to go to sleep for fear of never waking up again.

But I couldn't help it.

I laughed until my sides and stomach ached—laughed until tears were streaming down my face, until my laughter turned into wracking sobs of pain and despair. Without the strength to support myself, I slid to the floor where I curled up on myself. If they'd just left me, I could die in peace.

I did not care.

"Here we go again."

"Leave me alone," I muttered. "Keep your opinions to yourself."

"They're much better shared."

Did it not understand I just wanted to be left alone?

"Oh, I understand," the sword snorted derisively. *"I just don't care much for this self-pity. You knew what you were getting yourself into when you went to free Jaehyr. Now it's time to get yourself out of it. You're a* Tari—*a warrior, I might add*—*what in my owner's name is keeping you?"*

"What does it even matter," I murmured. "Nobody wants me on the throne anyway."

"I wasn't talking about Ilvanna, resha." If it could have, it would have grinned.

"Shalitha," a soft voice came from my side. "Come on, get up."

Z'tala helped me to my feet, placing her arm around my waist and mine around her shoulder to keep me upright. Kehran was looking down his nose at us, a gleeful shimmer in his eyes. Whatever he was about to tell me would be much to his enjoyment.

"You fight tomorrow," he said, his lips curling into a wicked grin, adding to his already twisted visage, "against Z'tala."

She stiffened beside me.

I stared at him. That day was bound to come, and it had been one I didn't relish. The fact it came now was no surprise either. He was going through fighters like some men went through their drinks—fast and furiously. The only fighter he couldn't seem to get rid of was me.

It was a satisfying notion.

"Only one of you leaves the *herrât*," he spat, "and it had better *not* be you." He looked at me with such intense hatred, it made my skin crawl.

"Why not just kill me?" I asked in a tremulous voice. By Esah, I was tired. "It would save you trouble and fighters."

He closed the distance between us, looking down at me. "It would also cost me a lot of money, but tomorrow... tomorrow my bet is not on you." He grinned and caressed my cheek. "Your reign in the *herrât* is coming to an end. There's no fight left in you. Look at you," he scoffed, giving me a once-over. "You can barely stand on your own feet. I doubt you'll be able to hold a sword tomorrow. Z'tala will finish this before it gets started."

My lips pulled up in a lopsided smile. "Sounds like a challenge to me, *Akyn.* We will see who walks out of there alive tomorrow."

Kehran's face fell momentarily. "You're in no state to fight," he sneered. "Don't be too confident, *Tarien.*"

It was the first time he'd acknowledged my title.

"He's afraid."

"Of what?" I felt like I should know the answer to that question.

The sword chuckled. *"You,* resha.*"

CHAPTER 24

HAERLYON

*a*zra was furious. Beyond furious.

Pacing up and down her bedroom—she rarely came out these days on account of being enormously pregnant— everything in her path found a new place of residence. Vases shattered against the wall, tables and chairs were overturned, and even smaller items weren't safe.

I was barely in time to duck when her washing bowl sailed in my direction.

"Where *is* he?" she screeched, picking up another vase. "Tell me you have found him!"

I inclined my head, but not without keeping an eye on her. "My apologies, *Tari*, but Eamryel Arolvyen knows how to keep a low profile."

A banshee-like wail tore from her lips as she threw the vase at me. I caught it and winced as it hit me square in the chest. My ribs were still a colourful shade of yellow and purple, courtesy of Eamryel's betrayal over a week ago. My lips flattened just thinking about it, but I couldn't dwell on it—couldn't dwell on the feelings that came with it.

"Tari," I began carefully, "perhaps you should sit down. In your condition, all this rage cannot be good."

She snarled at me so ferociously, I took an involuntary step back, halted only by the door behind me. Inhaling deeply, I crossed my arms in front of me, forcing down the annoyance at having to be the one to deal with her tantrums. Sometimes, I felt like a babysitter rather than the *Ohzheràn* of the Ilvannian army, son of the previous *Tari,* brother to the rightful *Tari.* I was so much more than Azra's personal lackey, and yet, here I was, being exactly that.

I couldn't help a scowl from appearing on my face.

"What are you looking so sour for?" Azra huffed, waddling over to the bed.

"Just the situation, *Tari,*" I replied. "It vexes me as much as it does you that he keeps slipping through our fingers."

She narrowed her eyes. "Do you now?"

Nohro, she knows.

"Of course," I said, cocking my head and arching a brow. "Clearly, security wasn't up to standards that night, *Tari,* and for that, I shall never forgive myself."

A snort escaped her lips. "I'd almost forgotten your way with words, Haerlyon."

I smirked. "A fox does not unlearn its tricks."

"So, you're a fox now?" She tilted her head, regarding me with pursed lips. "Are you trying to tell me something?"

"Not at all." I leaned back casually, inspecting my nails. "You know what I'm like, auntie. I haven't changed. Well, not much anyway."

Her lips curled up in a snarl at my endearment for her, something I hadn't called her since she returned to the palace. She quickly masked her dislike.

"I'm not so sure about that," she said at length. "Your lover's death hit you hard. You changed after that."

A low growl rumbled in my chest. "And all because of *her.*"

Azra smiled at that—a genuine smile—and her eyes lost some of the tension they'd been holding. A heavy sigh escaped from her lips as she lay back on the bed, stroking her belly with a grimace. I remembered Mother looking the same when she was heavily pregnant with my sister. On the one hand, I was glad I would never have to be there for my *wife*. On the other hand, the idea of having a child of my own was enticing.

I'd have loved to have a daughter.

"I need you to do something," Azra said, interrupting my wayward thoughts.

I glanced up, arching an eyebrow. "Of course, *Tari*. Anything."

"There have been rumours," she said, the look on her face predicting nothing good. "Sightings of the *Tarien*." She spat the last word, and her hatred for my sister became an almost palpable presence. "I need you to investigate these rumours, cut them short where necessary. I can't have my people believe in lies."

I inclined my head. "Of course, *Tari*. When?"

"You ride tonight. Take a couple of men and leave as quietly as you can."

"Yes, *Tari*."

As I placed my hand on the doorknob, she spoke. "And Haerlyon?"

"Yes, *Tari*?"

"Don't fail. Do not return before nobody dares even whisper her name."

My lips pulled up in a wicked grin as I turned to her. "Have I ever failed you before, *mey Tari*?"

She huffed. "Just go."

The tone in her voice sounded off—flat almost—as if she didn't particularly care whether I did or not. The hairs on the back of my neck stood on end as I left her bedroom, and in that moment, I wished so badly I had someone to discuss this with that my chest ached.

Before I left, there was one thing I had to do.

KALYANI REGARDED ME QUIETLY, tapping a finger against pursed lips as she mulled over my words.

"Do you think it's true?" she asked hopefully. "That the *Tarien* has returned?"

I shook my head and shrugged. "I honestly don't know. It could be true, it could be false. That's what I need to find out."

"You should be careful, Haerlyon. I don't trust her."

"Neither do I," I replied, my lips quirking up in a crooked smile. "But what can I do? If I refuse, she'll hang me like the *verathràh* I am."

Kalyani took a step closer and cupped my cheek in her hand. "You are no *verathràh*, Haerlyon. At first, I thought you were, but I've seen you move about. I see the shadows under your eyes, the sadness in them when you think nobody is looking. If you are what you say you are, none of this would have mattered. You wouldn't have bothered asking for help."

I exhaled loudly, the sound somewhere between a huff and a snort. "But I did all the things people accuse me of, Kalyani. I betrayed my friends, my family—everyone."

"Did you?" Her voice was soft. "Really?"

Rubbing the back of my neck, it was my turn to regard her. She was small in stature, reminding me painfully of Mother. Both Shal and Azra were much taller than her. Nevertheless, Mother had commanded respect with her presence, as did Kalyani. It was strange to think that such a small woman had produced such a bear of a son.

His death seemed a lifetime ago.

"How will they ever forgive me?" I whispered, fumbling with

my hands—a nervous habit I'd been able to suppress for a long time.

"It's not about whether they forgive you," she replied. "It's about whether you can forgive yourself."

I ran a hand through my hair and nodded even though I wasn't convinced. "I have no idea how long I'll be gone..."

"And you're afraid you may not be on time for the baby's birth?" Kalyani offered.

"Indeed."

"What needs to be done?"

She sounded so confident, so assured that it startled me. I blinked a few times and shook my head.

"How did you—?"

"You asked me to spy on her, *Irìn*." She looked smug. "Nobody pays attention to the servants. The higher up in society they are, the less they pay attention to those below. Plus that *Irà* Mehrean may or may not have asked for my assistance before she left the palace."

My jaw dropped. "Mehrean asked you?"

Kalyani chuckled softly. "Don't look so surprised, Haerlyon. As soon as she learned what you'd asked me, she looked me up, but she wasn't very specific. She merely told me to await your summons."

I pinched the bridge of my nose. "How does she always *know* things?"

"There is much more that we don't know," Kalyani said, her voice wistful. "Things that we have lost throughout history, things that should have remained hidden."

"What are you talking about?"

She looked at me curiously. "Do you believe in the Gods, Haerlyon?"

"Not particularly."

"Well," she patted my cheek. "Start praying, son. If I'm to believe your friend, we have seen nothing yet. Now, what is it

227

you need me to do?"

THAT NIGHT as I left the palace, my heart felt heavy. Although Kalyani had agreed to help once more, there was no assurance she would succeed, and if she did, if she could get away. A part of me was still annoyed Mehrean had already recruited her without telling me, the other part was grateful.

I couldn't shake the feeling something was about to go terribly wrong.

By the time the horizon began to turn a deep red and the sky began to lighten, the city was a speck in the distance, a mere memory of warm food, a hot bath, and comfort—three things I felt certain we would not enjoy for a long time, depending on whether the rumours were true or not. Something told me Shal wouldn't be as stupid as to make her presence known.

If she came back, and by now I was beginning to feel it was a big if, the last thing she would do was announce her presence. Her army was non-existent and trying to reach Denahryn was suicide no matter which route she took. And then there was the simple fact I expected more from her.

She was not that stupid.

The fact Azra believed in these rumours told me two things. One, she was much more paranoid than I'd initially believed, and two, she wasn't concerned enough about them to fortify the city and get ready. We'd been planning for so long, and yet there were no concrete plans. She kept going on about raising our army, training it to be ready without knowing what to be ready for. I didn't think she believed Shal would ever return, so she wasn't really preparing.

She's pretending.

Why then send me on this fool's mission?

"*Ohzheràn,*" a voice sounded next to me.

Rayadaen, a *sveràn* in the Ilvannian army I'd personally chosen to come along, had ridden up to my side, worry etching fine lines around his mouth and eyes.

"What's wrong?"

"Apologies," he said, glancing over his shoulder. "But I think we're being followed, *zhàn.*"

I arched a brow. "Followed?"

He nodded almost imperceptibly. "Ever since we left Ilvanna."

"You're absolutely certain of this?"

"Positive, *Serea.*"

"Thank you." I glanced over my shoulder but couldn't see anything directly. "Keep an eye out. Let me know if anything changes."

Rayadaen inclined his head and slowed his horse to fall back.

Naturally, we didn't see or hear anything for the rest of the day, nor when we set up camp in the forest. Two men set to tend the fire, three others went for firewood, and the rest either spread out bedrolls or took up guard duty. As *Ohzheràn*, I was exempt from standing guard—as *Zheràn* I had been, too—but I nevertheless took it up.

Shivers ran down my arms and spine as I stepped just beyond the circle of light. Anyone who'd ever stood on guard knew the stupidity of standing inside of it. For one thing, you couldn't see beyond the light, and for another, you'd be an easy target. The downside was that by stepping outside the circle of light, you also stepped away from its comfortable warmth.

I pulled my fur-lined cloak tighter around me, grateful for its comfort.

Without knowing how, I knew we were close to *Hanyarah*. I rubbed my arms underneath my cloak, but not because of the cold. Nightmares still haunted me every night. No matter what I tried, I couldn't get rid of the sightless eyes or the haunted screams, and I swore I could still smell the blood despite the time that had passed. But the one image that had me wake up in a cold sweat almost every night was the feeling of Tiroy's dead body in my arms as I carried him to the place where all the bodies were collected for the death rite.

Focus, an Ilvan.

A twig snapped up ahead. My hand was on the hilt of my sword instantly as I peered into the darkness.

"What was that?" a voice murmured from my left.

"Stay low and out of sight. Warn the others," I whispered back. "We're not alone."

If we were lucky, wild animals had found us. If we were less lucky, it were the ones who, according to Rayadaen, had been following us. At this point, I didn't like our odds to begin with. We were with enough to deal with predatory animals, but people were another matter entirely. It all depended on how many were out there, how trained they were, and what their objective was.

I had an inkling.

There were the hushed noises of conversation from the fire before it died down. Swords being unsheathed sounded loud in the deafening silence, and I realised it hadn't come from only behind me. There was more than one person out there. I withdrew deeper into the darkness of the forest, hoping my men would do the same.

There was no way of communicating without alerting the opposite side.

My heart picked up speed, and my ears were buzzing. Muscles strained as my body prepared for fight or flight while my brain went over the information I'd been given. Rayadaen had said we were being followed ever since we left Ilvanna. I'd not told anyone where we were going, and I'd kept my promise, which could only mean one thing.

Azra had sent them.

She doesn't trust me after all.

The thought came as no surprise—not really—it had only been a matter of time. The question was, why now? It didn't matter. What mattered was that I came out of this alive.

And continue to play the game.

The tell-tale *twang* of a bow disrupted the silence. I could almost hear the arrow zoom through the air, but I had no way of knowing if it had hit a target. After that, there was silence again. Nobody made the first move, and I had the distinct feeling our opponents were waiting for something. The arrow had merely been a distraction.

Nohro!

Staying low to the ground, I crept through the foliage, making my way back to the camp. Although I hadn't gone too far away, it felt like forever before I reached the first bedroll. My hand landed in something soft and sticky just as the scent of blood hit my nose, taking me back to *Hanyarah* almost immediately. I gulped in air and pushed myself back fast, heedless of the sound I made.

Someone beyond the firelight startled.

Without thinking twice, I scrambled to my feet, unsheathed my sword, and went after whoever was there. I stepped on soft tissue as I went, stumbled over limbs, but I didn't pause to think who they belonged to. I pursued the attacker deeper into the forest, hardly aware of where we were going or how far he—I assumed it was a he for convenience—was guiding me away from my horse, from safety.

It didn't matter.

Either I lived through this or I didn't, and the odds weren't stacked in my favour. They hadn't been from the beginning, so I bore no illusion they were now. I'd live or die. The simplicity of it was comforting, like a mother's kiss or a lover's hug.

I chased the shadow into a clearing and lost him. What little moonlight managed to peek through the canopy illuminated the small area, but as I turned and turned, I saw no sign of him. It made me wonder if I hadn't just imagined it.

No, there had been blood and dead bodies.

But the thought didn't convince me. My mind had been on the past, perhaps I'd dozed off and imagined all of it, and now I was somewhere in the middle of nowhere without any sense of direction as to where the camp could possibly be.

Well done, khirr.

Even so, I couldn't shake the feeling I was being watched. No matter how hard I peered into the darkness, however, nothing moved, nothing showed itself.

It had to be an animal.

It was no use trying to find my way back in the dark. Chances of getting even more lost were considerable. A part of me was desperate to sit down, close my eyes and get some rest, but the more rational part kept me on my feet, surveying my surroundings carefully.

I didn't feel like ending up on a bear's menu.

After a long time, I sat down with my back against a tree, my legs too tired after my headlong flight to keep me upright. I wouldn't fall asleep—I could keep my vigil, but I needed to sit down, if only for a bit. Placing my sword in my lap, I rested my head back against the bark of the tree, telling myself again and again I shouldn't fall asleep.

A sharp pain in my cheek jolted me awake almost simultaneously with a loud *thud* next to my ear. Looking sideways, I found an arrow quivering in the tree not an inch from my head.

A warning shot.

It was then I became aware of muffled footsteps on the foliage. I got my feet under me and crouched low, peering into the darkness of the forest in the faint hope of seeing what was there. Moonlight glinted off metal briefly, but it was enough to tell me there was a person there.

I rose to my feet.

"Show yourself!" I shouted. *"Nohro* coward!*"*

At least a dozen men stepped into the clearing, brandishing weapons of varying degrees of pain they could inflict. Some were Ilvannian judging by their white skin, others Therondian if their pinker skin was any indication, but there were others, too. In this light, it was hard to make out their origins, but I knew without a doubt they weren't from around.

"As you wish, princeling," a man twice my size in width drawled in a low rumble. "I don't like playing with my food."

I grimaced. "Who in Esah's name are you?"

His lips quirked up in a smile, but other than that, the expression on his face remained quite emotionless. "Someone who's been waiting for this moment for a long time."

That wasn't vague at all.

"You might just have to wait a little longer."

A noise like a cow mooing sounded up, and I realised it was the man. He was laughing, or what I assumed passed as laughing in his case. I couldn't help the snort escaping me.

"A cheeky princeling," he said, hoisting up his mace to rest on his shoulder. "She said to watch out for that tongue."

As I thought.

My lips pulled up in a lopsided smile. "Ah, I see," I drawled, taking up a relaxed stance. "I don't suppose we can come to an agreement?"

"The only agreement we will come to is your death."

"Yeah." I rubbed the back of my neck. "I was afraid you were going to say that. Guess my dear auntie finally caught on, didn't she?"

Their response was a coordinated attack. I parried the first blow from a sword and dodged an attack from a morning star, stilling momentarily as I felt it whoosh past my ear, much too close for comfort.

That moment cost me.

A quarterstaff connected with the elbow of my left arm. I

could have sworn I heard something snap, and I was convinced it wasn't the staff. The pain I had expected remained at bay, however, which was something to be grateful for at least. Between being a skilled fighter and having trained like this most of my life, I managed to stay upright much longer than I'd expected, but I was growing tired and the pain didn't help either. Even so, I killed one of them and disabled a second, but with four still standing, I was outmatched.

It would only be a matter of time.

I guess dying it is.

As the thought crossed my mind, another arrow flew past and embedded itself in an opponent's eye. He went down without a sound. The momentary confusion served as a window of escape for me, and I put some distance between myself and my enemies, moving in the direction where the arrow had come from. It was a risk, but whoever was picking off my enemies had to be a friend, and if not that, at least on the same side.

And if they weren't, I'd cross that bridge when I came to it.

Two more arrows took out two more opponents, leaving only their leader. He charged, raising his mace as if it weighed nothing, only bringing it down when he was close enough to hit me. As I side-stepped, the world turned on its side, and it took me a moment to realise I was falling. My foot had caught in a rabbit hole. The mace came at my head, but I rolled aside, flinching as it hit the ground with force. Although it took the man little effort to lift it again, it gave me an opportunity to stab him.

It wasn't enough to kill him.

He raised his mace again and brought it down with such force that if it were a hit, depending on the location, it could kill me. I rolled out of the way but wasn't fast enough, and the weapon connected painfully with my arm, sending me back to the ground forcefully. Stars danced in my vision as the world tilted and my stomach lurched.

I'm done for.

Resting in the knowledge I'd given this fight my all, I allowed the darkness to consume me. I'd see Tiroy again soon, and Mother.

And Father.

CHAPTER 25

TALNOVAR

*P*ortasâhn had been a remarkable city by day, but it
had nothing on its almost magical appearance at
night. Although Ilvanna had been alike during *Tari* Arayda's
reign, it had never felt so alive as here. Owing to the more
comfortable temperatures, people came out after the sun had
gone. Men and women strolled casually past the market stalls
set up along the longest and widest road of Portasâhn. Carts
carrying all kinds of wares trundled past, children were playing
in the street, women were hanging laundry while men sat in
rickety chairs, talking amiably with their companions, playing
board games the likes of which I'd never seen before.

My companion looked entirely relaxed as he took in our
surroundings, more relaxed than I felt anyway. People were
looking at me either curiously or apprehensively. Men ordered
their wives and daughters out of my way—women eyed me
with more interest, but always with covert glances. The notion
made me uncomfortable.

"You said you'd answer my questions," I began, redirecting
my focus to the matter at hand. "Let's begin with your name."

"It's Rashiìd." He flashed me an easy smile. "Pleased to meet you."

"If you say so. Why are we here?"

"Because you were ill, *eshen*," Rashiìd said, looking at me. "Dying even."

"Dying?"

I'd not been feeling too great for quite some time, but I'd never had the idea it was that bad. A memory of a beautiful woman resurfaced, her words lingering in my mind. She'd said I'd been dying as well, and she'd given me a choice.

Either you live or you die.

There had been more to it, but for some strange reason, that part of the memory was hazy, and I was unable to remember what it was.

It didn't matter.

"Why did you save me?"

He didn't respond to this question straight away. Instead, he rubbed the stubble on his jaw, staring off into the distance as if his answer was written in the stars.

"You're a fighter. I need people like you."

"What for?"

A laugh escaped his lips, and he shook his head, setting the golden hoops in his ears moving. "Why would I need fighters, *eshen*? To fight, obviously."

I bit back the retort, pressing my fist against my lips, and awarding him a deadpan stare. If the conversation was going to be like this, I'd much rather have him return me to his slave camp. The thought reminded me of Halueth.

"Is my friend still back at the caravan?"

Rashiìd's brows knitted together. "What friend?"

"Halueth," I said, sounding confused. "Tall guy, looks like me, a bit thinner, perhaps?"

A troubled look crossed his face, but he masked it quickly. He stopped and looked at me, his head cocked to the side as if he were trying to unravel the puzzle that was me.

"What?"

"I—" Pain surfaced in his eyes. Or was it pity? "I'm afraid Halueth doesn't exist, *eshen.*" He scratched the back of his neck and shook his head. "You were quite out of it when my men found you on the beach, half-delirious from lack of proper nutrition and the state of your injuries. They... reported you were talking, but not to them. They said it was as if you were living in your own world."

"No"—I shook my head firmly—"Halueth is real. Was real. I saved him on the merchant's ship. We made it o—"

I'd made it off.

"He died on that ship," I whispered, raking a hand through my hair. "I remember now. The ship made a sudden move, and he smashed his head against a support beam. He... he was dead on impact." I looked up at him. "So, the slave camp, what happened there..."

"Was real," Rashiid offered. "For the most part. I assume my version of events and yours might differ somewhat."

"What about Tariq and Nazeem?"

"Tariq is my healer." Rashiid smiled at that. "Nazeem is one of the men who found you half-dead on the beach. I had them keep an eye on you."

"And the man who attacked me?"

Although he smiled, the look in his eyes betrayed he wasn't pleased with that part. "I'm afraid you attacked him, *eshen.* You were paranoid, scared that everybody was out to get you. You got into several fights, actually."

Biting the inside of my cheek, I looked away from him. The notion I hadn't come out of everything as well as I thought unnerved me. Azra had done a number on me, that much had been clear, but I had no idea it had been this bad.

I had felt fine back at *Denahryn.*

"And now?" I asked tentatively.

"Tariq has cleared you," Rashiid said. "You'll have to take it easy for a little while longer, but the injury on your leg has healed quite well, as did your shoulder. Remarkably fast, too."

I remembered the warning in a female voice.

"My le—Oh, right. Yllinar's doing."

Rashiïd stilled at the name, and I could have sworn I saw him scowl as if he knew it. He quickly schooled his expression when he looked at me. "You might want to be careful overexerting yourself, but Tariq has said you can resume training if you'd like."

I inclined my head, unable to keep a smile from tugging my lips up. It had been so long since I'd done any proper training, and I found myself looking forward to it.

"So, this fighting," I said as we resumed our walk. "I assume it's not in an army."

Rashiïd laughed and shook his head. "No, *eshen*, nothing quite like that." He ran his hand through his hair as he regarded me, then dropped it with a heavy sigh. "I want you to fight in the *herrât*."

"In a what?"

Rashiïd arched a brow as if I was being intentionally obtuse. "An arena."

I'd heard the stories of Kyrinthan arena fighting from merchants back in Ilvanna, but I'd never seen them for myself on account of never having visited Kyrintha before. In that regard, for someone who'd lived as long as I had, I'd not seen much of the world before I went to find the *Tarien*.

I wasn't keen on doing so again if we ever get home.

If I ever find her.

"Why me?"

Rashiïd looked at me as if I'd asked him why he was breathing. "Because you can fight, Talnovar, and you can fight well. More importantly, you have a reason to. One doesn't survive the *herrât* by just being able to fight. One must know what he's doing if he wants to win."

"And if he doesn't?"

His face fell, a pained expression crossing his face. "He dies."

I'd figured as much. "Why *herrât* fighting? Why are you looking for men to do so?"

He remained silent for such a long time that I was afraid I'd asked too much, and he wasn't willing to answer any more. I didn't think the question was unreasonable. Straightforward perhaps, but not unreasonable. He was still the man who owned me, and the fact he was taking time to answer my questions was a courtesy on his part. Quite odd, all things considered, but I wasn't going to push my luck. For the first time in at least two years, I was treated like a person, not a commodity, although that thought was debatable considering what Rashiïd wanted me to do. But at least he spoke to me like an equal.

For now.

"Let's just say it's a family feud," he replied at length, avoiding my eyes. "My brother has a few of the best fighters in the country, and I want to teach him a lesson."

I frowned. "So, you'll have men killed for entertainment to do so?"

He had the decency to wince at my words, but he quickly composed himself. "I don't expect an outlander like yourself to understand."

"Try me," I said. "Must be some terrible family feud if you're willing to go to these lengths."

Rashiïd snorted at that, glancing at me. "That's one way to put it."

"What's in it for me?"

He glanced at me, his lips quirking up at the corners. "We'll discuss that when you win, *eshen.*"

We were silent for a while as we strolled across the market. Rashiïd greeted people here and there while I contemplated his words. Something about the whole situation was bugging me, but I couldn't quite put my finger on it. As I didn't want to push my luck, I decided to let it go, and in that moment, I noticed a small hand take a swipe at Rashiid's belt.

With success.

Without thinking twice, I pelted after the young child, weaving through the crowd with surprising ease. While nowhere near the speed or strength I used to have, it could have been worse, and despite myself, I smiled. This situation reminded me of times where I had chased another girl whose only desire had been to be free of the burden of her ancestry.

By Esah, I missed her.

The thought of Shal gave me new energy, and I pushed off hard against the ground as I followed the child into a side street. I almost collided with a group of men while taking the corner, but they jumped aside while I slowed down somewhat. I threw an apology over my shoulder and sped up, chasing the urchin around corners until I was properly lost.

All of a sudden, she halted and turned to me.

I stopped dead in my tracks, wincing at the strain it put on my legs. She tilted her head, big eyes looking me up and down.

"You look like her," the girl said.

My heart skipped a beat, and I stared at the child. "Excuse me?"

"You look like the nice white *amisha*." The girl flashed me a wide smile, and I couldn't help but notice the missing teeth.

My heart was hammering in my chest. A white lady whom I looked like. Had Shal passed through here? How long ago? Did the girl know where she was? Breathing in deeply, I lowered to one knee and regarded the child at eye-level.

"What's your name, *amisha*?"

"Prisha."

I smiled. "Nice to mee you, Prisha. My name is Talnovar, but my friends call me Tal. Do you know the name of this... *amisha*... I look like?"

She shook her head. "No, but she looked like you. She had

lines on her face. Blue lines in a pattern. Looked odd if you ask me."

My heart soared, and I whispered before I realised I was doing so, "Shalitha."

"Who?"

"Her name is Shalitha," I said, opting to sit down. "She's a... friend of mine."

Although Prisha smiled, her eyes narrowed. "So be *he*."

"He who?"

"The man I stole the pouch from," Prisha said, wrinkling her nose as if she smelled something foul. "He be her friend, too."

"What?" My voice came out in a noise between a hiss and a growl, but the girl didn't so much as flinch. Instead, she nodded vigorously, her smile turning brighter.

"I saved them." She thumped her chest. "They be chased when they be here last time. He be injured. She led bad men away, but they followed. I hid her and helped. They got out."

I inhaled deeply to steady my nerves and force back the anger coiling inside me like a restless snake. He *knew* her. It could explain how he'd known my name back at the slave camp. How much of what he had told me was true? How much of what he'd told me could I believe?

"Do you know his name?"

She shook her head. "No, but he be all right. Unlike other men. Other men bad."

"What other men?"

"The ones who steal us," she said.

I was about to ask more when a shout and the sound of running footsteps approached us. Getting to my feet, I turned to the girl.

"You'd better run, Prisha," I said. "But before you go, do you think I could have the pouch back?"

She pouted, eyes turning even bigger as tears gathered at the corners.

I grinned at her. "I'll give you some of its contents."

"There be more if I keep pouch," she said, folding her little arms in front of her chest.

Whatever became of this girl, I had no doubt she'd be fierce once she grew up. This time, I smiled at her before casting a look over my shoulder. Men were approaching fast.

"If they catch you, the bad men will take you," I said softly, "and we can't let that happen."

Prisha considered my words carefully, taking her sweet time doing so. Then she shrugged, flashing me a bright smile as she threw me the pouch. "I stole pouch in hopes you followed. You did. Goodbye, *mishan.*"

Without waiting for a reply, she dashed away into a side street before the men—guards if their attire was any proof—reached me. I rose to my feet, wincing at the imagined injury Prisha had just seen fit to give me before she ran off while tucking away the pouch underneath my shirt.

"Where did she go?" the leader of the guards asked gruffly.

"Don't know, *mishan.* She ran in that direction." I pointed at the opposite street I saw Prisha disappear in.

The leader issued orders for two of them to come with him and for the last to stay behind. He looked at me with a frown as I limped in his direction.

"Are you injured?"

"Nothing I can't handle," I replied. "If you'll excuse me, I must get back to my employer. How do I get out of this maze?"

The guard narrowed his eyes, sighed, and motioned for me to follow him. His shoulders slumped as if he'd just gotten the worst job in his entire life. I couldn't help a smirk creeping up on my face, having seen that look on people more often than I cared to count, especially after I'd been the one ordering them to do it.

Xaresh had hated chasing Shal.

Her name returned my thoughts to the matter at hand. He

had never told me how he'd known my name—the only logical explanation was if Shal had told him about me, which led me to wonder why she would ever tell a stranger such information. She wasn't stupid—she knew better than to trust just anyone.

What happened to you that you would?

RASHIÌD, if that was even his name, was waiting patiently at the stall where I'd left him. Perhaps a little too patiently. Not that it mattered. Before the night was out, I would have my answers, Esah willing, and there would be no more secrets between us. At this point, I wasn't beyond inflicting some pain myself to get what I wanted. I'd been on the receiving end long enough.

Now it was my turn.

"Had a good workout?"

"If you could call it that," I replied, forcing a smile to my face. "I was mostly trying not to slam into walls."

He arched a brow. "Interesting tactics."

"Necessity more than anything else."

"Did you retrieve my pouch?"

I shook my head. "No, the child disappeared before I could get to it."

He didn't look entirely convinced but didn't press the matter. Instead, he smiled, inviting me to continue our walk as if nothing had interrupted it. This time, however, it was much harder to pretend I knew nothing.

"So, this *herrât* fighting," I began, glancing at him. "Where does it take place?"

"Akhyr," Rashiìd replied. "The Kyrinthan capital."

"When?"

"The official games are two moons from now, but we should be there in a little over a moon. There's something else I need to see to first."

"Such as?"

"The caravan." He shot me a look as if to ask whether I was stupid.

I clenched my jaw and inclined my head. "Am I to be locked up in a cage again? Like an animal?"

Rashiïd stiffened for a flicker of an instant, barely noticeable to those who didn't know how to observe, but I had noticed.

"Do you want to be?" He grinned at me. "Saves you walking."

I snorted. "I'd rather walk if that's okay with you."

By the time we reached the inn, people had mostly disappeared inside the safety of their homes. The moon cast its pale glow over the city, a silent sentinel over those still endeavouring to find the bottom of their tankards or otherwise nightly entertainment. The raucous laughter of sailors drifted towards us as we stepped inside the inn.

Inside, it was blissfully silent.

"Feel free to have a drink on me," Rashiïd offered as he made his way up the stairs. "I'll be turning in for the night."

"I'm fine," I said, following. "I don't drink."

He looked at me appreciatively before nodding. "Very well. Good night, Talnovar."

"One more thing." I turned to him, cocking my head to the side. "Did you intend to sell Shalitha, too, or did you keep her for yourself?"

His hand stilled on the doorknob, his face ashen. I gave him no time to respond. Before I had actively decided what to do, I'd pushed him up against the door, elbow at his throat.

"No more lies."

CHAPTER 26

SHALITHA

*K*ehran had been right.

As much as I hated to admit it, I was in no state to fight. I barely had any strength to lift my sword, let alone deflect Z'tala's blows. She wasn't trying her hardest, I could tell as much, but she kept up a good show.

"I could help," the sword purred sinuously. *"Like all the other times."*

"No," I thought, gritting my teeth at the bone-jarring blow that just landed on my sword. *"Z'tala doesn't deserve to die."*

"You all die at some point."

"Thanks for the reminder."

With renewed strength, I blocked Z'tala's attack and pushed her back, but the reprieve was short and painful. We'd barely begun, and I was already short of breath. With every move I made, pain flared up inside of me, making it hard to focus on the task at hand. The look on Z'tala's face was one of quiet contemplation, as if she were meditating rather than fighting. As she brought her sword down from an overhead strike, I caught it. Our crossguards locked together, but neither of us put much effort into unbalancing the other.

"What are you doing?" I hissed.

"Stalling, *k'lele*," Z'tala replied under her breath. "We need a plan."

"For what?"

Her lips pulled up in a faint smile as she pulled her sword back. "To get you out of here."

"I like her."

"Hush," I mumbled, following it up by a cough.

She stormed me. I parried.

"*You* must live," Z'tala said as our weapons locked for the somanieth time. "Remember when I asked you about destinies, *k'lele?*"

I nodded and swung in a wide arc, aiming for her shoulder. She deflected my attack with relative ease. Around us, the crowd's jeers and praises blended into a single buzz.

"Your destiny lies beyond these walls." She hesitated. "I thought mine did, too."

"What do you mean?"

Z'tala grinned, spun and planted her elbow in my ribs. I staggered back with a grunt, glaring at her.

"I had a dream before I came here," she began, "about you, here, and so I went to find you."

Her words startled me, creating a moment in which I was unfocused enough for Z'tala to step past my defence and put her sword up against my throat. The crowd exploded into a cacophony of raucous sounds that wasn't too far off a flock of seagulls screeching at the docks. Glancing at the balcony to where Kehran sat, I found him staring at us intently.

This was a good moment to slit my throat.

"Of course," she said, making it appear as if we were struggling, "you weren't here, so I spent the last half a decade in Kehran's *herrât* waiting for you, praying to the Gods they had not sent me here without reason."

I attempted to push her away, but she would not budge. Kehran was watching us like a hawk watched its unaware prey.

"When you finally arrived," Z'tala continued, "you understand I was elated. Finally, my chance to get out of this place was here. But now—"

"—Kehran has made that impossible," I finished. "One of us must die."

"Not necessarily," she replied in a conspiratorial voice. "The *herriatâre* are fed up with the *Akyn's* whims, are done fighting for a dishonourable man. They are done with this lifestyle, *k'lele*. They will fight for you if you rally them. They will follow you if you promise them a future."

"And what future would that be?"

"Freedom, *k'lele*. Freedom. They want to see their families again. Rally them, fight with them, and give them their freedom in return."

"There's no way we can overpower Kehran's men," I objected. "They far outnumber us, and you forget the other *herriatâre* are still locked up!"

Z'tala clucked her tongue and swiped at my feet, a wicked grin on her face. "You must have more faith, *k'lele*."

"She's right, you know. I can almost taste the need for revenge," the sword added. *"Not necessarily from you. Where's that fighter spirit?"*

Anger boiled inside of me, lending me a strength I was sure I no longer possessed, and I pushed her away, taking up a defensive position. Without looking, I knew Kehran wouldn't be pleased with this turn of events.

The crowd, however, went wild.

"What do *you* propose then?" Z'tala asked with a wry smile, getting ready to attack. "If anyone can do this, it's you, *k'lele*. They will follow you because you have proven yourself. Nothing more is needed in a place like this."

She came at me in a flurry of blows. Sword, elbow, kick, sword, kick. It was more of a dance than combat, a blatant show of fighting skills the crowd would not be able to discern at this distance. Her sword barely nicked my skin, her kicks never landed in my sides, and as she pretended to plant her elbow in my chest, I was the one who doubled over, masking the fact I wasn't gulping for air at all. I staggered back and fell, landing on my back the way Tal had taught me long ago. If performed right, the air wouldn't be knocked out of your lungs.

While I feigned gasping for air, Z'tala grabbed a spear—weapons lay around the *herrât* randomly, just in case—and stabbed at me.

I rolled out of the way.

"You have to make a choice, *k'lele,*" Z'tala said fiercely. "Will you lead us into battle against the cruel *Akyn,* or"—she stabbed at me again— "do you choose death."

Although pretence, I was too slow this time. Act-fighting turned out to be as exhausting as real fighting, perhaps even more so. The spearhead broke my skin and pierced through muscle, sliding so easily past tendons it made my stomach churn. A howl of pain tore from my lips.

"*Nohro ahrae!*"

Z'tala quickly masked the look of horror on her face. "You must choose, or I have no choice but to follow orders. *T'maere k'tan, k'lele.* Choose your destiny. Get up. Fight."

Her words made sense. In the part of my brain that wasn't focused on the pain, I realised that, but my body was tired—I was tired. It was one injury too many. As I tried to get up, my arms trembled, and pushing myself to my knees proved an even harder struggle than this match. My stomach heaved at the exertion of rising to my feet. Sweat broke out across my face and back.

The crowd roared its approval.

Kehran screamed in rage.

"It has to be you, *k'lele,*" Z'tala whispered, glancing over her shoulder at the *Akyn*. "We don't have much time but trust me when I tell you everything is ready."

"For what?"

"For you, *Okleah*."

What's that supposed to mean?

I could barely keep myself upright, let alone continue fighting, but as that realisation dawned on me, the sound of rattling chains reached me. I spun around, swayed, and dropped to hands and knees, my gaze falling upon the dozen or so guards marching through the open gates.

It's too late.

"*Get up!*" the sword yelled at the same time as Z'tala.

"I can't," I gasped, feeling how tremors took hold of my body. "Just... kill me, Z'tala, I cannot fight. Kill me, and Kehran will be placated. It's fine."

She grabbed me by the arms and hauled me to my feet, wrapping an arm around my waist to support me. "I will neither kill you nor let you die on your knees."

"My fight is done, Z'tala. Let me go."

"*So be it.*"

The strangest sensation spread through me, starting at the tip of my toes, extending to my legs, my torso, arms, neck, and lastly, my head. An agonising flare of pain went through me. Then everything went numb. There was no more pain, no more fatigue—I felt reborn with renewed strength and an insurmountable amount of energy. As I watched the guards draw closer, I felt a grin pull up my lips.

It felt foreign on my face.

Beside me, Z'tala prepared for battle. As for me, I waited quietly, patiently, leisurely even, no weapon to my name. I stood there watching sure death approach, and all I did was wait. As if by instinct, I knew there was a sword lying not too far from me and beyond that, a shield and a mace. Ten feet to Z'tala's right lay a net and another spear.

Enough weapons for us to get around.

But we're only two. And how did I know that?

The thought didn't disturb me as much as I thought it should, so I pushed it to the back of my mind.

"Do what you must," I told Z'tala without looking at her. "Gather the *herriatâre*, as many as you can. I will lead them. His reign is over."

"Aye, *Okleah*," she said, a smile on her lips. "As you command."

The guards approached us with caution. I may have been more than halfway to death and without a weapon, but I wasn't defenceless. And then there was Z'tala, looking as fierce as ever.

"You need a weapon, *k'lele*."

"I am a weapon," I replied with a grin but did saunter over to the sword behind me and picked it up.

It wasn't the best quality, but it would do.

"Kill them!" Kehran roared. "Kill them both!"

So much for foreplay.

The guards obeyed their orders perfectly and attacked us, which was to say they followed every rule in the book lacking any finesse, skill, or surprise element. Between the two of us, we killed six of them without breaking a sweat. Three of the remaining eight looked as if they were about to soil themselves and barely put up a fight. In all fairness, they put up something, but I could not call it a fight—a half-arsed attempt, yes, but nothing more. They lay dead at my feet within the space of two heartbeats.

There was something oddly satisfying about it all.

Three were left. Two had decided to go after Z'tala, who had sprinted past their defences as soon as she saw an opportunity. Behind me, Kehran was positively screeching with fury. The sound was remarkably delightful.

He was finally making more of a fool out of himself than he already was.

Saves me the trouble.

I grinned at the three guards. "Well? I don't have all day."

"You've got somewhere to be?" the bravest of them asked.

"Absolutely, but I won't be telling you, will I?"

For some reason, my voice sounded unlike my own—playful, but with a hint of cruelty I'd never noticed before. Having nothing left to lose, the three men attacked. Unlike their comrades, they were a little more skilled, and definitely more coordinated, but they, too, didn't last very long.

It was barely a challenge at all.

While wiping the blood from the sword on my sleeves, I strolled over to one of the spears and picked it up while in the background, Kehran was yelling for more guards. I tested its weight in my hand before letting it slide until the end was on the ground, slowly turning toward the balcony. With his hands on the railing, Kehran was watching me with his skin flushed, lips pulled back to show his teeth. I trailed the spear behind me, drawing a lazy pattern as I flicked it from left to right. The motion was altogether soothing. Nevertheless, nothing about this situation felt calm. I felt like one of the tigresses I'd fought, ready to pounce the moment my opponent—*my prey*—was weak.

The thought of the kill almost made my mouth water.

What?

"Where are the guards!" Kehran screamed, a discernible squeak in his voice.

I cocked my head to the side and stalked closer to the balcony, my eyes never leaving Kehran. The crowd had fallen silent, watching my progress in silent anticipation. I felt that if I strained to listen, I could hear the rapid beating of their hearts in their chests.

"What's wrong, *Akyn?*" I shouted, my voice steady and strong —*but somehow off*—and loud enough for him and those in the vicinity to hear. "Not the outcome you had hoped for?"

He straightened and lifted his chin, but I could tell from the way he kept hold of the railing that he was afraid.

Afraid of you, Resha, I remembered the sword saying.

I tilted my head—not for Kehran, but to listen to the footsteps in the tunnels. Guards, I assumed, trotting to the *herrât* as fast as they could. When I looked over my shoulder, two squads appeared, one from each side. Behind them, hidden in the tunnels, were the *herriatâre.* I couldn't see them from this distance, but I could sense them.

Somehow.

This would be interesting indeed.

With a smile, I turned my attention to the *Akyn.* "Tell your men to stand down, and I'll allow them to live."

Kehran's eyes bulged as if I'd just proposed him to die of his own accord.

Perhaps I did.

"Kill her!" Kehran screeched. "What are you waiting for? Kill her!"

To everyone's surprise, including mine, they did not. Two men, captains I assumed, detached themselves from the squad and marched in my direction. When they knelt behind me, helms in hand, heads bowed, Kehran staggered back, held up only by the chair behind him. The clatter of armour and weapons drew both our attention, and looking over my shoulder, I watched the *herriatâre* take up position next to the squads.

Z'tala was at the head of one of them.

Jaehyr on the other.

Stubborn mule!

But even as the thought passed my mind, I knew these men —and women—and their squads were with me. The *herriatâre* were with me. Although I had but few people at my back, they were fierce, and they had a cause worth fighting for, but if I wanted to succeed, I needed more of his people on my side, and

I didn't have a lot of time. If he still had the support of his nobility, death would be our kindest fate.

As much as I hated politics, I'd been preparing for this my entire life. Perhaps not for the Kyrinthan throne, but a throne was a throne regardless of its position in the world.

"Kehran Ihn Gahr." My voice rang clearly through the *herrât*. "We, the people, are discontented with your tyranny, your destructive rule of Akhyr, and the fear-mongering among your own people. We no longer accept you as our *Akyn*. Step down and you may live."

For the count of three heartbeats, the *herrât* remained completely silent, but then... The crowd erupted in shouts, all of which were lost in the cacophony of their own voices, but there was agreement in the form of jeers, outrage in the form of screams, compliance in the form of people chanting my name in unison. It felt as if my skin hummed at their approval, the hairs on my arms and the back of my neck standing on end as goosebumps slithered down my back. As a feeling of pride rose inside of me, I realised there was more—a kind of excitement that pooled deep inside my body, reminding me acutely of the first night I'd lain with Elay.

The feeling was as exhilarating as it was disturbing.

I rose my arms in the air for good measure, lifting the spear along with it. A deep sound vibrated through the *herrât* as the shouts of the common people turned more intense, until I turned to the *Akyn*, pulled back my arm, and threw the spear.

A deep silence descended over the crowd.

Kehran stared at the spear protruding from his chest, the blood trickling from the corners of his mouth dripping on his pristine golden attire. He looked at me, disbelief contorting his speckled features into a ghastly mask as he staggered back and fell in his chair.

I'd done it.

I killed the Akyn.

The shock didn't register as I thought it should. In fact, it didn't register at all. Intense relief flooded me, but as I turned around to the guards and the *herriatâre*, anger replaced it. They were surrounded by a large contingency of the army, weapons drawn.

"Put down your weapons, *Tarien*," a young man bearing a striking similarity to Elay said. "If you don't, my men will kill you."

The corners of my lips curled in a smile. "You are brave, little man, to challenge your *Akynai*."

"Kehran is dead. Elay isn't present at court. In his absence, *I* am the rightful *Akyn* of Kyrintha." The boy sounded entirely more dignified than his half-brother.

"And I would not disagree," I purred, stalking towards him, "were it not for one thing."

Jahleal—I remembered his name now—squared his shoulders and stared at me. "And what would that be?"

I made sure my voice was loud when I spoke. "I am Elay Ihn Gahr's wife and in his absence, I believe it falls unto me to rule."

CHAPTER 27

TALNOVAR

The entire ride back to the caravan, Rashiïd—Elay, I reminded myself—looked as if he'd rather murder me in my sleep. The feeling was entirely mutual. We'd spoken the entire night, or rather, he had, and I'd listened, asking the odd question here and there to piece together what had happened to Shalitha during her time in Zihrin and Kyrintha. I felt certain he had left out some details to the story—some things didn't quite add up—but it was probably for the best. After hearing she was a fighter in the *herrât*, I'd been ready to kill him with my bare hands. Although that feeling still hadn't quite passed, Elay was useful. In fact, he was the only one I knew who could get me close to her, so our arrangements at this point were mutually beneficial.

I made no promises for after I found her.

Despite my feelings towards Elay, I felt elated. After so long, I was finally getting somewhere, and it wouldn't be long before I'd see her.

Hold her again.

If her feelings for me hadn't changed, that was. For all I knew, she hated my guts, and I couldn't blame her. Not really. It had, after all, taken me an awfully long time to find her. It hadn't been months. It had been nigh unto three years now.

Three years.

Did she still have that spark in her eyes when she fought? That ready smile? Her quick wit? My body practically thrummed with anticipation at the thought of seeing her again. According to Elay, between dealing with his affairs on the slave market and travelling to Akhyr, we shouldn't be more than a moon, maybe a moon and a half. Compared to three years, it was nothing—for an Elven life, it was a mere blink of an eye— but to me, it felt like eternity. Yet the only way I would ever find her was by following Elay to wherever he needed to go.

My mood soured even further.

By the time we reached the caravan, night had already fallen, and most of the camp was fast asleep. As promised, Elay didn't have me locked up in a cage and instead invited me into his tent. I considered refusing but had no good excuse.

Nobody liked to sleep outside, especially not in the desert.

I settled cross-legged on one of the many cushions close to the small fire, my eyes following Elay around the tent as he bustled about taking off his weapons, his coat, and his shoes, making himself more comfortable—more at home. My chest tightened at the thought of home, so I inhaled deeply and exhaled to the count of ten. I had a home to return to—I just had to fight for it.

We must fight for it.

"Tea?" Elay asked, taking a seat opposite me. "Or perhaps a cup of *keffah*?"

"*Keffah?*"

He flashed me a wide smile. "*Keffah* it is."

Stunned by his assumption I'd want whatever he'd just offered, I watched as he gathered two cups, a small black pot— heavy, judging by the way his muscles strained as he carried it —several jars on a serving tray, and carried it back to the fire.

There was a mesmerizing tranquillity about him as he prepared the *keffah*, a ritualistic air reminiscent of *iñaeique* about him. I tilted my head, watching him as he gathered coals a little away from the fire to place the black pot on. He proceeded by pouring small, dark-brown coloured pellets from a jar into a mortar and grinding them. The meticulousness with which he was preparing this drink was at odds with the man I'd come to know—a man who let everything be done by servants.

"Here," Elay said, offering me the mortar and pestle. "If you could grind the *keffah* beans some more, I'd be grateful."

I complied without comment, inhaling the deep, bitter aroma as I ground them to a pulp. I was of two minds considering the scent. It wasn't bad, just incredibly strong.

"That looks fine." Elay was leaning over to have a look at it.

"Do you always do this for a cup of *keffah*?" I asked, handing him back the mortar and pestle.

He chuckled as he spooned the beans, or what was left of them, in the cups before pouring boiling water over them. Steam billowed over them, and as he handed one to me, I could smell the bitterness. It was different now, more earthy, and I was quite curious as to how it tasted.

"Normally, I have a jar of powdered beans with me," Elay said. "But you are a guest in my tent, and both Zihrin and Kyrinthan hospitality demands one treats one's guests with the utmost respect and uphold the rituals of one's ancestors."

"Sounds familiar," I murmured, "except in Ilvanna, the women uphold the rituals rather than the men."

Elay looked quietly amused as he made himself comfortable against a pile of pillows behind him. "She did not strike me as the ritualistic kind of person. The *Tarien*, I mean."

Every muscle in my body tensed. He meant well, talking about her, but I hadn't yet forgiven him for not telling me the truth about his acquaintance with Shalitha. Despite that, I smiled. "No, she wasn't. She's made it her life's objective to go up against all rules and every tradition she didn't like."

He snorted. "I've noticed. Doesn't like no for an answer either."

"I'm surprised she even knows the meaning of the word," I confessed. "The amount of time she's disregarded her mother's..." I fell silent at that and let out a heavy sigh, holding the cup a little tighter in my hands, as if it would give me the comfort I was seeking. Her mother was dead.

But at least you're granting the Tari her last wish.

The thought was only mildly comforting.

"She knows her mother has passed away," Elay said, looking at me over the rim of the cup. "I don't know how she found out, but she did."

I released my breath in one slow, long exhale and nodded quietly.

"She may not be the woman you remember," he continued. "She's gone through a lot."

"And you left her at the mercy of that monster," I grumbled, glaring at him. "You should've stayed to look after her."

"And if I had, you would likely have died on that beach," Elay retorted. "Do you believe in fate, *irtehn?* In destiny?"

I snorted, my anger deflating somewhat. "I didn't use to."

"Neither did I," Elay replied, sitting up. "But I don't believe it was luck Shalitha robbed me that day, nor do I believe it was luck my men found you half dead on that beach."

"She robbed you?" All anger left me instantly, amusement rising in its stead. "How clever."

Elay smirked, taking a sip of *keffah*. "She was quite the accomplished thief for someone who was raised in a palace."

"She has always been a quick study," I muttered into my cup, taking a very careful sip of the dark substance.

I wasn't sure what to make of it, so I took another sip followed by a proper gulp. Despite its bitterness, *keffah* tasted quite well. Elay watched me, eyes sparkling, although it could have been a trick of the firelight.

"All I was trying to say," he began carefully, gauging my reaction, "is that whatever you had together before she was taken away might be something different now. If your... scars... are any indication of what you have been through, *irtehn,* I doubt Shalitha is the only one who's changed."

I winced at his words and looked away. What happened to me wasn't open for discussion.

"Let's turn in for the night," Elay remarked, getting up to gather the cups and jars. "We'll be leaving before the break of dawn. Selling slaves is a nasty, time-consuming business."

"Then why do you do it?"

"You wouldn't understand."

He tossed me a blanket and pillow and left me to my own devices while he made himself comfortable on his own pallet. Not wanting to bother with pillows for a few hours, I made myself comfortable on the ground near the fire, my gaze drifting over to Elay's back. As much as I disliked the man, I couldn't entirely fault him for his ways.

We all had our demons.

I had no idea about his.

THE SLAVE MARKET was quite a sight to behold, awe-inspiring, and not in the good sense of the word. Everywhere I looked, people sat huddled together, stood fastened to posts, were kept in cages, or hung from chains as if they were nothing but cattle. Unlike Elay's slave camp, there were no tents, no protection from the elements, and it was showing. Burns and blisters adorned skin both light and dark, lips were cracked, and bodies sat shivering.

If I'd thought Elay's slaves had looked bad, it was nothing on the ones here.

My emotions were in turmoil as I looked from left to right, my gut wrenching at the awful conditions these people were forced to live in. In Ilvanna, slavery was against the law, the penalty for doing so death if found guilty. Here, it seemed like a way of life and no discrimination was made. Elay had allowed me to look around 'to breathe in some culture' while he set up what few slaves he had brought.

If this was culture, I wanted no part of it.

Up ahead, a crowd of people had gathered around a podium on which stood a tall, well-dressed man. From this distance, he looked an awful lot like Elay, and I grimaced at the thought of him being up there—as if owning slaves wasn't enough, he had to openly sell them like this, too? Upon closer inspection, however, I realised it wasn't Elay. While the man looked as smooth as him, there was a hardness about his face that set him apart. At first, I thought it was just the look in his eyes until I noticed the scar pulling down the right side of his face.

He'd sure gotten on the wrong side of someone.

Standing off to the side, my arms crossed in front of me, I regarded the assembly and their host with ill-concealed disdain. The men were dressed in the gaudiest attires, the one outdoing the other just by the sheer size of his hat, and their women were no better. Dressed in opulent silks in ostentatious colours, they reminded me of a pride of peacocks on their most arrogant behaviour.

Like Ilvanna's courtiers.

It was a small relief to see courtiers were the same everywhere.

"*Eshen, Shena,*" the man on the podium began with a lisp on the 'sh'. "It is wonderful to see you on this very fine day. As you may have seen, we've got sensational fresh products for you today ranging in a variety of skills. From cleaning to guarding to looking after your... well-being." Men smiled a tad too lewdly at these words, the women let out little indignant gasps. "We have it all for you, and some of them look mighty fine, if I do say so myself. The first auction will begin momentarily."

The temperature suddenly seemed to drop, and tremors ran through my body as memories and emotions triggered by the man's words and the women's gasps and giggles assaulted me. I gritted my teeth at the memory of hands exploring my chest, my body, everywhere. I focused on the ground beneath my feet, on breathing in to the count of ten and letting go, on the words Soren had repeated to me night after night after they'd brought me to *Denahryn*.

Azra has no hold over you. Let her go.

As hard as it was, I managed to get through it even though the experience left me gasping for air. People were watching me, but the scowl on my face deterred them from further inquiry, and they turned their gaze away fast. I hadn't had one of these episodes in quite some time, probably owing to the fact I'd been delirious and dying, and before that, preoccupied with surviving, but it told me two things. I was sane and healthy and at ease. On guard, absolutely, but at ease.

I felt safe.

Granted, nothing about these surroundings was secure, but I had a sword on my back, armour on my chest, braces on my arms, and grieves on my legs. I was protected, and I could finally protect myself again. I might not have been at full health yet, but I hadn't felt this good—this strong—in a very long time.

One day, I will come to collect this debt.

The words came to me in a whisper, or was it just another memory? The voice sounded familiar, but I couldn't for the life of me remember who it belonged to.

It didn't matter.

Not now.

I returned my focus to the podium where five men and

women were cowering before the assembly. Although they'd been dressed in plain, proper clothes, it was clear they were malnourished. Shoulders and elbows stuck out sharply from sleeves, and dresses and shirts hung too wide around their frames. I wanted nothing more than to end this travesty, but I knew I couldn't. All I could hope for was that these people were bought by masters with a heart.

Reality wouldn't be so kind.

I watched as the assembly purchased one slave after the other. Some of them—those who looked too sick—were returned to their respective owners. I couldn't help but wonder what would happen to them and resolved to ask Elay later.

I wasn't convinced I wanted to know the answer.

A young woman was escorted onto the stage by two bulky men. As if a girl her size could do any harm. Despite myself, I smiled. I should know better than to estimate someone's lethality by their height, or gender for that matter. After all, my father before me and then I had trained a small ball of fury into a tall, deadly warrior.

I smirked.

I wiped the smirk off my face as fast as it had appeared. There, on stage, the less-than-savoury host grabbed hold of the woman and exposed her chest for the assembly to see. He squeezed her for good measure. My blood boiled inside my veins, and I wanted nothing more than to smash the man's head like an overripe melon.

Ai Sela'àn, Tal. *Ai Sela'àn.*

Balling my hands at my side, I forced myself to stay where I was. I should walk away, should find Elay and ask him for directions to Akhyr. No, I should punch him and *then* ask for directions. Every single one of these people, buyers and sellers, didn't deserve the air they were breathing, Elay among them. I didn't care he had saved Shalitha if he brought other people's life's in danger every single day.

The young woman's yelp brought my attention back to the stage.

Keeping her arms pinned between him and her, the host endeavoured to hike up her skirt to show the rest of her to the prospective buyers. My gaze flicked to the men there—all eyes were fixed on her. When the host's hand slid between her legs to expose her, I started forward.

"Get your filthy hands off of her," I snarled, jumping up on the stage without too much effort. "Filthy son of a *hehzèh.*"

People gasped. Men swore aloud. From the corner of my eyes, I saw the two bulky guards making their way back to the podium. The women giggled and gasped, whispering to each other behind their hands or fans. I scowled down at them, but it only made it worse.

"I'll buy him for ten gold pieces!" a woman called, the tone of her voice high and excited.

"Twenty!" another added.

Nohro ahrae.

I turned my focus to the host. "Let her go, or I swear to the Gods this will end in a bloodbath."

"You have balls," the host said, dropping the young woman's skirts but not letting her go. "I'll give you that, but there's no way you'll beat my men and live."

I felt my lips quirk up in a crooked smile. "You want to bet on that? I could use the money, and you seem to have enough of it."

"How about we bet on her life," the host said, stroking her cheek.

She tried to pull away, a disgusted look on her face, but he was stronger than her. Instead, he pulled her closer, allowing his hands to wander.

"Keep that up," I growled, "and you'll never touch a woman again."

"You've got a lot of talk, *eshen*," the host purred, "but that's all there is."

His eyes flickered to something behind me, and I grinned. Without waiting, I stepped back, swinging my elbow back in the same motion. A man grunted and staggered back. I spun around and clipped him underneath his jaw. He blinked, stumbled back, and fell as his eyes rolled back.

One down.

"Fifty gold!" a woman said, her voice bordering on hysteria.

I grunted in disgust and prepared myself for the second guard, who came lumbering up the platform holding a scimitar. As my hand went up for my own sword, a voice called out over the assembly.

"Stop!"

Looking up, I found Elay passing through the crowd which skittered to the side as if afraid to be touched by him. I dropped my hands alongside my body, glowering as he made his way to the platform.

"What's going on here?" he asked, his gaze wandering from the unconscious guard, to me, and to the host.

The host, who was still holding the young woman quite firmly, glared at me before turning to Elay with an elegant flourish of a bow.

Who is he?

"This man is ruining my auction, *Akynshan*," the host said.

Prince? Elay is a prince?

"He came charging up my platform without rhyme or reason. Scared my customers, he did."

I snorted at that. "Scared them? They were trying to buy me. I would hardly call that scared."

Elay glared at me. I returned a scowl but looked away quickly, deciding it wasn't in my best interest to get into a fight with the *Akynshan* in a place like this. I was sure we would get to that later.

"He wanted me to let go of *my* property." The host's voice rose in pitch. "*My* property, *Akynshan*, and he didn't offer to pay for it either."

Elay's lips quirked up in an easy smile. "I see."

I didn't like the smug look on his face. Instead of asking me my version of the story, he turned to have a look at the young woman before turning to the host.

"Five gold," he said.

"Five?" the host sounded indignant. "She's worth at least eight."

Elay scoffed. "Hardly. She's stunning, I'll give you that, but she's underfed and damaged. I'm not paying that much for damaged goods."

"Then someone else will," the host remarked.

Elay merely arched an eyebrow. "I could let him have his way. Makes for a nice bet. Easy money too. I wouldn't bet on your mortality rate, however. He's got quite the score."

The host's eyes narrowed as he looked at me. "Doesn't look much like a *herriatâre* to me."

"Trust me," Elay purred. "He is one and better. He only needs a reason to fight and from the looks of him, he has. Three gold, take it or leave it, it's the most generous offer you will receive for her."

The host looked from me to Elay, back to me and then to Elay, who was inspecting his fingernails as if this conversation was boring him. I narrowed my eyes at both, clenching my jaw to keep myself from hitting either of them over the head.

What is he playing at?

"Fine," the host spat at him. "Three gold, and you take this *terkan* away."

Elay handed him the gold, invited the young woman to come with him, and stepped down from the platform. Whispers fell silent the moment he passed but started as soon as I came within distance. My skin crawled at the suggestions of what the women would do with me if they could have bought me—the men discussed how to fast break my spirit.

I quickly caught up with them.

"Why did you buy her?" I asked.

Elay looked at me, amused. "Oh, I didn't, Talnovar. You did. Congratulations on owning your very first slave."

CHAPTER 28

HAERLYON

"*A*re you going to keep lying there feeling sorry for yourself, or are you going to open those pretty eyes and get a grip?"

"Eamryel?" I cracked one eye open.

Eamryel sat on his haunches next to me, a bow resting on his thighs, a wicked smile playing on his lips. I blinked and brought a hand to my face. To my horror, it didn't cooperate. When I tried to sit up, Eamryel pushed me back.

"Yeah, let's not go too fast, *mahnèh*. You got roughed up quite a bit."

"The arrows," I murmured. "It was you."

"And here I thought you were the biggest *khirr* in the realm," Eamryel scoffed. "You should've heeded the warning."

"Warning?"

He rolled his eyes, clenching his fist as if keeping himself from slapping me. "I told you not to trust anyone, didn't I?"

A low growl escaped my lips. "After you nearly kicked me to death."

"You told me to make it look believable."

I glowered at him. He smirked and rose to his feet.

"Keep still," he said. "I'd best finish your cot if I want to get you anywhere."

"I can ride," I said, pushing myself up.

As I did, a fierce pain exploded in my arm, my vision blurred, and the world tilted as I fell sideways. Eamryel caught me barely in time.

"You can't ride, Haer," he muttered. "*Grissin* destroyed your lower arm. If I don't get you to *Denahryn* fast..."

He shook his head and lowered me to the ground. "Lie still," he ordered gruffly as he turned away. I moved my head to follow him with my eyes and only then noticed the cloak covering me. I brought my good hand to my bad arm, and as I noticed the tremors running through it, questioned the sanity of wanting to feel the injury. Eamryel had said it was destroyed, and it hurt like a *hehzèh*.

That was all I should want to know.

Satisfying my curiosity had always gotten me in more trouble than I bargained for, so I rested my good hand on my lower arm. My stomach churned at what I felt. Dizziness rose to my head, and I had to take a few good gulps of air to keep fainting at bay.

"How did you know?" My voice was uncharacteristically shaky.

"You know how Azra likes to gloat when she believes she's winning," Eamryel replied, his voice coming from not too far off. "She told me a lot of things while she kept me in that dungeon, much more than anyone should ever be privy of."

A thought struck me. "Did you ever get the feeling something was... off... about her?"

"No more than usual," he replied. "She's gone full-on *qisera*. Her mental state is..."

"Fragile," I added. "More so now that she's pregnant."

"She must be close to giving birth."

"Too close," I muttered.

Mehrean had planned to be there. I had planned to be there. Now all we had was Kalyani to rely on. I prayed to the Gods and Goddesses she could get it done, especially after losing her own children.

What if she feels sorry for Azra?

The thought was disconcerting.

"I need to get back to the palace," I said, pushing myself up with my good arm.

I nearly passed out again from the pain flaring through my body, but somehow, I managed to keep it together. By the time I got to my feet, perspiration plastered my hair to my face, the world swayed and dipped, and my legs felt as if the bones had been taken out.

"Why are you in a hurry to return to that *hehzèh?*" Eamryel snapped, wrapping an arm around my waist to support me.

My heart fluttered at his nearness. I squelched it.

"Because," I said in between gasps. "Kalyani... needs... my help. We... need... to know."

"All very heroic." Eamryel helped me sit down. "And none of which you can do right now. I need to get you to Soren, Haer, if you want to use that arm ever again."

"Soren can't save this."

Eamryel smirked. "You'd be surprised. Come."

Somewhere between him telling me to lie still and my getting to my feet, he'd managed to build a cot. Lying down on it was pure agony. Eamryel had been right, I could not have ridden a horse, no matter how skilled a rider I was.

"If at any point we need to stop, you tell me," Eamryel said, tucking a blanket around me.

"What if I pass out and I can't?"

"We'll be at *Denahryn* all the quicker."

"*Grissin,*" I muttered.

He laughed and mounted his horse. This was going to be a long journey indeed.

WHEN WE ARRIVED AT *DENAHRYN*, I felt more dead than alive. The first two days I'd managed to keep up with the sun's progress in the sky. By the second day, night and day had woven into a single moment. After the third, I could no longer tell the days apart. I barely remembered anything from the journey aside from a few occasions where I'd woken to a cold touch to my forehead or cheeks. There were moments I could have sworn Tiroy was there, but then his face turned into Eamryel's, and I knew I had to be running a fever.

"What happened?" a familiar voice broke through the fog in my brain.

Soren.

"Ambush," Eamryel said. "His men were killed. Like a *khirr*, he chased the attacker through the dark forest, ending up alone and in the middle of now—"

"Not a full account." Soren sounded annoyed. "To his lower arm."

"Oh. Mace. Big fellow."

"Can you heal it?" a third voice asked.

This one, too, sounded familiar, but it took me a long time to remember who it belonged to. My mind drifted to the past as the voices above me swam in and out of focus. I was back at the training fields of Ilvanna with Evan, Talnovar, and Shal. We were going through the motions of a particularly difficult defence tactic and none of us seemed to get it right, not even Talnovar who usually understood attack and defence moves within a few tries. Shal looked positively annoyed—Cerindil was chuckling.

Cerindil, he's here.

"Haer?" Soren asked. "Are you with me?"

"In spirit," I murmured, opening one eye.

Soren cracked a wry smile. "I see you haven't lost your sense of humour."

"Nor you your temper."

He snorted and shook his head. "Not yet, but I'm close."

"That'd be the day," I mumbled, forcing myself to get the words out.

"I'm going to have to sedate you," Soren said as he placed something over my mouth and nose. "I promise you won't fe..."

I drifted off again, the voice flowing into nonsensical noise overhead. A welcoming warmth spread through me, as if I'd just stepped inside a heated cabin after having been outside in the snow for most of the day. It was a blissful relief.

"Haer!" Eamryel's voice snapped me back.

"What?" I grumbled, opening my eyes.

"No sleeping on the job, *mahnèh*," Eamryel said, a smirk on his lips. "If the *Tari* catches you..."

I sat up with a start, but a hand on my chest stopped me halfway.

"Just kidding," Eamryel murmured, his voice close—too close. "Lie down, you need to rest."

The pain was far less than I imagined and in a different place, too. I wanted to look, but it felt too heavy to move. Although I wasn't sure what, I instinctively knew something was wrong.

"Where's Soren?" I asked.

"Cleaning up," Eamryel said, his voice a tad too strained, his face a few shades too pale.

"What's wrong?"

Cerindil stepped into view, his expression more schooled but no less white than Eamryel's. Both looked like they'd seen a ghost.

"Don't be frightened," Cerindil said, clenching and unclenching his fist. "But... eh—" He rubbed the back of his neck, looking quite uncomfortable. "Soren couldn't save your arm."

I blinked at him.

"Not fully," he hastened to add. "Just... from the elbow down."

That explains why he's cleaning up.

"All right." I nodded, more to assure myself than anything else. "Very well. All right."

With help from Eamryel and Cerindil, I was able to sit up, propped up by one too many pillows. My right arm, although covered with bandages, looked normal. As I lifted my left arm, still numb from what Soren had done, my gaze settled on the stump at my elbow. I knew I should feel—something. Not pain, perhaps, but... something—anything.

I felt nothing.

"It's normal," Soren observed from my side, looking and sounding exhausted.

"What is?" My voice was flat, like my emotions.

"Not feeling anything," he replied, arching his brow. "Most people respond to an amputated limb that way. It's perfectly normal. At some point though, realisation will set in, and that's when it's going to be the hardest."

"Hardest how?"

"Acceptance."

He didn't need to explain that. After almost three years, I still had a hard time accepting Tiroy was dead. After more than a year, I still hadn't quite come to terms with the fact Mother was dead. Neither of them was coming back, and there was nothing I could change about it.

"You will have to get used to doing things right-handed." Soren looked as if it were his fault he'd had to amputate my arm.

"Time for a new boyfriend, I'd say."

Cerindil snorted and shook his head, Eamryel stared at me, blinking like an owl, but Soren looked as unperturbed as ever.

"What?" I shrugged, wincing at the motion. "You're not the only one who gets to crack jokes in dire situations."

At that, Soren let out a huff and rose to his feet. "You, *Ohzheràn*"—Cerindil winced at these words— "need to rest. I'll be around if you need me, but I suggest you get some sleep before anything else. Your body needs to recover from the journey *and* the injury."

"Doesn't sound like a bad idea," I murmured, feeling as if fatigue set in only after Soren had mentioned it.

Cerindil and Soren walked away while Eamryel helped me lay down, taking away two pillows from behind my back so I'd be more comfortable. He didn't speak—he didn't even meet my eyes. As he made to leave, I made to grab his wrist, only to realise I'd never grab anything with that hand again. Even so, Eamryel stopped, turning to me with resignation on his face.

"Thank you," I whispered. "I'd be dead without you."

He still refused to look at me when he spoke in a nasty tone of voice. "I don't like being indebted to anyone. The debt between us is fulfilled."

His words hurt more than I cared to admit out loud. "What do you mean, debt?"

Eamryel lifted his gaze, lips pressed tightly together. "You saved my life. I saved yours. There's nothing between us now."

Before I could respond, he stalked out of the room.

That was odd.

"He seemed genuinely worried earlier," Soren remarked. He'd returned. "Kept babbling about how bad it looked, apologising there hadn't been more he could have done."

I snorted. "He doesn't seem the apologising kind of person."

"Indeed." Soren offered me a bemused smile and held out a cup. "Drink, it'll help keep the worst of the pain at bay and allow for some proper rest. We'll talk in a few days when you feel a bit more like yourself."

"That'll be a long wait, *mahnèh*," I said with a heavy sigh. "I've not felt like myself since that day."

"I know..." He looked as if he was about to say more. Instead, he rose to his feet, wished me a good night, and moved out of view.

The concoction he'd given me tasted bitter, but it knocked me out as soon as I'd placed the cup on the bedside cabinet.

AFTER SEVERAL DAYS, once Soren believed I had rested enough, he allowed me to stroll through the garden adjacent to the healer's building. On the opposite side, the charred remains of another building stood in stark contrast to its surroundings. Vines wrapped around half-burnt poles, elegant blue-green foliage dotted with yellow, purple and red spread out over the ground like a carpet to soften the blow as to what had happened there. I wondered momentarily if *Hanyarah* would look the same.

"It's good to see you up," Cerindil said from behind me.

I turned and inclined my head. "*Ohzheràn* Imradien."

"I believe I no longer hold that title."

Although he was smiling, it didn't take away the sadness in his eyes. Now that he was gone, it struck me how much Talnovar looked like his father.

"The title is an atrocity these days," I replied. "People pronounce it as if it leaves a bad taste in their mouth, and the army is a far cry from what you've trained."

Cerindil exhaled slowly, shaking his head. "I'm afraid the royal line is considered an atrocity these days."

I winced at his words despite them being the truth. Between Azra and myself, we had ensured the *an Ilvan* line was hated—feared even. If Shalitha ever returned, she'd have a hard time convincing people not all of us were rotten to the core. I brought up my hand to run it through my hair, realising too late there was none to do that with. With an elongated sigh, I dropped my arm and shook my head.

"I've made a mess of things."

Cerindil arched a brow. "What makes you say that?"

"The plan was to have Azra trust me implicitly." I shook my head. "She tried to have me killed, *Serea*."

To my surprise, Cerindil was grinning. "Good. We can use that to our advantage."

CHAPTER 29

SHALITHA

*E*ver the paragon of patience, it was surprising to watch Z'tala pacing up and down the chamber, unrolling her fingers from a fist one by one as if she were counting. A nervous habit from the looks of it. Jaehyr had positioned himself next to the door, hands clasped together in front of him at the wrist. As for myself, I had taken up residence on one of the loungers, revelling in the luxury of the soft seat beneath me.

It had been a while.

"So." Z'tala looked at me with a frown. "You cannot actually prove you and Elay are married?"

I shrugged. "No. Not without him here."

She pinched the bridge of her nose and closed her eyes, shaking her head as if denying to herself any of this was happening.

"If you cannot prove it," Z'tala continued. "Jahleal has a rightful claim to the throne."

"I'm well aware of that fact," I retorted, swinging my legs over the side and pushing myself to my feet. "And if he does, I'll simply challenge him to a fight. Winner takes it all."

Both Z'tala and Jaehyr stared at me in horror.

"You would kill Elay's brother?" Z'tala asked in shock.

"I already did, didn't I?" I replied with a shrug, moving through the room to find something edible. I was starving. "Besides, I didn't say I'd kill him. I said winner takes it all."

"And how do you decide who wins?" Jaehyr asked.

"Whoever draws first blood." I grabbed a piece of fruit from a bowl and took a bite.

An intense sweetness overwhelmed my palate, and I couldn't help but moan at the deliciousness of the fruit. Juice trickled down my chin as I took another bite, and while wiping it away, I turned to Z'tala. "Jahleal will be no match for me," I said, dismissing him with a wave of my hand. "First blood will be easy, and then all we have to do is wait for Elay."

"All we have to do." Z'tala snorted, narrowing her eyes at me.

I could have sworn there was a warning in there. I grinned at her and returned to the lounger, dropping myself into it and sitting back relaxed. Jaehyr was watching me curiously but didn't say a word. Z'tala let out a heavy sigh and sat down in a wooden chair, leaning her elbows on her knees as she made a steeple of her fingers, contemplating the outrageously decorated tiles on the floor as if they held any answers.

"I suppose," she said, carefully choosing her words. "There are worse ways to go about it, but you have to make sure the people like you, *k'lele,* or you will end up like Kehran."

I grimaced. "I'm a thousand times better than that *khirr* by default. You've seen how they respond to me in the *herrât.*"

"Your arrogance will be your downfall," Z'tala said in warning. "Yes, people like you... as entertainment. As *Akynai,* it remains to be seen."

"That's a form of entertainment too, is it not? At least, that's how I perceived it at court in Ilvanna. It's nothing but a game."

"In any regard." Z'tala shot me a look. "We must wait for Jahlael to summon us."

"Why? Summon him. Jaehyr, fetch the princeling for me, please."

Jaehyr inclined his head and left the room.

"Are you mad?" Z'tala hissed, pushing herself off the chair so fast it toppled over. "We do not have the upper hand."

"You said yourself it could work." I tossed the remains of the fruit in a vase behind me and made myself comfortable. "Besides, it's good to put some pressure on the enemy while you can; makes them nervous."

"This is not a battle, *k'lele.*" Z'tala sounded desperate.

What is she so afraid of?

"Of course, it is. It's just a battle of wits, that's all."

She made a choked sound in her throat and walked to the archway leading to the garden, her back towards me. Judging by the rapid rise and fall of her shoulders, I figured she was fighting to regain her composure. It was quite amusing to get under her skin. Just by looking at her facial expressions I knew she felt like she wasn't getting through to me.

She couldn't be farther from the truth.

I had listened, and I'd come to my own conclusions. Unless Elay would magically appear out of thin air, my chances of proving our marriage was fairly non-existent. Jahlael was looking to prove himself, throwing in his weight and bravery to see how far it would get him, but he was young and inexperienced. As the youngest child, he wouldn't have been raised to be *Akyn*—a consultant perhaps, but no more. Like Evanyan and Haerlyon, he'd have a position in the army, but while his fighting skills might therefore be noteworthy, his political game might be less strong. I didn't doubt for a minute he would have advisers at his side.

It would be a challenge.

I loved challenges.

"*Irìn* Jahlael, *Tari,*" Jaehyr said from the archway he'd disappeared through earlier, "and his entourage."

I rose to my feet.

Jahlael's eyes swept over me as he entered the room with a flourish, lips slightly parted, head tilted. I supposed I looked quite the picture in my warrior regalia, coated in blood and whatnot. I flashed him a smile and inclined my head to acknowledge his presence.

It was the least I could do.

"Have you reconsidered your claim?" Jahlael asked almost curiously.

"Have you?"

"Unless you can prove you're my brother's wife, and I sincerely doubt that claim, as do my advisors, this—whatever this is—is over."

I arched a brow, folding my arms in front of me. "From the way I see it, you have two choices. Either you accept the fact I have told no lies and Elay's my husband or we settle this in a fight and the winner takes it all."

There was a gleam in Jahlael's eyes at the mention of a fight, a childlike exuberance I'd seen many times before in boys who felt the need to prove themselves. He opened his mouth to respond when a commotion at the archway caught our attention. Jahlael spun on his heels. My brows shot up in surprise.

"You?" Jahlael asked, incredulity in his voice. "What are you doing here?"

"I brought him here, brother," Naïda said, appearing around the corner.

"Whatever for?"

A smile ghosted across her lips as she stepped forward, motioning for R'tayan to follow her as she sashayed over to us. Jaehyr followed her every move closely.

"R'tayan?" Naïda held up her hand.

R'tayan handed her a scroll and bowed deeply, but not before catching my eyes and smiling, inclining his head ever so slightly. I merely stared at him.

"I hold here the marriage certificate of Elay è Rehmàh, better known as Elay Ihn Gahr, *Akynshan* of Kyrintha, husband to Shalitha an Ilvan, *Tarien* of Ilvanna," Naïda said, rolling it open and turning to the room. "You may have heard of her demise at sea, but one needs only look at her to know it to be her. By marriage, she's *Akynai*—Queen—of Kyrintha."

Jahlael opened his mouth, I assumed to say something, but nothing came out. He rather looked like a fish out of water and quite un-*Akyn*-like. Naïda glanced at me before turning to her brother.

"Elay will return," she said for our ears alone. "And when he does, he will be *Akyn*. You do not want this burden, Jahla. Let it go."

Jahlael squared his shoulders, then sighed and exhaled with a loud puff. "Fine," he muttered and turned to me, a wicked grin spreading across his lips. "Does the offer for the fight still stand?"

"Of course," I said at the same time as Z'tala, Naïda and Jaehyr yelled 'No'.

I smirked and whispered. "I'll let you know when."

Without pretending he was still anything more than a boy, Jahlael left the room to do the Gods know what, leaving his entourage staring after him, flabbergasted.

"Well, then." I clapped my hands together. "That's settled."

I HAD NOT BEEN PREPARED for the incredible tediousness of becoming *Akynai*. First, the council had come together to pore over the marriage certificate until every letter was properly scrutinised, labelled and agreed upon its authenticity. Next, a new document had to be drawn up stating I was to be *Akynai* until such time as Elay returned and assumed the mantle of

Akyn. After that, every council member signed the *nohro* paper, leaving me to sign last.

By that time, I was at my wit's end.

I'd never been one for politics, let alone the incessant discussions about—nothing.

"Are we done?" I asked after I signed the document. "I'd really like a bath now."

Not only did I smell as if I'd fought a pack of animals, I probably looked like one, too. I disgusted myself.

"And I will need some proper clothes," I added for good measure. "Silks. Satins. Anything that doesn't show more than I care for."

The council members inclined their heads and servants were sent off scurrying. I sighed in relief and turned away from the table, catching Z'tala's scrutinising gaze. I flashed her a mischievous grin. As soon as I left the room, Jaehyr fell in step behind me.

They'd become my guards.

No idea when that had happened.

"Where are the royal baths?" I demanded from a passing servant.

"Do you not remember?" Z'tala asked curiously.

"Bad sense of direction."

The look on her face told me she didn't quite believe me, but she didn't pursue the issue either. For now. Z'tala certainly had a mind of her own, and she wasn't afraid to speak it. Jaehyr, on the other hand, seemed to know when to stay quiet.

I liked him better for it.

The servant boy was still bowing deeply and awaiting my attention in silence. At least here they knew how to address their royalty properly. Ilvanna's courtiers could learn a thing or two. I snapped my fingers to get the boy's attention.

"Show us the way."

He scurried out in front of us and kept glancing over his

shoulder to make sure we were following. My pace was brisk, the thought of a proper bath adding a spring to my step. By Esah, even the thought of wearing a dress excited me, if only because it would be a good deal better than the blood- and sweat-stained clothing I'd been wearing for the past who knew how long.

A nice dive would be perfect.

THE BATHHOUSE WAS devoid of people when we arrived. I assumed it had been cleared out before my arrival.

Good.

They knew their place.

While Z'tala and Jaehyr checked the perimeter, making sure it really was completely empty, I struggled out of my armour. The leather was stiff with dried up blood, and my fingers were no longer nimble enough to undo the clasps easily.

"Let me help," Z'tala said from the doorway, her voice surprisingly gentle. I'd half expected a chewing out from her the moment we were alone.

Not that I would stand for it, but still.

With a heavy sigh, I relented and turned my side to her so she could undo the clasps. Even she had trouble getting them undone, so by the time she succeeded, it was a great relief to finally take off the thick leather garment.

It was beyond salvation.

"*Akynai,*" Z'tala began and frowned. "*Tari...* What will you do about the *herriatâre?*"

I looked at her as I pulled the shirt over my head. "I haven't considered that yet. Guess it depends on why they were there in the first place."

She narrowed her eyes. "You promised them freedom."

"Huh," I scoffed as I sidestepped her. "Can't remember that I did."

I left for the communal area without looking back, not feeling like getting into a discussion over what to do with a bunch of slaves. There would be time enough to deal with that, and that time wasn't now.

After the deafening noise in the *herrât* for the past fortnight and more, the silence was a blissful reprieve. A loud hiss escaped my lips as I lowered myself into one of the hot baths. All the cuts and injuries responded by pulsing, stabbing, and flaring, turning into a cacophony of pain that was hard to ignore. I assumed it was because the injuries might be getting properly cleaned for the first time since I'd sustained them, and after a while, the stabbing and flaring abated, leaving only a throbbing sensation where I'd been stitched or bruised.

Marks worthy of a warrior.

My thoughts returned to the battle with the guards. With their sheer size, they should have been able to overcome us without too much trouble, but what they had lacked in enthusiasm, the *herriatâre* had more than made up for, and it had made for a wonderful sight to behold. The sound of their battle cries had been music to my ears.

Z'tala's question came to mind.

If I were fair, I'd award them their freedom, although I could not remember promising it. Even so, their role had been vital in securing the throne. I might have managed against those guards —barely, but I might have—but I would not have been able to go after Kehran.

What happened to his body?

I shrugged at the idea and hoisted myself out of the water. Kehran was dead, a state of being he should have been in a long time ago, and I wasn't going to waste any more thoughts on him, although I did briefly wonder if I had to have a funeral arranged.

Does he even deserve one?

Deciding these were worries for later, I made my way to one of the bigger baths, quickened my step, and dove into it. Water rushed past me as I swam underwater. My lungs ached for air, but if I pushed just a little more, I'd be on the other side. As I glided through the water, all worries slid away from me as if they'd just been grease on my skin.

As I reached the edge of the pool, I slowly emerged, inhaling deeply.

Next thing I knew, the sharp blade of a dagger pressed against my throat.

"Who *are* you?" Z'tala hissed in my ear.

CHAPTER 30

TALNOVAR

*A*fter five days of our uncomfortable journey, Elay called for a halt. For the past half a day, he'd been conversing with Tariq while pointing in one direction and staring off into the other as if there was something to be seen. To me, everywhere I looked was the same—an endless sandbox without anywhere to make a campfire that wouldn't be seen for miles around. It was an open invitation for any miscreant out there.

Since leaving Portasâhn, Elay had not been very specific about how long the journey would take. Anywhere between a moon and a moon and a half, he'd said, depending on the weather and circumstances he hadn't cared to define.

Stop whining, Imradien. You've served on less information than this.

With a heavy sigh, I set to pitching the tent as Nazeem had instructed, diverting my thoughts from the downward spiral they tended to follow these days. While I may have been saved from my plight as a slave, I wasn't exactly free either.

"Oi!" Nazeem yelled. "Keep that pole straight!"

I kicked the lower part of the pole towards the middle while keeping the upper part in place. With the canvas tight around it, it took a few proper kicks to get the pole sorted. A muttered grunt from outside told me it was enough. Once everything was in place, I let go of the pole and ducked out of the tent, squinting against the sudden bright light.

"C'mon, pretty boy." Nazeem grinned and clapped me on the back. "Three more tents."

"Why are we stopping here, of all places?" I asked while hoisting a second tent from the cart. "Surely there are better places to camp?"

Nazeem snorted. "Have you looked around? This is as good a place as any to sit out the storm."

"What storm?"

He arched a brow at me, eyes crinkling at the corners. "You have a lot to learn about dessert life, *irtehn*. Why do you think Elay's been on edge the past two days, checking charts, the wind, the sun... everything?"

"Because he's got an unhealthy obsession with the weather?" I offered, dumping the tent in front of Nazeem's feet. "Truth be told, I'd been wondering. He does seem awfully out of sorts."

He let out a non-committal grunt as he began to unfold the canvas. "Desert storms are lethal if they catch you unprepared, but if you are an experienced traveller like Elay and Tariq, you might be able to survive."

"Loads of ifs and maybes," I murmured, lifting the tent pole. "But it doesn't sound unlike snowstorms in the mountains. If you're caught unawares, you better hope you find a place to hide or you'll freeze to death in no time."

"Snow?"

My lips quirked up. "It's like sand, but white, less scratchy when it's in your clothes, and freezing-your-balls-off cold."

Nazeem made a choking sound at that. I looked up sharply to see if he was okay, only to find out he was laughing. With a shake of my head and a chuckle, I crawled underneath the canvas, fixed the pole to the top and lifted it upright. Outside,

Nazeem set to fixing the pegs and guy-lines and tested how much they could handle by pushing and pulling until he was satisfied the tent was going nowhere.

We repeated the same process for the other two tents.

By the time we finished, Inenn and Qiras, two other men Elay had brought along, had built us a firepit and gotten a fire going. I might have scoffed at the idea of bringing a cart loaded with various supplies when we left Portasâhn, but it all started to make sense. Unlike in a forest, there was precious little firewood to be found in a dessert, and rivers were far and few between. The last body of water I'd laid eyes on was Portasâhn's harbour on the morning of our departure.

"Would you like some tea, *Masran?*" Lujaeyn asked.

I winced. Even after five days of her asking me this question and many others besides, I still hadn't gotten used to her presence. Whenever I asked Elay why he'd bought her, he smiled in that mysterious way of his that could mean anything. It only served to add to my growing list of things I was frustrated about, but it wasn't her fault, so I made sure not to lash out at her.

"That would be welcome," I replied, rubbing the back of my neck without looking at her.

Lujaeyn smiled at me and set about making tea. Qiras was watching her like a hawk would its prey. Noticing my watching him, he flashed me a grin and returned his attention to the conversation with Inenn. I risked a glance at Nazeem, but his attention was on Tariq and Elay conversing in the distance.

After I sat down, I kept my attention inconspicuously on Lujaeyn as she prepared the tea above the campfire. The way she went about it reminded me of how Elay had made the *keffah* and the tea ritual we had at home. A soft chuckle escaped my lips as I remembered Shal's downright loathing whenever her Mother had demanded she do it.

She may not have liked it, but she had been good at it.

The first difference between our ritual and the one Lujaeyn was performing was the amount of spices used. I counted at least four of them, and the combination smelled divine. The second difference lay in the pouring of the tea. In our ceremony, the focus remained on the pouring. Although I'd never been taught how to do it—it was a woman's ceremony after all—I'd seen and heard Mother teach Varayna, and she'd always been adamant about the proper way of holding the teapot, the hands, the wrists.

Truth be told, I'd always thought it sounded exhausting.

Lujaeyn poured the tea with less flourish, but the details were in how she handed me the cup. Rather than doing just that, she settled on her knees in front of me before raising the cup in her hands and offering it to me, all the while without even looking at me.

I took the cup with a smile. "Thank you."

She risked a glance up, and as she did, I could see a spark of hope igniting in her eyes.

Hope for what?

"Where's our tea, *amisha?*" Qiras asked, stressing the word *amisha* a bit too much to my liking.

Grissin.

Lujaeyn glanced at me, insecurity masking the hope I'd seen before. I inclined my head with a smile.

"It's fine, *shareye.* Pour the men some tea."

Although she did, she left out the ceremonial side of things, even in handing out the cups. My gaze was on Qiras as she gave him his tea, but he took it graciously. Judging by the set of his jaw, however, I could tell he wasn't pleased.

"Keep her close, *irtehn,*" Nazeem whispered. "Qiras has got a nasty temper on him, more so after a couple of shots of *cahrtin.* His respect for other people's property diminishes with each sip."

"Duly noted."

Inenn thanked her kindly enough for the tea, happy with the offer. Nazeem declined with a polite gesture of his hand.

"I'm a *keffah* man through and through," he said with a grin. "Nothing better to get your heart pumping."

"With the amount you drink," Inenn observed. "You should be careful your heart doesn't explode."

There were laughs all around, except for Qiras, whose gaze had returned to Lujaeyn as she packed up the ingredients she'd used.

Keep her close.

A stone settled in my stomach. "Lujaeyn, come here."

She obeyed without question and knelt in front of me, hands in her lap, eyes downcast. "Yes, *Masran?*"

"Sit with me." I patted the spot between Nazeem and myself.

"Of course, *Masran.*"

My gut coiled tight as she settled herself beside me. Discomfort radiated from her like heat, and I noticed her shuffling as if she had no idea how to sit. Nazeem was looking at me over her head, one brow arched in question.

I wasn't sure what I was doing either.

"When you lazy donkeys are done," Elay remarked from above and behind me. "The carts need to be emptied and everything needs to be stored in one of the tents. The horses and donkey need to go in another, and someone has to stay with them to keep them calm."

I was about to offer when Inenn spoke up to say he would.

"Very well. Tariq and Nazeem join in my tent. Qiras, Talnovar, and the girl will stay in the other. The storm's going to be rough, *eshen.* Whatever you do, if you value your life, don't venture out during it."

Everybody nodded, the other men a bit more sagely and determined than I. I was more concerned with the fact Qiras would sleep in the same tent we did.

"Perhaps you can get our bedrolls ready," I murmured to Lujaeyn. "Don't go anywhere near Qiras."

"Yes, *Masran*."

BY THE TIME WE FINISHED, the wind had picked up speed and sand dervishes were frolicking through our camp. We'd killed the fire a while ago, so the only light in the camp came from the lanterns hanging inside the tents. Those, too, would have to go off once everyone was safely inside. Before I did, I relieved myself for the night, Elay's warning firm in my mind.

Would be a shame to die with my trousers around my ankles.

As I returned, Qiras' tone of voice coming from the tent alerted me, and I quickly ducked inside. Qiras was sitting cross-legged on his bedroll, his hand clasped around Lujaeyn's wrist. She stood rigid, chest rising and falling, her eyes wide as she regarded him.

"Release her." My voice was calm, controlled, but on the inside, I was shaking with fury, just like I had the day Elay bought her.

Qiras' grin widened. "Or what, *terkan*? You will kill me?"

"Or I will take what's most precious to you."

He snorted, not letting go. "Your threats fall empty, white hair. You are a stranger here. You do not understand our customs. Here, a slave is shared."

"I don't care," I replied icily. "I told you to let her go."

"And you do not command me," Qiras spat, tightening his grip around her wrist.

Although Lujaeyn's whimper was soft and her flinch barely noticeable, it set me off regardless. I was on him before he realised I'd moved and punched him on the nose hard enough to hear something snap. Qiras yelped in pain and grabbed his nose. I didn't need to look to see he was bleeding all over the place.

Lujaeyn rushed over to me, wrapping her arms around my waist and burying her face against my chest as if she were a small child.

My scalp prickled.

I ran my hands through my hair and glanced down at her, quickly looking away when she tilted up her face to look at me. Without sparing Qiras any more of my attention, I steered Lujaeyn away from him and to the other side of the tent. I stared at the single bedroll, resigning myself to an uncomfortable night.

"Something wrong, *Masran*?" The innocence in her voice did not go by unnoticed, and I couldn't help but wonder if it was real or acted.

"Nothing," I replied, glancing around the tent to see if there was anything I could use to sleep on, but aside from two saddlebags, there was precious little equipment in our tent. Outside, the wind sounded positively fiendish—the storm had arrived.

"Get some sleep," I murmured to Lujaeyn. "You'll be safe."

Qiras, still cursing me in every way he knew how to, was pressing a piece of fabric to his nose. He was glowering at me. I stared back unimpressed as I settled down beside the bedroll. If he did at some point decide to go for her, he'd had to go through me first. Lujaeyn looked at me as if she was about to ask me something, thought better of it and lay down, her back towards us. I leaned over to pull the blanket on top of her and felt her still beneath my hand as it touched her shoulder.

A shudder went through her, and she curled deeper in on herself.

"You won't always be there to protect her," Qiras muttered, his scowl deepening as he took a swig of his wineskin. "And when that day comes..."

"Spare me the threats, Qiras." I sighed. "You're hardly the first and definitely won't be the last. I'm tired. There's a storm. Do us all a favour and drink yourself into a stupor."

A hiss escaped his lips, but he spoke no more. Sure enough, while the wind continued its relentless tug-of-war with the tent, its high keen adding an eerie note to the tempest outside, Qiras drank and drank until he passed out.

His snores barely made it above the din of the storm.

My eyelids were heavy, and more than once, I caught myself dozing off. I tried to fight it but there came a point where I kept yawning, and there was nothing I could do to stop it. If my *sehvelle* habits had taught me anything, it was that Qiras would likely be out of it till morning.

I could catch a few hours of sleep.

I AWOKE to the touch of a hand on my bare chest. Still in that lucid place between sleeping and being awake, I put it down to a dream and let it go. It had been a while since I'd felt a touch that wasn't meant to hurt me. It trailed from my shoulder, down my side, to the waistband of my trousers. A pleasant tingle ran down my spine. When the hand moved beneath my waistband something in the back of my mind jolted me to alertness. Before I'd struggled through the web of sleepiness, that same hand began to stroke the length of me.

Azra.

I sat up, looking wide-eyed around the tent, my breathing coming hard and fast. Still with her hand in my trousers, Lujaeyn stared at me, mouth half-open, posture rigid as if she was caught doing something she shouldn't have been.

Not too far from the truth.

Realising it wasn't Azra playing her tricks, I fell back, willing my frantic heart to calm down. Lujaeyn neither spoke nor moved, but her hand on me was enough to draw out a deep groan.

"What are you doing?" I murmured, my voice huskier than I liked.

She swallowed hard and licked her bottom lip, looking anywhere but at me. "I thought... perhaps... you looked like..." She fell silent and looked away. "You're so tense, *Masran*. I thought I could perhaps ease that tension."

I wanted to yell at her, tell her that she thought wrong, but by the Gods, I could not deny how good it felt. Letting out a shuddering sigh, I closed my eyes, my mind at war with the wrong head. I knew I should tell her to withdraw her hand, to let me go, to tell her I was fine and that if I wanted something— needed something—I would tell her.

Would I?

As I opened my eyes, I found her watching me, her head cocked slightly to the side as if waiting for an answer. Her lips quirked up on one side, just slightly, but in that same moment, she lay down next to me and continued her stroking.

"Let me take care of you, *Masran*," she whispered in my ear. "You deserve a moment of happiness."

I gritted my teeth and closed my eyes, inhaling deeply and exhaling slowly to keep my composure, but when she wrapped her hand around me and began placing soft kisses on my neck, all caution left the tent, and an internal hunger took over.

She's mine.

CHAPTER 31

SHALITHA

ho are you?
The question was as irrelevant as its answer but not at all unexpected. Although the knife against my throat was an inconvenience, I knew without a doubt Z'tala wouldn't go through with killing me. There was too much at stake.

She just wanted an answer.

It was no surprise. I'd made a few errors in judgement, but who knew someone could be so mortally afraid of water? And how had she expected me to remember the way to the baths after only having been there once? Small errors, nothing I couldn't fix. I just had to be quick on my feet.

"What kind of question is that?" I muttered, leaning my head back to ease the pressure against my throat. "You know who I am."

A light, shallow cut, enough to draw blood but not enough to kill me, came in answer. "I don't believe you."

I refrained from shrugging, keeping very still instead. "Then don't, but whether you like it or not, I'm your superior, and if you don't release me right now, I'll call for Jaehyr and I doubt he'll be very pleased to see you attacking his *Tarien*."

Z'tala growled in my ear, making no move to ease the pressure.

"It'll be worth it," she hissed. "Because you're *not* the *Tarien.*"

A cackle escaped my lips. "And who do you think I'm supposed to be then?"

"I don't know, but I will find out."

If I didn't settle this now, not a day would go by where I didn't have to watch my back, which would be incredibly annoying considering the fact she was there all the time. She was supposed to watch it, not me. But how could I convince her I was who I said I was?

Not without proof.

A grin spread across my lips. Moving fast to catch her off guard, I grabbed her hand, twisted the knife from it, and tossed it farther into the pool. Z'tala yelped in surprise and fought against my hold, but I was stronger. It was then I realised I shouldn't be, so I eased up, giving her the illusion she was fighting an equal, possibly even someone lesser.

It worked like a charm.

Confident in her own skills, she used her elevated position to her advantage, locking me in place with her arms around my neck. There was just one thing she hadn't thought of.

I still had room to move.

Inhaling deeply, I dragged myself underwater, pulling Z'tala down with me. The need for self-preservation kicked in on her side, and she released her grip. Without waiting for her to gather her bearings, I kicked off against the floor and hauled myself up on the edge, quickly pulling my feet out of the water. Z'tala came up spluttering and coughing, wiping water from her eyes with the back of her hand. I rose to my feet to grab towels, keeping an eye on her as she hauled herself out of the pool.

"Here," I said, handing her a towel. "Sorry for pulling you in."

Z'tala grunted noncommittally, jerking the towel out of my hand. She wasn't pleased with my actions and rightly so, but if she needed proof of my being Shalitha, that was all I was going to give her. The *Tarien* had a wicked streak, and she knew that, so if this didn't persuade her, at least for the time being, nothing else would.

Wrapping the towel around me for the *Tarien's* modesty, I glanced at her. "I'm going to get dressed. Don't attack me again."

She scowled at me but didn't press the issue any further. Instead, she followed me in silence, the look on her face sullen, thoughtful.

I wasn't out of the woods yet.

Watching my back it is.

A decorated box was waiting for me inside the dressing room, but as I made to open it, Z'tala slapped my hand away, her scowl deepening.

"Let me do it," she muttered. "You never know what's inside."

I arched a brow. "I assume clothing."

"You wouldn't be the first royalty to make the wrong assumption, *Akynai*," she said. "And perhaps in your country, it is not a practice, but sending elaborate packages with a poisonous animal inside is quite the scheme around these parts. A single bite from a snake or the sting of a scorpion will see you dead within hours."

"Inconvenient."

"For you, *Akynai*," she stated, lifting the lid with the tip of her sword. "Absolutely. For your enemies, it would be rather beneficial."

Enemies, huh?

I'd not even considered that notion. Surely people were glad to be rid of that tyrant, except, I supposed, those who'd made money from his tyranny, and I wouldn't have been surprised if that were more than a handful of people. As Z'tala flipped the lid off the box, a snake reared its flat, ugly head, hissing at the both of us. If it hadn't been for her, it'd have gotten a taste of me. Z'tala made short work of the snake by decapitating it in one swift movement. She picked up its head and dropped it back in the box, a look of disdain on her face.

"No clothes then?"

She shook her head, the faintest of smiles ghosting her lips. "I'm afraid not. I'll ask Jaehyr to get some."

"No," I replied. "Tell him to give me his shirt. I have no time to wait for him to return.

She inclined her head. "As you wish, *Akynai.*"

Z'tala returned in short order, carrying a shirt in her arms that would cover the essentials but was still considered highly indecent. Without waiting for her to finish dressing, I stepped out into the bathhouse corridor where I was greeted by a silent, bare chested Jaehyr. Upon seeing me, he inclined his head, never showing any emotion about his state of dress.

As *herriatâre*, he'd worn less than trousers.

PEOPLE STARED EVERYWHERE WE PASSED—THEY bowed, but they also stared, and I made my displeasure of my state of undress clearly known as we marched through the corridors, stating that if I found out who was responsible for this, I'd have them hanged, or decapitated, or anything that tickled my fancy. Z'tala and Jaehyr were one step behind me, both scowling enough for people to keep their distance.

As soon as I reached my chambers, I issued commands for food, drinks, and a dress in a voice that brooked no argument. Servants scattered to the four winds, keeping their heads down so low I wouldn't have been surprised to find some tripping over their own feet. I settled on one of the loungers and leaned back, draping my arm across my face to block out the light.

"Is something amiss, *Tarie—Tari?*" Jaehyr asked.

"Not at all. Just waiting for these incompetent fools to get me clothing rather than a snake."

"A snake?" he asked, worry slipping into his voice.

How adorable.

The notion of cuteness made me sick. I glanced at Z'tala from under my arm, but she was occupied studying the tapestries on the wall.

"Yes." I sat up, looking at him. "A snake in a box. A good thing Z'tala was there or it would have bitten me." I rose to my feet and sashayed over to him, my eyes never leaving his. "Tell me this. What has two eyes but cannot see?"

Jaehyr looked confused. Z'tala's head snapped up at my words.

"*Tari?* I—I'm not sure what—"

"A servant must have passed you," I interjected, stepping close to him. "Am I right?"

"Y—yes, but—"

"And they would have been carrying a decorated box?"

Jaehyr swallowed and nodded. "Yes, but I checked it. There was nothing in there except for a dress."

I stepped back as if he'd backhanded me, a frown creasing my brow. Jaehyr looked uncomfortable by my presence, but if the shocked and confused look on his face was any indication, he wasn't lying. Turning away, I began to pace, tapping pursed lips as I mulled over his words.

"How did that snake get there then?"

"The servant may have carried it on his person, *Akynai,*" Z'tala offered. "Kept it hidden underneath his clothing."

"Find me that servant," I said, turning on Jaehyr so fast he stiffened. "Do not return until you've found him."

Jaehyr inclined his head. "As you wish, *Tari.*"

"And get dressed first."

He pivoted on his heel and left the room just as two servants returned with carefully wrapped packages teetering precariously on top of one another. Z'tala stepped forward and took the packages from them, tearing them open without any regard for its contents. A chuckle escaped my lips upon laying eyes on the servants, their eyes bulging.

"It's clear," Z'tala said, turning to me.

I nodded, then turned to the servants, tapping a foot. "What took you so long?"

They dropped to their knees and bowed until their foreheads touched the tiles. "Apologies, *Akynai*. We had to scour the palace for a dress that would befit your status."

Scrutinising them longer than necessary—I really did enjoy watching them squirm—reminded me of the conclusion I'd just come to with Jaehyr and Z'tala, and that I'd sent away the only one who knew which servant had tried to kill me.

"Undress," I ordered.

They stared at me dumbfounded.

"Did I pronounce that incorrectly? Did I speak a different language?" I stalked closer. "Undress, now."

Both obeyed with lightning speed. They untied sashes, took off robes, shirts and trousers with trembling hands until all they wore nothing but their undergarments. I gathered their clothes and shook them violently in case something was hiding in them, much to the horror of both servants. Only when I was satisfied did I return their clothing and with it, undoubtedly, their dignity.

I didn't apologise.

"Get me dressed."

Just as they finished adding the sash to my attire, there was a tentative knock on the door, and it opened without me having invited anyone. Z'tala opened the door and was greeted by Naïda and R'tayan, the man who should have bought the *Tarien* for the night, had failed to do so, but had redeemed himself by providing me with a marriage certificate and thus, the throne.

"Yes?" I asked, sitting down in front of the mirror.

"We were hoping to have a word with you, *Akynai*," Naïda said, bowing slightly.

Via the mirror, I saw R'tayan follow suit, but his eyes never left mine. There was a curiosity in them that went beyond propriety.

"Then speak." I motioned for one of the servants to come closer and do my hair.

"We were hoping it could be a private affair, *Akynai*." Naïda's voice was kind, gentle, but there was an edge to it. Glancing at her via the mirror, I noticed her stiff posture. Her fingers were twisting the rings on her index finger, obviously a nervous habit. It piqued my interest enough to send the servants out.

Without looking at any of them, I rose to my feet and made my way to the table laden with fruits and drinks. Grabbing one of the first pitchers and a cup, I began to pour myself some wine, but before I could put the cup against my lips, R'tayan took it from me and emptied it in one of the plants.

"Not a wise decision, *Akynai*." Although he sounded kind, there was a clear admonishment hidden in the undertones. "You must realise you've made more enemies than friends at the palace, and you cannot trust anything without having it checked first."

"It's why I had my servants undress before you came in," I replied nonchalantly.

His brows shot up in surprise. "You must have had your reasons."

"Of course." I turned to him, folding my arms. "So, what brings you here? What did you so desperately need to talk to me about that you neglected proper etiquette?"

R'tayan lifted his chin. "You need people on your side, *Akynai*. People you can trust, people you can confide in, people who can tell you the most current news and the trivial gossip. Your servants will answer whatever you want them to answer, your guards are with you night and day. None of them can do what we can do."

"And that is to spy for me?" I asked, my lips curving up in a smile.

"Yes, *Akynai.*"

"What if people find out you are working for me?"

R'tayan shrugged. "I've lived at this court long enough to know whom I can trust and whom I should avoid. I'm a valuable asset, *Akynai,* if only because the list of people I can depend on here is longer than yours."

I arched a brow. "The real question is," I began, looking from him to Naïda and back. "What's in it for you?"

He smiled brightly at that, revealing a row of perfect white teeth. "That, *Akynai,* is something I cannot divulge."

"Then why should I trust you?"

R'tayan whistled, a short, sharp sound that was unpleasant on the ears. The door to my bedroom opened and two guards stepped in, dragging a dishevelled-looking servant between them. The angle of his lower legs suggested they'd broken them in order to keep him from running away. Effective, but not quite what I'd had in mind for when he was caught.

"What's this?"

"After the announcement of your supervising the throne while *Akyn* Elay is still away, I assumed somebody would try something," R'tayan said. "So, I had my men posted out of sight of the bathhouse, just in case. This man went in with a box, came out carrying a piece of cloth. I think we both know what happened, *Akynai.*"

I inclined my head. "It's a good start. What else do you have to offer?"

R'tayan produced a folded piece of paper from inside his brocade jacket and handed it to me without speaking a word. Names were written in neat, elegant lines, but it was the information after them that caught my eye.

"What's this?"

He smiled. "A... peace offering, *Akynai,* to convince you of my sincerity."

I stared at the piece of parchment a while longer before folding it and tucking it inside my dress.

"Offer accepted."

IF ONLY BECAUSE I want to keep an eye on you, too.

"Bring him to the courtyard," I ordered, turning to the guards. "Assemble everyone in the palace, no excuses.

They glanced at each other briefly, then inclined their heads. "Yes, *Akynai.*"

Jaehyr slipped back into my room, his mouth half-open to speak when his gaze fell on the half-conscious captive hanging between the two guards.

"Oh," was all he said, and snapped his mouth shut, surveying the room quickly while taking up his place beside the door.

I liked his solidity. A man after my own heart. Someone who took orders without questioning them into infinity. One of those was more than enough. I watched as the guards dragged the man away, heedless of his broken legs banging into things. The cries of anguish echoing through the corridors sent a delightful shiver down my spine and settled deep in my stomach.

I all but purred at the sound.

"What do you plan on doing, *Akynai?*" Naïda asked tentatively.

She was spinning her rings again.

"Make an example out of him, of course," I said, as if this was the most common thing in the world. Without waiting for a reply, I swept out of the room, the uneven fall of footsteps behind me indicating they were all following me.

"Do not turn into *him, Akynai,*" Z'tala hissed from slightly behind me. "You're better than that tyrant. Show them your grace and your mercy rather than your wrath."

I stopped and pivoted on my heel.

She nearly bumped into me.

"And show weakness?" I growled under my breath. "They've given me no choice but to make an example out of him without mercy. If they'd not broken his legs, I'd have had more options."

"Forgiveness goes a long way," she pointed out, staring at me.

"Not when you've got a target on your back. Now either you trust me and accept what I'm doing, or you don't, but if you choose the latter, you'd best leave before I change my mind about not punishing you after your stunt in the bathhouse."

Z'tala gritted her teeth and inclined her head. "Yes, *Akynai.*"

I turned around and began walking in the direction of the courtyard, the rest following on my heel. Everyone we passed bowed first and scurried after us at a respectable distance, so by the time we arrived, a remarkable party filtered out into the courtyard from behind me. Both Z'tala and Jaehyr remained close by me, and I could just imagine their gazes sweeping over the crowd to catch any signs of trouble. Palace guards formed a wide circle around the prisoner, staying close to the people to keep them away from what was about to transpire.

I didn't want anyone to help him.

"Give me your dagger," I said, turning to Jaehyr.

He obeyed without question, although the look in his eyes told me he didn't quite seem to agree with the idea either.

I was fine with that.

Neither of them had to agree for this to work out the way I wanted to. I wasn't Kehran, but I couldn't let an attempt on my life go unpunished. I could have him thrown out of the palace and issue a decree he was to be helped by no one, but that was just as cruel as what I intended on doing, perhaps even more so. No, he needed to be made an example of to dissuade anyone stupid enough to be considering another attempt.

I bore no illusions it would work on everyone.

Those who had nothing to lose would still try, but those who bore the slightest bit of doubt would be discouraged, if only because they valued their lives more than mine.

As for this man, he'd made his choice, and I'd be doing him a service.

"*Eshen, Shena,*" I began, slowly moving in a circle so that I could look at everybody present. I knew this would piss Z'tala off, big time. "You may be wondering why I have gathered you here today. I will not keep you long, and I will make this simple." I stopped behind the captive and yanked him up by the hair.

Another yelp. Another surge of pleasure going through me.

"This man made an attempt on my life earlier today." I paused. People gasped. "For that, he shall be punished. Under any other circumstances, I would have given him a chance to defend himself, but as you can see, he's lost control of his legs. If I were magnanimous, I would offer him a healer, wait out his recovery, and still give him his chance, but you must understand the severity of this case. If I were malevolent, I would kick him out on the streets, punish anyone who'd help him with a similar fate, and leave him to die, but that would be barbaric. So"—I placed the dagger against his throat— "I've decided that killing him is the best course of action."

In one swift motion, I slit his throat.

His body crumpled to the floor.

A high keen erupted from somewhere in the crowd.

"Let this be a warning!" I declared, turning around and around to face the crowd. "His fate was easy. Yours will be worse. Promised."

I stepped over the dead body and marched back to Z'tala and Jaehyr, handing the latter his dagger. R'tayan and Naïda fell in step behind us.

"Now what, *Akynai?*" R'tayan asked.

My lips curved into a bright smile. "Now we wait."

CHAPTER 32

HAERLYON

*I*n the three weeks following my accident, I'd more or less come to terms with the fact I would never have two hands again. According to Soren, the process of acceptance could take years—years that I didn't have, so I put mind over matter and got on with things as though nothing had changed. It wasn't always easy. One thing I had to learn anew was how to dress. It turned out to be quite the challenge to button up either trousers or jacket with just one hand.

Not impossible.

Difficult.

To be fair, it was a lot easier—albeit a good deal more awkward—to get help with such things. As long as I didn't need help to relieve myself, I was confident I would manage, one way or another. Nevertheless, colourful expletives left my lips after the sixth failed attempt at buttoning up my trousers.

A cough sounded up behind me, and I spun around.

"Need help?" Eamryel asked, a light blush colouring his cheeks as he nodded towards my hand holding up my pants.

I caught myself from saying I could manage and relented

with a sigh. "Please. I'm getting nowhere fast, and Cerindil is expecting me."

Eamryel's lips lifted. "Yeah, I came to fetch you."

He closed the distance between us and began to button up my trousers. The touch of his fingers so close to my private parts sent electric jolts down my spine, and I had to bite back an involuntary gasp as his hand accidentally grazed bare skin just below my navel. He stilled, breathing in sharply. The tension between us increased, more so than it had before, and I couldn't help but wonder where it had come from. I may be interested in Eamryel, but he'd always been a lady's man.

I stood a snowball's chance in summer.

And yet, something was going on between us. I just couldn't put my finger on what it was.

Never the matter. He won't reciprocate.

I coughed, leaned around Eamryel to grab my shirt from the bed and wrestled it over my head. Next came a leather overcoat which mercifully came with belts. I'd already found out they were a good deal easier than buttons.

"Why does Cerindil want to see me?"

Eamryel glanced up. "Not sure, but knowing him, he wants to make plans."

I scowled. "Best not keep the man waiting then."

Eamryel's lips quirked up, but his face quickly fell, looking as if he was at war with himself, his mouth and throat working as if he needed to force out the words that came next, "I'm sorry."

"What for?"

"Being too late," he said, his voice soft, strained. "If I'd been faster, I could've saved your arm."

I flashed him a lopsided smile. "You saved my life, *mahnèh*. I thought I was done for."

Eamryel growled in the back of his throat, jerking his hand through his hair in obvious frustration. "Don't patronise me. I was too late, too slow. I could have saved your life *and* your arm.

I cannot... this—" He swept his hand to encompass all of me. "It's hard to see you struggle and kn—"

Before he could finish his sentence, I pressed my lips to his.

He didn't pull away—not immediately—but when he did, confusion lit up in his eyes and on his face. I swallowed hard, watching him bring a trembling hand to his lips, touching them.

He bolted out of the infirmary without a backwards glance.

Khirr.

I slumped back to the bed with a heavy sigh, lowering my chin to my chest.

What have I done?

I closed my eyes, contemplating what was possibly the stupidest action in Ilvannian history. Why had I kissed him? Why had I given in so suddenly? I sighed again and pulled my boots from under the bed. My mood soured as I struggled into them, realising I could have had help if I hadn't acted like a lovesick teenager.

Nothing to be done about that now.

Gathering my courage, I rose to my feet, grabbed my cloak, and donned it as I walked out of the infirmary. The permanent crispness in the air was a welcome relief after the sweltering heat inside the building. Fires roared in the fireplaces all day every day. In my opinion, they could take it down a notch, but I'd been informed after several complaints that it was important to keep it warm inside in case they had patients. Unlike the *Haniya*, the *Dena* actively participated in the mountain society and frequently had visitors and patients over. Even now, harbouring Ilvannian fugitives and rebels, their daily activities had not ceased.

Pulling my cloak tighter about me, I wandered around until I found someone who could tell me where to find Cerindil, but most of them scurried in a different direction as soon as I approached. I rubbed my arm—the part still left—trying to ignore the bitterness surfacing. My reputation had preceded me even here.

Guess I deserve it.

"No," I told myself quietly. "You did what you were ordered to do."

Had I?

At the same time as the thought appeared, the hair on the back of my neck rose as goosebumps slithered down my arms and body. Next thing I knew, the world tilted as something slammed into my back, and I went down to the ground. Years of training kicked in, and although slightly out of balance with my lower arm missing, I didn't miss a beat rolling out of the way and back to my feet.

A prone man was a dead man.

Taking up a defensive stance, I looked up at my assailant and felt the air knocked right out of me as I recognised her face. A sigh of relief escaped my lips.

"You made it," I whispered, eyes widening. "Thank the Gods."

Samehya didn't share my relief. Her eyes were blazing furiously, and without a word, she attacked. I was lucky she was unarmed, too, because dodging her kicks and blows was hard enough without a weapon. I shuddered to think of the consequences had she borne a weapon.

"How dare you!" she hissed, landing a punch on my shoulder.

I winced and staggered back. "What are you talking ab—"

Before she could land her kick, I blocked it, but the move made me unsteady, and I had to hop back to regain my balance.

It was all she needed.

"*Ai Sela'an,*" a voice commanded, and both Samehya and I stilled.

At ease, soldier.

The words had been drilled into me from a very young age. Samehya was a quick study. Cerindil strolled up to us, looking as if he was merely enjoying the scenery. Samehya pressed her lips together in a thin line and avoided looking at me. I made to clasp my wrists behind my back and realised a bit too late this was no longer possible. Swallowing hard, I lifted my chin and avoided looking at Cerindil.

"What's going on here?" Cerindil asked.

I glanced at him. "Just a friendly exercise."

"Is that why she attacked you from the back?"

"One must always be prepared, *Ohzheràn*," I said, catching the quirk of his lips at the mention of his old title.

Old habits die hard.

"I see you haven't lost your touch," Cerindil said and turned to Samehya. "Go see if Soren needs help in the infirmary."

Samehya scowled but inclined her head, spun on her heel and stalked off, fists balled at her sides. I let out a sigh of relief.

"I probably deserved that," I said, rubbing my neck.

Cerindil looked at me. "Maybe. Maybe not. She's been harbouring a lot of anger lately."

"Eamryel said you wanted to see me to make plans?"

His eyes sparkled in amusement as he looked at me, motioning for me to follow. "Yes, and no. First, I think there are other matters to discuss, unless I am mistaken?"

I shook my head. "No."

"Is it true Yllinar is dead?" he asked after a while.

"I think so," I replied, worrying at my lip as I pondered the next words. "It really set Azra off, so I assume it must be true."

He nodded quietly. "Tal?"

"I don't know."

He released an explosive breath and looked up at the sky where dark clouds heavy with rain had gathered, blocking out the feeble rays of the sun.

"He must be fine," I said, more because I felt I had to say it than anything else. "He's resourceful, strong, and he's on a mission. Nothing will stop him from finding Shal."

Cerindil nodded again, his face tightening. "News from the palace?"

"She's gathering more troops," I replied. "Not just from Ilvanna, but from across the borders as well. Therondian *lerdas* with nothing left to lose have promised their allegiance to her."

"What about the Therondian King?"

"He's been remarkably quiet." I frowned, trying to remember the last correspondence with him. "But I do not think he'll align himself with Azra if history is any indication."

"Let's hope so," Cerindil muttered. "If Therondia musters all their forces in favour of Azra, the *Tarien* stands no chance."

I snorted. "Knowing my sister, she'll have found some way around that."

He chuckled at that and shook his head. "She always was rather creative, but unless she's found a way into court somewhere, I doubt she'd be that successful."

"I just have to have faith in something," I muttered, clutching the stump at my elbow. "There's already precious little of it left."

Cerindil glanced at me but remained quiet. I offered no response either, so we followed the path in silence, both of us lost in thought. It wasn't until we had nearly arrived at the infirmary that Cerindil spoke again.

"You must return."

"I know."

BREATHING IN DEEPLY, I knocked on the door to the cottage Cerindil had pointed me to. A familiar voice called for me to wait a moment, but it wasn't the one I'd expected to hear, so when the door opened, revealing a tousled looking Mehrean, I'd already pulled my face straight. In her arms, bundled in a layer of blankets, slept the prettiest baby girl I'd ever seen.

"She's gorgeous," I murmured, hovering between wanting to touch her and not wanting to impose.

"Come in," Mehr said in a whisper. "Be quiet though. Evan's taking a nap."

"A father's life must be hard on him."

She smiled gently. "Not as hard as losing his wife was."

I winced as if she'd slapped me even though there had been no cruelty in her voice. She'd gone back to the Mehrean I'd known for years instead of the one I'd spoken to back at the palace.

"Did you find what you were loo—"

"Not here," she interjected with a hiss.

The baby immediately began to fuss, setting Mehrean into motion. I watched her dance through the cabin while singing softly, swaying back and forth. In no time, the girl was quiet again. On the bed, Evan lay sprawled on his front, feet hanging over the edge as if he'd dropped there and fallen asleep straight away.

I wouldn't be surprised if that were the case.

Mehrean, judging by the dark circles under her eyes and the falter in her step, wasn't faring much better. I stepped forward and lay a hand on her shoulder.

"Why don't you take a nap as well," I offered. "I can look after her until she wakes."

Mehr turned to me, her eyes moving down to my mangled arm, and she bit her lip.

I smirked. "I won't drop her." To prove my point, I sat down in the only comfortable chair in the room and held out my good arm. "The both of us can sit here."

"She doesn't like it when you sit still," Mehrean said, stifling a yawn. "She wants to move."

"Mehr..."

She scowled at me, but rather than malice, there was gratitude in her eyes. "Just... when she wakes up, feel free to wake us, too. She might want to eat."

"What's her name?"

"Naraysha," Mehrean replied, a tender smile on her lips as she placed the sleeping baby in my arms. "He wanted to honour the three most important women in his life."

I arched a brow. "He's missed one."

She just smiled at that. "Thank you, Haer."

I watched her prod Evan in the side so he'd move, and when he didn't, she simply snuggled up against his back, hooking her leg over his so she wouldn't fall off. Within no time, her breathing slowed and Mehr had joined Evan in the land of dreams. I looked down at Naraysha, at her little button nose, the dark lashes against her ivory skin, the translucency of her eyelids, and the curly fuzz peeking out from under the blanket she was wrapped in. Her pink lips were curled up in a small smile, as if she were enjoying whatever it was.

She's perfect.

Despite holding such a lovely little creature, my heart was heavy, my chest tight. No matter how much I longed for it, I would never have this—never have a child to call my own. I swallowed hard and forced myself to smile as my gaze settled back on Naraysha.

I may never have children of my own, but I would have her.

And whatever spawn Shal may bring into the world.

I'd be the fun uncle who'd allow everything, much to the despair of the parents. I chuckled softly. Naraysha immediately stirred, but after a bit of swaying back and forth, she settled again.

"I'll teach you all the things your father doesn't want you to know," I whispered. "All the things a lady shouldn't know, but those I'm certain your aunt will approve off. I'll teach you how to swim, how to climb trees and ride horses. It'll be so much fun."

It hit me then.

How was I supposed to teach her if I couldn't do most of those things myself?

Stop it. You'll figure it out. Soren will help you figure it out.

Provided I live through it.

Cerindil's words—while a blow to the gut—hadn't exactly come as a surprise. Azra had never intended for me to survive the mission, so therefore I wouldn't be surprised if she believed me dead, and *that* I could use to my advantage.

My reappearance could rattle her just enough.

Just enough for what?

Not that it mattered.

Somewhere between then and now, she had to be giving birth to her baby and she would be told it had died. I instantly returned my focus to Naraysha and couldn't help but feel sorry for Talnovar's unborn child. If Kalyani didn't manage to do what I had entrusted her with, and if Azra won the war instead of my sister, it would grow up in the clutches of a madwoman. The thought alone sent shivers down my spine.

Naraysha woke up from the shudder, blinked at me and yawned.

For a moment, I believed we were good—then she started bawling. I got to my feet, supporting her with my stump, and began to walk back and forth through the cottage, trying to calm her down with hushing noises. When that didn't work, I tried singing, keeping my voice low as not to wake up Evan and Mehrean.

To no avail, Naraysha was producing enough noise for the both of us.

"Hush, *shareye*," I cooed. "*Naie i'fean.* All is well."

Her sobs became hiccoughs, but she wouldn't stop crying entirely.

"Here," Evan said from my side, sounding tired. "She's hungry."

He handed me a warm bottle after twirling it around for a bit. I looked at him, at the bottle, and then to my arm, smiling ruefully.

"I'm afraid you'll have to do that," I said. "I'm one arm short."

"One arm sh— oh..." He rubbed the back of his neck, a sheepish smile on his face. "Apologies. It's quite something to get used to."

"Tell me about it."

He jutted his chin to the chair. "Sit down."

I offered him his daughter, but he shook his head.

"Sit down with her."

A little taken aback by this, I lowered myself into the chair and watched as Evan pulled forth a footstool, seemingly unperturbed by the situation. Although he'd come and seen me a few days after I arrived, we hadn't spoken to each other. I had no idea how he felt towards me after what I'd done to him and his wife, to Mehrean supposedly, and to his friends.

Yet he trusted me with his daughter.

"Put your feet on the stool," he said. "You can place her on your legs."

It was awkward at first and truth be told, plain scary. When Evan lay her on my lap, I was afraid she'd roll off, and I wouldn't be able to catch her. Apparently more experienced with this, Evan arranged us so that rolling off couldn't happen, and to my surprise, Naraysha settled comfortably in this position, as if she'd done this a thousand times before.

She probably has.

Evan handed me the bottle. "Just hold it up and she'll do the rest."

He sure hadn't been lying. Naraysha emptied the bottle in record time and then wailed for more. Evan chuckled softly and shook his head.

"She's a hungry one," he said. "Mehr says it's fine. She's

growing. I can only marvel at the thought of how women put up with this."

I looked amused. "Just like you do, *mahnèh*. One day at the time."

He smiled at that, but it didn't quite reach his eyes. Just hovering behind his gaze now focused on his daughter was something I couldn't quite place. It wasn't worry exactly, nor fear, but a mix I'd never seen on Evan before.

"She'll be fine," I said, startling him out of his reverie. "You know that, right?"

He let out a heavy sigh. "I hope so, Haer. I really do, especially with Azra still on the throne. If she gets her hands on Naraysha..."

I had nothing to say to that.

She'd already sent men to deal with the baby, but none of them—well, none except for one—had returned, and after he had delivered the message from the rebels, Azra had killed him for good measure. She'd been furious at their failure, but not more so than at her own for sending an incompetent *hehzèh* to do it for her.

I'd managed to talk her out of taking the army to *Denahryn*.

"She's safe," I murmured. "For now."

Or so I hope.

With luck, Azra would be preoccupied right about now and Naraysha would be furthest from her thoughts, but I had no doubt whatsoever that at one point, her attention would return, and if her response to my sister was any indication, all bets were off.

"Haer?" Evan sounded as if he'd been repeating my name.

I glanced up, heat creeping up my cheeks. "Yeah?"

"How are you holding up?"

Naraysha fussing pulled my attention away from him, and I watched intrigued as the little girl fought to get the wrappings away from her. Evan leaned over and lifted her to his shoulder, patting her back gently. I rubbed my arm just above the stump, tongue in cheek as I pondered his question.

"Not sure," I said at length, furrowing my brow. "I suppose, all things considered, I could be doing a lot worse."

Evan let out a sound halfway between a snort and a chuckle at the same time as Naraysha let out a good, healthy burp. We burst out laughing at the surprised look on her face.

"Good girl," murmured Evan as he moved from the stool to the floor with her.

He placed her on her back, and as soon as he unwrapped the blanket, I understood why. I turned my head away fast, biting back on a gag.

"By Vehda," I muttered. "That's... intense."

Evan snorted loud at that. "Maybe you can lend me a hand..."

I scowled at him.

He laughed. "Too soon?"

After I'd peeled myself from the chair, staying as far away from the smelly child as possible, I tapped him on the back of the head. "*Khirr.* What do you need?"

"A triangle piece of fabric and wet cloth. They're over by the fireplace."

When I'd gathered what he needed, I placed everything close at hand. Sinking to my knees, I lost my balance and by instinct, my arm shot out. If it hadn't been for Evan's hand steadying me, I'd have fallen over regardless. Neither of us addressed the issue, so Evan set to changing his daughter while I distracted her with silly faces. The moment I leaned over, one of her chubby hands grabbed a strand of my hair and pulled.

I yelped.

"Friendly bit of advice." Evan chuckled. "Do not let her near your hair."

"Duly noted," I grunted.

Prying those little fingers from my hair proved to be quite a challenge. Who knew babies had such a death grip?

After Evan finished, he set to cleaning all the cloths he used while I kept an eye on Naraysha. Although unable to roll on her tummy yet, she was quite endeavouring, scooting across the floor on her back. I kept hurrying after her to avoid collision with items much sturdier than her head.

"I can see why you're tired," I said as Evan picked her up from the floor and returned her to the deerskin where she'd started. "Quite the adventurous sort. Reminds me of someone we know."

Evan awarded me a deadpan stare before it turned into a deep frown. "Has there been any news of her?"

"Last bit of news came from Kyrintha," I replied, settling back in the chair. "She'd been seen in Portasâhn where she gave Azra's hunters the slip."

He smiled, albeit faintly. "Sounds like her, all right." It took a while before he spoke again. "How are things at the palace?"

I stilled. "Unlike anything we ever imagined."

"Are you going back?"

"I have to."

Evan nodded, biting his lip as his gaze settled on the baby in front of him. "I could never have done it."

"Done what?"

"Betray my own family like you did."

CHAPTER 33

TALNOVAR

*E*lay, despite his calm, collected, and snobbish exterior, looked as if he was witnessing either a blood bath or an orgy, neither of which I had thought would affect him much. Yet here he was, sitting still as a statue on his *camelle*, eyes wide, jaw slack, and blinking so rapidly his lashes must be fanning him. I couldn't help the snort escaping my lips.

"Not what you expected?" I asked Elay more cheerfully than I had a right to be.

It felt good to see him off his game.

He glared daggers my way and didn't respond, but my question had jolted him from his stupor. Shock made way for curiosity and something else—something I couldn't quite place. His eyes narrowed the tiniest bit as he surveyed the area. I followed his gaze but couldn't pinpoint what he was looking for or at exactly.

There was a lot to be seen.

In the distance upon the only hill I'd seen in Kyrintha, eight white, spiraling towers with golden roofs glittering in the sunlight jutted into the sky like silent sentinels. In their midst, a massive golden dome dominated the scenery. The rest of Akhyr, houses as white as snow, sprawled across the slope of the hill in a haphazard kind of way from what I could tell. No doubt it wasn't as haphazard as I thought. Akhyr, for all its gaudy appearance, looked a good deal more welcoming than Portasâhn, and I had liked that city.

"Better dismount," Elay said, checking the fabric covering all but his eyes for good measure.

After three tries to make my beast of burden follow suit, it was Lujaeyn who got it to its knees with a simple click of her tongue. I grunted, slid off its back and turned around just in time to catch her before her feet hit the ground.

She beamed up at me. "Thank you, *Masran.*"

A shiver slithered down my back. Even after more than a moon, more than one shared night, I still hadn't gotten used to the title. I glared at Elay over the neck of my *camelle*, but he was preoccupied talking to Nazreem, Tariq, Inenn and Qiras, the latter of whom was only paying half attention to his employer's words, his eyes on a scandalously clad woman standing at the corner of a street. My gaze settled on the sling around his neck, and I felt my lips pull down in a scowl.

After that night during the storm, he had tried again with Lujaeyn.

I'd broken his arm.

Qiras' howls had echoed through the night, waking everyone in a ten-mile radius, and Elay had been angry with me, admonishing me for not understanding their culture, for purposefully undermining his authority and the gods knew what else (I'd stopped listening shortly after he'd begun).

"She's *mine,*" I'd snapped back, snarling like a feral cat. "In my country that means she belongs to *me*, not to *everybody*, so unless the meaning of *mine* is different here, he'd better stay away from her before I break his other arm."

But I had no intention of keeping her.

As soon as I found a decent place for her to stay, I'd release her. Until then, she was in my care.

And I in hers.

The thought was accompanied by an unpleasant feeling in the pit of my stomach. I quickly pushed it away and placed my hand on the small of Lujaeyn's back to guide her to Elay. Nazeem grabbed me by the wrist in farewell and grinned.

"Be well, Talnovar," he said. "Until we meet again."

I snorted. "I doubt we will, *mahnèh.*"

Nazreem clucked his tongue and shook his head. "Never say never."

Tariq followed, his goodbye in rapid Kyrinthan a lot more eloquent than his brother's. I caught about half of what he said and opted for a smile and well wishes. Qiras had taken his pay from Elay, grabbed his bag from one of the *camelles,* and stomped off to the woman I'd seen him ogling moments before. Inenn kept his distance, waiting for Tariq and Nazeem to grab their belongings. We hadn't spoken much during the journey, but he was a solid kind of guy, and had not been easily pulled into Qiras' drama.

He reminded me of Evan.

Elay sighed in relief. "Good riddance."

"And here I thought you actually liked that *grissin.*"

He rolled his eyes, deciding I wasn't worth an answer. I sniggered. "So, where to next?"

"The palace," Elay replied, shielding his eyes as he stared in the direction of the golden dome. "Whatever you do, be civil to the *Akyn.*" A frown creased his brow as he turned to me. "He's got somewhat of a temper..."

"Yeah," I began, rubbing my cheek. "You mentioned it."

"I'm serious." He folded his arms in front of him. "He has no scruples, no conscience. He'll throw you in front of his pets just for amusement."

"He can try."

"If he finds out how important Shalitha is to you"—he gave me an arched stare— "he will use it to his advantage, so you must keep your head down and your temper at bay. He's taken it out on her before, he will do it again. He does not care whether she lives or dies."

I gritted my teeth and balled my fists at my side. I wanted nothing more than to punch this *Akyn* in the face. Elay's expression made me realise this was exactly what he was warning me about. I relented with a heavy sigh, releasing the tension in my body.

"Fine," I muttered, following his example of gathering our items from the *camelles*. "But I will do my job when she's in danger."

Elay shrugged. "I won't stop you. I'm just warning you."

Lujaeyn made to help me with my bags but stepped back when she saw the scowl on my face. It wasn't even directed at her.

"You can get the saddlebags," I said, going for kindness. "These are easier for me than for you."

She glowered at me, hands on her hips, and I bet she was close to stomping her foot. She did that sometimes when she thought I wasn't looking.

"I'm not a frail girl," she commented. "I can carry heavy bags."

"Sure you can," I replied. "But you're not going to. Grab the saddlebags."

Elay looked quietly amused as he slung his bags over his shoulder but said nothing. As soon as we turned to the palace, the look on his face changed, his lips set in a thin line, and his brows knitted together.

Something was wrong.

I didn't ask and instead wrapped the *Hiijr* around my face. After Portasâhn, Elay had thought it wise to hide my features, hair, and skin—hide *me*, because I stood out like a beacon in the night, he'd said. That being the last thing we wanted, I'd complied with his suggestion. As it turned out, it was also a good way not to get sunburned.

After my experiences in the slave camp, it was a welcome reprieve.

But this sun still was far from comfortable, and I couldn't help but long for the Ilvannian mountains and snow—lots of it.

As if frostbite is any better.

It reminded me of the snowstorm Eamryel and I had ended up in after leaving *Denahryn*. When he'd fallen off his horse and slid over the ledge, I had been sure he was dead. When he started shouting for help, there had been a brief moment where I'd considered abandoning him, abandoning the plan and make my own.

I was glad I hadn't.

Without his help, I would not have gotten where I was now.

Is he still alive?

He'd sacrificed himself to give me a chance. I'd better find the *Tarien* if I didn't want to make that sacrifice meaningless.

Is she really here?

I let out a shuddering breath at the thought that after almost three years, I'd be seeing her again, but I couldn't help but wonder what she would be like. Elay's words had lodged themselves in my memory like an unwanted guest, constantly reminding me of the fact that if I was no longer the same person, there was no chance she was. But had she changed for the better or the worse?

I guess I'll find out.

"Are you all right?" Lujaeyn whispered from my side.

Looking down at her, a pang of guilt knifed its way through my gut. I nodded in response. "I'm fine."

She didn't know exactly why I was here, and I wanted to keep it that way. As far as I was concerned, I'd find her a place here in Akhyr and leave this sandy horror behind as soon as I'd found Shal.

"You don't look fine," she said pointedly. "You look like you're in pain."

"It's nothing."

"Very well." She relented with a heavy sigh, and I noticed her taking a step away from me.

"Lujaeyn, I—"

"Apologies, *Masran*," she said under her breath. "I have no right to question you. It is not my place."

I let out a snort, glancing at her. "It hasn't stopped you before. Don't start now."

She looked up at me, her head tilted as if she wasn't sure what to make of me. Truth be told, she probably didn't and just pretended she did out of a misconstrued sense of belonging. Granted, she had been good company, I just didn't know if I could continue with that once I found *her*.

"You are unlike the others," she murmured when she looked away.

I smirked.

She has no idea.

Because of my conversation with Lujaeyn, I nearly missed it —that prickling sensation at the back of my neck as if we were being watched. Surveying the area inconspicuously yielded nothing, and I could hardly turn around to look. If we were indeed being followed, that would surely give away my intentions. No, our best move was to keep walking.

I just couldn't allow myself to get distracted again.

I hitched the bags higher up my shoulder to free up my arm, my hand hovering near my sword. Beside me, Lujaeyn looked tense. Up ahead, Elay still appeared determined judging by the set of his shoulders and the firm stride. I could keep up easily, but Lujaeyn had to quicken her pace to keep up.

"What's the rush?" I called forward.

Elay glanced over his shoulder, a grim look in his eyes. "Something's not right. We need to get to the palace as fast as we can."

"You said that before. Why then didn't we take the *camelles?*"

"Too obvious," he replied. "I want to keep m—our—arrival under wraps, for as long as that's possible."

I arched a brow. "First you warn me of Kehran, and now you want to get in without being seen?"

Elay stopped and turned to me, anger blazing in his eyes. "I told you. Something's off. The whole atmosphere is just... wrong. The market? Wasn't there last time I came in. There were guards at every corner, and the streets were silent. Now? Well, look around you, Talnovar. What do *you* think?"

"That maybe Kehran lightened up?"

He snorted. "He's not the kind of person to *lighten up.* If anything, he'd be even more strict and controlling."

"So then what?"

He shook his head, gaze turning back to the palace. "I don't know, but we're about to find out."

DESPITE THE CONSTANT feeling of being watched, nothing untoward happened during our trip up to the palace. The closer we got, the more tense Elay became, and the more clipped his answers were. By the time we'd almost made it to the gates, he was all but snapping at us. Lujaeyn had opted to walk half a step behind me, head bowed, hands clasped together in front of her, effectively making herself as small as possible.

"Whatever you do," Elay bit back at me as I stopped next to him, "do not open your mouth, do not take off your *hiijr*, do not move. Let me do the talking."

I shrugged. "Sure. I've got nothing to say to those guards anyway."

Elay glared at me, shook his head and stepped forward, pulling himself up to his full height. As opposed to what he had ordered me to do, he took off his *hiijr*, and as soon as he did, the guards took a step forward and fell to their knees, fists against their chest in salute.

"*Akyn,*" one of them said loud enough for everyone close in the vicinity to her.

"King?" I muttered. "Huh, I'll be damned."

Around us, people stopped and stared. Beside me, Lujaeyn's head snapped up and her eyes widened. Before I could stop her, she was on her knees, head resting on the cobblestones. As for myself, I remained standing. If there was one thing I'd learned as an *Arathrien*, it was to never bow to any royal member, whether it was customary or not.

All it took was a moment's loss of focus.

Instead, I took a step forward to stand closer to Elay, ignoring the hand signal for me to stop. Last time I checked, he'd hired me as his bodyguard, so that was exactly what I would be doing in the right circumstances. The captain of the guard looked at me, taking in my appearance, my choice of weapon, and my stance all in one glance.

He'd have been a horrible captain if he hadn't sized me up.

"Your return comes at an auspicious time, *Akyn,*" the captain said, his eyes sliding from Elay back to me.

He had noticed something was off, but Elay spoke unperturbed, "Then let us continue."

The captain inclined his head. "I'll have you escorted to your quarters, *Akyn,* and send a messenger to the *Akynai* of your return. She will be pleased."

Akynai? Queen?

Elay stilled at the words, but only momentarily. He inclined his head and motioned for the captain to go ahead, following him. I beckoned Lujaeyn to come along with a snap of my fingers, feeling bad about it in the process. You snapped your fingers at an animal, not a person. Even so, I didn't know how to catch her attention short of calling her name, and I wasn't sure what the correct protocol was for that in a place like this. One thing was for sure, Elay had been right, and it had set him on edge even more.

Who is this Akynai?

Deep down inside, I had a feeling I knew, but that couldn't be true. Elay had told me she was a *herriatâre*—a fighter for entertainment in King Kehran's *herrât*. It couldn't be her. It just didn't make sense, if only because Shal had always loathed the idea of becoming *Tari* one day.

It's too farfetched.

When we passed the gates, people dropped to their knees left and right, not just guards, but well-dressed men and women, servants—everyone. Elay looked around the courtyard with the wild-eyed wonder of a child.

They were kneeling for *him*.

"You could have told me you were *Akyn*," I muttered under my breath.

"I wasn't when I left," he hissed in return.

"An *Akynshan* then."

Elay looked at me, one brow arched. "You knew I was. That auctioneer was quite vocal about it."

I growled under my breath. "Don't play coy with me, Elay. I've had enough of these mysteries and lies."

His lips quirked up in a wry smile. "I pray you have enough patience to see it through a little longer. There are things I cannot yet explain. Whatever happens next, I beg you to keep your calm."

"Even if it's not Kehran sitting on that throne?"

"Especially because it's not Kehran on the throne," he replied, more in a hiss than a whisper. He opened his mouth to say more, but the captain of the guard urged him along, and I had to take an extra step to catch up.

Elay's words did nothing to comfort me.

If what he said was true, something had changed recently. When he left, Kehran had been on the throne and now he was not. It didn't take a genius to figure out what had happened to him—he was either imprisoned or dead. What worried me was Elay's response to it all. By all accounts, he should have been relieved, but he looked a far cry from it. His jaw was set, shoulders locked, and he walked like a man on his way to be hanged.

Something was still wrong.

But what?

Upon entering the palace, the captain made to guide Elay to a corridor on the right, but Elay refused.

"Where's the *Akynai?*"

The captain looked a bit stricken. "She's dealing with some minor issues, *Akyn.* Come, you must be weary from your travels. You'd best get freshened up before you see her."

I could have cut the tension with my sword if I'd wanted to.

"No," Elay said. "Bring me to her. I need to see my wife."

A feeling of dread spread through me, wrapping its tentacles around my muscles and squeezing them until not just the room was full of tension. A gentle hand on my arm had me look down, and I found myself staring into Lujaeyn's deep brown eyes.

"Are you well, *Masran?*" she whispered, sounding honestly worried.

I dispelled the feeling with a shake of my head. "Yeah, everything's fine." I smiled at her, then realised she couldn't see it behind the *hiijr.* "I promise."

She nodded softly but didn't look convinced.

"Perhaps I can show your guard to his room?" the captain offered.

"Show her his room," Elay said, nodding in Lujaeyn's direction. "He's coming with me."

Lujaeyn stared at me wide-eyed, insecurity washing over her

features as a servant walked up and invited her to come along. I inclined my head in permission and watched her trail off sullenly. I felt suddenly light and released a huge breath.

Whatever was about to happen wasn't going to be pretty.

The guards created a cordon around us and escorted us at a brisk pace through the corridors. I caught sight of servants huddled together, watching our party in silent anticipation. Elay walked stiffly, his chin lifted ever so slightly, eyes focused on the back of the captain's head. He'd have looked through it if he could have.

Shouting reached us from up ahead, and the closer we moved, the more intense it became. The captain looked incredibly uneasy, as if he'd rather be anywhere else but here. The rest of the guards shared the captain's feelings, their expressions strained.

"Perhaps we should go in alone," I murmured in Elay's ear. "With a bit of luck, we can blend in. Sounds to me like there's quite the crowd inside, and they aren't happy. If you come in with a group of guards, we have no idea what it will set off."

Elay acknowledged me with the barest of nods. "Leave," he ordered.

And they did, almost tumbling over each other to get out of this corridor. Only the captain's retreat was more graceful.

"I don't know what your wife's doing," I mused, "but it sounds like she's handling things quite... well."

He shot me a look, and without saying anything, pushed the double doors open. Inside, the crowd was bigger than I'd imagined and most of them looked angry indeed. We slipped inside and closed the doors. Elay quickly fixed his *hiijr* before moving farther through the assembly. I followed him on his heel, hand hovering near my sword. My gaze swept over the crowd, taking in what I could. I noticed the surrounding group of people were dressed in silks and satins—rich, wealthy people then, come to look at the spectacle going on in the centre.

Everyone in the middle of the throne room was dressed in leather and chain, a few even in a mismatched set of plates either on their legs, shoulders or chest, but not anything fully. These had to be the *herriatâre* Elay had mentioned. I looked to see if I could spot Shal amongst them, but the crowd was too thick. They were blocking the view to the throne, so I couldn't see the *Akynai*, but as my gaze slid over the crowd, it settled on a white-haired, white-skinned man who looked both out-of-place and exactly where he was supposed to be at the same time.

There was also something strangely familiar about him.

I had just placed my hand on Elay's shoulder to tell him to move, even though the onlookers didn't seem happy with our disturbance, when suddenly all pandemonium broke out. The fighters roared and surged forward, stumbling and tumbling over one another at the same time as Elay pulled the fabric from his head and yelled, "*Sêtt!*"

As if he'd spoken a magic word, everybody stopped, slamming into their comrades' backs and toppling over one another. Around us, people turned, and as they did, dropped either to their knees or a deep bow befitting their status. Even the *herriatâre*, who had turned around to look in the direction of the voice, stared and went down to one knee.

Behind them, a woman dressed in the finest silks rose from the throne. Her white hair was done up elegantly and finished with an elaborate headdress. Along one side of her face ran an *Araîth* in various shades of blue, I remembered. It disappeared beneath the cropped shirt she was wearing and surfaced again on her ribs, coiling down her side, her hips, her legs, all the way down to the sole of her foot.

I couldn't see it, but I knew.

Silver eyes glanced over me and settled instead on Elay. Her lips pulled up into a smile, but there was something off about it, almost as if it were forced. Elay let out a sigh of relief, his lips

quirking up as well, and as he took a step towards her, it all came crashing down on me.

She's the Akynai. She is his wife.

In a daze, I staggered back, pulling the *hiijr* from my head in defeat. As I did, her eyes settled on me. At first, there was nothing, no awareness of who I was, and it felt like Yllinar stabbing me all over again. But then her eyes widened, and recognition dawned on her face.

"Shal," I whispered.

CHAPTER 34

SHALITHA

That voice.

Everything came rushing back at me at once—like waking up from a deep sleep and having to find my bearings. I felt unsteady and staggered as if I'd forgotten how to use my legs properly. Sounds registered horrifyingly distorted as if my ears had not heard for quite some time. My thoughts were slow to the point of being sluggish, and I had a hard time making sense of things. It wasn't just like waking up from a deep sleep, it was like waking up from a deep sleep after a night of partying, having had too much *ithri*, and perhaps even more. Not that I knew what that felt like, but I'd seen it on Haerlyon a long time ago, and I just assumed he had looked how I felt right about now.

What happened?

All thoughts left me as the face that belonged to the voice—a voice I'd longed to hear for so many nights I'd lost count, a voice I thought I'd never hear again—came into focus.

"Tal?" I whispered.

I'd expected my voice to be hoarse.

It surprised me it wasn't.

I took a tentative step forward, another, and another, down the three steps, my eyes never leaving his. As I placed my right foot on the floor, it suddenly gave way, and I felt myself falling, I just never felt myself reaching the floor. It was like submerging and sinking, deeper and deeper until your chest aches from lack of air, and your thoughts dim and blink out of existence.

And yet, this was different.

When I came around, the throne room was devoid of people, devoid of anything. As I pushed myself to my knees, I realised there was no pain, no blood—there should have been blood after crashing to those tiles—just a vague sense of awareness of something not being as it should be.

"Interesting," a voice said from behind me as I was getting to my feet.

I twirled around.

On the throne sat a man I thought looked vaguely familiar but couldn't remember ever having seen before. Perhaps it was in his jawline reminding me painfully of Evan, or the shaved hair on one side, long on the other that was Haerlyon. Perhaps it was in the emerald coloured eyes or the skin colour which was neither bronze nor ivory. It was in the nonchalant way he sat on the throne, the way he made a steeple of his fingers and the look of dismay in his eyes.

He was everyone I'd ever known.

But who was he?

Rubbing my arm, I stood there forlornly, watching him just as he was watching me. The most obvious question was on the tip of my tongue, but I didn't ask because deep down inside I knew—I knew who he was.

"Why are we here?" I asked, looking around.

"Because this is where I am," he replied, looking smug. "And you, although you're not actually aware of it. Neither are they."

"Aware of what?"

He smiled as if the answer to that question was common

knowledge. It triggered my annoyance, and I felt my temper flare, but before I could say anything, he spoke. "I had to do it."

"Do what?"

The look on his face was that of an adult looking at a child who'd asked the so-manieth 'why' on something it didn't really want an answer to. It just liked to ask that question. I rolled my eyes and folded my arms.

"Listen," I began. "You clearly have the upper hand, and I'm in no mood for games. Judging by your response, neither do you, so how about we deal with this like proper adults."

His lips curved up in a wicked grin. "Very well, but I do not think your simple mind will be able to comprehend the full extent of your situation without driving you mad."

"Try me."

"What is the last thing you actually remember, *Tarien?*"

I arched a brow. What kind of question was that? The last thing I remembered was—I couldn't recall. No matter how hard I tried, I could not summon my last real memory.

"What have you done to me?"

"I saved your life," he replied calm and collected, and with a wave of his hand added, "And I decided I'm quite enjoying this."

"Enjoying what exactly?"

"Living your—my—life." He couldn't have sounded more casual had he tried.

I blinked at him, opened my mouth to say something, and closed it again. Surely, I'd heard it wrong. This wasn't possible, couldn't be possible.

Neither is a talking sword.

And so, I asked the obvious question. "Who *are* you?"

"That, *shareye*—or should I call you *mithri*—is a very long, boring story," he replied, "Really, it'll only put you to sleep."

My lips pulled up into a smile of my own. "That's fine. I've got nothing else to do apparently, so I have all the time in the world."

He leaned forward, a malicious gleam in his eyes. "Not quite, *shareye.* You see, the longer you are here, the less aware you become—the less aware you are, the less resistance you'll put up until, eventually, you fade into the background, content to let it all just be, and I... oh I can do whatever I want pretending to be you, and in *your* position, imagine what that could be."

So, all I have to do is keep you engaged and find a way out?

He chuckled. "I'm afraid it doesn't quite work that way, but you are welcome to try."

That's what I thought.

"Doesn't it?" I asked, lifting my chin. "Is that why you pulled me back forcefully when you momentarily lost control?"

He narrowed his eyes and rose to his feet. "I didn't lose control. I allowed you to come back just so you could see him, both of them, before I do away with you completely. You no longer serve a purpose and quite frankly, having you in my head's been giving me quite the headache."

"No," I said, staring at him. "It doesn't work that way, either. You can't just do away with me, or you would have done that the moment you took possession of my body. Something is preventing you from doing so, and you're just scared I'll find out what it is, so you're trying to logic me into submission. You didn't allow anything, you didn't want that to happen, which means..."

I didn't finish my thoughts on purpose and instead focused on keeping my mind blank, watching his face contort into incredulity first, fear second, and rage third. It had been a guess, a gamble, but I had been right.

All I had to do was find out how to outwit him and regain control of my body.

How hard could it possibly be?

Before I could respond, he stood in front of me, his fingers digging into my jaw. Again, I expected pain, but there was none.

Because this is all in my mind. Or is it his mind?

He smirked. "My mind, and this is as far as I'm allowing you to go."

If there was no pain, I doubted there was any damage, at least, not physically.

"Again with the allowance," I muttered. "You have no idea how to go about this either, except for keeping me subdued. As long as I put up a fight, there's nothing you can do."

At that, he grinned. "Oh, there's absolutely something I can do, *Tarien*, but it will be much more detrimental to you than to me."

"You wouldn't."

"No?" The sweet tone in his voice was at complete odds with the snarl that came next. "Watch me."

Tired of his threats and desperate to get out of this situation, I raised my arms and brought them down on his, breaking his hold on my jaw. Normally, there would have been a howl of pain, but as it was, neither pain nor damage—physical damage anyway—applied here. I figured that while this may appear to be an actual fight, it was nothing but a battle of wits.

It didn't matter.

I attacked, possessed by every bit of anger and frustration that had built up inside me since being aware. The attack took him by surprise, and he staggered back. His foot caught on the first step up, and he fell with a grunt. A sword materialised in my hand as I stepped forward, and I pushed the blade up underneath his jaw.

"I told you," I hissed. "I am done playing games. Yield, or I'll carve you out of my mind with everything I have."

"Do that," he growled in response, "and I'll let you die. See how you save your people then."

I glared at him. The sword disappeared, and I stepped back, watching him rise to his feet and tug his clothing in order with my lips curled up in a silent snarl.

"I won't give up," I said. "No matter what you threaten me with."

At that, he stopped what he was doing, amusement dancing in his eyes. "Are you sure? I could kill your husband, and you wouldn't even know, or perhaps that handsome Ilvannian man —Talnovar, was it?"

I bared my teeth in a snarl, my body tensing, my heartbeat racing—or the equivalent of that in here. Whether I liked it or not, he did have the upper hand, and there was nothing I could do. Not now, anyway. I relented with a heavy sigh, took a step back and bowed slightly.

"Very well."

"You cede?"

"Yes."

WAKING up to a pounding headache was the least of my concerns. Inches from my face was the *Tarien's* husband, the gravely worried look on his face a clear indication of how much he cared about her, and judging by the look on Talnovar's face, it hadn't gone by unnoticed by him either.

Love rivals. Convenient.

It meant my threat to her held even more strength than I'd initially thought, and these men could easily be blackmailed to do anything for me, as long as I kept her safe, I assumed. That all hinged on the fact how well I'd play my role from here on out. I hadn't been able to convince Z'tala yet, but these two were an entirely different matter. To them, a bit of change might make sense as long as I didn't go all out in my enthusiasm.

This could work.

"Elay?" I moaned softly.

"I'm here, *mithri*," he murmured, stroking a few wisps of hair out of my face. "How are you feeling?"

"I've had better days," I replied. "Feels like I cracked open my skull."

He bit his lip and looked away. "That's because you have. Well, sort of. It's not that bad, but you've hit your head on the tiles. The healer's said to take it easy the next few days to assess the full extent of the injury to your head."

So that's why neither of us was in control.

Ending up in the empty throne room with the *Tarien* had been quite the surprise. I'd been confident she was not aware of what was going on, and I had been right until that moment. I had not accounted for both our awarenesses to meet or for us to have an actual conversation, let alone give her answers she didn't even know she was looking for.

Well done.

But I liked to think I handled the situation well enough. Either I killed the men she loved, or I killed her. That should shut her up for a while.

I hoped.

"Will I be okay?" I asked softly, turning my head to watch Elay.

"I don't know, *mithri*," he said quietly, shaking his head, gripping my hand just that bit harder. "The healer said there might be swelling in the brain after the fall you made, but there's no telling how bad it is until a few days have passed."

It explained the pounding headache.

"I'm not sure what happened," I murmured, looking away from him. "One moment, everything was fine, and all of a sudden, it felt as if my legs lost all their strength."

"Did you feel ill before?"

I shook my head. "No, not at all."

Elay smiled and placed a kiss on my forehead. "You just rest, all right? If there's anything you need, ring a bell and somebody will come to help you."

I nodded slowly as not to upset my head too much. My gaze

339

flicked past him to Talnovar, who didn't look impressed at all, and to Z'tala, who was standing guard at the door, eyes narrowed as she looked at me.

"When you feel better," Elay said, "we must talk."

I began to nod but stopped halfway as the pounding increased.

"I guess so," I whispered, giving him a faint smile. "I'd really like to sleep now."

"Of course. I'll wake you up in a little while, though. Healer's orders."

I smiled. Elay placed a kiss on my lips, and I had to force down the urge to push him away and wipe my mouth. Glancing aside, I found Talnovar watching us, jaw set tight, eyes flashing, but other than that, he looked in control. That was until I grinned at him, and I answered the kiss wholeheartedly. The door banging shut reverberated inside my head painfully.

One down, one to go.

CHAPTER 35

TALNOVAR

I didn't watch where I was going.

Anywhere other than that room was good. If it hadn't been for the fact something felt completely wrong, I'd have happily gone back to Ilvanna after that atrocity. A shudder ran down my spine at the memory of her kissing him, of the look in her eyes as she did so, the wicked gleam I knew she'd meant just for me. She had never been that cruel, and I sincerely doubted that whatever she had endured had made her so. I'd expected bitterness, resentment, perhaps even hatred towards me for not having come sooner.

Not cruelty.

Never cruelty.

I slowed down after a while, rubbing my temples to keep the headache at bay. It was useless, I knew, but I had to do something. I released the breath I was holding with an explosive sigh and ran a hand through my hair.

This was not how I'd imagined our first meeting to be like.

I snorted. *What had you expected, khirr? For her to run into your arms and kiss you?*

While not exactly that, I'd certainly hoped for a warmer

welcome, a look of recognition beyond what she'd shown in the throne room. Not in my wildest dreams had I imagined her playing court and dealing with politics in a different country.

Let alone wear a dress voluntarily.

Things didn't add up but curse me if I knew what was wrong. It didn't matter. I'd finally found the *Tarien*, alive and—well, alive, at least. I couldn't exactly say she was well. Not yet. As I rounded a corner, I stepped into a lush garden of greens and bright-hued flowers, a shrill contrast to the endless desert surrounding the city. I breathed in deeply and closed my eyes, indulging in the calmness this garden exuded.

After I'd stood there for the Gods knew how long, I continued following the path, my thoughts returning to the *Tarien* and our current situation. It would have been a lot easier if she weren't married to the *Akyn* of Kyrintha, but here we were. Another hurdle, another problem to solve, and I had no idea how to go about it. Would she even want to leave him? Soft footsteps drew me from my reverie, but whoever it was didn't come up to me straightaway, so I continued down the path until I found a bench where I could sit.

Despite the fact I'd just arrived, not being inside the palace seemed a good idea right about now.

He should have told me.

Reluctantly, I admitted I wasn't so much angry at Shal as I was at Elay. For some reason that was beyond me, he'd failed to mention he had married her. It would have been nice to know, not to have been blindsided, but he didn't owe me. If anything, I owed him much more, so he was entitled to his secrets.

Nevertheless, I felt bitter towards him—towards them.

The *Tarien* had obviously found a place and made a name for herself. Perhaps she didn't even want to return to Ilvanna.

She was finally free.

If you can call being married free.

A headache began to form behind my eyes, and my chest felt

tight. I'd had my chance back then, and I should have told her sooner how much she meant to me. I should have taken her up on her offer that night to take her away from the palace—to flee. Perhaps we wouldn't have been here now, and it had taken me forever to find her. I could hardly blame her for moving on.

No. She did what she had to do to survive, even marrying.

As long as I hadn't spoken to her personally, I had no right to judge her, especially not after what I'd done to survive. I'd found her, but between finding someone and getting to know someone again was a world of difference. Instead of it feeling like an end, it should feel like another beginning. Even if she were married, her life was not here and maybe, just maybe, we still had a chance.

If I could get us home.

But not only didn't I have a plan for when we reached the other side of the map, I didn't even have a plan to get us away from here. We could hardly go straight back to Ilvanna.

Azra would kill us on sight.

Out of the corner of my eye, something caught my attention. I tensed at first, only to relax moments later, forcing a gentle smile on my face.

"You can come out now."

Lujaeyn stepped from behind a massive potted plant, her eyes downcast, shoulders hunched as if she expected to be punished for her behaviour. When I patted the bench beside me, all colour drained from her face, and she looked ready to bolt.

"M... *Masran*, I can't," she murmured, glancing around to see if there was anybody close enough to have seen.

"There's nobody here," I replied. "Come, sit with me."

Call me an idiot, but I could do with some company.

Lujaeyn reluctantly sat down at the other side of the bench, keeping a good distance between us. I rolled my eyes but said nothing.

"How's the room?" I asked.

She glanced at me. "Spacious, *Masran*. Clean. It looks out over this garden."

"Is that how you knew where to find me?"

She nodded without looking at me. Her focus was on the threadbare skirt she was wearing, more specifically on a thread that was unravelling at the side. She looked as if she was about to say something while still at war over whether she should or not.

"You can talk to me," I remarked, looking at her. "I won't punish you."

"I know," Lujaeyn whispered, and swallowed hard. "I... I was just wondering, *Masran,* what you will do when you go back?"

I knew she wasn't asking this just because—she was asking out of self-interest, but if she wanted something, she had to ask for it.

"What do you mean?"

Judging by the way she inhaled, I assumed she was gathering her courage to ask me whatever was on her mind.

"Take me with you," she said, turning to me. "Please, *Masran?* I can be useful wherever you go. I won't be in the way. I'll do whatever you want, just... don't leave me here."

I frowned, trying not to show how surprised I was by her question. "Why?"

Letting out her breath in one big whoosh, she looked away and began plucking at the threads on her skirt. I practically had to sit on my own hands to stop her from doing that.

"Because here I'll always be a slave, *Masran*," she replied at length. "Whether you would set me free or not. That is what you had planned, isn't it? Our culture, it just works that way. With you, I may be a slave, but you do not treat me that way."

I smiled faintly. "Where I came from, slavery is illegal. We do have servants, but they get paid for their work, as it should be."

"I could be your servant."

It wasn't as much a question as it was an offer, and a loaded one at that. On the one hand, I wanted to provide her with safety and protection. On the other hand, I knew it would be nigh impossible with a war looming in my future. If I agreed, she'd have to come with me wherever I went until it was safe enough to go back home, and safe enough meant Azra was dead and Shalitha finally *Tari*. Until then, Lujaeyn would be at as much risk of getting killed as she would be here.

What kind of future was that?

"Lujaeyn," I began, twisting my upper body so I could look at her. "Listen." Rubbing the back of my neck, I sighed and shook my head slowly, unsure of how to proceed. "There will be a war where I'm going, one I cannot ignore or walk away from. It will determine whether I have a home to return to, provided that we win and I survive. If I were to agree, and I'm not saying that I will, you must know the danger you will be in un—"

"I don't care," she interjected, lifting her face to look at me. Tears were rolling down her cheeks. "It will still be better than the life I will be resigned to here. If I'm lucky, and that's a big if, a gentle lady will take me on to do household chores, and she may treat me kindly, but I'll be working for next to nothing. Chances of me ending up in a *Gemshin* are much more likely, and I'd rather face the possibility of death than end up in one of those again."

I looked at her. Outside the pressure of social convention, she was a lot fiercer and had little trouble speaking her mind, even to me. Before, she'd spoken her mind once or twice, but only when we'd been alone, and she'd rarely spoken in the presence of the other men.

"Very well," I said, sitting up straighter. "You can come."

She perked up.

"On two conditions," I added, and her shoulders hunched.

"Yes, *Masran*?"

"You stop calling me that the moment we leave this place," I said, raising one finger, then adding the second. "Two, I want you to be straightforward with me from now on when we're alone. I understand your culture doesn't much allow women to have a mind of their own, but I like women who can think for themselves. If you can promise me that, we have a deal."

Her eyes lit up at my words, and she nodded eagerly. "Yes, *Masran*. Of course."

I smiled. "That's settled then. Now, all we have to do is buy you some decent clothing."

She gaped at me. "*M... Masran?*"

"You're neither on display nor a piece of meat," I replied, resting my arm on the backrest of the bench. "That skirt will unravel faster than you can say *Wannenyah*, and I refuse to let you walk around in it any longer."

"Thank you, *Masran*," she whispered.

"That's quite the offer you made her," a deep voice said from my left.

Lujaeyn all but jumped off the bench, scooting out of reach. I glanced up, surprise filling me upon finding myself face to face with the Ilvannian stranger I'd seen in the throne room. He was eyeing me as quizzically as I was eyeing him.

"Have we met before?" he asked in accented Ilvannian.

I shook my head. "No, not that I know of."

"You look familiar."

"I've got one of those faces."

He shook his head. "No, that's not it. I..." It looked as if he was about to say more, but instead, he straightened. "*Akyn* Elay sent me to find you. He wishes to speak with you"—he glanced at Lujaeyn—"in private."

At the mention of Elay's name, my mood darkened instantly. Rather than responding to him, I turned to Lujaeyn. "Go back to our room. I'll meet you there."

She curtsied. "Yes, *Masran*."

I watched her leave and didn't rise to my feet until she was well out of sight, turning to the stranger with a scowl on my face. "I'm minded to send you back with the message I don't *nohro* care if he wants to see me or not," I said through gritted teeth. "But I'm curious to hear what excuses he'll come up with this time."

He arched a brow. "Excuses?"

As I made to reply, something else dawned on me, and I turned to look at him. "How long have you been here?"

"Much longer than I liked to," he replied, a wistful look in his eyes. "Long enough to meet our *Tarien.*"

I nodded slowly. "How... is she?"

"The fights changed her," he replied, motioning for me to follow him, and I did, reluctantly. "She's a skilled fighter... skilled enough that she managed to fight her way into being Akhyr's favourite, skilled enough to fight a battle a day for more than a fortnight, and then..." He swallowed hard and looked away. "She snapped and killed *Akyn* Kehran. She's not been the same since."

I stared at him.

First of all, he was much too talkative to someone he didn't know, although I could appreciate the notion it might be the case because I was Ilvannian. From the sounds of it, he'd been deprived of his home country for a long time. Second, he hadn't even offered me a name. Not that I had, but I was just following his example here.

"What do you mean, not the same?"

He shrugged. "There's an edge to her that hadn't been there when I met her. She was kind, looked out for others, for herself, but now it's as if she's lost all control and doesn't much care about the consequences."

I snorted. "The latter sounds more like her than the first."

His brows shot up in surprise. "You knew her before?"

"I'm her *Anahràn,*" I replied with a heavy sigh and turned to him to offer my hand. "Talnovar Imradien, at your service."

He stopped dead in his tracks, his face turning ashen. "Imradien?"

"Yes."

"You're... you're Cerindil's son?"

Now it was my turn to stare and feel as if all the strength had left me. I noddy slowly. "Yeah, how do you know?"

"He's my only brother," he whispered softly.

My jaw dropped and I stared. I didn't even try to conceal the fact I was gaping at him like an utter *khirr*.

"You're Jaehyr," I whispered, disbelief in my voice. "You disappeared when I was a baby."

A faint smile ghosted his lips. "I didn't exactly vanish. *Tari Arayda* knew perfectly well where I was—I just couldn't return."

I snorted. "She sure had a way of getting people to do what she wanted. I wouldn't have been here otherwise."

Jaehyr smiled wryly. "She was an excellent strategist and was always three steps ahead of everybody else."

"Until she wasn't," I muttered.

"Why would you say that?"

"Azra poisoned her," I said, looking up at him as pain twisted my gut. "She died a while ago."

Jaehyr's lips thinned. "The *Tarien* told me, but she didn't tell me how."

"I doubt she knew," I said. "I'm surprised she knew at all. She wasn't there when it happened."

Jaehyr arched a brow. "How then?"

"Wish I knew," I shrugged. "Your guess is as good as mine, but Elay told me she knew."

"Perhaps he told her?"

I shook my head. "I doubt he would have known, although I suppose rumours travel."

He fell silent, chewing his lip with a thoughtful expression on his face. "How's Ilvanna under *her* reign."

"Not a place where you'd want to be found dead," I whispered. "I've been told this Kehran was a tyrant. I think he paled in comparison to her."

He cursed in both Ilvannian and Kyrinthan and proceeded to hit the wall next to him. I didn't move—I didn't even flinch—if only because I could relate to how he must be feeling.

"We must get her home," he whispered at length, looking at me. "The *Tarien*."

"That's why I'm here." I smiled wryly.

Jaehyr rubbed his jaw and nodded slowly. I could see his brain working behind his eyes, but whatever he came up with wasn't something he shared. Instead, we continued our way through the maze of corridors.

How had I ever found that garden?

Jaehyr halted in front of an archway, a deep frown on his face. "Whatever you do in there, don't hit him."

"Why would I do that?"

"Because you were contemplating murder when you left the room." Jaehyr was smirking. "If the look on your face was any indication."

"I make no promises."

"Fine. Just promise me you'll hear him out," he said. "I think he has something to say that might be of interest." He began walking away. "Do *not* hit him. He's the *Akyn!*"

"Where are you going?" I asked incredulously.

"I've got some things to arrange," he replied, a wide grin on his lips. "No worries, we'll see each other again."

Of that, I had no doubt.

I watched as he strode around the corner, breathed in deeply and entered the room through the archway. Elay was standing near the window—or what passed as a window since everything was open here—a cup in his hand.

He turned when he heard me.

"Tal, I'm glad you could co—"

Before he could finish his sentence, I punched him in the

349

face. Something cracked, and he cursed. Blood spurted from his nose and even though he tried to stop it by tilting his head back and pinching the bridge of his nose, which had to be painful considering the fact I'd just broken it, it still poured on his chin, down his neck, and on his clothing.

"Start talking," I growled, offering him a kerchief. "And stop lying."

CHAPTER 36

HAERLYON

"*Querta* for your thoughts?" Eamryel said, looking at me over our modest campfire.

I shook my head. "Just thinking."

"Don't let his words get under your skin. He's exhausted, in pain, and dealing with entirely different things than you are. He has no idea."

"Maybe," I mumbled, not entirely convinced by this rhetoric.

Evan had always followed the rules to the letter, never stepped a toe out of line. It had been no wonder Mother had asked me instead of him, but he wasn't wrong. I did have to forsake my family for it, and everyone else I'd ever cared about. I suppose I should have been grateful for the fact some had been in on the plan from the beginning, but Evan hadn't been one of them.

As far as he was concerned, I did betray them.

Perhaps it was for the best that he believed that. It would keep him safe, keep Naraysha safe, and right now, that was all I cared about. He may believe I had deceived him, but I would do everything in my power to show him otherwise, even if he never got to see it. But that success all hinged on the maniacal idea that Azra would welcome me back after trying to get me killed.

The odds were not in my favour.

I glanced up at Eamryel, watching him as he stirred the contents of the pot. Earlier, he'd shot rabbits while I'd prepared the carrots, potatoes, and onions for the stew—quite a challenge if you only had one hand to use. After being on the road for seven days, we'd fallen into a comfortable routine.

It had been like that with—

Stop that, khirr. Stop comparing everything.

I rose to my feet with a heavy sigh, stepping behind the log I'd been sitting on to pace back and forth, mulling over everything that had happened in the last two moons, trying to make sense of things I knew deep down inside there was no making sense of. Not everything happened for a reason. Sometimes, things just happened because you're in the wrong place at the wrong time, and I'd always had a habit of that.

"Could you stop that? You're making me nervous."

I scowled at Eamryel. "It helps me think."

"Of what?"

"Everything. Nothing."

Eamryel snorted. "You realise it only makes it worse, right?"

"Easy for you to say," I muttered. "You're not about to go back to the lion's den and pretend it didn't try to eat you for breakfast."

"Perhaps," he replied, "but I am getting close enough and last time I checked, I was a wanted fugitive. I only need one person to recognise me and Azra will send her bloodhounds after me."

"I didn't ask you to come," I snapped more vehemently than I intended. I sighed, swallowed, and sat down. "Apologies..."

He was looking at me, his head slightly tilted, a thoughtful expression on his face. "Evan asked me, actually. He didn't like the idea of you going on a journey alone without being able to properly look after yourself."

"I'm not a cripple."

"And I'm the *nohro Tari*," he replied, a smirk on his face. "It's commendable how well you deal with it, Haer, but you've got to face the truth. You *are* crippled, whether you like it or not. Evan may have been wrong in saying what he did, but he wasn't wrong in this. Could you have made a fire? Shot rabbits for food? Look after your horse?"

I scowled at him and sat down, my mood plummeting to the soles of my feet. Eamryel was right. As much as I hated the idea, I could have done none of those things by myself, and truth be told, it frightened me. I was going back to court sans one arm, without backup or allies.

I would be alone.

"What am I even doing?" I ran a hand through my hair, looking up at Eamryel with desperation clinging to me like a soaked shirt. "This is insanity. She'll have me hanged in no time."

"Not if you stick to the plan," Eamryel replied. "I'll admit it's not flawless, and it has about as many holes as a fishing net, but until we hear anything from the *Tarien*, it's all we've got." He looked at me then, the sorrow on his face barely visible in the firelight. "I'm sorry it has to be you. You've already given enough to the cause."

"We all have," I replied, shaking my head. "Let's just hope Mehr is right with her gut-feeling that my sister is coming back, because if she's wrong..."

"Yeah, I know."

We fell silent.

Eamryel stirred the stew, tasting it a few times until he was satisfied with the result and proceeded to pour each of us a bowl. After adding some seasoning, he took the small wooden board he carried around to chop vegetables and herbs, placed it on my lap—like he'd done every night since we left—and set the bowl on it, handing me the spoon.

I hadn't been able to shake the impression he still felt guilty. *That makes us even.*

Although I didn't really feel guilty about kissing him—awkward perhaps, but not guilty, I still had no idea what his feelings on the matter were. We'd not spoken of it at all, and he seemed perfectly content pretending it never happened. He was even being incredibly civil and kind to me, like he had been before, as if nothing at all had changed for him.

Everything had changed for me.

I glanced at him inconspicuously during dinner and caught him looking at me. His lips pulled up in a faint smile as he returned his attention to his bowl, eating heartily. My heart was thudding in my chest—what was wrong with me? I breathed out a sigh, finished the stew and set the bowl aside.

It was a while before I spoke, "Eam, about that day."

"Don't mention it," he said a little strained, but not unkindly. "It's fine."

"I wanted to apologise," I said, ignoring his protests.

He didn't respond to that—not straightaway. Instead, he collected the bowls and set to cleaning them with as little water as possible. I'd noticed before how meticulous he was about it, more so even than most of the kitchen staff at the palace.

He was used to this kind of life.

"Have you always known?" Eamryel asked without looking at me.

I didn't need to ask to know what he was talking about. "Yes. Well, I think I did, I never really considered it."

"Your family seemed fine with it," he replied, softer this time. "They accepted it, didn't they?"

"I think they knew before I ever did. It's probably why Evan was always at my side, and Shal would give anyone who ever said anything wrong about me an earful. It wasn't easy being who I was—especially because of who I was."

Eamryel nodded, biting his lip as he contemplated my words. Although hard to tell by firelight, I deduced he was working through something of his own, at war with himself whether to tell me or not.

I didn't press him.

"Father never approved." His voice was hushed, barely audible over the crackling of the fire. "Always said he did not understand why your parents didn't cast you out, said you were an abomination, that you and your... kind should be eradicated. He was so vocal about it, I never dared take that step, never dared to explore, but I knew... I knew I was different."

I tilted my head slightly. "But you went after my sister. You hurt her because she loved somebody else."

He pressed his lips in a thin line and rested his head in his hands. "What I did to the *Tarien* is unforgivable. I... wasn't myself then, certain... opiates, they make life bearable, they can also make you psychotic. I—" He lifted his head to look at me. "I can never repair what I did in those weeks, can never make it up, but I'm trying. You have no idea what it was like growing up with him, living with him."

"He wasn't exactly a delight to have around the palace either," I replied, a faint smile on my lips. "As for Shal... that's between you and her. As far as I'm concerned, you've proven your worth and loyalty and paid for your mistakes."

"Thank you."

In truth, the image of Shal on the day of her return after her time with him still haunted me, but I meant what I said to him. He'd redeemed himself—in my eyes. As for Shal, I doubted she would ever forgive him, no matter what he did in her favour, but I wasn't going to tell him that. He seemed to be struggling enough as it was.

"I like both," Eamryel said after a bit, "but I have a stronger affinity towards"—he paused, swallowing audibly—"men."

Was that an admission?

A jolt went through me, but I quickly pushed down all the hopeful feelings that surfaced in case I was reading too much into it. I couldn't afford any hope. Not now.

"When you kissed me," Eamryel continued, staring into the fire, "everything I'd kept locked away for so long came out, and"—he bit his lip again, looking down—"I didn't want you to see me fall apart."

My brows shot up in surprise. "I wouldn't have judged you."

"You would have," he said. "I didn't cry, Haer, not at first. I screamed, I yelled, I cursed—cursed you in every language I knew, wished I'd let that man kill you, wished a thousand deaths upon you, and then I cried."

"I still wouldn't have judged you," I replied, keeping my voice gentle.

I wanted nothing more than to hold him, to comfort him, and tell him it was all perfectly normal, but it was easy for me. I'd never really had to hide, not like him, obviously. Sure, children my age had bullied me, called me names behind my back, even picked fights with me the few times Evan or Shal hadn't been around to shield me from them.

I'd not grown up with someone like Yllinar.

No matter how much I'd tell him it was normal, no matter how much I would try to comfort him, he would believe and feel none of it until he felt comfortable with the idea—with himself. So, I stayed where I was, watching him work through this from a distance.

"I didn't want to come at first," he said, flashing me an apologetic smile, "but then I realised my saving your life would have been poor judgement if I allowed you to die now."

I smiled. "It is appreciated."

He returned the smile this time. A moment later he coughed and rose to his feet, looking around for something to do.

This conversation was over.

"Get some sleep," he said. "I'll keep first watch."

He'd keep watch all night. For a brief moment, I considered arguing, but decided against it and made myself comfortable on my bedroll instead. Well, as comfortable as one could be anyway. It would never beat a featherdown mattress. I listened to Eamryel's receding footsteps. He wouldn't go far, just beyond the circle of light from where he could observe our little camp. I thought it'd make him an easy target for wolves and bears, but he had scoffed at my protest the first night, so I didn't voice my opinion on the matter again.

He knew how to survive in the forest.

Who was I to doubt him?

MORE THAN EIGHT days after Eamryel's confession, we reached the mountain pass from which a single road snaked towards the main road to the city. There were trees on either side of the road, obscuring anyone travelling that way from view, but Eamryel would go no farther. This was where we'd say goodbye, for better or for worse, and each go our own way. Although we hadn't spoken of it, I assumed Eamryel would return to *Denahryn*—he was an Ilvannian fugitive after all—but I wouldn't be surprised if he'd hang around simply because he could.

We sat on our horses side by side, looking down at the city sprawled at the foot of the mountain, the palace towering over it like a silent protector. Ironically, it offered no protection at all, not to its denizens within, nor to the people without.

Not anymore.

A knot formed in my stomach at the thought of having to go

back. I'd much rather turn around and join forces with Cerindil and the rebels.

With Eamryel.

I almost made myself want to throw up at this cliche. I had a job to do—I didn't have time for daydreams of romance and happily ever afters. It wasn't in the cards for me, would never be in the cards for me. After everything I'd done, I deserved to die in the upcoming war.

Along with many others.

The thought was sobering.

As I turned to Eamryel, my horse began to prance underneath me, and I barely managed to cling to its back when it reared. If it hadn't been for Eamryel grabbing the reins, there was no telling what would have happened.

It fed into my anxiety of going back.

How was I going to survive court if there were so many things I couldn't do by myself? Soren had helped me as much as he could, but two moons had been too little time, and Cerindil figured I couldn't stay away much longer. I inhaled deeply and exhaled to the count of ten, calming myself down.

I had one thing to my advantage.

"Be careful out there," Eamryel said, looking back at the city now. "Scouts have come back with the most horrendous stories."

I flashed him a lopsided smile. "I thrive underneath a bit of danger. Makes life interesting."

He didn't buy it. "I'm serious. Rumour has it Azra gave birth, but her baby died. She's been even more dangerous since."

"I didn't know there was a stage above genocidal maniac," I replied. "Although if anyone could reach it, I suppose it's her."

"Do you ever take anything seriously?" Eamryel looked a bit taken aback.

I shrugged. "Humour is my coping mechanism. It's how I survived court intrigue for as long as I have being who I am."

He shook his head slowly, but there was the hint of a smile on his lips. They'd tasted so good. I pulled my thoughts away from them and instead focused on his eyes, sobering up.

"Don't worry," I said. "I realise the gravity of the situation, and I'm not going in believing it's going to be easy. It never was. It never will be. I only hope I survive long enough to see Azra's face when Shal returns."

Eamryel snorted at that. "I doubt she'll welcome her with open arms."

"Oh, definitely with open arms," I remarked, "and a hidden dagger."

At that, he rolled his eyes. "You should get going. The gates close at dusk, and they will let nobody in after that. I wouldn't want you to freeze to death."

"Would you miss me if I did?" The words were out of my mouth before I could stop them, and I looked away, discomfort nestling in my stomach in a way it never had before.

"I would," Eamryel said.

My head snapped up at his words, and I stared at him like a half-wit. He chuckled softly and guided his horse closer to mine so that our legs were almost touching.

"Who else am I supposed to save then?" he added with a wicked grin.

I rolled my eyes. "I'm sure you'll find someone."

It was hard to keep the bite out of my voice, but his words had stung worse than I'd imagined. It was my own fault. I had secretly built up the hope there was something going on between us. I'd acted on it back at *Denahryn*, and his confession had only bolstered that belief. There had been moments the past days where I'd thought he'd open up, but clearly it wasn't in the way I'd expected.

Happiness is for those who deserve it.

We clasped a hand on each other's wrist, a solid goodbye—a

man's goodbye—and looked at each other much longer than any man should. Then Eamryel let go and inclined his head.

"I'll look for you on the battlefield, *mahnèh.*"

My friend.

I watched him ride in the direction we'd come from until he was out of sight, then sighed heavily, returning my attention to the city below.

"Meet you on the battlefield."

CHAPTER 37

SHALITHA

It took the better part of six days for the healer to decide I was well enough to get out of bed, six days in which Elay had been able to ascertain his hold on the throne and his people. This wasn't how it had supposed to play out. I'd hoped for more time, but with his return, I could no longer lay claim to anything in any other position than his wife.

Suffice to say, I was annoyed.

"Not the way you like it?"

I stilled at the sound of that voice. Her voice.

That's impossible.

She didn't respond. I slung my legs over the side of the bed and waited for it to happen again. It didn't. It must have been a figment of my imagination. I'd slept for most of those six days, and I simply hadn't quite woken up yet.

That was it.

I was just imagining things.

Pushing myself to my feet, I staggered forward, caught myself by grabbing the back of a chair and breathed deeply for a few moments to regain my bearings. A servant girl shuffled forward, keeping her eyes downcast, waiting for an order. Strangely enough, I wasn't sure what to go for. Food, clothing, something to drink?

"I'd go for food first," Shalitha spoke in my mind. *"Food always makes me feel better, especially after I've been ill. Fluids are supposed to help, too. Well, according to Soren anyway."*

A low growl escaped my throat, startling the servant girl and drawing attention from someone at the door. I glanced up to find Jaehyr hovering at the edges of my peripherals and dismissed him with a wave of my hand.

"Get me something to eat and drink," I told the girl without looking at her. "And get me something to wear that won't hamper my movements."

"Oh, are we training?"

I ignored her. Perhaps if I did that long enough, she would stop talking. What was it they said about paying attention to enemies?

"It makes them stronger," Shalitha offered. *"So, we're enemies now?"*

"Shut up," I hissed.

It was a strange sensation to be spoken to in my mind—I'd always been on the providing comments end of the spectrum, not the receiving end, and in a strange way, I began to understand the *Tarien's* annoyance when I'd done it to her. I quickly shoved my feelings away. It didn't matter. She didn't matter.

None of this did.

I was alive, albeit not exactly in the form and shape I preferred, but it wasn't all bad. If anything, I had options— better options than I'd ever had before, and I would make the best of it. I just had to make sure nobody would defy and expose me.

I'll have to keep a close eye on Z'tala.

Half-expecting a comment from the *Tarien*, I was surprised

none was forthcoming, and I heaved a sigh in relief. I could still keep her out if I really wanted to. My thoughts returned to the matter at hand, to Elay having had six days to determine his power over his people and the position it left me in. Ideas swirled on the edges of my mind, not quite within reach, and they stayed stubbornly out of it no matter how hard I tried to grasp them.

As if they were being kept back.

Is that even possible?

"Not really, it's just how the brain works. Think of it for a while, and your ideas become more tangible. Surely, you knew that. Doesn't it work the same for you?"

"I was sentient," I muttered. "Not alive. Makes a difference."

"But you used to be alive..."

"How did you—"

A cough startled me and looking up, I found Jaehyr standing at my side, a concerned look etched around his eyes.

"Everything all right, *Tari?*" he asked.

I nodded. "Fine, just... still a bit tired, I guess."

He narrowed his eyes but inclined his head. "Very well. Breakfast is here. Would you like to remain indoors or sit out in the garden?"

"The garden," I replied, deciding a bit of fresh air would do me good.

On his command, servants carried plates and bowls of food outside. Soon after, the sound of them preparing the table reached me inside, and I rose to my feet unsteadily. Jaehyr's hand shot out to keep me from falling over.

"I'm fine," I snapped. "Let go of me."

He did, but not without casting me a suspicious look. At least, I thought he did, because when I looked at him directly, his face was impassive. I slipped into my robe and tightened the sash around my waist. It wasn't enough to hurt—just enough to be noticeable. I needed the pain to comfort me this was real, to tell me I wasn't going slightly mad. Outside, the air was less stifling than inside, the fragrance of flowers heavy enough you could taste it. Even so, I felt better just being here, if only because I wasn't surrounded by four walls.

The table was set up for two.

"The *Akyn* will join you shortly, *Akynai*," a servant said from somewhere behind me. "He bids you do not wait for him."

Of course, he would.

I sat down heavily and leaned back, closing my eyes. This day kept getting better and better.

"Self-pity really doesn't become you, or me for that matter. I've never understood how it helps a person feel better. It's only ever made me feel worse."

I didn't reply, but as much as I hated to admit it, she was right. Self-pity wasn't for the likes of us—I'd told her the same— and as much as she annoyed me, a part of me took pride in the fact she was putting up a fight. As the daughter of the God of War, I'd expected no less.

She was still a nuisance.

Looking around the table, I settled for a variety of fruit and nuts. The scent of meat made my stomach churn. Who ate meat for breakfast anyway? I was halfway through my plate when Elay appeared, shadows under his eyes and around his jaw. He flopped in the empty chair across from me and stretched out his legs.

"You look tired," I observed, sitting back.

Not just tired.

The shadows under his eyes weren't just that—they were bruises, and his nose looked a little crooked as well, as if someone had punched him. Purple and yellow spots still surrounded his eyes. Whoever had punched him, had gotten him good.

I had the silly notion to put a plate of food together for him.

As his wife, I probably should, and though it would help keep up appearances, I wondered if the *Tarien* was the kind of partner who would do that for her husband. She'd never struck me that way, but I couldn't risk it. I was of half a mind to ask her, but I didn't think she'd respond.

What is happening to me?

Rather than focusing on that disturbing notion, I began piling food on a plate and placed it in front of him. At first, I didn't think he'd even noticed, but then he took a piece of meat between thumb and forefinger and brought it to his mouth.

"I've been in council all morning," he said, sounding tired, too, "just like I have the past mornings to undo the mess Kehran made of things."

I merely nodded and sat back, watching him rub his jaw and grimacing.

"Is it true you told them to gather every man able to fight?" he asked after a while, looking up at me.

"I did," I replied, lifting my chin. "That was part of the deal to get you back on the throne. I'd help you—you'd help me."

"I know. I haven't forgotten," he said. "The council hadn't honoured your request yet."

I scowled at that. "Let me guess. Because I'm a woman?"

He smiled faintly at that. "I wouldn't be surprised. The first thing they did was shove the agreement under my nose, which said you were appointed *Akynai* until my return and had me sign a boatload of documents in order to observe that I was indeed who I said I was and more of that nonsense. They even had the audacity to question our marriage certificate."

"As did I," I replied with a shrug. "I was ready to fight your younger brother over the position."

He stared at me. "What?"

I shrugged. "It would only be till first blood. I wouldn't have killed him."

A groan escaped his lips. He closed his eyes and leaned back as if to ask the Gods to witness my stupidity.

I was sure they did already.

"He took you up on the offer, I presume?" Elay asked, opening one eye to look at me.

"Absolutely," I grinned. "He even asked if we could still do it after R'tayan settled the dilemma with producing the marriage certificate. I promised we could."

He sighed heavily and murmured, "Remind me to ask Talnovar how he kept up with you."

I merely shrugged.

I had no idea either.

"The royal tailor is coming by later to take your measurements," Elay said. "I'd have asked you this morning, but you were still asleep."

"Why does he need my measurements?"

Elay's brows shot up in surprise, but he quickly masked it. "For a dress for the coronation, of course."

That's the first time I've heard of it.

"I could have told you," Shalitha said, sounding quite smug. *"Quite the obvious follow up on events, don't you think?"*

I didn't like how that sounded, but as much as I'd love a little one-on-one time with the *Tarien,* now was not it. Out of the corner of my eye, I noticed movement, and I looked up to find Z'tala coming our way.

"Your presence is required, *Akyn,*" she said, glancing at me. "Jaehyr will go with you."

I inclined my head. "Thank you, Z'tala."

He pushed himself to his feet and turned to me, obviously about to say something, but he snapped his mouth shut and turned away, the look on his face as if I'd hurt him. I frowned but didn't say anything.

I had no idea.

Z'tala turned to me as soon as he left, her eyes full of suspicion. Again, I had no idea why, but I got the impression I had done things I wasn't aware of.

Had I?

"The tailor is here, *Akynai*," she said. "Do you wish to receive him here or inside?"

"Inside," I replied, if only because I felt that's what the *Tarien* would have chosen.

As we moved into the room, I couldn't shake the disturbing feeling settling in my gut. Elay had behaved out of the norm, nowhere near the doting husband I'd seen the first few days. Z'tala was naturally suspicious, so that didn't count, and then there was the *Tarien's* voice in my head.

How did that happen?

"You don't want to know," Shalitha commented. *"But you don't have to worry. They don't know. Yet."*

"And you do know?" I thought in annoyance.

"Nope. No idea."

An image of her walking away appeared in my mind like a thought, except that I was quite sure it hadn't been something I consciously thought of. Had I appeared to her like that?

Get it together.

Breathing in deeply, I counted to ten and released my breath in a loud exhale, drawing the attention of a man dressed in the finest silks. He turned in a flurry of colour, the scowl on his face deepening once he laid eyes on me.

"I don't like the look of you either," I said snidely, "but can we get on with this? I've got more to do than standing around all afternoon."

The royal tailor turned a darker shade but inclined his head and whistled. A moment later, a young boy hurried into the room, carrying two bags and several rolls of cloth underneath his arm. He dumped them on a table and ran off, only to return a little while later carrying even more cloth.

This wasn't just going to be a measurement session.

BY THE TIME evening came around, my feet were sore from standing, and I was no longer sure I could move my shoulders if I wanted to. I'd endured hours of mumbling, poking, and prodding, and while the royal tailor hadn't been unkind about it, I still just felt sore. But he'd gotten everything he needed and promised me a dress the likes of which had never been seen in either the Kyrinthan or Ilvannian court.

I couldn't help feeling impressed and even excited.

Just after the tailor left, there was a knock on the door. It sounded hesitant, as if the person behind it wasn't sure whether to knock at all, and then it came again, more purposeful this time. I motioned for Z'tala to open it, expecting R'tayan or perhaps Naïda.

I did not expect Talnovar to step into the room.

Nohro.

The moment I laid my eyes on him, something changed. It was as if I forgot how to breathe, forgot how to think, forgot how to be alive, and I knew.

"*Hehzèh!*" I yelled. "*I will kill you! I will kill them. You won't win this!*"

Shalitha didn't respond, but I knew she'd taken over control, just like she had that day in the throne room when she'd first seen him. Talnovar was more of a threat than I'd initially thought.

Something had to be done about that.

So, I lay dormant, waiting, experiencing her life yet again as a spectator. Unlike her, it seemed, I could hear what was being said, see what she saw. It was the only upside of having been sentient for centuries.

To my surprise, there wasn't much to hear.

Talnovar kept his distance, lips pressed in a thin line,

watching her as if he were looking at a stranger. When she stepped forward, he took a step back, shaking his head.

"Don't," he said. "Just... don't."

"Tal, please," the *Tarien* whispered, taking another step forward. "Let me explain."

I had missed part of their conversation.

"It's fine, *Tarien.*" The tone in his voice revealed it was anything but fine. "As your *Anahràn,* I merely wanted to see how you were doing. Seeing you up is good. I'm sure your husband is looking after you."

She stiffened, her thoughts a turmoil.

"I thought he loved you," I sneered. *"By Esah, the amount of times you thought of him and now he doesn't want you? Harsh!"*

She didn't respond.

"Let him go, Tarien. He obviously doesn't want you. Can't blame him. You haven't exactly been yourself lately. Do you think I should have let you run into his arms? Would that have helped?"

Still no response.

She was ignoring me as I'd been ignoring her. I would have rolled my eyes if I could have. This conversation had lasted long enough.

"My turn, Tarien."

Breathing in deeply, I was relieved to find taking back control was easier than I'd thought. Talnovar's cold shoulder had obviously done the trick. Maybe I could lend her a hand.

"As a matter of fact," I said. "He does. Better than you ever have."

He stilled, staring at me.

"I've always looked after you," he replied, voice devoid of emotions. He was a trained warrior, of course, he knew how to keep them under control.

"And yet it's taken you three years to find me," I spat, baring my teeth in a snarl. "You didn't even bother to go after me! You didn't even bother to rescue me. You just stood there! You allowed Eamryel to take me!"

He narrowed his eyes, lips pressed in a thin line, and before I could say anything else, he'd pivoted on his heel and left the room.

"It wasn't Eamryel who took me."

I cursed.

CHAPTER 38

TALNOVAR

"*W*e need to talk."

Elay looked up from his training but didn't stop. While not exactly scowling, he wasn't pleased to see me either, for which I couldn't blame him. I'd broken his nose, after all.

We'd not spoken again since.

"It's about the *Tarien*," I continued and cleared my throat, "about Shal."

His movement slowed until he halted completely. He didn't look at me straight away, his focus determinedly on the tiles, clenching his hands into fists, and releasing them as if he were debating whether to return the favour.

"I think something's wrong."

"She's been through trauma," he said through gritted teeth, "even before you arrived, Talnovar."

"Yes, and through trauma even before then," I snapped, quickly reigning in my anger before I continued, "and she didn't behave the way she does now. She's never been this... cruel."

He spun toward me so fast I thought he'd lunge for me. "Then perhaps this was the final straw, and she broke."

"Listen to me," I growled. "It's not her. She blamed me for not coming after her, for just standing there, for letting Eamryel take her!"

His eyes narrowed at the name, but he wasn't perturbed. "So?"

"It was never Eamryel who took her."

Elay had opened his mouth to retort something, but snapped it shut upon hearing my words. He sank back on the lounger, dropping his head in his hands.

"I thought it was me," he said after a while. "I thought I was the only one who'd noticed."

"No," a female voice said from the garden side of the room. "Not just you, *Akyn*. Jaehyr and I have noticed it, too."

I looked up at Z'tala, a frown on my face. "How long have you known?"

"Known is a big word, *k'lele*," she said. "I suspected."

"How?" Elay asked. "When?"

Z'tala shrugged and shook her head. "I'm not entirely sure, *Akyn*. Perhaps during the last battle? By all accounts, she should not have made it. The *Tarien* of Ilvanna should have been dead... like me. She'd been too injured to fight, too exhausted to lift her sword. I'd told her to say the word and I would rally the *herri-atâre*. Naïda and Jaehyr were already waiting. She told me..." She swallowed and looked away. "She asked me to kill her, told me her fight was done. Everything would be fine, she said, if I just killed her. Kehran would have been appeased, and nobody else had to die."

"Sounds like her all right," I muttered.

She shot me a look. "Then suddenly, something changed. She did. It was as if she'd gotten her strength back, as if she'd gotten a new burst of energy that burned all the pain and exhaustion away, but..." Her brows furrowed in a thoughtful V-shape, tongue between her teeth as she tried to remember. "She had this grin on her face, a gleam in her eye. She'd always had that during a fight—she was good, good enough to have survived so many battles, and if Kehran had treated her better, she could have been up there with the best, but it had never been so wicked, so insane. And the way she killed Kehran—"

"How did she?" Elay and I asked at the same time.

"She threw a spear at him," Z'tala said. "From a distance."

My jaw dropped. Elay looked impressed. Z'tala on the other hand shook her head again, confusion written all over her face.

"You don't understand. She should not have been able to do that either. She was halfway across the *herrât* when she threw it, and she did not miss." She ran a hand through her braids and began pacing. "Afterwards, when we went to the bathhouse, she couldn't remember the way, and once there... she dove into the water."

Elay looked puzzled at that.

I didn't.

"She would never do that," I observed quietly. "She'd bathe, but she'd never dive into the water."

"I know," Z'tala replied. "The first time we went to the bathhouse, she panicked when I told her to go under. She never did explain what happened, but I assume she was afraid."

I nodded, not surprised by this. "She nearly drowned when she was young."

"And at sea," Elay offered quietly, a look of comprehension dawning on his face.

"So, the question is," I said at length. "What is wrong with her and how can we undo it?"

Neither of them answered, shaking their head, or shrugging instead.

"We must pretend we know nothing," Z'tala said. "Or at least the two of you do. She already knows I don't trust her."

"How come?" Elay looked up at her.

"Because I asked her outright who she was with a knife at her throat."

"She must not have been pleased with that."

Z'tala smirked. "No. She tried very hard to convince me it was her. I figured it would be easiest to keep an eye on her if I pretended that she had, and it has worked—so far."

"How are we going to help her?" Elay's voice was soft, tired, the look on his face of a man who was defeated, who'd gained everything and shortly after lost it.

I knew exactly how it felt.

"As long as we don't know what's changing her," I ventured, "I don't think there's much we can do. Although"—something occurred to me then—"when I went to see her tonight, something about her changed briefly, but it did. She recognised me— really recognised me, said she wanted to explain. I told her I was doing my job to check up on her as her *Anahràn*, to see how she was doing, to ensure that everything was fine." My gaze settled on Elay, but he wasn't looking at me. "And then she started shouting and blaming me for not coming after her. It was then she twisted the truth. Why would she do that?"

"What does it matter?" Elay suddenly rose to his feet, clenching his hands into fists. "As long as we don't know what's wrong with her, there's nothing we can do."

I wanted to smack him.

Hard.

Z'tala was there before me, but a lot kinder than I would have been. "Get some rest, *Akyn*. You're worn thin and worried about her. Talnovar and I will go over everything we know and see if we can come up with something."

"What if you don't?"

"We'll go from there," she replied, sounding like a mother putting her child at ease.

Elay walked out of the room in a sullen mood, all but dragging his feet as he left us. Z'tala turned to me, a worried expression on her face.

"There's something else you must know, something I have

yet to tell Elay," she said, glancing at the archway to make sure nobody was lurking there. A fleeting look of uncertainty crossed her face, and then she sighed. "She was raped, not too long ago."

Her lips were moving, but I could hear no sound beyond the sudden rush in my ears. My heart pounded as if it were trying to break free from my ribcage and take on a life of its own. A hand on my shoulder jerked me back to awareness, and I found myself staring at Z'tala, breathing hard and fast.

"I'll kill him," I hissed.

"Don't bother," Z'tala replied. "She already did."

That knocked the wind right out of me. "She did?"

"Listen, Talnovar. You seem like a good guy, which is why I'm telling you this, no offense meant. A lot has happened to her, I do not know to which extent. Elay knows more, but I know what happened to her here. Kehran did everything he could to make her life miserable—more than miserable. He did everything within his power to break her—he enjoyed watching her struggle. She defied him every step of the way until she no longer could. I know you punched Elay, and I can tell by the way you're looking at them you're not happy with the arrangements, but here's something you need to remember..."

"What's that?"

"She did it to survive," Z'tala said, softer this time. "She did it so she could live and return to you."

"She told you that?"

"She didn't have to. It was clear from the way she spoke about you."

"What about Elay?" I asked, not quite sure what to make of this.

"I think she loves him, too."

The pain would have been less had she gutted me with a knife.

"Thank you," I said, inclining my head. "For helping me convince Elay."

I turned on my heel and left, needing to be alone with the emotions running rampant. I wasn't yet sure how to get it out of my system, but I knew I didn't want to stay inside.

IT WAS WELL into the night when I entered my bedroom. I assumed Lujaeyn was already asleep, but I found her sitting on the windowsill, knees pulled up, head resting on them, staring out into the garden. The fire had died down to smouldering embers, and what little light illuminated the room came from a few candles that hadn't yet sputtered and died.

She looked up when I closed the door behind me.

"You're back," she said in a soft voice, turning her head to look at me. "How is your *Tarien?*"

"She's fine," I snapped, then quickly added, "sorry, Lujaeyn, it's been a long day."

I sat down on the side of the bed, my elbows resting on my legs, my head bowed. Although training helped get rid of some of the emotions, I was still tense and more than a little angry, at Elay, at Kehran, but mostly at myself.

The bed dipped as Lujaeyn sat down beside me. "Are you all right, *Mas*—are you okay?"

"I'm not sure." I winced at the vulnerability in my voice.

"Here," she murmured, seating herself behind me. "Sit up. Let me massage out those knots."

Without waiting for me to do or say anything, she ran her hands from my neck down my back, repeating the motion several times. I straightened and was soon lost in the rhythmic movement of her hands massaging my neck and shoulders.

"If you lie down," she murmured, "I can do your back, too."

By then I was too languid to protest. She moved out of the way, and I rolled on my stomach before scooting up on the bed. I swallowed hard when she straddled me and placed her hands on the small of my back. A sound between a sigh and a moan escaped me as she began to massage the muscles along my spine.

"This is... amazing," I murmured, half-asleep. "Don't stop."

She chuckled softly. "I won't, *Masran*."

A moment later, she placed a kiss between my shoulder blades, sending a shiver rolling down my spine, and I couldn't help grunting in response.

"Just relax," she whispered. "Let me take care of you."

I remembered what that meant and was of half a mind to tell her to stop until I realised I didn't want her to. Massaging had turned into caressing as her fingers trailed the *Araîth* coiling down my side.

"What does it mean?" she whispered softly. "Your tattoo, I mean?"

She'd never asked me before.

With a bit of wriggling, I managed to turn around underneath her so I could look at her. Her eyes widened just a little as she sat back down on top of me. These kinds of trousers hid everything and nothing.

"Every Ilvannian has one," I said softly, watching her as she trailed the design on my shoulder, gritting my teeth as she followed it all the way down to my waistband. "The bigger the *Araîth*, the higher in rank."

"Is that why the *Tarien* had her face done?"

The thought of Shal was almost like a cold shower. I swallowed hard and nodded, taking Lujaeyn's hands in mine to kiss her knuckles to prevent myself from responding too much to her caresses.

"Yes. Hers starts underneath the sole of her foot and winds all the way up into her hairline," I said.

"You must be high nobility, too," she remarked, her eyes roving over my chest. "Yours is quite sizeable."

The bright smile on her face made me wonder if she was still talking about the *Araîth*.

"Not quite," I chuckled, placing a kiss on the inside of her wrists. "As her *Anahràn*, captain, I received her mark, too. Only my arm is the mark of my family."

Lujaeyn pursed her lips, mulling over my words. "What if you do not want to be her captain anymore?"

I smiled faintly at that. "I either die in my position or cede it to someone younger if offered a higher position. In either case, I'd still be in her service."

"Sounds complicated," Lujaeyn murmured. "Do you enjoy it?"

"I enjoy this," I said under my breath and pulled her in for a deep kiss.

She melted against me, and for some time, nothing existed but us. The guilt that had gnawed at me before vanished with each gentle touch and each scorching kiss until it was nothing but a whisper in my mind. Lujaeyn's caretaking had been welcome on our journey here, but we'd never gone further than that. I hadn't felt the need to share that with whomever we shared our tent with.

But now?

The tenderness of her hands and the curiosity in her eyes nearly undid me. She was young perhaps, but she wanted it as much as I did.

No, I need it.

I needed it like I needed air to breathe and water to drink—I needed to know, feel, sense that there was still something good in this world, something whole. It felt like my life was falling apart around me, each day bringing to light a new problem to deal with, but here, now, there was just us.

A low growl escaped my lips when she kissed my throat and

proceeded a steady trail down, but before she could get much farther, I spun us around, so she lay beneath me. She bit her lip, squirming beneath me in a way that sent my body into a frenzy. I swallowed hard, looking at her, my breathing coming in ragged gasps.

"My turn," I murmured.

I LISTENED to Luyaen's even breaths, felt her chest rise and fall underneath my arm, and wished upon a star it was Shal in my arms. Our lovemaking had been wonderful, no doubt about it—gentle, sweet, slow, nothing like what I'd ever experienced with Cehyan, or Azra for that matter, but it wasn't Lujaeyn I wanted to wake up next to.

I miss you.

Without rousing her, I extricated my arm and slipped out of bed. My mind was much too awake, my thoughts much too dark to find the bliss of sleep I'd hoped to be in by now. I stifled a yawn as I pulled on my trousers and made my way over to the window. Except for the occasional call of a bird, there was absolutely no sound—the palace had drifted off into a deep slumber.

At this time of night, the palace was quiet.

I didn't like the quiet.

Not anymore.

I considered going for a walk to clear my head and think things over, but by the time I finally made a decision, I couldn't stop yawning, so instead, I slipped back into bed. I remained on the edge and turned on my side, drawing up my knees.

I awoke to a rustle just in time to see the shimmer of a blade coming down at me.

CHAPTER 39

SHALITHA

A loud scream tore through the room—a feminine scream, but not one I recognised.

I was on my stomach on the floor, my arm twisted painfully behind me, a knee pressed firmly on my back. The weight pushing me down made it hard to breathe. My thoughts raced past every possible option to get out of this, but no solution presented itself. I struggled, but it only resulted in my cheek being pushed even firmer against the tiles.

"Who sent you?" a voice hissed.

His voice.

My heart fluttered and skipped a beat, not just because Tal was here, but because I'd beaten *him*. I'd made it back. I swallowed hard, tried to speak, but it was hard with Tal's weight on top of me. Then his question hit me.

Who sent you?

Sent me to do what?

The fireplace suddenly roared to life, blinding me, and it took me a moment or two to make out a silhouette coming my way. Judging by the way they walked, it was a woman, and she was carrying a candle in our direction.

Why is there a woman in Tal's room?

"Please," I whimpered. "You're hurting me."

He pushed firmer on my arm. "Which one are you?"

"Shal."

Tal eased his hold on me, but only a little. Judging by the way his fingers were digging into my arm, he didn't quite believe me.

"Tell me something only you know."

"I asked you to take me away from the palace," I whispered. "In the caves. You said it'd be kidnapping, and I replied it wasn't kidnapping if I'd go voluntarily."

As the pressure on my back lifted, I pushed myself to a sitting position and leaned against whatever was behind me. It was only then I noticed the blade lying a few feet away. Wide-eyed, I turned my attention to Tal, looked at his feet, and let it travel upwards until my eyes locked with his.

"What did I do?"

He'd folded his arms in front of him, pressed his lips in a tight line and for a moment, I was taken back to a time where he'd looked much the same—a time in which we'd been happy.

Happier.

I couldn't see his eyes in this darkness, and I wasn't sure I wanted to. I touched my face with a trembling hand, ran my tongue over my lips, only to find them split, and gingerly touched the bruise I could feel forming on the side of my head.

"You tried to kill me," Tal said, his voice devoid of emotions.

"I—" I wished I could say it hadn't been me, that I'd been possessed by some sentient being I'd picked up through a sword given to me by Esahbyen.

As if he would believe me.

"I'm sorry."

He arched a brow. "You're sorry? That's all you've got to say to me. Sorry?" He ran a hand through his tousled hair, looking for all the world like a caged tiger ready to pounce.

"Calm down, *Masran*," a soft voice said from behind him, and it was only then I noticed the girl standing there.

As she cupped his face in her hand, I wanted nothing more than to grab the dagger and plunge it deep into her heart. The sudden rush of jealousy startled me, and I scooted back against the bed hard enough for the wooden base to prick uncomfortably in my shoulder blades.

I kicked the dagger away for good measure.

"Master?" I asked, forcing to keep my voice level. "You have a... a slave?"

"A servant," he replied through gritted teeth.

I nodded, swallowed, and let my eyes wander over him. As the girl went about lighting the candles throughout the room, Tal emerged from the shadows more and more. My eyes were drawn to the black lines starting at the base of his jaw, disappearing beneath the waistband of his trousers. Tears pricked my eyes upon recognising the design.

"You..." I swallowed again, staring at it.

My hand went up of its own accord even though he was nowhere near enough to touch and hung there trembling. I dropped it as soon as my gaze settled on the white line just barely visible on his abdomen.

"By Esah," I gasped and looked away.

I'd almost added another scar.

I looked at him—really looked at him. The harshness in his eyes had softened, but only a little. Emotions were swirling in their emerald midst, and I wanted nothing more than to rise to my feet and throw my arms around him, to kiss him, but I didn't dare.

I'd tried to kill him.

"I warned you."

A sob escaped my lips upon hearing that voice. Dread slithered through my body and settled heavily in my bones. Fear rose higher and higher until I found myself gasping for air and clawing at my throat. My heart was racing, and my chest felt as if Tal was sitting on it again. Nausea threatened to overwhelm me. I tried to fight it back, tell myself to calm down, think of the times where I'd managed to breathe it away.

And then he was there, on his knees in front of me, placing my hand against his chest.

"Breathe," he murmured. "Count my heartbeats and breathe to them. You can do it. You know you can."

I did.

I breathed, I calmed down, and I burst out sobbing, burying my face in my hands. Tal shifted, sat down next to me and pulled me into his lap, letting out a deep, shuddering sigh as his arms came around me.

We sat like that until my sobs subsided into sniffles.

"Here," the girl said and handed me a kerchief. "I... made some tea, if you want?"

I looked up at her, surprise washing over me. "For... me?"

"Of course," she replied gently, "and *Ma*—ehm, Talnovar, if he wants?"

He waved his hand in dismissal as he helped me to my feet. "I think I might try Elay's *keffah* again. It tastes vile, but it sure keeps you awake."

I stilled. "You've met Elay?"

"He brought me here," he replied, a faint smile on his lips. "Although he left out you two were married."

"I—" He placed a finger on my lips to keep me from speaking.

"We'll talk about it later." Worry etched lines into his face I'd never seen before. "Have a seat." The awkwardness with which he conducted himself around me was almost adorable but completely opposite to the man I'd known and loved.

What happened to you, sharyen?

As he guided me to a chair, the girl returned with two cups and a teapot. The scent reminded me of *ithri* in a way, except there was no vanilla as far as I could detect. Tal sat down opposite me, rubbing the back of his neck as if contemplating what to talk about next. There was so much I wanted to say to him, but I didn't know where to start.

I doubted he did.

"Your mother passed away," he said after a while, coughing to clear his throat. "She... didn't suffer."

"I know," I whispered. "I've been told."

"By whom?" He sounded surprised.

"Esahbyen."

He stared at me incredulously. "Esahbyen? As in, the God of War Esahbyen?"

I nodded miserably. "Yes. There's... a lot I need to tell you, Tal. A lot has happened since Yllinar took me away from you." I swallowed hard, glancing up. "H... how are my brothers?"

Tal looked as if he was going to be sick. "Evan's all right, considering the circumstances. He had a baby girl, but"—he chewed his lip, and it took me some effort not to stop him —"Nathaïr died in childbirth. From what I gathered, it was either her or the child. She sacrificed herself."

I stared at him for what felt like forever. "A daughter? What about Azra? Did she...?"

"She tried to come after the girl, but we stopped her. At least, we did before I left. I have no idea what happened after I went."

I clasped my hands firmly between my knees to keep them from shaking. "What about Haer?"

Tal's mood soured instantly. I could tell from the storm in his eyes. "Your brother is a *verathràh*. As soon as your mother's pyre was cold, he turned to Azra. He's her *Ohzheràn* now."

I felt all warmth leaving my body. "No... no, he couldn't—he wouldn't. He..."

"Losing both you and Tiroy and then your mother, it must have driven him over the edge." Tal was scowling. "He blames you for it, incidentally."

"For what?"

"Tiroy's death."

"I would, too," the sword—or whatever it was now—purred. *"You've gotten quite the name,* resha.*"*

I closed my eyes and counted to ten. I had the sinking feeling I was running out of time, fast, but I somehow had to let Tal know.

"Let him know, and I will kill both of you."

I cursed under my breath.

"What's wrong?" Tal asked, narrowing his eyes.

"Kicked my foot against the table's leg."

It was obvious he didn't believe me.

"You've gotten my *Araith*," I remarked, forcing a smile to my lips. "How?"

Tal managed a faint smile of his own, but the look in his eyes betrayed his thoughts were entirely elsewhere. "Ione."

I sighed in relief. "She survived *Hanyarah* then?"

"She did," he replied, his mouth half open as if to say more, except that he didn't.

"I loved how she incorporated the sword on my hip," I offered, "and made a bracelet of the lines around my wrist."

Tal looked at me, obviously confused.

"She did remarkable work," I continued. "I know they're there, but one has to look closely to the design to actually see it."

"If you say so," he replied, a bit nonplussed.

An awkward silence between us followed. My gaze kept being drawn to his torso, to the *Araith* and to his scar. I wanted nothing more than to touch them—touch him—be close to him like I had been during my breakdown.

"I—I'm keeping you awake," I blurted, looking around the room.

A soft light came through the curtains, heralding the arrival of a new day. A new kind of fear settled in the pit of my stomach, and I prayed to the Gods this moment would never end, but a deep unease settled in my bones, and I knew I had to leave. I quickly rose to my feet and stepped away from the table, wrapping my arms around me as if I were cold.

Tal rose to his feet as well.

"I need to go," I whispered, looking up at him. "It's for the best if I do."

As I turned to leave, his hand shot out and circled my wrist. I stopped, breathing out a shaky sigh and closing my eyes. When I opened them, he was standing a few inches away from me, face close to mine.

"I don't know what you're afraid of," he whispered, "or why you think you must leave, but I've only just found you, and I'm not letting go."

I looked away, my eyes drawn yet again to the scar. He'd survived that time, the Gods knew how since Soren had been taken along with me. It had happened because of me, and I didn't want it to happen again.

"You only get hurt around me," I murmured. "I can't let that happen again."

"Then talk to me, *shareye*," he said, lifting my chin gently. "What's going on with you? Why are you so afraid?"

I shook my head, tears brimming my eyes. "Drop it, Tal. Please, if you know what's good for you, drop it."

He narrowed his eyes. "The *Tarien* I knew was afraid of nothing."

"The *Tarien* you knew is dead," I snapped. "She died at sea."

I made to step past him, but he was faster. He took my hands in his, stepped back, and bowed ever so slightly, placing two kisses on the inside of my wrists.

It sent pleasurable shivers down my spine.

"I'm still your *Anahràn*." He brushed my cheek with the back of his hand. "I've gone through torment to find you, and I'm not leaving without you."

He rested his forehead against mine, rubbing his thumbs over his knuckles. "Promise me one thing, *shareye.*"

"You always taught me making promises is for those who have nothing left to lose."

"I've got nothing left to lose," he murmured. "Promise me you'll fight?"

I frowned at that. "Fight what?"

He didn't answer.

Instead, he kissed me.

My surroundings dissolved as if they'd been made of smoke and were blown away. I screamed at the top of my lungs, but sound didn't travel here.

Grissin!

"SHE DID SAY you were a magnificent kisser," I purred, stepping back from the handsome captain.

I could see why the *Tarien* had fallen for him even though he was a bit too pale for my liking. If I had a choice in the matter, I'd have gone for Elay.

Talnovar narrowed his eyes at me. "Who are you? What have you done to her?"

"She's still here, for now."

"What's that supposed to mean?" He narrowed his eyes.

"It means that if you do not keep your mouth shut, I will kill her."

He straightened his shoulders, pulling himself up to full height, but the remarkable thing about the *Tarien* was her height. As much as I hated to point it out to him, he wasn't all that impressive, and judging by the expression on his face, he knew I knew.

"What do you want from us?"

"From you?" I grinned. "Nothing. Although a body like yours

instead of hers… It *does* suit me better. How about we swap? You for her?"

I could tell he was considering the offer, but he was a proud man, and he wouldn't just agree to something like this without at least trying to save the woman he loved.

He wasn't stupid, that much was clear.

"And you promise to release her if I agree?"

He's seriously considering it? How adorable!

"*You're insane,*" Shalitha growled in my mind. "*Whyever did Esahbyen give me you?*"

I chuckled, earning a frown from Talnovar.

"Just talking to your *Tarien.*" I waved my hand in dismissal. "She can be quite foulmouthed, did you know? Did you teach her that?"

"Answer my question."

I tapped my lips in thought, pretending to consider it. While the offer of his body was tempting, to say the least—he did have a good, well-trained warrior's body and all the right tools—I liked what the *Tarien* had to offer.

"*You keep your filthy paws off him,*" she shouted loud enough to make me wince, "Or I—"

Or you what? Kill me?

I laughed at the notion, drawing surprised looks from both Talnovar and his little girl. If memory served me correctly, and if the *Tarien's* did, too, she could marry him—marry me then—and I'd be in almost the same position.

Almost, but not quite. Shame.

"No," I said at length, looking up at him. "I think I'll keep her."

388

CHAPTER 40

HAERLYON

H *ere goes.*

I pushed open the doors to the council chambers with alacrity, striding in as if nothing had changed, wearing my cocky grin and cavalier attitude. Twelve pairs of eyes were on me instantly, but only one of them widened.

I smiled jovially and bowed deeply, much deeper than any of them deserved, no doubt. "*Tari. Irìn.*"

"Haerlyon," Azra whispered, rising to her feet. "You're... alive?"

"Of course," I said with a smirk, wriggling my eyebrows as I took a seat, making myself comfortable. "What else would I be?"

She just stared at me, blinking like a demented owl. Whatever she had expected, it had not been this, and it was utterly satisfying to see her caught off guard. Not many people had ever managed that.

I put my feet on the table and leaned back, folding my arms across my stomach. "I'm alive and whole, auntie. Well, almost whole, anyway..." I lifted my arm to show her the stump. "But you should see the other guy. Ugly mug. Dead, too."

"How did you—," she began.

"Survive?" I interjected and shrugged. "Obviously the better warrior."

"Scouts returned with reports your entire squad was killed," Azra replied, regaining some of her wit judging by the tone in her voice. "They hadn't found you, but it was assumed the wolves might have gotten you."

I chuckled and tutted, shaking my head. "*Tari*, surely you know what they say about assumptions?"

"You've been gone for more than two moons."

"As you can see," I replied, "I wasn't completely lucky. Thank be the Gods a passerby found me and brought me to a healer. Did you know *Hanyarah* survived your attack? The *haniya* have returned."

Her eyes narrowed. "They do not allow men inside."

"True." I waved my stump around. "They didn't use to, but they've gotten a little less uptight about it. Something to do with the fact they were nearly decimated, I think."

"Who is this *kailenn?*" one of the men asked gruffly.

My attention turned to him. His pinker skin and lesser elongated ears marked him as Therondian; I assumed one of the *Lerdas* Azra had been buttering up since before ascending the throne. I'd never seen any of them at court before, so the fact they were here did not bode well.

"This *kailenn*," Azra said stiffly, regarding the man with a murderous look, "is my nephew and *Ohzheràn* of the Ilvannian army, Haerlyon an Ilvan. Insult him again, and I will cut out your tongue with the dullest knife I can find."

I returned my attention to her, and it was then I noticed she was no longer pregnant. The baby had been born.

So, the rumours are true.

I took a closer look at my aunt, taking note of the haunted expression in her eyes and the dark circles underneath them as if she hadn't slept in weeks. Her skin was more ashen than ivory, and even her lips had lost some of their shine.

She looked like a hollow version of her previous self.

I resolved to get some answers once this circus was out of the way—a circus I had every intention of interfering with for as long as I could. Azra may have come to my defence, but she was not well-pleased with my return.

Not yet anyway.

"Pleasure to meet, I'm sure," I waved my stump in a flourish. "Please, don't let me interrupt whatever it is you were discussing. Just pretend I'm not here."

Azra scowled

After introducing me the way she did, she could not exactly send me away from their meeting, not without a very good reason, and we both knew she didn't have one. She couldn't very well tell them she tried to have me assassinated because it could lose her the support she so desperately needed if she wanted to win this war.

She sat down, her back stiff, hands flat on the table. She was furious.

Good.

"We were discussing where to best gather the army," she said, staring at me, "should it be necessary."

I arched a brow, forcing myself not to perk up. "There's news then?"

"Just rumours," she replied, letting out a heavy sigh. "Rumours of a white-skinned, white-haired woman in Akhyr winning the hearts of its people while fighting the scum of the world in a *herrât.*"

My heart picked up speed. "You think it's the *Tarien?*"

Azra's scowl deepened. "Who else could it be, *khirr?* Is there another missing Ilvannian woman who has the prowess and skill to survive a Kyrinthan *herrât* I don't know of?"

I shrugged. "I wouldn't be able to tell, *Tari.* I've never been in one, although it sounds absolutely exciting."

The cup she threw at my head shattered against the wall behind me. I didn't so much as flinch as she stared me down.

"Calm down, *Tari*. Akhyr is a long way from here, and my sister may be a skilled fighter, but I doubt she could survive a *herrât*. It's not what she was trained for."

"Desperate people take desperate measures," another man offered. "Your sister is a fierce woman, *Ohzheràn*. Can you safely say she will not find a way out of there? She's defied the odds more than once from what I've heard."

"Then we must assume her return." I shrugged. "Isn't it what we've been preparing for?"

"If she does return," a third man chimed in. "She'd have to land on Therondian shores, unless there's a place in Ilvanna we're not aware of where she could land?"

I smirked.

I'd had this same conversation with Cerindil only a few weeks before.

"There's a bit of no man's land between Ilvanna and Naehr, accessible from the sea," I offered. "But that mountain range is nigh impossible to traverse."

"Nigh impossible doesn't make it impossible," Azra said, drumming her fingers on the table. "It would be right up her alley."

"There's no way she could get an army through the mountains." It was the man who'd called me *Kailenn*.

"She wouldn't have to." I took my feet off the table and leaned forward. "If memory serves me correctly, there's already an army waiting for her in *Denahryn*."

Azra scoffed. "That's hardly an army. It's a rebel group. There can be no more than a hundred."

If only you knew.

"Perhaps." I put my feet back up, placing my hand behind my head. "But if I were the enemy, that's what I would like you to think, too. I wouldn't be surprised if their numbers are more substantial than that."

"Impossible."

My gaze settled on the man who'd spoken. He was Ilvannian by the looks of him, but I couldn't recall ever having seen him before. The wrinkles on his face indicated old age, but how old was hard to say. We usually didn't start showing age until after six-hundred-and-fifty, give or take, which meant this man had to have been around for a long time.

He must have known Mother, too.

"Why would you say that?" I asked.

"Because there is no room for them there," he explained. "*Denahryn* can hold about two-hundred, two-hundred-fifty at most. I'd say that with the *Dena* already living there, it's filled to the brim. They wouldn't hide an army in the mountains for years while waiting for a *Tarien* who may never return. Cerindil would not be stupid, which means he has other plans."

Nohro.

"Such as?" Azra asked, eyes narrowing suspiciously.

"He's got allies elsewhere," the old man said with a shrug. "Naehr, Therondia, perhaps even the clans beyond the mountains. Who knows?"

"No." Azra shook her head. "Naehr would never get involved in a war, and even if Cerindil somehow managed to persuade the Therondian king, Shalitha would never agree."

"Why is that?" I asked, unable to hide my curiosity.

She was inspecting her nails, a catlike smile on her lips. "Because he's the one who sold her off."

It felt as if the floor fell away beneath me, but I quickly recovered. I couldn't show her how much this news affected me. She hadn't just sent my sister off—she'd sold her as if she were a piece of meat.

Despite my feelings, I grinned.

"That surely makes it a lot easier for us. She will have a

hard time finding allies anywhere, and the rebels will be nowhere near our numbers. This isn't a war. This is a skirmish!"

Around the table, the men laughed, except for the old one. He was looking at me with barely concealed interest. Azra didn't partake in the merriment either. The thoughtful expression on her face told me she was still thinking, unconvinced by my words.

"She's resourceful," she mused, her voice barely audible over the din the men were making. "She'll find allies somewhere."

"*Tari,* even if she married the *Akyn* of Kyrintha, she would not have an army big enough. There is no way she could bring them across the sea," one of the men offered, a bright smile on his face. "This is a done deal."

"She won't marry that *Akyn,*" Azra murmured. "Trust me."

"So, we've eliminated all her options," I said, looking at Azra. "We have the upper hand, *Tari.* You've more than secured your position on the throne. Besides, she may never come back at all, not if she's fighting in that *herrât.*"

Azra sat back in her chair, resting her arms on the armrests, drumming her fingers as she stared absently out the window. She wasn't convinced of any of this, and I couldn't exactly blame her. Shal had always found unconventional solutions to unconventional problems, and if there was something she wanted, she'd get it, one way or another. I couldn't shake the feeling there was more to Azra's mood, though.

"It's getting late, *Tari,*" the old man offered. "Why not retire for the night and pick this up in the morning? I doubt the *Tarien* will be knocking on our doors soon."

Her only response was a dismissive wave.

The sound of scraping chairs echoed through the room as everyone rose to their feet simultaneously. Without fault, barring myself and the old man, everyone bowed before they left, and I couldn't help but notice how fast they were doing so.

The old man left at a more leisurely pace, clearly unperturbed by the presence he was in.

I supposed at that age, one simply no longer cared.

"Stay," Azra said as I turned to leave.

I halted, bit my lip, and spun around with a flourish, a smile on my face. "Yes, *Tari?*"

"Why did you return?"

"I thought you'd never ask."

"A WORD, OHZHERÀN." The voice came from the darkness opposite my bedroom, and I spun around to find the old man shuffling my way. "Not here, of course."

I opened the door, glanced around and invited him in. After I closed it behind us, I leaned back against it, grabbing the stump of my arm in an imitation of folding my arms. He turned to look at me, a kind smile on his face.

"You look a lot like your mother."

I arched a brow. "You're one of the first to say that."

"It's in the calculating look in your eyes."

"Why are you here?" I asked. "And more importantly, who are you?"

"I'm a friend," he replied. "It doesn't matter who I am in the grand scheme of things, but if it eases your conscience, Cerindil asked me to keep an eye on things here while you were... healing."

My brows shot up in surprise. The old man chuckled.

"Not what you expected?"

"I'm just surprised you're still alive," I replied, pushing myself off the door to light some candles. "Azra usually kills everyone who is even remotely close to him or any of the others for that matter."

"Yet you are still alive."

"Not for lack of trying." I held up my crippled arm with a grimace.

He smiled at that and inclined his head. "She doesn't remember me, Cerindil figured she wouldn't. I've not been at court in hundreds of years."

"How come she opened a spot at the table for you?"

He sat down in one of the chairs, releasing a sigh of relief as he made himself comfortable. I watched him from the corner of my eye as I got two glasses and a bottle of *ithri*. He'd closed his eyes, and as I sat down, I was under the impression he'd fallen asleep.

Until he spoke.

"I had information," he said, opening his eyes. "Like you, I used it to secure my position, at least for the time being."

I poured him a glass, not looking at him. "What kind of information?"

"The kind that's lethal in the wrong hands."

"I assume we're not exchanging then." I offered him one of the glasses and picked up my own, taking a good, long sip as I settled back, regarding him.

"No."

"I assume Cerindil told you not to either?" I asked, a wry smile on my face. "That man is up to something."

The old man chuckled. "Of course, he did, and of course he is. He would not be much of an *Ohzheràn* if he didn't."

I frowned at that, wondering momentarily if I should take that as a personal affront. I wasn't scheming my way in all the four wind directions.

No, you're just playing two sides.

"You said we needed to talk."

"I said I needed a word." The old man looked amused. "A word of warning, Haerlyon. The *Tari* may not be at her best right now, not after losing her child, but trust me when I tell you her wickedness has reached a new level. She doesn't trust anyone anymore, not really. She hardly leaves her room these days, and only if she absolutely must. Azra may look vulnerable, but she's anything but. Her failed assassination attempt will not keep her from trying again."

"Does she suspect me?"

He lifted one shoulder as he took his sip. "I do not know. I haven't been around long enough, and she hardly ever speaks aside from giving commands. What I do know is that people have been disappearing left and right. Their bodies are usually found somewhere within the perimeter of the palace, and they look like they've been mauled."

A cold shiver ran down my back, reminding me of the night she attacked me and most importantly, the morning after.

"What has done this?" I asked, trying to sound neutral. "Has a wolf or a bear somehow made it through the mountain pass?"

"It's possible. Not likely, but possible."

"Why not likely?"

"Bears and wolves avoid us as much as we avoid them unless we present ourselves on a silver platter. The mountain pass is in the farthest corner of the palace grounds and barely accessible. One would have to know where it is, and I highly doubt an animal would be smart enough for it."

"Someone could have brought it in?" I offered, but it sounded weak even to me.

I had a good idea what was going on, but claiming the *Tari* was some kind of animal would only land me in the dungeons— if I were lucky. Nobody would believe me, except maybe Mehrean, but she wasn't here.

"Do you know the tale of the twin sisters, Haerlyon?" the old man asked after a while, his gaze distant, as if remembering something. "The Goddesses of dark and light?"

"Some say it's just a myth."

"What if it wasn't?" he mused. "We know the Gods walked our lands many centuries ago and created us in their image."

I made to reply, but he held up his hand to stop me.

"Hear me out," he continued. "When the Gods walked among us, they bestowed us with powers, with *magic*. Not a lot, but enough to get simpler tasks done like growing food no matter the conditions, healing others, some could even catch glimpses of the future. Of course, there were those who used these powers for good, and there were those who didn't. You know, I assume, what Xiomara stands for?"

I nodded.

Everyone knew.

"Do you know what her sister stood for at that time?"

I shook my head. "No, she's not discussed in theology nor ever mentioned in the Temple. It's as if she never existed, which is why this is just a myth."

"Xarala was the Goddess of death, darkness, and loneliness." He went on as if I'd never said a thing. "But you'd be surprised to learn how much of a following she had. Those who used their powers for evil worshipped her. You see, our worshipping them was what gave them power in the first place. As an outcast amongst her brothers and sisters, Xarala enjoyed the attention we mortals gave her, and she bestowed upon her followers power the likes of which had never been seen, but they paid a price for that—a blood price."

He paused to take another sip of his drink, smacking his lips in the process as if it was something he hadn't had in a long time. "At some point, they realised they were doing more harm than good with their power, so they decided to leave us, taking their *magic* with them. All the Gods and Goddesses agreed, and they made themselves a home amongst the stars. They would seal their world from ours, to protect us. But when the time came, Xarala was nowhere to be found, and the sealing process had already begun. There was no time for them to find her. Xarala had hidden amongst her followers," he continued, his voice more intense than before, "as a mortal woman with immense powers. As time wore on, her mortal body withered and died, as did her *magic.*"

"What happened to Xarala?" I asked, unable to shake the feeling this was supposed to mean something, but for the life of me I couldn't imagine what it was.

"Nobody knows exactly," he replied with a shrug, finishing his glass. "Everybody believes she died at some point. Some believe she survived."

"How?"

"Now that," he said on a chuckle, "is the real question, isn't it? Your guess is as good as mine."

"Why are you telling me this?"

The old man smirked. "To pass the time and the night. No assassin in his right mind would attempt to take on both of us, even if we are crippled."

"You think she sent one?"

"I know she did. You don't happen to have a spare blanket, do you?"

I stared at him incredulously, opened my mouth to say something and snapped it shut, no words adequate enough to respond to a situation like this. I downed the rest of my *ithri,* grabbed a blanket from the trunk at the foot of my bed and tossed it at the old man.

He smiled. "Thank you. Goodnight, Haerlyon."

"Good night, *Irìn,*" I mumbled as I sat down on the bed, a deep frown creasing my brow as I mulled things over.

He hadn't told me this story just to tell me a story. There was a message behind it, I was certain of it. I had my suspicions, but without anything to solidify them, they would remain that—suspicions. Frustration boiled to the surface, but I could hardly let it out, least of all because I didn't want to wake the old man. I rubbed the back of my neck and stretched myself, going over the story again and again, but no matter how deep I looked at it, I could not make out the reason for the old man telling me.

Yet I knew the answer was staring me right in the face.

I SHOT AWAKE, blinking at the light streaming in through my windows. Sweat beaded my brow, had soaked my shirt, and I was gasping for air as if I'd been running away from something. Come to think of it, I had, hadn't I? In my dream, I was sure someone had been chasing me, but as I tried to grab the last remnants of my dream, they dissolved into nothing.

As I swung my legs over the bed, I noticed the empty chair and blinked at the folded blanket and the note on top of it.

Had someone been here?

I rose to my feet, scratching my head, and picked up the note.

Thank you for the ithri *and the blanket to keep an old man warm, Haerlyon, and thank you for listening to my ramblings. It has been quite some time since anyone has been so gracious as you. I know you have questions, and I'm sorry I could not give you the answers, but I can give you this.*

The first four lines were the prophecy that had hung over my sister's head since the day she was born. As I continued reading, my heart began to thump faster, my hands began to tremble until, when I finally came to the end, I cursed.

"Son of a *hehzèh!*"

CHAPTER 41

TALNOVAR

"*I*'m going to kill him. Her. It."

"Sit down, *Masran*." Lujaeyn patted my arm gingerly. "You're not going to kill anyone this morning."

I growled under my breath, but she continued unperturbed. "Just... sit down, will you? You're wearing the floor thin with your pacing."

"What would you have me do then?" I muttered. "Sitting down isn't going to solve anything either."

"No, but a cup of *keffah* and some food might clear your head," she replied. "You've barely slept the last few nights, barely eaten, too, and you almost got killed tonight. To learn that your *Tarien* is possessed would make anyone go mad, but you'll not be able to help her if you die from starvation."

I scowled at her but sat down. She pushed a platter with an assortment of fruit in front of me, followed by a cup of steaming hot *keffah*. Before, she wouldn't have promptly sat down opposite me—she'd have asked, if I hadn't yet invited her.

Not today.

It was as if something had taken over Lujaeyn, too, and made her someone fierce.

"I need to talk to Elay," I muttered, pushing my food around my plate with my fork. "He needs to know what happened, and we need to figure out what to do about it. Soon. It's up to something, although I can't for the life of me imagine what."

"How long has she been like this?" Lujaeyn asked quietly, a thoughtful expression on her face.

"Z'tala said since the last fight in the *herrât.*"

"The one where the tyrant was killed."

It wasn't a question.

I nodded, pricking my fork into a particularly juicy looking slab of meat and popping it into my mouth. "How did you know?"

"Servants talk." She smiled. "You'd be surprised how much information you can get by pretending you don't exist and listening."

Arching a brow at her, I shook my head. "You shouldn't do that."

"Do what? Listening?"

"Pretending you don't exist."

She chuckled. "For someone who grew up at court, *Masran,* you are quite dim."

I blinked at her, then narrowed my eyes. "Who are you and what have you done to Lujaeyn? Don't tell me something's possessing you, too?"

A loud snort was all the answer I got from her.

"People do not pay attention to servants," she continued, "much less so to slaves. We're a nuisance, dirt under the soles of their dainty slippers. Half-wits. Idiots. Incapable of thought and logic." She waved her hand. "You get the idea. As long as they keep thinking that, we keep pretending we don't exist and obtain the most valuable information."

I blinked at her.

"For example." She was grinning now. "Did you know the

previous *Akyn* preferred boys over girls and would dress up as a woman when he thought nobody was looking?"

Something about the gleeful look in her eyes made me chuckle, and I shook my head, feeling the tension in my body ease somewhat.

"And," she began talking animatedly, looking the happiest I'd seen her yet, "the Master of Coin has a serious gambling problem. I suppose the previous *Akyn* didn't mind as much because he was just as bad, but *Akyn* Elay was not pleased when he found out."

I looked quietly amused as I listened to her stories, finding myself calming down more and more. My stomach growled in protest after the first few bites, and by the time Lujaeyn finished up a particularly nasty detail about another one of Elay's staff, I'd shovelled in all the food she'd put on my plate.

"I also heard things about the *Tarien*," she said right after I'd finished, looking more solemn this time. "People admired her, even after she killed *Akyn* Kehran, but after that, when she assumed the mantle of *Akynai*, the narrative changed. People have begun to fear her. Did you know she slit a man's throat because he tried to kill her? A snake, or so the rumours go."

"Well, you've seen the change," I muttered. "You know why."

She nodded, biting her lip.

"What?" I asked.

"I'm not entirely sure," she began, glancing up. "But it's something the *Tarien*—the real one—said during your conversation."

"What do you mean?"

"You said your *Araith* is mostly similar to hers, right?" She was tapping her fingers against pursed lips. "You have a part on your hip that's not the same as the rest, but there's no sword."

Heat crept up my throat at the mention of Azra's part of the *Araith,* but that feeling cleared the moment she mentioned a sword.

"I'm not sure I—"

"The *Tarien* said the detail of the *Araîth* astounded her, that this Ione's work was remarkable, and that she loved how she'd incorporated a sword on her hip. If you haven't got it, I assume she doesn't either."

"And there is no bracelets on her wrist, either," I whispered, comprehension all but slamming into me. "The lines go up her hand and her fingers."

Nohro ahrae!

Without waiting for Lujaeyn's reply, I pushed the chair back and bolted out of our room. Although I slowed down in the corridors, I kept a brisk pace as I made my way to Elay's bedroom—Shalitha's room, I realised belatedly.

Jaehyr stood guard, and he didn't look happy about it.

As I neared the door, it became obvious why. Elay and Shalitha—*not Shalitha*—were enjoying their marital status quite vocally, she more than he. Bile rose in my throat, but I forced one foot in front of the other. While I should have expected this, it wasn't something anyone wanted to consider. Truth be told, I never minded hearing it—living in the barracks, it had been hard to ignore the sounds—but hearing *them* together made my blood boil. The only solace lay in the fact it wasn't Shalitha he was doing it with.

"Guess you're not here to switch shifts?" Jaehyr remarked dully.

"Thank the Gods, no. I am here to talk to Elay."

His lips quirked up in a wry smile. "He's currently busy."

"Could've fooled me."

"I'm sure you won't have to wait long," Jaehyr replied

"I could just storm in," I offered.

"It's your sanity, *mahnèh.*"

To spare myself the details, I decided against it and sat down on the open windowsill close to Jaehyr. Silence stretched out between us, and it was obvious both of us were trying to focus on anything but the indoor activities. He shuffled from foot to foot, his jaw working as if he were about to say something but was still contemplating how to phrase it.

"How's Cerindil?"

"Leading a rebellion, last I knew," I replied, my lips curving up in a lopsided smile. "Not the kind of person to sit down quietly."

Jaehyr let out a snort. "Hardly surprising. He's always been a hard worker, but I suppose that came with the territory of being the oldest brother to three younger ones."

"Three?" My brows shot up in surprise.

A shadow darkened his features. "Our brothers died in a skirmish at the borders a long time ago, before the war even. Cerindil survived, but Mother never forgave him."

I bit my lip, nodding absently.

I knew that feeling.

"I had a sister. She died because of me."

Jaehyr arched a brow. "What happened?"

"She drowned," I murmured. "She had come to the lake with my friends and me, but I hardly paid attention to her. Truth be told, I didn't want her there. I had... other... interests at the time. She was a good deal younger than I was, too. A child still, and while I loved her, at the time I resented being used as her nursemaid."

"You never forgave yourself?"

I shook my head.

"It's a heavy burden to bear, Talnovar," Jaehyr observed, "but ultimately she was your parents' responsibility. Not yours."

Easy for him to say.

"It happened a long time ago," I muttered, folding my arms across my chest by way of protection.

The door opened and a haggard looking Elay slipped out of the room, hair tousled, robe askew, looking for all the world like a secret paramour sneaking out of the *Tari's* chambers as not to get caught by her husband.

"Had fun?" I asked, perhaps a bit more snidely than intended.

Elay jumped at my voice, spinning on his heel to stare at me. It took him a few moments to gather his bearings.

"It wasn't—"

"What I think it was?" I offered.

He opened his mouth, blinked, and snapped it shut. "Fine," he muttered. "We had sex, but I can tell you it was anything but satisfactory."

"Didn't sound like it."

Out of the corner of my eyes, I noticed Jaehyr studiously ignoring us, lower lip between his teeth, probably to keep himself from laughing if the dimples in his cheeks were any indication. Elay turned a few shades darker.

"This is not her either," he snapped, scowling at me. "I feel... used."

Jaehyr burst out in a coughing fit, turning away with a muttered apology. I snorted, surprisingly unable to feel pity for the *Akyn*.

"Why are you here again?" Elay retied the sash on his robe and combed his hair with his fingers

"It's about her, actually." I jerked my head in the direction of the door and lowered my voice. "Not here, though."

Elay motioned for me to follow him.

Our footsteps echoed through the otherwise silent corridors. The palace was starting to awake, but in the few days I'd been here, I'd learned only the servants rose before dawn, and they were silent as ghosts while going about their work. In Ilvanna, it had been much the same, except by the time dawn arrived, I was already training the *Arathrien*, so I was never inside to notice anyone waking up. When I finally did enter the palace, it had been bustling with people.

Unlike here.

Even during the day, a hushed kind of silence spread throughout the palace. I had to admit it was more sizable than Ilvanna's, and I had the distinct impression fewer people lived here.

"Care to join me in the bathhouse?" Elay asked, glancing sideways. "I could do with a proper wash."

His request reminded me of the bathhouse in Portasâhn, how people had stared at me and how uncomfortable it had made me feel. At the same time, I hadn't felt so good in a long time.

What did I have to lose aside from my dignity?

"If that is what you wish, *Akyn*," I replied, inclining my head.

Elay's lips quirked up, but the amusement never quite reached his eyes. He'd changed since returning to Akhyr, but at least he was still mostly himself. Perhaps more exhausted, but still the quick-witted man I owed my life to, whether I liked it or not.

"We'll be alone," he said. "Perks of ruling this country, I guess."

I nodded. The moment we stepped into the courtyard, my gaze swept left and right, and I cursed myself for having run out without a weapon.

"One would be stupid to assault me here, Tal," Elay offered, glancing at me. "Guards are stationed all around the perimeter and on the walls."

"It only takes one desperate attempt," I replied unperturbed. "If it hadn't been for Z'tala, Shalitha would have been dead. Snake bite."

If I was being honest with myself, this felt good. This is what I did, this is where my strength lay—not in politics and figuring out the world's problems but in protecting those who did. Elay looked disturbed.

"You didn't know?"

He shook his head. "The *Tarien* and I, we don't speak much."

"A good thing it's not the *Tarien* then," I remarked. "Should make you feel less guilty about it."

Elay spun toward me, and I nearly barrelled into him. His nostrils flared, his chest rising and falling with fast, shallow breaths. He took a step closer, balled hand level with my face. I arched a brow, unimpressed with the sudden change in behaviour.

"If you want to have a go at me, let's go to the training room instead," I offered, "and you can take all that frustration out, but I promise I won't hold back either."

He looked as if he was seriously considering the offer, then stepped back, inhaled deeply, and exhaled torturously slowly. Without saying another word, he turned around and continued his way to where I presumed was the bathhouse.

I kept a two-step distance from him this time around.

As PROMISED, the bathhouse was empty save for a couple of servants scurrying about to prepare everything for our arrival. Robes had been laid out along with a double set of towels for each. When the head of the bathhouse staff inquired about our wishes for additional services, Elay sent the man off with instructions to not let anybody in under any circumstance save Z'tala or Jaehyr, and only if it were an emergency. Before I allowed Elay to go inside, I checked every nook and cranny just in case the *Tarien,* or anyone else for that matter, had decided to make an attempt on his life, too.

"You're awfully thorough and mistrusting," he observed as he submerged himself into one of the hot baths.

I followed suit. "You would be, too, if you'd seen what I've seen."

"Who says I haven't?"

He had a point there.

After only a short while, I could feel the tension in my body ease up, and I almost groaned in relief. I closed my eyes, allowing the sensation to absorb me, knowing full well this would only last as long as I was in here.

"So," Elay began. "What had you waiting outside my bedroom, anyway?"

My eyes snapped open, and I couldn't help but scowl. "Hey, let a man enjoy his repose. I allowed you yours."

Elay snorted at that. "And you were only too happy to make it awkward the moment I stepped out of my room."

"The two of you were loud." I shrugged. "Anyway, she tried to kill me."

He blinked rapidly, shaking his head as if to clear his head. "What?"

"Tell me something," I continued as if I hadn't heard his question, "since you've seen her naked up close much more recently than I have. Does her *Araith* form a sword anywhere on her hip?"

He looked thoughtful at that. "I'm... I'm not sure. Why do you ask?"

"I awoke just in time to find Shalitha standing over me ready to plunge a dagger in my heart, but she looked a little dazed, as if she wasn't quite there. After I wrestled her to the ground, she asked me to let go," I explained. "*Asked* me, and she sounded like... like *her*, so I asked her a question only she could know the answer to." I sighed at the memory, and continued softer, "It was her, Elay, I swear. It was her, but... she was afraid."

"Of what?"

I shrugged. "Your guess is as good as mine. Perhaps for whatever is keeping her imprisoned? She changed right before my eyes, and it spoke to me, offered a trade. Me for her, or so I thought..."

"You are actually considered taking it?" Elay asked, sounding almost shocked.

"I'll do anything for her," I replied, my voice barely audible. "Anything, Elay. I would have gladly taken it from her, but it pulled back in the end, said it would rather keep her."

"So, we still don't know how to help her?"

I shook my head. "No, yes. Maybe. Lujaeyn... she figured it out, I think."

"How?"

Heat crept up my neck and settled there. "Last night, she began with a back massage and ended with trailing her fingers over my *Araîth*."

"I can see where that ended," Elay said, a smug look on his face. "Go on."

"Let's just say she's had a thorough inspection of it," I continued, trying not to glower too much. "The thing is most of our *Araîths* match."

He looked a little less pleased with that notion but nodded.

"During our conversation, after Shal had noticed my *Araîth* had been finished, she remarked how much she loved the sword hidden in the design on her hip and the way the *Araîtiste* had wrapped the ink around her wrist like a bracelet."

"Get to the point, will you?"

"Lujaeyn pointed out if Shal has that design on her body, so would I," I said. "But I don't."

Elay narrowed his eyes suspiciously, as if he didn't quite believe me. Not feeling like a discussion over this, I heaved myself on the side of the pool and showed the side where the *Araîth* flowed in neat, precise lines from my jaw to my ankle.

"While I can't see it well from this vantage point," I remarked dryly. "I'm fairly certain there's no sword on this design. Besides, I trust Lujaeyn to have told me the truth."

"So, you think Shal was giving you a hidden message?"

I nodded. "Same as with the distinction as to who took her in Ilvanna."

He made a steeple of his fingers, tapping them against his

lips as he contemplated the water in front of him. His focus was so deep, I almost began to wonder if the answers would appear on the surface somewhere, and I couldn't help but stare at the same spot.

"So, we just have to figure out what it means?" Elay asked at length.

I shrugged. "I guess. Did she ever obtain a sword or a bracelet?"

"She would obviously have gotten her hands on a sword in the *herrât*," Elay offered, shaking his head, "but those barely make a dent in anything, let alone be imbued with... with what? Magic?"

Before Soren, I would have snorted at the idea of magic. Now, I wasn't so sure. I pursed my lips in thought as I considered his remark. Eventually, I shook my head with a heavy sigh. "I have no idea, *mahnèh*, but something tells me we're about to find out. If whatever is controlling her came after me, I have no doubt it will come after you."

"Why would it?"

"For the same reason anyone in this position does anything," I replied. "Power."

CHAPTER 42

SHALITHA

*I*t's now or never.

As our wagon rounded the last corner on our way back to the palace, the cheers and chants of the people of Akhyr died down. My ears were buzzing, and my head was aching in a dull, persistent throb, scattering all thoughts to the four wind directions.

I had to keep my wits about me.

The coronation ceremony hadn't even begun yet.

The parade had been a spectacle for the people to include them on this special day, an opportunity to show off the new regents of Akhyr, and a sign to them that while we were above them, we were also among them. Neither time nor expenses had been spared to demonstrate that the new *Akyn* and his wife had Akhyr's best interests at heart.

That remains to be seen.

I felt my lips pull up at one corner at the notion but masked it quickly. If any of them—Elay, Z'tala, Talnovar, even Jaehyr—

caught wind of my intentions, they wouldn't hesitate to kill me. Since my botched attempt on Talnovar's life, their behaviour had not changed. To add to the matter, the *Tarien* had been remarkably quiet, too. Not once had she endeavoured to take back control, but she was there, lurking in the background, just beyond the edges of my conscious mind. Between their semblance of normalcy and her silence, I was suspicious.

They were up to something.

I just couldn't figure out what it was.

Not that it mattered. It would all be over soon. Although my plan wasn't flawless, I was confident that by the time they realised something was amiss, it would be too late. I just had to wait for the right time, the right moment. My heart soared in anticipation—that moment would be soon.

"Shalitha." Elay sounded as if he was repeating himself.

Looking up, I found him standing next to the ladder leading down from the parade wagon, offering his hand to guide me down the steps. With the layers of clothing making up my dress, and the elaborate piece perching precariously on top of my head, navigating any kind of stairs on my own had proven a challenge. I allowed him to help me down, taking one careful step after another, briefly cursing myself for not having taken Talnovar up on his offer.

He looked much more comfortable in his warrior's attire.

"How are you holding up, *mithri*?" Elay murmured at my side as we glided across the red carpet to the palace.

A line of people knelt on either side—arms outstretched, foreheads touching the ground—reaching all the way up to the palace entrance. Servants, guards, kitchen staff—everyone who had a job at the palace displayed themselves in this fashion. How I loved them subservient.

"I'm fine," I replied, flashing him a smile I hoped assured him. "It's such a wonderful day, isn't it?"

He merely returned my smile.

He knows.

My awareness of Z'tala and the two Ilvannian men behind us increased, as did the feeling of being watched. My skin tingled. Perspiration beaded my brow, my upper lip, and neck, and I hastened to dab it away. The last thing I wanted was to accidentally lick my lips. I breathed in deeply and exhaled a bit more shakily.

Why did it have to be so warm?

It wasn't as hot inside the palace, and when we stepped inside, the headache decreased in intensity, and I felt like I could breathe again. But the reprieve was short. As soon as we entered the throne room, the assembly of nobles waiting inside was stifling on its own. I had to refrain myself from curling up my lips in disdain, because unlike the staff, they merely bowed from the waist down. Elay inclined his head and shook hands left and right as we passed.

I flashed a forced smile.

"You might as well enjoy it," the *Tarien* commented. *"Isn't this exactly what you wanted?"*

The sudden sound of her voice in my mind nearly sent me stumbling to the ground. Elay caught me at the elbow, looking worried.

"Tripped over the hem of my dress," I muttered.

He nodded and replied in a soft voice, "We're almost there."

The fact she had spoken added to my unease, a feeling I was not well-acquainted with and hoped never to experience again. How could these mortals even function like this? I half-expected the *Tarien* to answer that question, but she remained silent.

She was there. I knew she was.

An officiant of the law was awaiting us on the dais, looking rather dismal in his dark attire as opposed to our festive colours. Elay had been dressed in gold and emerald whereas I had been adorned in midnight-blue and silver.

Night versus Day. Sun versus Moon.

The irony wasn't lost on me.

Without wasting any time, the coronation ceremony began with a tedious recollection of all past regents of Kyrintha and all the good they had done for their country. To my surprise, Kehran was mentioned, too, although the list of his magnanimity was small in comparison to his predecessors. The monotonous tone of the officiant's voice allowed my thoughts to drift off again.

"You'll miss the fun part," the *Tarien* remarked.

She was sitting on the steps to the dais, one foot propped on a higher step than the other. Her elbows rested on her thighs, and she was leaning forward, hands clasped together. Her attire was simple, leather pants, a blouse, and deerskin boots. It was the attire I knew she was most comfortable in.

"—Elay Ihn Gahr," the voice pulled me back to reality.

I snapped my attention back to Elay's coronation.

He was down on one knee, the end of a golden sceptre resting on his knee, his hand wrapped around the staff just below the orb adorning the top. The crown hovered above his head, held by the officiant as he recited yet again the name of all the *Akyn* before Elay, asking them for their blessing and guidance during his reign. The crowd erupted in clapping and cheers as he was crowned.

I was next.

My heart was beating so fast, I was afraid everyone would hear. Soon. Very soon. Gleeful anticipation slithered and coiled inside of me like the snake they'd sent to kill me. A smile tugged at my lips, and I lifted my head. Movement in my peripherals caught my attention, but when I looked, there was nobody there except for our bodyguards, and all of them stood rigid.

"I've never seen you this nervous," the *Tarien* mused. *"One would think you're up to something."*

She hadn't left her place on the dais, but she was now

cleaning her nails with a dagger I knew hadn't been there before. The nonchalance oozing from her was disconcerting. When she looked up, she flashed me a grin. *"Better pay attention now."*

A low growl rumbled in the back of my throat, earning me a startled look from the officiant. Elay narrowed his eyes.

"Please, kneel," the officiant murmured, sounding irked.

I knelt.

I had an urge so deep and profound to lick my lips that I began to wonder why. Surely my will to survive was stronger than that? A sudden realisation hit me, and I was just in time to bite back the snarl threatening to pour forth.

"It's you," I hissed.

The *Tarien* looked up, head tilted. *"I have no idea what you are talking about."*

"Don't play coy with me, Resha. I'm not that stupid."

A soft chuckle escaped her lips and instead of responding, she turned her attention back to her nails, inspecting their cleanliness.

"—Shalitha an Ilvan."

Curse it.

Ignoring the *Tarien*, I returned my attention back to present affairs, looked out at the crowd so I would not see her sitting just within sight. She was taunting me, distracting me, trying to get me to lose focus.

I won't allow her.

Because they hardly knew anything about me, and the *Tarien* had been reluctant providing me with any information concerning her predecessors, my list of former *Akynai* was short. At least it made this part of the ceremony a good deal less soporific. When the time came to crown me, one of the servants who'd dressed me helped take off the headpiece. In comparison, the crown weighed nothing when it settled on top of my head.

This time, the crowd was less cheerful, but I didn't care.

Excitement coursed through me as Elay helped me to my feet. It was time for our ceremonial vows. While holding my hand, Elay recited his speech—his promise to both me as his wife, and to his country and his people. It was a formality, tradition, and if I'd learned anything during my time here, it was that Kyrinthans loved their tradition.

It was time to make new ones.

"Do you ever get tired of yourself?" the *Tarien* was looking at me now, standing just next to Elay.

The longing to touch him was paramount in her eyes, and it only served to fuel my eagerness to see this through. Just a few more words, and it would be over.

"Why don't you just sit back and enjoy the view, Tarien?" I purred.

"Oh, I'm watching with bated breath," she replied, her lips quirking up, eyes twinkling.

What was that supposed to mean?

"Mithri," Elay hissed. "Your vows."

Startled, I looked at him, only to recite my vows automatically, promising him my time, my diligence, my undying love, and a couple of other things I could scarcely remember. He was watching me with a gentle smile on his lips, a loving look in his eyes, but there was an emotion hidden in their emerald depths I couldn't quite place.

Sadness? Melancholy?

I put it down to a figment of my imagination.

"Those were beautiful," he whispered as I finished my vows. "You are beautiful."

I managed a smile even though his words made me nauseous. This saccharine display of emotions just wasn't for me, but I had to go along, just for a little while. He brought my hands to his lips and kissed my knuckles, his eyes never leaving me. Applause echoed through the throne room, and I closed the distance between us.

All I had to do was kiss him, and it would be over.

"Forgive me, *shareye*," a voice murmured behind me seconds before everything went black.

SHE STEPPED out of the shadows dressed in full warrior regalia, a full plate harness with Ilvanna's crest etched into the chest plate. She had braided her hair on the side and pulled it back into a ponytail, showing off high cheekbones, elongated ears, and a sharpness to her face I'd never noticed in the mirror. I staggered back as she approached me, tripped over the hemline of the dress and went down in a flurry of silks.

"This is impossible," I muttered, staring at her wide-eyed.

"*Is it?*" she asked, tilting her head slightly. "*Impossible for me or for you?*"

"You have no power here."

Her eyes twinkled mischievously. "*Don't I? And here I thought this was my body—my mind.*"

"Why now?"

"*Why not? Don't you think your reign of terror has lasted long enough? I know what it is you want, but I cannot let another tyrant rule Ilvanna, or Kyrintha.*"

"I'm not a—"

"*You are,*" she interjected, stepping even closer. "*You have no regard for any other life but your own, so you will do anything to keep it safe. It wasn't hard to figure out. You'll believe anything that inflates your ego.*"

I narrowed my eyes at her. "What are you saying?"

Sadness touched her eyes. "*It's over.*"

Anger simmered underneath my skin, humming to the discordant tunes of my desire for revenge. I wasn't done yet, and I certainly wasn't going to let someone like her win. With a snap of my fingers, plated armour replaced the dress, and my hand wrapped around the hilt of a sword, sending a feeling of comfort through me.

"It's not over until *I* say it is."

"You're arrogant. Arrogance kills people."

"People kill people."

She shrugged at that. *"They do, but it usually stems from either arrogance or fear to lose power they believe they have that they feel the need to do so."*

"What is this?" I scowled. "A philosophy lesson?"

"Consider it a life lesson."

She attacked without preamble, a sword materialising in her hand out of nowhere. A smile tugged at my lips—she had learned a thing or two while I thought she was out of commission. Unfortunately for her, I'd spent enough time here to know every rule of this place, every limit, every boundary.

"This will be fun." I parried her first attack. "You really think you can beat me?"

She grinned. *"With one hand tied behind my back."*

"That can be arranged."

I hardly had to think about it, and sure enough, ropes coiled around the *Tarien's* waist and wrist, binding her hand there. To my surprise, she never flinched—she didn't even look worried, but she didn't immediately attack either. It was almost as if she were waiting for something. Narrowing my eyes, I regarded her, waiting for her next move. None was forthcoming.

This time, I was the one to attack.

She parried me in an elegant twirl, as if this were a dancing lesson rather than a fight. I struck for her shoulder, but she stepped out of the way. I aimed a kick at her side, but she was faster. No matter what I did, she always seemed to be just one step ahead, knowing exactly what I was going to do.

"Of course, you do," I growled, annoyed with myself.

It was only happening in my mind.

A sudden thought struck me, hitting me as if it were a slap in the face. "You're stalling."

"I thought you'd never figure it out."

I ceased my attacks, jerking a hand through my hair as I observed her. She watched me, silver-eyes calm, curious even, head tilted slightly to the side. She gently shook her head as if to say she felt sorry for me.

She pitied *me*.

"What have you done?" I asked through clenched teeth.

"You know what I did," she replied, pity making way for solemnity. *"You knew it before you even got here."*

It took me a moment to realise what it was. "You poisoned yourself? You'd rather die than allow me to live?"

"It's the lesser of two evils."

I didn't believe her—didn't want to believe her.

Letting out a roar of frustration, I charged her again, hammering into her defences until I was gaining ground. Even with her hand tied behind her back, she kept up a steady pace, not showing any sign of weakness, and I hated her for it, even if it was exactly what I'd demanded of her during her last fight in the *herrât*.

But she'd grow tired. Eventually.

"Nobody would willingly kill themselves like this," I said between explosive breaths, continuing my assault. "Nobody's this... brave, this stupid."

"You wouldn't, no." She began to tire. Her parries became slower. *"But the thing is. I already died. Twice. Almost three times if you count that time when Esahbyen stepped in and gave me you. I'm not afraid to go."*

"You have a duty to your country!" I yelled, pushing her back.

She staggered and stumbled against the steps to the throne,

the sword clattering out of her hand. I placed the tip of my blade against the hollow of her throat.

"It's over, *Tarien*."

The serene look and the soft smile on her lips caught me off guard. "I know."

EPILOGUE

Talnovar

*R*esting my elbows on the railing of the balcony, I let my gaze wander over Akhyr, watching the people in the streets scurry about like ants. A part of me envied them for the chance of going about their lives, unaware of what plays above their heads. I bore no illusions. Their life wasn't easy. It was different and vastly so, but I couldn't help but wonder what life was like if you didn't have to worry about the running of a country, court politics or wars. Although, the latter was usually started by the rich and fought by the poor. I sighed heavily, my gaze flicking from the city to the endless desert beyond. Someday soon we would have to cross it, find a ship and sail for the shores on the other side of the sea. But before we did, we needed a plan.

For that, we needed the *Tarien*.

I glanced over my shoulder at the room behind me just in time to see Elay stepping out, the shadows under his eyes an indication of how little he had slept the past ten days.

That makes two of us.

"How is she?" I asked, turning around to lean back against the balustrade.

Elay shrugged and shook his head. "It's hard to say. My healers have no idea what's wrong or if she will pull through, and if she does, what the lasting effects might be."

I jerked a hand through my hair and looked up at the sky. In the distance, I could barely make out a circling bird, a predator most likely, ready to swoop down and catch its prey. With a deep sigh, I turned to Elay.

"Do you think we made the right decision?"

"I've been asking myself that every day since," he replied. "We had no choice."

"Didn't we?"

Elay raked a hand through his hair, shaking his head. "I've gone over it a thousand times and more, trying to come up with other solutions, but no matter how I look at it—"

"There's only this one," I interjected.

He sighed. "We must have faith she is strong enough to get through this, too."

"But what if she isn't?" My voice sounded small even to me. "What if this was the last straw?"

"Then we will fight her war for her."

It was the kind of promise dangerous for two men about to lose everything that they loved, but if anything, it would get us through. There was no doubt in my mind Elay cared deeply for her, nor that he would raze Ilvanna to get his revenge if she died.

If anything, Azra would not expect that.

"If she does wake up," Elay said after a while. "What is your plan?"

"To be honest? I have no idea." I glanced at the room in front of me, peered through the curtains blowing gently in the afternoon breeze. Beyond it stood the canopied bed with Shal in it, asleep, oblivious to the world and everything around her. Every night, I prayed to whatever God would listen to a desperate man's pleas to let her wake up and be herself, to come out of this alive and well because she deserved it.

After everything she'd been through, she deserved it.

I would have swapped with her in a heartbeat, no questions asked. I'd still lay down my life for her if it meant keeping her alive, even if she did not love me anymore. After all, there was Elay to contend with now, and he sure had his life more in order than I did. I was a broken man—no longer the one she'd kissed that night, no longer the one she'd begged to take her away from the palace, the one who had been at her side almost night and day because he was too much of a *khirr* to show his feelings for her.

And now it may be too late.

I lifted my shoulders and turned back to lean my elbows on the railing. "I go back to being her *Anahràn,* I suppose. Fight the war at her side, hope we both survive, find a woman who can love a man like me and settle down."

Elay assumed a similar position, staring off into the distance. "She never stopped loving you, you know. Our marriage was one of convenience, although I will not deny that eventually, our feelings got involved, too. Even so, we spoke of her life back in Ilvanna, of her brothers, her mother, and you. I could tell she was struggling with guilt—she never told me why, and I never asked. Whenever she spoke of you, her eyes lit up and there was a smile on her lips, you know, the kind where her entire face lights up, and it's just so genuine you can't help but smile in return?" He waved his hand as if to dismiss that thought. "Anyway, it's how I knew who you were the moment my men dragged you into my camp. I recognised you from her stories."

I glanced at him, unsure what to say to this. "But you... you are married."

"As said, it's one of convenience," he replied with a shrug. "I'll have it annulled before you leave." He chuckled then, looking at me. "Besides, I doubt it has any value beyond the borders of Kyrintha and Zihrin, *eshen.* As soon as she sets foot on a ship, she's her own woman."

"You're saying she ever listened to you?"

He snorted. "Oh, no. Shalitha did whatever she pleased, and she never stopped doing that. I promise you it wasn't my idea to have her fight in the *herrât.*"

"Why am I not surprised?"

Elay shook his head, his lips curved up in a smile that means his thoughts are going down memory lane.

"Do you love her?"

His head snapped up, and he stared at me, looking as if he got caught stealing the cookies his mother just baked. A blush darkened his cheeks, and he looked away.

"I do," he said at length, "but neither her heart nor she belong here."

I nodded sagely, finding I was without words to comfort him. My heart ached for him, for both of us. No matter what happened, one of us would have it broken.

"It will give me a chance to settle down," Elay mused. "Find a wife who is perhaps a little less adventurous, although she'll probably be much more high maintenance than your *Tarien.* Give that woman men's attire and a sword, and she's happy."

It sounded so typically Shalitha, I couldn't help but laugh. Elay looked amused until his eye caught something in front of me and he frowned. Looking down, I realised I'd been twisting the ring on my finger.

"I see you kept it?"

"Something tells me we may yet need it," I said, halting the fidgeting. "I don't know how she got it, but she must have gotten it for a reason. Jaehyr tells me she had it on the night she killed that man, that she told him she had to have it and nearly tumbled out of his arms trying to retrieve it. She isn't the sentimental kind."

Elay nodded, lips pressed in a thin line. "After everything that has happened, she may not forgive you for it, *eshen.*"

"I wouldn't blame her."

I'm sure this arrangement will be mutually beneficial.

Kalyani

AT THIS TIME OF YEAR, the mountains were rough going due to the snow and storms, but I could at least be certain I wasn't followed. The little bundle wrapped against my chest had finally fallen asleep after an extended time of wailing. No matter what I tried, I couldn't calm him down. My heart broke with each agonising cry, but other than giving him the milk I'd collected before our departure, there wasn't much I could do. I would have to find a place soon if I wanted us both to survive. I sang him a lullaby under my breath as the horse picked its pace across the mountain path.

The longer we travelled, the more doubt crept into my heart, gnawing its way to its centre, whispering in my mind what a wicked being I was. Haerlyon had bidden me to go to *Denahryn,* to bring the child to a safe environment, and yet I had diverted from the path, leading the horse deeper into the mountains, farther away from Ilvanna and *Denahryn* with every step.

Had I made the right choice or a selfish one?

Looking down at the sleeping baby, my heart tore in half. How could I let it grow up in a country on the brink of war, a country whose *Tari* held no regard for her people and killed them on a whim? She wasn't fit to rule.

She wouldn't have been fit to raise a child.

And yet, when she was told her baby hadn't made it, the *Tari* had cried—heart-wrenching sobs and wails like any other mother. I had taken the child despite it.

The palace was no place to raise him and *Denahryn* was no better.

The rebels had made their base there—were planning a war from there. It was bad enough one of my own children was a part of it, I couldn't allow them to raise a baby that had no part in this. It wasn't a good, safe environment. He was innocent in all of this, the result of a madwoman who never considered the consequences of her actions.

No, I'd made the right decision.

And a selfish one.

This was my second chance, a new start. I had raised three fine children, Xaresh had been the perfect gentleman—I could do it again. This boy would have a loving, doting mother whose life revolved around him. He'd not know his real mother was a tyrant or that nobody knew who his father was. I'd raise him as one of my own, far away from Ilvanna, far away from war.

He would be living a lie.

But one that will keep him alive.

BOOK 4 EXCERPT

TALNOVAR

*T*ime has a habit of getting away from you when you're not paying attention to it, even more so when there are lives on the line or, in my case, when the one person you love more than anything in the world has been asleep for over a moon without showing any signs of waking up. Nothing the healers tried had worked, and none of them were able to tell us anything other than that she'd suffered a severe trauma, warning us she might never wake up again.

Elay had not been happy with that answer.

I was too stubborn to accept it.

"Tal?" Jaehyr said, sounding as if he had been repeating himself for the hundredth time. "The plan won't make itself."

"Apologies," I muttered, rubbing my forehead. "I got distracted."

My uncle's lips quirked up in a half-smile. As an Ilvannian— a loyal one at that—he understood more than most where my thoughts were exactly. Our plan was contingent on the fact the *Tarien* would wake up, but we allowed for the possibility it might not happen.

We had to.

Jaehyr was poring over a detailed map Elay had provided him with, trailing his fingers over lines to find the best possible route to the coast. I followed his progress with my eyes, arms folded in front of me.

"If the *Tarien* awakens," he said, "we can cut through the desert and be in Portasâhn in a moon."

"Provided we have someone who knows the way," I remarked, fighting to keep my voice neutral. "Without one, it could easily take a year."

"Of course."

Somehow, Jaehyr had mastered keeping his emotions under control. After all his time here, I would have expected him to be bristling with anger and boiling with revenge, but he was as calm and collected as *Tari* Arayda had been, regardless of the circumstances.

How I used to be, I thought bitterly.

It was one of the reasons why it was hard to keep the cynical tone from my voice. He had been away from Ilvanna for almost three hundred years, had failed to kill Azra, and had been a prisoner for perhaps as long. And yet, he bore no grudge against Elay or his family, nor had he any trouble whatsoever keeping his everlasting patience.

I almost growled out loud.

"If the *Tarien* hasn't woken up," Jaehyr continued, gauging my reaction, "we had better take the caravan routes, but that might take us up to three moons or more."

"It's a moot point," I replied. "We're not leaving her here."

"Moving her while she's still unconscious might prove disastrous," Elay commented from the archway.

My gaze snapped to him, but I recoiled from the haunted expression on his face and the dark circles under his eyes. I had avoided looking in a mirror for the past fortnight and couldn't help but wonder if my appearance resembled his.

Lujaeyn kept telling me to get some rest.

"That may be well and true," I muttered, "but she's not staying here. If she doesn't wake up, her home is still Ilvanna."

"Where she will be in danger if Azra is not defeated," Elay countered. "Is that what you wish for her?"

I gritted my teeth. "Of course not. Are you suggesting I am not capable of doing my job?"

Elay's lips lifted into a half-hearted, lopsided smirk. "I am suggesting you think things through, Talnovar. Defending a woman who wields a sword as well as any warrior is much easier than defending a woman whose only ability is breathing. She'll be an easy target for anyone out to hurt her, especially for Azra."

I shook my head. "You don't understand. I *must* take her to Ilvanna, or as close as I can get her, especially if she doesn't wake up."

Not until then had I really thought this through, but I knew I was right. Maybe the healers in Kyrintha couldn't help her, but I knew one who could. All I had to do was get her to Soren, and he would do the rest.

Just take her across a desert, a sea, and a war-torn country. What can possibly go wrong?

Jaehyr looked at me curiously. Elay wore a frown, the look on his face of someone trying to come to terms with something unpleasant. In the end, he sighed, not convinced by my words by any measure.

"I'm not sure I can let you do that," he said, pulling himself up to his full height. "Not as *Akyn*, but as a... friend." I opened my mouth to retort a few colourful insults, but he held up his hand and continued quickly, effectively cutting me off. "I understand why she must return, believe me, I do, but there is no point in risking her life. I will provide you with everything you need. You can return to Ilvanna within two moons and assess the situation there. We can communicate through messengers, and when she awakes, I will personally escort her to a meeting point of your choice."

"Perhaps—," Jaehyr began, but I cut him off with a resolute 'no'.

"She's coming with us." I growled. "Awake or asleep, end of discussion."

Elay's lips thinned. "Very well. Suit yourself. If you do not accept the warning of a friend, heed an order from the *Akyn* of Kyrintha. By law, Shalitha an Ilvan is my wife, and I will not release her into your custody while still in a coma."

"You son of a *he*—"

"Be careful, *Anahràn*," Elay interrupted, his voice remarkably cold. "You are speaking to this country's sovereign. Your words may be misconstrued."

"Tal," Jaehyr murmured. "Leave it be."

I scowled at him, then returned my focus to Elay. He may have saved my life, offered me the sanctity of his home, but he would not keep me from fulfilling my mission. Jaehyr shot me a warning glare, the look in his eyes urging me to simmer down.

So, I did.

Not because of him.

Because of her.

I lowered my gaze and inclined my head, clenching my jaw as I did. "Understood, *Akyn*."

Elay stared at me a moment longer, then nodded and pivoted on his heel, leaving the room in a flurry of robes.

"What in *Esahbyen's* name do you think you're doing?" Jaehyr hissed, momentarily losing his calm. "Are you insane?"

"No," I replied, scrambling around for the right words. "You have to believe me, uncle. If we can get her to Ilvanna, to *Denahryn*, I know someone who can wake her."

His brows shot up in surprise. "*Denahryn?* By the Gods, I haven't heard that name in forever. It still exists?"

"Thriving, actually." I smiled wryly. "That's where your brother is amassing a rebel army."

Jaehyr scoffed. "Leave it up to Cerindil." He exhaled slowly, rubbing the back of his neck as he considered me. "You are sure this person can help?"

"Positive."

He nodded slowly, the look in his eyes betraying the fact his mind was already ten steps ahead. "Very well. I'll see what I can do about Elay."

A GENTLE SUMMER breeze wafted through the room, sending the curtains at the window dancing to an unheard tune. My gaze was drawn to the oversized canopy bed to the left of the entrance, heavy curtains preventing anyone coming in from seeing its inhabitant. Lujaeyn was sitting on a chair near the window, hemming one of my shirts, while Z'tala stood on guard only a few feet away.

Neither woman would leave the *Tarien* for longer than was necessary.

"Please," I said, exhaustion lining my voice. "Could you... please... leave us alone?"

Lujaeyn rose to her feet and left without contesting my request. Z'tala arched a brow at me, lips pressed in a thin line, looking as if she were about to deny me, but something on my face softened her resolve, and she inclined her head.

"I'll be just outside," she murmured as she passed me.

"*Teralé, Irà.*"

Once the room had emptied from everyone, I sauntered to the bed, my heartbeat picking up speed with every step I took. When I opened the curtains, my heart sank like it did every day.

She still hadn't woken up.

The bed dipped underneath me, and I took her hand in

mine, swallowing hard at how frail it felt. As I stroked a lock of hair out of her face, I couldn't help but notice how prominent her cheekbones were. Her skin, usually a warm ivory, was now ashen, highlighted more so by the dark circles around her eyes. I stroked her cheek with the back of my hand, my eyes searching her face as if trying to find a hint of her former self.

I couldn't find it.

"We're making plans to go home," I said, my voice hoarser than I liked. I coughed to clear my throat. "When you wake up, we'll go straight for Portasâhn and find our way to *Denahryn*. Evan's there, and Mehrean. You can meet your little niece."

Biting my lip, I looked down at our hands, heat creeping up my neck. "Soren's there, too. If you... should you—" I took a deep breath. "If you don't wake up before we leave, we will take you with us. Soren, he'll be able to help you. I'm sure of it..."

Even as I spoke those words, I felt agitated. So many things hinged on uncertainties. Even if we did take her along, there was no guarantee she'd survive the journey. As much as I resented Elay for his earlier words, deep down inside, I knew he was right.

Was I really that convinced of Soren's skills that I was willing to risk her life?

As my gaze returned to Shal, a memory of *Tari* Arayda the night she ordered me to find her daughter came to mind, and my chest constricted so painfully remembering, I thought my ribs would crack from the sheer force of it. The *Tari* had been thin and frail, a mere shell of her former self. How much of a contrast had she been to her daughter then.

How similar to her mother she looks now.

I let out a sound between a chuckle and a sob. "Of all the stupid things you've done, *Tarien*, this is probably the stupidest of all."

She didn't reply. Of course, she didn't. A man could hope.

"When you wake up," I muttered, stroking my thumb over

the back of her hand. "I'll be yelling at you for the next moon, just a fair warning."

"Yell all you want, Anahràn," I imagined her saying, *"You'll run out of breath, eventually."*

I snorted at the thought. It wasn't quite her, but her response would have been close—wittier though. She was good at those kinds of comments.

"Anyway," I continued in a more hushed voice. "I'm counting the days till you open your eyes and"—I snorted and shook my head—"you start yelling at me, or give me the slip, or beg me for a training. After your endeavours in the arena, I doubt there's anything left for me to teach you, but I'll try. Jaehyr and Z'tala told me you were a force to be reckoned with in there. Earned the respect of almost every *herriatâre* in Kehran's dungeons. Jaehyr also tells me they would still fight for you despite what happened."

I gulped and ran a hand through my hair. "You're also driving Elay completely mad by not waking up. The man looks even worse than you do." A heavy sigh escaped my lips. "I'm just praying to whatever God will listen that you will wake up eventually, so we can go home."

It was a lie.

She wasn't driving just Elay mad with worry but me as well, and although I did pray to the Gods, it wasn't to ask them for her to wake up; it was to curse them for allowing something like this to happen in the first place. Not that they could be of help— at least, I didn't think they could—but I had to yell at someone.

I didn't think they could hear me, anyway.

But she can.

"Actually," I whispered, lifting her hand to place a gentle kiss on her knuckles. "That was a lie. You're driving me insane, *Tarien.* Utterly and completely insane. You've no idea what I've gone through to find you, and then to find you"—I swallowed away the lump in my throat—"Possessed, dangerous, and... crazy. Like her..."

My voice trailed off.

I pressed her hand against my forehead, gritting my teeth at the assault of emotions rushing through me at the memory of Azra. When I'd finally calmed down, I looked back at Shalitha, my eyes searching her face, hoping against all hope she'd heard me and was returning to us.

She wasn't.

Defeated, I lay down beside her, resting our entwined hands on her chest while I turned on my side, staying as close to her as I could. I inhaled deeply. Gone was the scent of orange and vanilla and an earthy fragrance that was her. It wasn't that she smelled bad—servants sponged her every day—but she rather smelled of flowers, a scent that in my mind did not belong to her.

At all.

But being this close to her after all this time, after all the suppressed feelings I'd never shown her until the night Xaresh was killed, I was hard-pressed not to pull her into my arms and hold her, perhaps even kiss her.

It's not appropriate, I chided myself.

It had never been appropriate, but she was the last one who would care about propriety. Yet under the current circumstances, it felt wrong, even lying here did. At the same time, it felt right where I should be.

"*Mey tahre beleth'ien è istilma.*"

My heart belongs to you forever.

ILVANNIAN CHARACTERS

TARI ARAYDA AN ILVAN, Queen of Ilvanna. *Deceased.*
TARIEN SHALITHA AN ILVAN, daughter of Arayda. Princess of Ilvanna.
EVANYAN AN ILVAN, first born son of Arayda.
HAERLYON AN ILVAN, second son of Arayda. General of the army.
AZRA AN ILVAN, sister of Arayda. Queen of Ilvanna.
GAERVIN AN ILVAN, husband of Arayda. *Deceased.*
NARAYSHA AN ILVAN, daughter of Evanyan and Nathaïr.

CERINDIL IMRADIEN, Father of Talnovar.
TALNOVAR IMRADIEN, Captain of the Arathrien. Son of Cerindil.
LEYANDRA IMRADIEN, mother of Talnovar and Varayna. *Deceased.*
VARAYNA IMRADIEN, sister of Talnovar. *Deceased.*
JAEHYR IMRADIEN, brother of Cerindil.

YLLINAR AROLVYEN, noble. Father of Eamryel, Nathaïr and Caleena.
EAMRYEL AROLVYEN, noble. Son of Yllinar.
NATHAÏR AROLVYEN, noble. Daughter of Yllinar. Betrothed to Evanyan an Ilvan. *Deceased.*
CALEENA AROLVYEN, Daughter of Yllinar. Half-sister to Nathaïr and Eamryel. *Deceased.*

ANHANYAH LAELLE, former leader of *Hanyarah* (sisterhood). *Deceased.*
ANHANYAH MEHREAN, leader of *Hanyarah*.
IONE AN HANYA, sister at *Hanyarah*. Araîtiste.

SOREN AN DENA, master healer at the palace.

ELARA SEHLYN, noble. *Arathrien. Deceased.*
QUERAN PAHLEANAN, noble. Arathrien. *Deceased.*
RURIN TRIQUELLEAN, noble. *Arathri. Deceased.*
CAERLEYAN VIRS, noble. Arathrien. *Deceased.*
XARESH NEHMREAN, commoner. Arathrien. *Deceased.*

SAMEHYA NEHMREAN, commoner. Sister of Xaresh.
KALYANI NEHMREAN, commoner. Mother of Xaresh.
TYNSERAH NEHMREAN, commoner. Sister of Xaresh.

GRAYDEN VERITHRIEN, commoner. *Àn* in the Ilvannian
Army.
CEHYAN NE HIRAEN, commoner.
HALUETH, a prisoner Talnovar meets on the ship.
RAYADAEN, Sveràn in the army.
EHRLAHN, Ilvannian guard.

KYRINTHAN CHARACTERS

Ship

FEHRAN, captain
ARAV, ship's healer

Akhyr

ELAY È REHMÀH /ELAY IHN GAHR, Akynshan of Y'zdrah.
Prince of Kyrintha.
KEHRAN IHN GAHR, *Akyn* of Kyrintha. Half-brother of Elay
NAÏDA IHN GAHR, sister of Elay.
JEHLEAL IHN GAHR, brother of Elay.
NAHRAM IHN GAHR, brother of Elay. *Deceased.*
MA'LEK, Shalitha's buyer.

Portasâhn

PRISHA, homeless girl.
SADEREH, Kyrinthan woman in employment of Elay.

Slavecamp/on the road

RASHIÌD, Elay
TARIQ, Elay's healer.
NAZEEM, Elay's bodyguard.
INENN, Elay's caravan guard.
QIRAS, Elay's caravan guard.
LUJAEYN, slave girl bought by Elay owned by Talnovar.

NIHBERAN CHARACTERS

Z'TALA, Shalitha's friend. *Herriatâre.*
R'TAYAN, Elay's confidant.

ILVANNIAN PANTHEON

AESON, God of music, arts, and medicine.
ARRAN, God of fire, inventions and crafts.
ESAHBYEN, God of war, violence and bloodshed.
ESLANDAH, Goddess of wisdom, knowledge and reason.
NAVA, Goddess of love and passion, pleasure and beauty.
RAWEND, God of travel, communication and diplomacy.
SAVEA, Goddess of harvest, nature and seasons.
SEYDEH, God of water and seas.
VEHDA, Goddess of hunt, protection, and the moon.
XANTHIER, God of law, order, and justice.
XIOMARA, Goddess of life, marriage, women, and childbirth.
XARALA, Goddess of death, darkness and loneliness.
ZORAY, Goddess of hearth and home, and family.

ZIHRIN/KYRINTHAN PANTHEON

ALEYA, Goddess of harvest, nature and seasons.
BEAHDEH, God of music, arts, and medicine.
DERANA, Goddess of hunt, protection, and the moon.
FAYRA, Goddess of life, marriage, women, and childbirth.
GHAYETH, God of water and seas.
HEZA, Goddess of death, darkness and loneliness.
KEHMARI, Goddess of hearth and home, and family.
LAROS, God of war, violence and bloodshed.
LEYALLEH, Goddess of love and passion, pleasure and beauty.
MEDHA, Goddess of wisdom, knowledge and reason.
RESHAD, God of travel, communication and diplomacy.
SAQIB, God of fire, inventions and crafts.
YDRES, God of law, order, and justice.

ILVANNIAN GLOSSARY

Royal terms

TARI, Queen
TARIEN, princess
ARATHRI, Queen's guard
ARATHRIEN, Princess' guard

Military terms

OHZHERÀN, General of the army
ZHERÀN, General
INZHERÀN, Lieutenant-general
IMHRÀN, Colonel
INIMHRÀN, Lieutenant-colonel
MAHRÀN, Major
ANAHRÀN, Captain
SVERÀN, Lieutenant
ÀN, Men-at-arms

Sisterhood

HANYARAH, sisterhood
ANHANYAH, leader of the sisterhood
HANIYA, sister

Brotherhood

DENAHRYN, brotherhood
DENA, brother

General

AI SELA, stand down
AI SELA'AN, eat ease, soldier

ARAÎTH, tattoo; the size depends on what class someone is
born into
ARAÎTIN, feast held in honour of the one receiving their full
Araîth
DIRESH, porridge
DENM, pawn in Sihnmihràn
DOCHTAER, daughter
IÑAEIQUE, a sense of tranquillity obtained through specific
moves
INÀN, a pawn in Sihnmihràn
IRÌN, lord(s)

IRÀ, lady(ies)

ITHRI, an alcoholic beverage of vanilla, often drunk with oranges and ice

KHIRR, idiot (m)

LYADRIN, beggar

MAHNÈH, my friend

MEHRA SAEN, sleep well

METÂH, mate

MEY, my

OUKOUROU, heavy, hallucinating drugs

PEHRÎN, hopscotch

QIRA, idiot (f)

QISERA, insane

Q'LERAHN, mortal

QUERTA, copper

RUESTA, rest

SALLELLES, seals

SEHVELLE, drugs similar to weed

SEREA, sir

SEVAETHTAER, projections of the Gods.

SHAREYE, my dear/my love (f)

SHARYEN, my love (m)

SIHNMIHRÀN, a strategic board game similar to chess

SIHRA, miss

TERALÉ, thank you

TAHRASH, an herb used as anti-conception

VERATHRÀH, traitor

ZHAN, short for OHZHERÀN

Expletives

GRISSIN, bastard
HEHZÈH, bitch
NOHRO AHRAE, damnit!

Phrases

DANE ÍL RUESTA, may you rest peacefully
NAIE I'FEAN, Don't fuss

ZIHRIN/KYRINTHAN GLOSSARY

Royal terms

AKYN, king
AKYNAI, queen
AKYNSHAN, prince

General

AMISHA, my lady. Miss (Zihrin)
CAHRTIN, brand of wine
CAMELLE, camel
CH'ITI, porridge
DEKIATÂRE, doctore. The one who trains the herriatâre
DIYENKA, thank you
ESHEN, my lord (Kyrinthan)
GEMSHA, whoremaster
GEMSHAN, whorehouse

HAVV, move
HARSHÂH, wedding
HERRÂT, arena
HERRIATÂRE, gladiator
HIJRATH, a garment worn by women to cover their hair
HIIJR, a garment worn by men to cover their hair and face
Ì, and
IRTEHN, my friend
KEFFAH, coffee
K'YNSHAN, palace
MASRAN, master
MISHAN, my lord. Sir (Zihrin)
MITHRI, my dear. My love
SA'ANEH, spa
SÊTT, stop
SHENA, my lady, miss (Kyrinthan)
TALEH, calm
TAZUR, steam house
YGR'ETH, feast
ZRAYETH, whore

Expletives

KOHPÈ, fuck
TEKKA, bitch
TERKAN, asshole

Phrases

IHR ENA DEN KELAR, you are an idiot.

DEN KELAR SIN K'IRAI, you are the idiot.

Places/people

AKHYR, capital of Kyrintha
PORTASÂHN, main port of Kyrintha
T'ERZA MAHRZAL, the mountain people

NIHBEHRAN GLOSSARY

General

K'LELE, my friend (used only for women)
N'ERA, not a problem
OKLEAH, my queen
RESHA, *she who will conquer.*
TEMARÌN, Nihbehran name for Vehda, goddess of the hunt
T'MAERE K'TAN, whatever comes next

THERONDIAN GLOSSARY

General

KAILENN, idiot
LERDAS, lords

FROM KARA

ear Reader,

I WOULD LIKE to thank you for taking time to read Whispers of War, the third instalment of The Ilvannian Chronicles. I hope you enjoyed reading it as much as I enjoyed writing it, even though it did give me a headache at times. There have been moments where I seriously doubted myself, and the story, but I'm glad I persisted and got to share it with you. After all, you, my readers, are what I'm doing this for.

Follow me on Instagram or Facebook, and you will be kept up-to-date on my daily activities. If you sign up for my newsletter on my website www.karasweaver.com, not only can you download the prequel to Crown of Conspiracy and Dance of Despair for free, you will also receive a snippet of a story each month, and you'll be the first to know about upcoming releases, cover reveals and all that.

Before you go, I'd like to ask you one more thing. If you enjoyed Whispers of War, please consider leaving a review on

Amazon and/or Goodreads. As an Indie author, your review is invaluable to me. Thank you in advance for taking the time.

Until next time, and happy reading.

Love,
Kara

ACKNOWLEDGMENTS

After three books and working with the same people, writing the acknowledgements becomes a bit of a repetitive affair. Even so, I think it's important to give gratitude and thanks where it is due.

Natalie, thank you for being the best critique partner and friend a girl can have. Without you, it would have been 2023 before I dared publish this book (if not later). Again, you've created a stunner of a cover. I don't know where I'd be without you, but I know this series wouldn't have been the same. I wouldn't have been the same (and I would never have published, I think).

Jodie and Cassidy, thank you for putting up with the thousands of snippets I left in our chat, for the kind, uplifting words, for believing in me, for being there when I needed you. Honestly, your faith in me has helped me get this far. You're amazing people and amazing authors. Thank you for being my friends and critique partners.

Soma, Luc, you guys rock! Thank you for reading the very first, ugliest version of this book and still love it. Your continuous support keeps me going.

In no particular order, thank you Michelle, Ciara, Courtney, Lisa, Jessa, Brandi, Douglas, Jeroen, Candyce, MJ Vaughn, and World Indie Warriors.

To all the people on Instagram who have been following me on this journey, who cheer my every accomplishment, who have told me how much they love my book or even yelled at me in my DMs. Thank you.

Last but not least, to my husband. Thank you for putting up with my crazy writing quirks, keeping me fed and hydrated, and listening to my rants about characters doing stupid things.

ALSO BY KARA S. WEAVER

The Ilvannian Chronicles

In reading order

Crown of Conspiracy

Song of Shadows (available for subscribers)

Dance of Despair

Whispers of War

ABOUT THE AUTHOR

Kara S. Weaver currently lives in the Netherlands with her husband, two children, and Kita the cat. English teacher by day, and aspiring author by night, Kara has always loved creating fantasy worlds and characters. Not all of them have found their way on paper yet.

When not teaching or writing, Kara is well versed in the mysterious ways of binge-watching Netflix, and speed-reading books. Occasionally, she whips out her DSLR camera to take pictures, but those days are far and few between.

If you would like to share your thoughts, ideas, or comments on the current books in the Ilvannian Chronicles feel free to contact Kara S. Weaver at: weaver.kara.s@gmail.com .

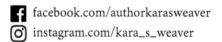

facebook.com/authorkarasweaver
instagram.com/kara_s_weaver

Printed in Great Britain
by Amazon

64143623R00284